THE BOOK OF LOST CHILDREN

JENNY O'BRIEN

This is a work of fiction. Names, characters, businesses, places, events and incidents are either the products of the author's imagination or used in a fictitious manner. Any resemblance to actual persons, living or dead, or actual events is purely coincidental.

Copyright © Jenny O'Brien, 2025

The moral right of the author has been asserted.

All rights reserved. No part of this book may be reproduced or used in any manner without the prior written permission of the copyright owner. This prohibition includes, but is not limited to, any reproduction or use for the purpose of training artificial intelligence technologies or systems.

To request permissions, contact the publisher at rights@stormpublishing.co

Ebook ISBN: 978-1-80508-893-6
Paperback ISBN: 978-1-80508-895-0

Cover design: Ghost
Cover images: Trevillion, Shutterstock

Published by Storm Publishing.
For further information, visit:
www.stormpublishing.co

In memory of Brenda Hervé and Dave Le Page

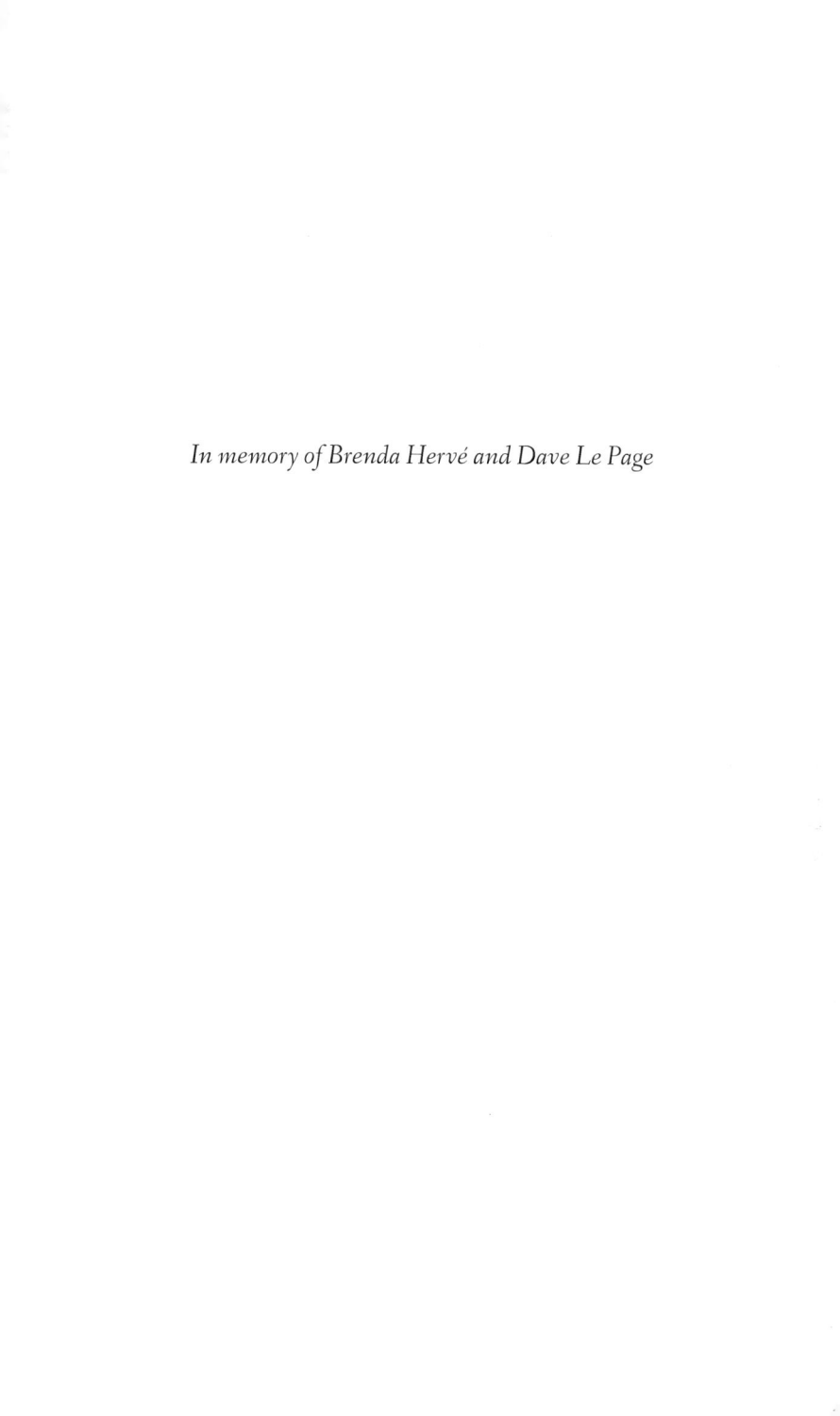

'...Live as if you were going to die tomorrow.' Paul Bocuse

PROLOGUE

6 June, 1944 – Guernsey

The sky overhead was murky grey, the moon hidden by a thick layer of cloud. There was no trace of sunset. The day had slipped from pale grey to dark almost at the flick of a switch.

Camille thought the weather a blessing, a sign that it was time to leave. They wouldn't get another chance. If she told herself that, she might begin to believe it. All she cared about were the children.

The children, and him.

The breeze lifted her black hair back from her face and tugged at her clothing as she clambered on board, one hand grabbing onto the gunwale, the other pressed against her chest to where the baby lay swaddled in a thick scarf. The boat rocked and swayed underfoot, causing her to launch herself onto the bench at the back. She tucked her skirt around her to make room for her charges.

'Here's the first one, dearest. Come on, little man. Big brave boy.'

'Thank you, *cheri*.' She circled the small wriggling body

with her arm, drawing him close. 'Don't be afraid. We're going on a big adventure. It's going to be great fun. Here, huddle under my cloak. That's right. Let's pretend we're hiding.' She smoothed his white-blond hair briefly before adjusting the black fabric so that only his face was visible. 'A little closer. As close as you can to make room for the babies.'

The couple spoke in whispers as they arranged the children in the flimsy boat. There was just enough room for his feet as he worked on fixing the oars into place. Words carried across water and the last thing they wanted was to announce their presence. She kept her gaze on the road and the buildings beyond, searching for movement. Searching for *him*. If he caught her, there'd be no reprieve, no second chance.

Camille placed her hand on top of the baby's head, her fingers briefly touching the gold locket secured at her throat. The cool metal was a reminder of what they were escaping from. She cast a silent prayer out to sea, her lips barely moving as the boat slipped away from the shore. The soft lapping of the water against the sides was in sharp contrast to the pounding of her heart. She didn't look back. Instead she turned to face the uncertain future that lay in the swell of the waves and the inky blackness of the ocean ahead.

ONE
KITTY

Wednesday, 19 December, 2018 – Dublin

'You'll be alright minding the shop, luv. I'm just heading out for a bit.'

Kitty glanced up from her book, her finger marking the page, noting the way her dad couldn't quite meet her gaze, his overcoat already draped over his arm, his cap squashed flat on his head.

Out for a bit meant tottering along the road to the bar on the corner for a pint. There was nothing new she could say to change that. Her deep sigh said it all.

'I'll be fine. If you're going to be late best to remember your keys, Da.'

'I don't plan on being that long,' he snapped, but that didn't stop him from searching in his pocket a second and brandishing the small bunch like a prize before pulling the door open, the little old-fashioned brass bell chiming his departure.

Kitty swapped her finger for her bookmark and pushed away from the table to carefully shut the door behind him. The heater might be blasting out hot air but there was no point in wasting money. The sign on the glass declaring they were open, in both English and Gaelic, was enough of an invitation.

Instead of returning to her book, she took a moment to look out the window and watch as her dad negotiated the street, his capped head bent against the raw drizzle of rain that seemed to have set in for the day, his hand clenched around his walking stick. It wasn't that she was worried about him, but he was ageing before her eyes. His sisters often teased that he'd kissed the Blarney Stone, as well as drunk from the fountain of youth, but his birth certificate didn't lie. Seventy-four last birthday and, over the last few months, starting to look every year of it. He was as lost as she felt following the death of her mother but there seemed nothing she could do except sweep up the pieces when he finally returned home later. He always turned up, an inebriated smirk on his face and an apology on his lips, his feet thumping on the crooked stairs that led from the shop to their tiny apartment above.

She only stopped watching when he disappeared round the corner, her attention skittering to the throng of pedestrians wandering up and down the street, mostly glued to their phones instead of looking at the quaint buildings found along the quayside or peering at the delights in their shop window. Kitty had spent hours arranging the eclectic display of china and curios in a way to attract the most reluctant of spenders and she took it as a personal affront when their shop was ignored in favour of Facebook or TikTok.

Dressing the window had been her job ever since she was a schoolgirl, a chore that had quickly grown into a passion. She spent hours poring over magazines and Pinterest trying to magic up impossible arrangements on little or no budget. Sometimes she went with the current trend. Hearts for Valentine's, spiders for Halloween, eggs for Easter – but this Christmas, she couldn't stomach anything festive with the memory of her mother, almost a year to the day, slipping away on a bed in St John of God's Hospital.

She had lain beside her mother's emaciated body, staring at the ceiling strung with paper garlands and counting the circles to the sound of her shallow breaths, a bitterness for Christmas sinking deep into her heart.

No, Christmas was on the back burner this year. It had been a silent agreement between Kitty and her dad as they navigated the unchartered territory of grief. What came after was a question that neither of them felt in a fit place to think about let alone discuss.

Kitty glanced over at the window display on her way back to her chair. This week's theme was the sea: the Edwardian mahogany table dressed in Victorian placemats embroidered with blue hummingbirds, and a particularly ugly Vaseline glass epergne included as the centrepiece only because of its azure lustre. Her father had insisted on bringing it back from a house clearance six months ago and she'd moved it from shelf to shelf ever since, trying to make *the thing* catch someone's eye.

She spent a few seconds sweeping a feather duster across it before adjusting one of the Sheffield silver forks and returning to her chair. Her attention was pulled to the door and the impeccably dressed man entering, shaking raindrops from his umbrella all over the clean floor. Slate-grey overcoat over matching trousers and accompanied by an attitude to match, if his arrogant smile was anything to go by.

Serving customers was the part of the business she hated the most, particularly those who took her youthfulness as an indication of inexperience. While Kitty might look to be in her mid-to-late twenties, she was clutching onto her thirties by the tips of her fingers. She also had an art history degree under her belt and was currently studying for a master's in her spare time. After growing up in an antique shop, there was little she didn't know on the subject of what the uninitiated often called junk.

'Afternoon, lovely to see a shop without a bunch of holly or glitzy bauble in evidence. I'm interested in the epergne.' The man waved in the direction of the window as if she needed clarification, his speech staccato clear.

Kitty eyed him briefly before turning back to the piece, her lips pressing into a thin line as she regarded the hideous monstrosity with barely concealed disdain. He was probably around her age and good-looking, although a tad serious for her taste.

'A particularly fine example.' It pained her to lie but she'd been trained by both her parents on people's different views when it came to beauty, and the impact a stray comment could make to a sale. There was the gas bill to pay as well as the electricity. Integrity came with a high price tag, often impossible to repay.

'I have a few questions if there's someone?' He glanced around the shop before turning back, one heavy eyebrow raised.

'Certainly, sir. What would you like to know, and I'll see if I can be of help.'

'Well, the age for a start and... and...' He hesitated, seeming suddenly at a loss for words.

'It's really beautiful, isn't it? A perfect example. The four crimped flutes and scalloped tray at the base are simply stunning. Of course, very popular as a central table piece during the late nineteenth century.' She ran her finger carefully down the side of one flute, the opaque glass doing nothing for her, her smile powered by thoughts of a possible sale and not the piece. 'This one comes with a full provenance from a manor house in County Clare, which we'll supply on purchase.'

'And what's the best you can do on the price?'

Kitty was expecting the question, even though disappointed with it—disappointed in him. It was common enough for most people to barter them down when they came into the shop. Her father invariably gave in. Kitty was learning not to. Second hand didn't mean cheap, and it wasn't as if they could pop out the back and magic up another epergne, hideous though it was.

She took a moment to study him from the top of his short brown hair, serious glasses, plain tie and fashionable, albeit conservative overcoat. *Clearly well-off, one would think he'd have little need for haggling.*

'Doctor... dentist. No, silly me. Accountant?'

They got all sorts wandering into the shop, conveniently situated on the bank of the River Liffey, but there was something about the way he was dressed that screamed of someone working in financial services.

She gave herself a mental kick, her smile still in place but only just. Her father was always telling her off for yapping at the hand that fed but she couldn't seem to help herself. There was no chance of him buying off her as she had no intention of dropping the price. She'd already dropped it to rock bottom in the hope of shifting it.

'Excuse me?' His eyes met hers for the first time. Startled grey.

'Your profession?'

'I'm not sure the interest, or indeed the relevance, but I'm a solicitor.'

'Ah, so it's common practice to haggle over your fees then?' She placed her finger under her chin, holding his gaze. 'Good to know. You might as well leave your card on your way out.'

'Pardon?' He looked and sounded affronted, a slight wash of pink colouring his cheeks.

'The price is on the ticket. A perfectly fair price given the tenure of the piece.'

Kitty moved towards the desk and deliberately picked up the book she was reading in preparation for her next assignment. The use of light and dark, and how Vermeer and Caravaggio changed art forever. It was a heavy tome, requiring her full concentration, which was proving difficult as he was still in the shop. She glanced up, only to find him hovering nearby, his expression now one of contrition.

'Are you able to gift wrap?'

By ten to five the street was starting to thin. Kitty washed out her mug ready for tomorrow morning and placed her books and laptop in a neat pile to take upstairs when the doorbell rang.

The woman was tall and thin, mid-to-late fifties with pale blonde hair stuffed haphazardly under her red woollen cap, a plastic carrier clutched between her fingers. They got all sorts in the shop and Kitty could tell a shopper from a seller in less than a blink. The cut of the coat was more Primark than Prada, the plastic of the Co-op bag crinkled and faded, its red handles stretched to breaking point, the sides bulging with the weight of what it held.

Kitty felt her heart soften at the air of dejection and defeat in the woman's face and the slump of her shoulders. If her dad was a sop when it came to giving discounts, Kitty was the one more likely to be swayed by a hard luck story.

However, being generous didn't mean she could afford to be on the wrong side of the Garda Síochána. She kept away from anything with the whiff of stolen about it. Buying off the street was one of the hazards of the trade.

'Hello there. You just managed to catch me. What have you got?'

'I was wondering if you'd be interested in an old violin?' the woman asked with a nervous laugh, fumbling with the plastic bag before pulling out a battered, black leather case and placing it on the mahogany table in the centre of the shop.

Kitty's breath hitched at the sight of the case, dust ingrained in the seams. The woman had chosen their shop over others for a reason. She'd done her research. While her father handled the china and furniture, it was her mother, Hilary, who had breathed life into old musical instruments – the older and quirkier, the better. A gifted musician, Hilary could coax a tune out of anything. She already had a violin. A perfectly good dusty violin, Kitty remembered with a flash of guilt.

Now, standing in the shop, staring down at the case, it felt like a door opening in her mind – a door that had been locked for too long. Her brilliant, talented mother.

Memories surged, so strong they made Kitty cough into her hand. Evenings spent above the shop, practising together, her mother's laughter filling the room.

She skimmed her fingers over the leather before reaching for the clasp, her heart thumping a little faster in anticipation. 'May I?'

'Please do.'

The violin was nestled on a bed of faded and torn red velvet, the wood dull and lifeless. The strings were loose and one had snapped completely, but it was the size of the two F holes that got her attention, the elongation a mark of quality. The first clue that it might be something very special indeed.

'Don't get too excited, luv. It's only a copy. There.' She pointed at the F hole, where the label was clearly visible. 'My da told me it would be worth a mint if the label were right.' The woman's voice faded as she cast her eyes downwards. 'I'm not asking for much being as it's not the real deal. Shame to leave it in the attic and no one to play it.'

'Right. I'll just take it over to the light if I may.'

Kitty walked to the desk, the instrument balanced between her hands as she held it under the anglepoise lamp, and read the words '*Made in Germany*'.

The wood was tacky under her fingers and in need of a good polish. More than a polish, she thought, watching the finish flake off onto the top of the desk. The violin was a complete mess. It would take weeks of painstaking repair to even begin to get it into a condition where they'd see a return for their money.

It would be far easier to dust off her own violin than to take on a new project, if her need to play persisted when the seller left their shop.

The woman was obviously desperate to sell but there was no value in the item as it stood, and when would she find the time to work on it? A little part of her wanted to buy it, for the enjoyment of restoring it to its former glory before picking up her bow and running it over the strings, but it wasn't a big enough part for her to open the till.

She replaced the violin and closed the case, taking a moment to press the fastening, her fingertips lingering on the leather with regret. Her father had told her to look out for something for herself, his rheumy gaze earnest, intent. They both knew that her ma had always been the one to buy her gifts.

'Two hundred euro and it's yours,' the woman offered, her tone as desperate as her expression.

'It's not as simple as that, Mrs...' Kitty said gently.

'Miss Raven. Caroline.'

'Tell me about the violin. How it got to be in such a state for a start, Caroline?'

'I don't know much.' She fumbled with the strap of her handbag, hitching it over her shoulder. 'Been in me da's family for years and, to be honest, I'm loath to sell it.' She smoothed her hair behind her ears, her fingers reddened and unadorned by rings. 'He told me before he died that if ever I was in need of a bit of cash, to come to White's as you'd know its worth and that I wasn't to sell it to anyone else.'

Kitty was surprised by her answer, surprised and more than a little intrigued. While her mother had built up a significant reputation as a specialist in musical instruments, that was a long time ago. The woman looked ordinary enough. World worn but no different to many such women trying to navigate the rising costs. Kitty was fairly sure she had never met her before, but they got a lot of callers into the shop, most of whom she turned away, albeit with a heavy heart and, on a couple of occasions, with a tenner from the till for the cost of a meal.

She blinked at where her thoughts were taking her. It was Christmas after all.

'I'm afraid it's not worth anything in this state, Caroline. It needs so much work doing to it that I'm not even sure where to begin.' She spread her hands in resignation, trying to let her down as gently as possible. 'It has no resale value as it is and trying to repair it, bearing in mind—'

'Hundred and fifty then. Please. I'm desperate.'

Kitty knew about desperation. The months following her mother's death when the shop had been closed and the bills racking up while her father had languished in the pub. It was a habit he'd failed to break when the fog of grief had lifted enough for him to return to work.

'There's more too. I almost forgot.' Caroline rummaged in her bag, her hands shaking as she removed an A4 brown envelope and poured the contents on the table along with a small velvet pouch. 'I think the original sales invoice. They were altogether so I brought the lot.'

Along with the invoice there was a sheet of yellowing music and a few photographs. Old black-and-whites featuring people and scenery Kitty didn't recognise. Mostly of countryside. Possibly the Dublin outskirts but she didn't think so. The car number plates were a giveaway, along with the absence of the steel and glass office blocks that seemed to be taking over the city.

Kitty picked up the images, one by one, before lining them up in a neat pile. A hundred and fifty euros was still a lot for what was essentially a restoration project, but she'd had a good afternoon, a great one, so she could afford to be generous, and she still had to buy and wrap a gift for her dad to give to her. It would make for an easier Christmas Day.

'And this. Look.' Kitty watched as Caroline opened the

velvet pouch, a signet ring tumbling into the palm of her hand. The gold tarnished and dull and with a build-up of grime obscuring the engraving. A humble piece but someone must have loved it once. Kitty was a sucker for stories, and it had that air about it, hidden under the neglect. There were so many possibilities as to its history. A violin, a bunch of old photographs. A signet ring. What could it all mean. In that second, she knew she was determined to find out.

'Can I have a name and address for the sale, Caroline?' she said, noting the swift look of relief pass across the woman's face. Buying off the street came with an element of trust and there was something familiar about the woman. She didn't recognise her. In fact, she was positive she'd never met her before and yet the feeling remained.

Afterwards, Kitty followed the woman to the door, locking it behind her and turning the wooden sign over. The shop was closed.

The ring intrigued her more than the violin or even the photographs. She picked up a small magnifying glass and peered at the hallmark on the inside.

TWO
KITTY

Tuesday, 25 December, 2018 – Dublin

'You've been had, my girl. I'm happy enough to reimburse you the cost as it's meant to be a gift, but I can't see the fiddle will ever be worth anything.' Her father pushed his glasses up his forehead, a sure sign he'd lost interest in the conversation.

Kitty slipped off the ring from her thumb. There had always been complete honesty between them and the freshly polished signet ring was part of that. 'There was this too.' She placed it in his palm. 'German, made after 1888 unless I've read the hallmark wrong. I thought I'd wear it for a bit before deciding what to do with it.'

'A substantial piece.' He weighed it in his hand, the glasses back in place. 'Mmm, could be worth something to the right buyer. Less if melted for scrap.'

'Da! Trust you.' She replaced it on her thumb, running her finger over the engraving on the front. 'I thought the violin could be a project. And anyway, I wasn't thinking of selling it. More like playing it,' she said quietly.

Her father's sudden silence was a shock until she saw his

expression, a slow burn of a smile, which caused her heart to trip. It had been a long time since she'd seen her father's face light up like that.

'You don't know how happy that would make me. Your mother always said that you never realised how talented you were.' He coughed, clearing his throat, quickly steering the conversation away from dangerous ground. 'That said, I'm not sure this is the right violin. We still have a stock. You could find something better suited to your needs.' She watched as he picked up the instrument, his hands bearing the marks of repairing and oiling old relics. 'The wood is in a terrible state and as for the varnish... It also needs a complete set of strings and a new bridge.'

'Any idea how old it is, Da? It has the shape and feel of a Strad, but I was thinking much later.'

He laughed. 'You'd be lucky to find a Stradivarius that isn't already accounted for. I reckon, probably late nineteenth or early twentieth at a guess. The market was flooded with the blessed things from Germany made especially for the American market but a few finding their way over here. I remember your poor dear mother getting very excited by a similar fiddle way before you were born. In fact, it might have been the same one come to think of it. I've a funny feeling I've seen this before.' He paused a second. A beat. Two beats before reaching for his wine glass and taking a long sip.

They rarely talked about her mother, and now they'd mentioned her twice in as many minutes. Kitty swallowed hard as she watched him place his glass back on the table, his gaze on the intricate embroidered cloth that her mother had worked on as part of her trousseau. It was impossible to lock away their memories. She should have realised that before now. Hilary's presence was felt in every room, every item and all the spaces between. The tablecloth was only a very small part of that.

'Da?'

'The case, on the other hand, is a completely different animal.' His voice was brisk, matching his fingers as he shifted it an inch closer. The tempo of their conversation changed. 'I'd go so far as to say that it has the potential to be very special indeed.'

He ran a finger across the plain leather, concentrating on where the top met the sides and bottom. 'Calfskin most probably, on a hard wood base. The earliest violins would have had the case lined with paper and no place for the bow, which meant scuff marks on the body of the violin from having the stick bouncing around inside.'

'So, not that old then as mine is covered in velvet,' she said, suddenly eager to dig out her dusty violin and play... anything.

'Not necessarily,' he hedged. 'It's all about the glue, which would have had to be some kind of animal base instead of a modern-day synthetic polymer adhesive. We'd need to peel back a portion of the velvet to see what's underneath.'

'And how can you tell the difference?' she asked, as he flicked open his pocketknife and extended the thin blade, slipping the point between the leather and the lining with the finesse of a surgeon in an operating theatre.

'Not all that difficult. It makes sense that animal glue will have a yellow undertone, unless bones have been used, but in old glue like this it might even be brown. The early synthetic glues on the other hand were milky white.'

He peeled back a corner, revealing an amber-coloured residue on the fabric and, interestingly a corner of what looked like paper.

'What's that?'

'I'm not sure. I'm also not sure what you've got here, KitKat,' he said, using her nickname for the first time in ages. 'The glue is old so probably some time in the 1920s or 1930s which, if it means what I think it means, then the case pre-dates the lining. You might want to talk to an expert. I could be doing more damage than not.'

'I think we should carry on.' She shrugged. 'We know the violin isn't worth much and a case on its own without any provenance isn't going to be worth that much either. A few hundred either way and it's already been tampered with. Call it restoration. Restoring the case to its former glory before someone lined it in red plush.'

'On your head be it.' But he picked up his penknife again and painstakingly continued working down one side until there was room to tease back the fabric, leaving enough room to slip his hand underneath. 'Would you like to do the honours? It is meant to be your present...'

'You're doing a fine job, Da.'

The corner of the paper turned out to be a photograph. An old sepia image of a small group of people sitting on the grass under a tree.

'Looks like some kind of old manor house. What's on the back?'

'Nothing.'

Kitty took the image off him, holding it up to the art deco lamp. Two women, one dressed in a nun's habit, the other in a dark cloak, and between them three small children, no more than toddlers. She reluctantly put it down. There was more to learn from the image but there'd be time enough later. 'Anything else?'

'Another photograph and what appears to be a notebook,' he said, his words slow and deliberate.

Kitty lifted her head from the image of a young woman with coal-black hair in a pretty dress, a soldier by her side, his grey uniform immaculate. There was something about her father's fixed expression and the way his hand gripped his glass that made her call out to him, her voice sharper than she intended.

'Da?'

'Who did you say you bought it from again?' His voice was small and narrow. Contained.

'I didn't. A woman called Caroline Raven.'

The room contracted in the sudden silence, the only noise the sound of the clock ticking in the corner. Tick. Tick. Tick.

He shoved back from the table, the glass slipping from his fingers and snapping in two, showering her mother's best linen tablecloth in red wine drops, not that either of them noticed. Kitty would later. She'd remember that exact moment every time she carefully unfolded the fabric, the faintest of stain visible to those who knew where to look.

'What the hell, Da!'

'I thought as much. Coming to stir up a hornets' nest I'll bet. You'd be wise to realise that the past is best left in the past, dead and buried where it belongs, my girl,' he hissed. 'Bag the lot up and drop it in the nearest bin. If I see it again that's where it's going.'

He lumbered to his feet and swiftly left the room, the remains of their lunch lying between them. His lopsided party hat at war with his angry words. The festivities were over for another year. She was at a loss as to why.

The room felt colder despite the heat from the blazing fire. Kitty rubbed her hands up and down her arms, trying to get warm, the threat of sudden tears an ache in the back of her throat. She stared in confusion at the slim green notebook splattered with wine as she struggled to make sense of what had just happened between them.

It looked like an old school journal, with the pupil's name on the cover. Very similar to the ones stored in the attic from her own school days but somehow, she knew that it was more than that. It had to be for her father to react in the way he had.

She focused on the name penned on the front, her eyes stinging with unshed tears. The ink faded but easy enough to read.

Miss E Nightingale.

THREE

EVELYN NIGHTINGALE

21 June, 1940 – Guernsey

'One small bag only, madame.' The official eyed her case in alarm, his mouth a thin line of disapproval.

'I'm sorry. It's the only one I could find.'

'I don't care about that. That suitcase is too large for the boat,' the man said, his expression as belligerent as his posture. All bull neck and beady eyes, his attention switching between the people behind and the gangway ahead, the customs barrier the only thing separating the two. Evelyn would have made a run for it if she thought she could get away with it, but not without leaving the case, which defeated the exercise somewhat. It was bad enough being shipped off home soil to an uncertain future, but she needed her things. Not that there were many. Her clothes. A few mementos. Her life.

Evelyn clenched her embarkation ticket in her hand, the card thin between her gloved fingers, the couple behind jostling into the back of her at the delay, the passenger steamer being loaded up ahead. The group of fellow teachers turned to watch, their expressions laced with a combination of fear and confusion. They didn't know what was coming, not exactly, but with France occupied there was only one thing standing between the German troops and the UK and that was the Channel Islands.

She shook her head at them in dismay. The suitcase was the only one she had. With everyone else leaving the island too, the shops in St Peter Port town had sold out. Evelyn had found her parents' case on top of the wardrobe in her father's bedroom. It was a heavy, sturdy case made from thick leather designed to last. Full of all her possessions. It was almost impossible to drag along the quay, the bottom scraping against the ground, her muscles bunching under the effort, the sun hot and thick overhead. The sweat causing her best dress to stick to her back.

'I don't know what to do.'

'Move aside now, madame. There are other people to board. We leave on the half hour.'

She stepped back, watching as the crowd surged around her, filling the space she'd left, an assortment of small cases and carrier bags clutched between anxious hands.

Evelyn held on to the railings, boats bobbing round on their moorings to the backdrop of Castle Cornet beyond, the screech of herring gulls overhead. She hadn't wanted to leave. Now that decision had been taken out of her hands. Guernsey was her home, the only place she'd known. There were so many memories that tied her to the island. Memories of her mother and the picnics they used to take at a moment's notice. The weekends spent on her father's small fishing boat as they rock hopped to Herm for a swim when the weather allowed. The precious time with her fiancé, Joseph, that she couldn't bear to let fade into oblivion. Losing those memories would be akin to losing him all over again. There was also her father to consider, her father as he was now. A difficult man who'd lost his way when her mother had died. A man who was keen for her to leave the past behind. But how could she? It had shaped her into who she'd become.

While White Rock Quay was busy with last-minute passengers, the town was deathly quiet as were the surrounding roads. She'd heard rumour that twenty thousand boat tickets had been printed, which she could well believe. Most of their friends and neighbours had left. All the children in the schools, accompanied by their teachers, or most of them. A ghost island inhabited by essential workers and the odd stupid woman with a too large suitcase and a guilt that far outweighed any actual need to assuage it. She shouldn't have listened to her father. Her place was with him, whether he liked it or not.

St Julian's Avenue had never seemed so steep, the case growing heavier with every step. Nothing to distract her. No boys to be seen loitering through the railings of Elizabeth College since they'd suspended the term the day before. A couple raced past the Gaumont Cinema, their jackets flying out behind them, a bulging pillowcase gripped between them. She walked along until she came to Candie Road and the Georgian townhouse where she had lived with her father for as long as she could remember. It was an imposing white building buttressed up to the pavement and surrounded by an impressive set of black railings. Now that there were only the two of them, the four bedrooms were two too many. It was difficult to keep clean and difficult to heat, tasks that fell on her shoulders now.

The front door creaked when she pushed it open. There was no front door key or none that she knew the location of. No one locked their homes. There was no point as crime was non-existent on the small island, although she feared that might be about to change.

She slipped off her shoes and left them under the hall table before glancing into the lounge. The overstuffed horsehair sofa that had been bought when her parents had married, the radio taking pride of place on the mahogany sideboard. Coal in the fireplace as well as a full scuttle now it was being rationed, a stack of old newspapers beside it. The sound of a glass chinking against bottle caused her to blink hard.

The whisky bottle sat in the centre of the table, the top discarded on the work surface along with the seal, the glass half full. Beside it, the ham sandwich she'd made for him before she left lay untouched, the bread glistening and curling in the warmth streaming in through the sparkling windows. She'd spent yesterday washing and scrubbing, polishing and darning. Getting things ready for her departure and for what? The bent head, the grey hair wispy and uncombed. No acknowledgement as to her presence apart from a brief flexing of his fingers around the glass before raising it to his lips and downing it in one.

'I'm back, Father.'

'I can see that. Miss the boat, did you?' He lifted his head briefly, his mouth compressed in his unshaven face.

'No. They wouldn't let me on.' She forced a laugh. 'How stupid. Said the case was too big.'

The excuse lay thick and heavy. An excuse that was anything but. She could have managed without her things, everything except a couple of treasured photographs. No, she'd chosen to stay. The decision was hers alone. Some might call it cowardly, or even selfish when she knew she wasn't wanted. She'd promised her mother to look out for him. That promise was a heavier burden than any suitcase.

'As you like.'

She went up to change out of her Sunday best dress. What to wear when you're being evacuated was yesterday's problem. With the dress back on its hanger and her little brown hat on the shelf above, she smoothed her frock over her hips before stooping to check her face in the oval mirror set into her dressing table. She still had a few minutes to unpack.

It was the sight of the small pile of spelling notebooks lying beside her case that made her sink onto the edge of the bed, her head in her hands. In her haste to remain she'd forgotten about her duty as a teacher. Her duty to her pupils, who'd been whisked away from their parents and everything they'd ever known. It was too late to change her mind now, with the last boat having already set sail. Only time would tell if her decision had been the right one.

FOUR
EVELYN

28 June, 1940 – Guernsey

There was nothing unusual about Evelyn's morning. The day was hotter than the one before, the azure, cloudless sky stretching out into the distance as far as the eye could see. There was perhaps even a trace of confidence in the air, the news beating out, on the hour every hour. The military expert opinion was that there was nothing to fear from the Germans taking advantage of the British military pulling out of the islands. It wasn't a confidence Evelyn shared. She'd seen the low German aircraft flying overhead yesterday and again this morning as had anyone who'd bothered to glance out of their windows at the roaring thunder filling the skies. She couldn't make out a Junker from a Messerschmitt. She wouldn't even be able to recognise a British plane from a German one if it wasn't for the swastikas emblazoning the side.

It was a trifle unkind to consider the day run-of-the-mill. It was also Evelyn's birthday. A strange day to be celebrating turning forty with the streets empty and the onset of ration books making everyone think twice before splurging on anything that wasn't essential. There was flour in the kitchen cupboard and a spare sack in the shed but to use it on a cake instead of bread when all stocks of the stuff had now been taken over by someone called the Food Controller would be extravagant and that was something Evelyn wasn't. Her father might be manager of Grange Lodge Hotel and bring home a good salary along with the occasional treats from the kitchen but there wasn't money to waste. There would be no cake. Instead, she'd arranged to cycle up to Fermain with her best friend, ditch their bikes in the hedge along Gypsy Lane before wandering down to the beach for a sunbath and a swim in the crystal blue of the seas that surrounded the island. A stolen day before the two currently unemployed teachers decided what to do with themselves now their charges had been whisked away from their classrooms.

'I can't believe you're forty,' Alice said, starting to sift through her bag.

'Neither can I!' Evelyn didn't know where the years had flown to. Forty and still single. A spinster of the parish no less. What a horrible term but with a large element of truth hidden between the consonants. Spinster. Someone who spins. Knitster would be more apt but, in the same way she'd had no say in taking her place on the shelf alongside other unweds, she had no say in how she was labelled.

'Here. This is for you. Don't get too excited.'

'You shouldn't have.' Evelyn took the squashed package, fingering the neatly tied ribbon with a beaming smile, her eyes dancing with delight.

'I didn't! You know me and handiwork of any sort. Ma knitted them but I did buy the wool and choose the colour,' Alice carried on, obviously keen to make up for her failings in the crafts department. Evelyn had sat beside the younger woman in the staff room for the last three years, while she'd mangled her way through an assortment of woollens from scarfs to socks. It didn't matter. What did was that Alice hadn't been shipped off the island along with the rest of her friends and colleagues.

'I love them.' She slipped on the cherry-red gloves with no regard for the temperature shooting up to the high seventies. 'The colour is perfect, and thank your mother too,' she said, swishing her hands backwards and forwards to catch the light.

'Enough of that. We have beer, only one each but...'

'But perfect. Thank you, Alice. It will go great with our sandwiches.' Evelyn removed her gloves, making sure to tuck them deep into the bottom of her swim bag, one foot on the pavement, the other on the pedal, her eyes scrunched up against the brightness of the sun. 'If we pedal hard, we'll be there in twenty minutes.'

'Another swim?'

I'm not sure I should after all those sandwiches,' Alice replied from her position stretched out on the sand, her blue one-piece a perfect foil for her bright blonde hair.

They'd been baking for three hours but now, with the time well past six and the beach emptying, it was time to think about the journey home. There'd be an evening relaxing in the front room listening to the radio with her knitting. In truth, Evelyn would have preferred the cinema, but they'd closed all dance halls and entertainment venues earlier in the week.

'Go on. It will cool us off before the cycle home.'

With their hair tucked underneath their swim caps they raced to the waterline and launched themselves into the sea, splashing round like the children they looked after. Memories of happier times flickered. Her parents anchoring their boat and swimming to shore, the sun hot on her shoulders and back, her eyes wide in anticipation at the thought of ice cream.

They were on their way home, halfway down the Val des

Terres – the twisty hill at one end of St Peter Port – when the air raid sirens shrieked and within seconds came the now familiar roar of airplanes overhead.

'Quick, into the hedge.'

With their bikes abandoned, they hurried across to the other side of the road where the bushes were easier to get to, their hands covering their ears as the pulsing thump of explosion after explosion caused the ground to shake and the birds to scatter, the azure sky almost obliterated by thick columns of smoke.

'We're going to die,' Alice screeched, her head now in her hands, tears leaking between her fingers, no trace of the confident thirty-year-old of earlier.

'No, we're fine.' Evelyn tried to reassure her, her own heart beating fast. 'If we can't see them then they can't see us.' Evelyn pulled Alice into an awkward hug, her hand on her back, and they stayed like that until the sirens petered out.

'Come on.'

'I don't think I want to...'

'Alice, either you come with me, or I leave you here by yourself.'

They left their bikes by the Slaughterhouse and carried on by foot, the pavements and roads glistening with shards of broken glass. A beautiful sight. Like something out of a fairy story except that it wasn't.

'That's a lot of broken windows.'

'If all we've got is smashed windows then...'

They'd reached the Ship and Crown pub, the harbour opposite and the White Rock Quay, the wail of screams overtaken by the wail of ambulance sirens streaming down St Julian's Avenue. People wandered around in a daze, their hands, their faces, their clothes streaked in red. The air filled with a thick, heavy smoke, flames clearly visible from the line of trucks, the smell of burning causing Evelyn's nose to itch and her throat to tighten.

'Mother of...' Alice started to say.

'She can't help but we can.'

'I think I'm going to be sick.' And with that Alice bent over and lost the contents of her stomach.

Evelyn scooped her friend's hair away from her forehead and mopped her up with her hanky, her first aid training coming back to her.

'You stay right there. Well, not right there.' She took her by the hand like a child, leading her away from the vomit before sitting her down on a convenient wall in front of the States Office. 'I'll be back as soon as I can.'

'Don't go.' Alice grabbed her hand. 'Please. I should have left. Why didn't we leave when we had the chance? God, we're all going to be murdered in our beds.'

'Now that's silly talk. They're going to do nothing of the sort.' Evelyn sounded more confident than she felt. Her legs were shaking, the skin scratched red raw from where her shins had landed in the middle of a bramble bush. 'I'm going to offer my services to that ambulance man over there. I'll be back in a minute.'

The ground crunched under her feet, the air heavy with the smell of burning, mingling with the pungent odour of squashed tomatoes. The normal sounds from the town seemed muted. Cars had been abandoned in the road, their doors open as people ran down to help, now the planes had retreated into the distance. The screams had changed to keening moans of despair from near the long line of blackened lorries lined up in their usual position waiting for the ferry to dock, one or two still slick with flames.

'Need a hand? I have my first aid certificate,' she said, approaching one of the ambulance men who was on his knees rummaging in a large green bag.

'Well, I won't say no, miss. I'm Mr Le Page, and you are?'

Evelyn would have smiled as she swapped names but there

was nothing remotely amusing about the man still finding the space for the usual civilities between strangers on first meeting. There was nothing usual about the situation they found themselves in and a strange kind of comfort in the normality of their exchange.

'Leave your things in the front of the ambulance, Miss Nightingale. They will be safe there. There's bandages, tweezers and antiseptic on a tray. If you can attend to the minors. I've been asking them to line up against the sea wall.' He nodded in the direction of a group of men and women holding an assortment of scarves, towels and other makeshift dressings to various body parts. 'Mostly bits of flying glass and other bits of shrapnel. Anything you can't handle or anyone you think more seriously injured then holler. I'll just be over there with my colleague.'

Evelyn blinked as she separated out what she was seeing into its constituent parts. The two ambulance men and what looked like a pair of blackened legs poking out from under the burned-out chassis, the pool of water indication that the fire buckets had been put to good use. A tarpaulin in one of their hands no doubt ready to disguise the worst from the members of the public still milling about.

The minute she'd promised Alice quickly slithered into three hours, the worst three hours she'd ever experienced, hours she'd relive over and over again later when there was nothing to distract her. Twenty-two lives lost, the bodies that they could get to all carefully transported up the hill to the hospital.

The daylight was starting to fade by the time she remembered Alice.

Turning to Mr Le Page, she asked, 'You haven't seen my friend, have you? Blonde, pretty. She was sitting on the wall along a bit.'

'One of my mates said they'd give her a lift home. Looked in a bit of a state.'

'That was good of him.'

'He was happy to. Here, don't forget your bag.'

Evelyn barely registered the bag dangling from his fingers with her swim things and the remains of their beach picnic. It all seemed so long ago.

'Sorry, thank you, I forgot. And call me Evelyn. I'm sure we can allow normal protocol to drop after what we've been through.'

'I'm Dave, hop in the back and I'll drop you home. Nothing more we can do until the morning.'

'My bike,' Evelyn said, suddenly remembering.

'If you tell me where you've left it, I'll collect it on the way past. Save you a walk in the morning. Least I can do. Not many I've met who'd do what you've done today.'

'Thank you.' Evelyn waved away the rest of his words, concentrating instead on her breathing and the strong, pressing thought that she was about to disgrace herself by throwing up in front of him. Practising bandaging within the confines of the ambulance station had proved to be very different to patching up the assortment of men, women and children who'd restlessly waited her ministrations. The reality of the day suddenly came crashing down. She'd been alright when she'd been too busy to think but now... Now her thoughts were back in abundance and she wasn't in a fit state for any of them.

She gripped her bag between clenched fists. The creeping sense of anxiety that she'd probably caused more harm than good made her chest tighten and her hands tremble.

'If you could drop me off just before Elizabeth College, please,' she managed, her voice tight. 'It's only a few steps from there and won't be taking you out of your way.' She wasn't in a fit state for her father's questions. She wasn't in a fit state for anything.

. . .

Twenty minutes later found her wearily pushing open the front door.

'Dad, where are you?' She placed her gloves on the hall table, staring at the cherry red and only seeing blood.

'Evelyn!'

'Dad.' She ran to him, her arms reaching out in the same way she used to as a child, breathing in the smell of him, a combination of smoke, whisky and sandalwood soap.

They didn't hug, not really. As soon as her arms stretched around his back, he shifted away. They didn't have that sort of a father-daughter relationship. Sometimes it was difficult for her to remember that.

'I was worried out of my mind. Alice was back hours ago.'

'I'm sorry. I stopped to help.'

She noticed his expression souring at her words and, glancing down, took stock of her appearance for the first time since that morning. The red streaks on her shirt and shorts. The scratch marks on her legs mingled with dirt from kneeling on the ground while attending to the children, and a quick glance in the hall mirror showed her hair was a bird's nest of tangles.

Evelyn's dark hair was already starting to streak with grey and she had a preference for practical clothes over flattering ones. If life had been kinder, she'd have been married to Joseph these last twenty years or more. Instead, she had no children of her own. She tried to tell herself that it was a blessing being able to give her charges back at the end of the school day but it didn't make any difference. She missed out on being a mother as much as she mourned not being Joseph's wife.

Her father shook his head at her before turning away and making for the kitchen, his old slippers slapping against the linoleum flooring, disappointment etched in every step.

'Let me get changed and I'll make tea.'

'I've already eaten.'

Evelyn had always known she was a disappointment. Her

father had wanted a son, a not-so-secret secret that he'd blurted out one day when she was being a particularly trying teenager. At least he'd kept it to himself until then, but it had still hurt. It still hurt now but she was old enough not to show it.

'That's good,' was all she said, running her hands through her hair.

She was tired from her day and tired from trying to act in control in front of a pile of terrified friends, neighbours and, in a few instances, strangers. But mostly she was tired from the stress and strain of trying to live up to her father's unrealistic expectations.

Instead of heading upstairs to change, she followed him into the kitchen, noting the dirty plates from his meal stacked beside the sink, the lingering smell of smoked mackerel filling her nostrils. Evelyn hated the dish but it made a frequent appearance as many of the guests at the Grange Lodge Hotel, where her father worked, couldn't or wouldn't eat the breakfast staple either. There was also a brown paper bag in the centre of the table, sitting alongside a prettily wrapped box, tied with a scrap of string fashioned into an intricate knot.

He placed his finger on the box first, pushing it across. 'Your aunt asked me to pass this on. She didn't have time to stop.'

'Thank you. I'll write and thank her,' she said.

It was difficult to remember the slight bespectacled woman in any other light than her role as nun at the local Les Cotils Convent. Sister Thérèse's black and white habit seemed to swallow her small frame, making it easy for Evelyn to forget that beneath it all, she was still her aunt. She remembered how the nun had set aside all hopes of marriage following the death of her betrothed in the Battle of the Somme. Sister Thérèse, from the Order of Sisters of Mary of the Presentation, was one of the many spinsters manufactured by the Great War. When her mother had told her the sad tale, Evelyn had struggled to understand her aunt's decision. Following the death of Joseph, it had been something she'd toyed with. She envied her aunt's serenity following her decision but she could never imagine having that spiritual certainty for herself. She knew that her own faith wasn't strong enough.

The box was small and with a scrap of paper with the word *fragile* written in her aunt's sloping hand. Evelyn quickly realised why when she removed the lid to find two brown speckled eggs lying on a little nest of hay. 'The darling. I can't remember the last time I had an egg.'

'Not sure when you'll next get one either. Food is getting scarcer and scarcer, not that we're getting many guests at the hotel. Right twitched with everyone leaving. We've had more cancellations than bookings.'

She stared at the eggs, trying to recall the last time she and her da had spoken about anything more adventurous than the weather. The intricacies of conversation had died along with her mother. She missed that. She only realised just now how much.

'Here. There's two.' She went to remove one only to stop at her father's expression.

'No, you mustn't. I get fed well enough,' he said, brushing off her offer with a gruff shake of his head.

Do you? Do you really, Da? I don't think so the way the skin is almost falling from your bones. The thought remained unsaid. Her father wasn't the type to take advice, especially not from a woman even if she was his daughter.

'I insist. Couldn't manage two anyway.'

'Thank you. There's this too. It's not much.' The words tumbled out as he focused on his feet instead of meeting her gaze. 'Only something from the lost and found cupboard but, well, I know you'll make good use of it. Happy birthday.'

'I'm sure it's wonderful, whatever it is.'

Evelyn knew what it was, unless her father had decided to play a trick on her by disguising her gift into the shape of something else. But that wasn't his way; he wasn't one for surprises. Her fingers brushed the edges of the parcel and suddenly she was eight again, sitting at the kitchen table with her mother, the smell of freshly baked sponge cake filling the room. She remembered the way her mother had smiled, lighting the candles with such care, her eyes bright with the joy of the moment. They'd spent the morning together, Evelyn's small hands helping to ice the cake, smearing more on her face than on the sponge. That birthday her present had been a music box.

She ruthlessly blinked the memory away until later. Her father's gift couldn't bring back that time, but for a moment, holding the package in her hands, it felt like a connection to the past.

Firmly back in the present, she unfastened the clasp of the case and couldn't help a small gasp of astonishment. The violin might be old and discarded but Evelyn saw beyond the peeling varnish and broken strings. Until recently, she'd been using one of the school's instruments but that had all stopped now the school had been packed up and the pupils evacuated to safety. That she could play again forged a lump in her throat too heavy to swallow. With her father all but forgotten, she lifted the violin out and balanced it on her hands. The shape and the feel spoke of quality. It didn't matter how it looked. For Evelyn it was all about the depth and breadth of the notes hidden within.

She couldn't resist running the bow across the strings, her eyes slipping closed briefly at the sweetest of chords, only to snap open again. It was too soon to play, not with the sound of those screams from the harbour competing for attention.

Evelyn replaced the violin and bow gently back in their nest, using the time to marshal her thoughts and control her emotions. 'It's wonderful. The best of presents. Thank you, Dad.'

'I'm glad you like it. Something no one else wanted.' His words were harsh but Evelyn saw them for what they were. The flush of embarrassment that stained his cheeks was a visual reminder of what they'd both lost when her mother had died. Their emotional anchor.

She worked on snapping the clasp shut. 'Oh. Why's that?'

'Because of its origins.'

He tapped on the case with a bony finger.

'German.'

FIVE
EVELYN

19 November, 1940 – Guernsey

'Tell me a little about yourself, Miss Nightingale.'

Evelyn managed a small smile, her gloved hands lying loosely on her lap, her knees pressed together to stop them shaking. When Dave Le Page had encouraged her to apply to the recently formed Emergency Hospital in the nearby parish of the Câtel, she hadn't given a thought to the fact she might get an interview. But with the island completely shut off from its neighbours, getting trained nursing staff was impossible. Five months out of work had shrunk Evelyn's savings to nothing. She'd kept herself busy by volunteering at the ambulance station but now she needed work. It was this job or working in the greenhouses because she couldn't countenance working for the Germans. Her father had decided to take a job with the *Feldkommandant*. It wasn't that difficult a decision since the *Feldkommandant* had set up residence at her father's place of work. However, in Evelyn's opinion, one Nightingale working for the enemy was one too many.

The room she'd been shown into was small and dark with

one tiny window partially obscured by a blackout blind. The desk took up most of the available space, the top clear apart from a pen and a blank sheet of paper. Sitting behind it, statue still, was the matron of the medical wing. Matron Rabey was formidable, her hair pressed into knife-pleat waves, her long-sleeved, navy uniform topped with a gleaming white frilly collar and matching cuffs. Over the years Evelyn had managed to control a class full of unruly teenagers and their equally unruly parents, but Matron Rabey was a completely different proposition.

'I'm a teacher. That is, I was a teacher until the school evacuated,' she answered, her hands folded in her lap, her voice quiet but steady.

'Of what?'

'Languages and music.'

'Languages as in English?' Matron leant forward, her eyes wide with sudden curiosity.

'I'm afraid not. Languages as in French, Spanish and German.' Evelyn's accompanying smile was small, almost apologetic.

'Mmm.' She tutted. 'I don't allow German to be spoken on the wards. Distressing for the patients and unnecessary with the Germans having their own hospital. Indeed, there should be no need for them to enter ours, but they do. Constantly. However, the music will be an asset to our social club. What instrument do you play?'

'The violin.'

'Charming. I've always thought the violin very dignified. Are you in a relationship, Miss Nightingale?' she asked, the change in topic causing Evelyn to blink.

'No, not currently.'

'For the record, our nurses aren't allowed romantic entanglements.'

'That's a relief.' Her joke fell on stony ground, causing her to mumble through an embellishment. 'I live with my father. No husband, boyfriend or significant other and not likely to be.'

'And your father is happy to lose you to us?'

Evelyn hadn't asked him. With German officers occupying the Grange Lodge Hotel she'd barely seen him. She couldn't blame him for working for the Germans. He needed to eat and it was only a continuation of the job he'd been doing previously.

'He won't mind.' The truth was that he probably wouldn't notice.

Matron picked up her pen, removed the cap and spent a moment writing something on the top of the page. 'And what makes you think you'll be a good nurse, Miss Nightingale? The work is hard and the hours long,' she said, eyeing her up and down. 'If you don't mind me saying, you don't appear to be very strong.'

'I'm stronger than I look.' Evelyn adjusted the hem of her second best skirt over her bony knees before continuing, her voice taking on a thread of steel. She needed this job and she knew she could do it, at least as well as anyone else. 'I'm also used to hard work, and I'm not scared of what I might come across.' She paused before continuing, her gaze direct, her chin lifted in defiance. 'It was my great misfortune to be nearby during the harbour bombings but I managed to do what I could to help. Volunteering for the ambulance service has been an… enlightening experience.'

'I am sure of that.' Matron smiled, her face lighting up briefly before returning into its composed lines and grooves. 'It's a live-in post. Two afternoons off a week and one full day off a month. I'll start you on day duty, male medical to get your bearings then a month of nights. Thirty-one on, three off. Then back on to days. Seven o'clock tomorrow morning, sharp, Miss Nightingale. When you've adjusted to us, I'll consider where you'll be most suited to work.' She hesitated briefly. 'I take it you've come across the term *Freudenhaus* during your studies?'

Evelyn had difficulty in controlling her expression at the swift conversation change and the use of the term.

'I know of it, yes but I'm not sure of the context?'

'Brothels, Miss Nightingale.' The statement was unadorned, Matron's displeasure clear by her tone. 'The invaders are in the process of setting up numerous bordellos across the bailiwick and filling them with foreigners, mostly French and Russian. As we are the only hospital set up to take women they will be treated here.' She leant back, clearly waiting for Evelyn's response.

Evelyn's heart pounded, unsure whether what she was about to say was right or wrong, only that it felt right to her. 'Which is as it should be.'

'Exactly.' Matron nodded briefly before returning to the matter in hand. 'One of the maids will be expecting you this evening to show you the nurses' accommodation. Between six and half past. I'll have her leave out two uniforms for you. Any questions?'

Evelyn had a long list of them in her bag but not the courage required to fish out the scrap of paper in the woman's presence. 'No. Thank you for taking me on, Matron.'

'You might want to reserve your thanks until you know what you're letting yourself in for.' She held out her hand. 'Welcome to the Emergency Hospital, Nurse Nightingale.'

Evelyn exchanged her best Sunday gloves for her red ones as she made her way to the entrance, hunched against the biting wind, unsure of what had just happened during the most bizarre of interviews. Dave Le Page must have been right about their desperation for staff. She'd have to remember to tell him next time she saw him, she thought, walking through the high white gate and over to where she'd left her bicycle. If she saw him. Two afternoons a week and one day off a month would be barely enough time to do her laundry.

. . .

Six thirty the following morning and she was queuing up for a free sink in her new uniform, her toothbrush in her hand, wondering what she'd let herself in for. The other women seemed nice enough from what she'd seen of them last night, but they were all younger and more interested in chatting among themselves than to the new girl.

The woman in front turned slightly, a smile on her face. 'New? I'm Ivy. It's far worse than it looks.'

'I'm Evelyn and, so I'm gathering.' She managed a laugh.

'Which ward are you on?'

'Male medical. Days for a week then nights.'

'They always stick the new ones on nights. You can't do as much damage or that's the theory.' Ivy turned back to the mirror before smoothing a stray hair and fixing her cap on top. 'Never turn your back on the men and remember, the old ones are always the worst.'

After twenty years of exclusively teaching girls, Evelyn had little experience of men outside of her father and her fiancé, Joseph.

'Thanks for the warning. I can probably guess why!' She spat out her toothpaste and, glancing in the mirror, tweaked her collar and cuffs in a passing imitation of her new friend.

'You're welcome. Male medical is out the doors and straight opposite. It's report first, which is always in Sister's office. You'll soon catch on.' Ivy scanned the room, her tightly knotted black hair gleaming under her cap. 'Hey, Violet, you're on male medical. Look after Evelyn, will you?'

'Sure. Follow me and do as I do.' Violet added another hairpin to her cap, her hair a cloud of unruly curls. 'Oh, and don't speak until you're spoken to, especially to anything in a white coat. In fact, the sluice is the best place when there's a doctor's round. You'll be able to keep the rest of us juniors company.' Evelyn didn't know if she was joking. There was a faint glimmer of a smile and then she almost, but not quite, ran for the door before dropping her speed to a fast walk, saying over her shoulder, 'Another thing. We don't run unless it's a fire, or a haemorrhage. Got it?'

'Absolutely,' she replied, mirroring Violet's stride and already feeling the pull on her calf muscles. She had an idea that she wasn't as fit as she thought from all the cycling she'd had to do recently.

The Sister in charge of male medical was a slight Irish woman called Margaret Murphy with enviable ankles and a manner that could curdle milk at fifty paces. All the nurses feared her, along with most of the patients.

'Don't underestimate her pretty face and sweet smile, Evelyn,' Violet whispered out the side of her mouth. 'Sister is a real harridan, but Matron thinks differently, as do the doctors.'

'What's so important that you feel you have to interrupt my report, Nurse Gaudion?' Sister snapped, looking up from the large book she was writing in, her dulcet Northern Irish accent at war with her intransigent stare.

'Nothing, Sister. Sorry, Sister.'

With report over, of which Evelyn hadn't understood a word outside of the names and ages of the patients, she was surprised to be paired with Violet for the remainder of the shift instead of one of the other two older staff on duty.

'She knows I'm a good teacher as well as quick on my feet. Come on. I'll take you on a tour, but it will have to be short, mind. There're thirty-four patients to sort before we even get a whiff of breakfast. First the blackout blinds so we can at least see what we're doing. Then it's bottles, bedpans, bed baths, bed-making and breakfasts. All the B's this time of the day and here's me gasping for a cuppa.'

Evelyn was feeling dizzy by the time the tour was over. Violet had whizzed in front of her, pointing out this and that at a speed she feared she'd never emulate. Working at the ambulance station doing the odd dressing and rolling up bandages was very different to the span of duties she'd have to carry out, with one eye on the clock and the other on Sister. What had felt like an amazing opportunity now felt anything but, as she tried to recap everything she'd been told. Apparently, the sluice was temperamental as was the kitchen maid. The steriliser a relic from the last century and likely to burn the skin from your hands. The linen cupboard now padlocked, the key dangling off a chain hanging from Sister's belt since the loss of ten sheets and pillow cases to people or persons unknown. The only thing in the ward kitchen not carefully rationed, and only because the hospital was situated on a farm, was milk.

'If you don't like the stuff then tough. Sister is a great believer in egg flips for the undernourished, which is most of the ward with Jerry the German hogging the best for themselves but with eggs now in short supply it's more flip than egg, if you get my meaning.' Violet headed to the supply of towels and flannels on the back trolley. 'It's important we keep the egg whites for the pressure sores. Best thing on the market. Works a treat with a bit of oxygen.'

Evelyn nodded and smiled as if she understood.

'Right, it's time for the colonel's bed bath. I like to get him out the way first while there's a bit of heat left in the water.' Violet secured her cuffs higher up her arms and, with a bowl under one arm and towels in the other, approached the end of the ward as if going into battle.

Male medical was made up of two oblong wards with sixteen beds each, separated by two side rooms. The beds, with their smart red blankets and white counterpanes, hugged the wall, each identical to its partner with a locker, a bed table and a chair. There was also a light dangling over each bed and a distinct smell of some cleaning product Evelyn always associated with sickness clinging to the air.

'Okay, there's a few things you need to know about the colonel, or Lieutenant Colonel Mark Carter to give him his full title,' Violet said, picking up a large earthenware jug and filling the bottom of the bowl with an inch of steaming water before topping it up with cold. 'He's a bit of a hero is our colonel. Served in the Western Front as a teenager during the first war, earning himself a DSO. If that wasn't enough, he decided to join up for the second. Shot in the leg somewhere in France at the start of the year and lost his leg in the process but not before he'd managed to save his unit from capture. Forty men owe him their life. Got the Victoria Cross for that little bit of heroism. Returned home to Guernsey to convalesce before taking up a desk job in Whitehall, only days before Hitler's army decided to pay us a protracted visit.' She spoke rapidly, her quick steps making short work of the long ward. 'Sadly, he's also a diabetic.'

'Ah.'

Evelyn looked at the man resting back against the sheets, his eyes closed, his skin loose around saggy jowls in a concertina of wrinkles. She remembered from the report that he was only forty-nine, which made him only nine years older than her. He looked twice that age and more. Part of her job at the ambulance station had been to restock their cupboards. When she'd started, the storage cupboard had been ceiling high with boxes containing everything from dressings, bandages to drugs. Now it was a constant battle to even get the most rudimentary of supplies.

'Technically now his wound has healed we could discharge him but we're fond of the colonel, so we've decided to keep him.'

Violet adjusted the portable screen to shield the bed from prying eyes, not that any of the other patients were interested in what was happening in the other end of the ward. There was a game of chess underway in one corner and a few newspapers being passed between the men on the opposite side of the room while they waited for breakfast. Sister was standing in front of the medicine trolley, her apron folded across her dress to form a V, her sleeves rolled up and secured by white elasticated cuffs.

'Morning, Colonel. Hope you had a good night?'

'Fair. Here to annoy me, I take it.'

'Here to freshen you up, if that's what you mean. Fresh sheets and pyjamas too, as it's a Wednesday. This is Nurse Nightingale. Her first day so I'm holding you responsible to help show her the ropes.'

'First name Florence by any chance?'

Evelyn chuckled. She'd been waiting for that sort of comment ever since she'd decided to apply to the hospital. She opened her mouth but Violet got in first.

'You know better than that, Colonel. Sister will string us up by our garters if we divulge our Christian names to you. It's nurse this and nurse that as you very well know.' Evelyn watched as Violet leant forward on the pretext of unbuttoning his pyjama top and helping him slip it over his head. 'First name Evelyn.' Then a little louder. 'Nurse Nightingale, we start at the top and work our way down, using towels for privacy and to prevent the colonel becoming cold with the hot water limited to lukewarm. Then it's a rub of the heel with methylated spirit and a sprinkle of talc. Circular motions with the flat of your hand to get the blood flowing.'

'Speak a little louder, why don't you, Nurse Gaudion. They might be able to hear you in the upper parishes as well as the lower,' Sister hissed from outside the screens. 'And do get a move on. The breakfast trolley is nearly here.'

'Is she always like that?' Evelyn whispered, drying the colonel's arm before moving on to dry his chest. Walking out during the first day wasn't what she'd envisioned but that was the way things were looking. At forty, Evelyn had imagined that she'd finished with being treated like a child. It was galling to realise that was far from the case.

'Pretty much but with a heart of gold under all the bluster, eh, Colonel?' Violet whispered back, trying to get a lather from the small disc of soap and failing miserably.

'If it wasn't for Sister, they'd have turfed me out long ago.'

Evelyn nodded, her head bent as she worked on the colonel's right leg, trying to avoid looking at the stump where there should have been his left.

It was all too new and emotional. Every patient had a story, a heavy burden which settled like a dead weight in her chest. The colonel was only one of the patients on the ward. There were many more. As a teacher, she'd mostly been able to leave her job at the school gates, apart from the occasional stack of marking. After what she'd seen that morning, she knew that she'd be carrying the worry of every one of her patients back to the nurses' home tonight. Only time would tell if she had the strength and stamina for nursing.

Evelyn placed the leg down and started rubbing in cream, following Violet's lead. She'd give it a fortnight and if things hadn't improved by then she'd get a job in the greenhouses. Plants didn't have the emotional entanglement that came with nursing.

SIX
EVELYN

25 March, 1943

'Nightingale, it's already gone 6 p.m. Time to get up.'

Evelyn groaned, tugging the pile of blankets further up her neck, an act of resistance at the thought of clambering out of bed into the cold.

The second day had followed a similar path, as had the third then it was the first week, the first month, the first year. Every day was different and yet eerily the same. She got to feel a rhythm for the ward, and the patients and staff within it.

Evelyn had noticed a pattern to nursing, the shape of her day, which wasn't that dissimilar to the shape of a teacher's one. Being at the beck and call of others while trying to keep some sort of order. Hospital corners and straight counterpanes instead of lined notebooks and cursive script. The main difference was her feet. Whatever she did she couldn't avoid standing while she did it. Soaking them in a bucket of water now featured as part of her daily routine. It had become as important as music. A soporific for skin, muscles and bone instead of for her soul.

She'd been billeted out of the nurses' home to a cottage a twenty-minute walk away for the last six months, along with Violet. It was a lovely, traditional two-up two-down white-washed cottage with foot thick walls, no heating or bathroom, only an outside toilet in what was one of the coldest winters on record. She'd barely made it home earlier, a snow-laden tree branch breaking off within an inch of her face, giving her the shock of her life. When she had finally made it to bed, she'd struggled to sleep with the sound of the wind hurtling through the rafters and rattling the slates. It must have been the afternoon when she'd finally dropped off. Four hours' sleep to take her through the walk back to work in what could quite conceivably be worse conditions, followed by a twelve-hour shift.

'Come on, Evelyn. If you don't get a move on, you'll make me late or have you forgotten it's my first night. I've made you a cuppa too,' Violet said, trying to coax her out of bed.

She stuck her nose out of the blanket, managing a smile at the sight of her friend carrying a tray with two cups and nothing else. There were no biscuits, not even the broken ones they used to be able to buy at the shop in the arcade in St Peter Port town. All treats had disappeared along with any drink worth drinking.

'Please say you managed to secure some darjeeling in return for favours rendered,' she said, her voice set to optimistic. Violet was the least likely person she knew to be influenced by the Germans. She was also her dearest friend now that Alice had got a job working at the Royal Hotel in town. They were still pals, exchanging letters almost weekly but she never had any spare time in her day to see her.

Violet giggled. 'If you think I'm dropping my drawers for a piddly mug of tea then you can think again. He'd at least need to throw in a box of silk stockings, some French perfume and ten chocolate bars and even then, the answer would still be a resounding no. Walter would have a hissy fit.' She settled on the edge of the bed, the bare fingers of her left hand spread out, a frequent occurrence with her recent engagement. It was either agree to wait for her ring or wear something second hand and, with the bottom fallen out of the second-hand market, it wasn't really a choice. With Walter in the clergy neither of them could afford black-market prices. 'Anyway, I heard from one of the doctors that bramble leaf tea is meant to be good for you.'

'Well, you can carry on believing it. I won't.' But Evelyn didn't demur further. She didn't even grimace when she lifted the cup and took a small sip of the liquid, the sharp flavour catching at the back of her throat, with no milk to alleviate the taste. Violet would have gone out of her way to eke out wood from their meagre pile for the stove to boil the kettle, the only means they had of heating both water and food. 'That reminds me.' She leant out of bed, as far as she could go without toppling onto the floor, and pulled out a large branch. 'Nearly killed me earlier. I thought I'd return the favour.'

Violet eyed the long branch with a frown. 'I'm not sure what we're going to do with it and what if Lili finds it?'

'I'll hide it with the crystal set and my violin behind the outside loo before we leave.'

Lili was the German maid foisted on them two days a week to help with the heavy work while they were up to their necks in equally heavy, albeit very different work over at the hospital. They didn't want her, and they certainly didn't trust her, but they hadn't had a choice in the matter. They were convinced it was Jerry the German's way of spying on them. Things hadn't disappeared since she'd started working for them, but they'd been moved and their belongings rifled, which was another reason Violet was holding out for a ring until a time when she could be assured of its safety.

Getting ready for the walk to work was like preparing for battle. A change from hopping on their bicycles for the five-minute journey freewheeling down to the hospital but their bicycles were now their most precious of possessions as there were no parts to fix them. Taking them out in snow was asking for disaster. Their only other option was to walk.

They had no wellington boots; they didn't even own a pair of boots between them. Their shoes were worn at the sole and the heel, patched up by an extremely busy cobbler in the heart of St Peter Port with whatever he had to hand, which invariably wasn't leather. Instead, they both wore trousers with the ends wrapped in hessian sacking, tied in place with string: a look frowned upon by Matron but essential if they weren't to catch a chill. With their uniforms in their bags, they donned their nursing capes simply because they were the thickest items of clothing they owned and left the safety of the cottage for the lane directly in front of them, their arms entwined for balance.

'This is ridiculous. We'll be lucky we don't catch pneumonia.' Violet was shorter than Evelyn, barely five foot, and the snow was reaching well past her ankles.

'We'll be fine. Think of it as an adventure.' Evelyn hurried her along the track bordered by two high banks, everything draped in white. 'It looks like we're the first to walk this way. Think what it will be like when it turns to slush.'

'Something to look forward to in the morning then,' Violet replied, the sarcasm crystal clear.

They reached the end of the lane, pausing to catch their breath in the icy cold wind, the sight of dark looming shapes etched against the stormy sky drawing their gaze and, in Evelyn's case, hardening her resolve. She'd only been working at the hospital a few months when the Germans had commandeered the building bordering the farm behind for one of their gun batteries. The peaceful location of the country hospital was destroyed in a blink by the earth-shattering sounds of gunfire overhead every time the allies dared to fly overhead on their way to the continent.

'Halt!'

They were halfway down the hill, eyes on the ground when

one of the sentries jumped out in front of them, a rifle lying across his arms.

'Heil Hitler.'

'Er... Heil Hitler.'

Their words were soft, barely audible in the breeze. Meaningless words that they had to comply with or suffer the consequences. It wasn't easy to be brave when the sentences for even tiny breaches were as swift as they were severe. Six weeks in the cells for the most minor indiscretion and with the threat of deportation to Germany, and all the horrific tales that accompanied it, for anything else. Evelyn and Violet had quickly learnt that it was better to act the collaborator even though it was against everything they believed in.

'It is not good weather to be out, yah?'

Evelyn took charge, squeezing tightly onto her friend's hand. 'Heading into work and we're going to be late.'

While she was prepared to play their petty little games to carry on as she wanted, she wasn't a scared young miss cowed by his presence. Yes, he was tall and striking in the way the Germans were. Immaculately dressed in his pressed uniform when they had to make do with whatever they had left in their wardrobe. But he had no reason to stop them walking down the road, unless there was some new rule about not being allowed out in snow. It wasn't even curfew, nowhere near. And anyway, as shift workers, they had exemption slips.

He wasn't going to let them go straight away; it was there in the way he stood a little straighter, his blue-eyed stare unwavering. 'Your ID cards, *bitte*.'

'Certainly.' They unlinked arms briefly to search their pockets before handing them over. They'd all been issued with little cardboard cards with their name, address, date and place of birth along with a small photograph, at the start of the occupation. It was an offence not to carry it.

'You are nurses?' he questioned, tilting his head down the hill in the direction of the hospital.

Evelyn managed a brief nod instead of replying. There was no point. He had no reason to detain them further except for bloody-mindedness. The card stated their occupation, along with the rest of their details. He'd also be able to work out their unmarried status, she remembered, a little niggle of apprehension exploding like an itch she couldn't scratch.

So far, the soldiers she'd come across had been polite, almost gentlemanly. There was always the exception to any rule but thankfully, not in this case as he clicked his heels with a little bow. 'Be careful on the bend. It's like an ice rink.' He stepped back, waving them on with a tilt of his rifle.

'What do you think that was about?' Violet said, her voice a little shaky.

'I'm not sure.' Evelyn chanced a look over her shoulder, only to find the German watching their progress. Something was up, but she had no way of guessing what. 'I wouldn't worry about it. Probably bored,' she said, with far more conviction than she felt, but the last thing she wanted was to ignite Violet's overactive imagination. They'd both been lucky so far in their dealings with the enemy. Long might that luck continue.

After a long stint on female medical, she was now back on male medical with Sister Murphy again at the helm. Nights were very different to day duty with a staff nurse in charge and two untrained staff to support. Tonight, it was her and a new male orderly called Tim Le Clair along with a tall, thin staff called Roberta Draper who everyone called The Rottweiler.

It might have been snowing all day and the temperature dropping to below freezing but that made no difference to the five patients housed in the annex, a long thin corridor of a room bordering the side balcony that skirted the building, the double doors of which were pulled open. The men lived day and night on the balcony in all weathers apart from driving rain and snow: the reality of nursing tuberculosis patients while the scientists tried to find a cure. The only concessions to the cold were the extra blankets piled on top of their beds, hot water bottles tucked down the sides, topped off by mackintoshes and a large tarpaulin canopy attached by a series of batons screwed into the fabric of the building.

Evelyn popped to check on them as soon as the ward settled, a tray of bramble tea between her hands. Her gown was wrapped twice around her thin middle, her soft brown gaze the only thing visible above her mask.

'Alright, chaps?'

'All the better for seeing you, darling,' Pete Grant replied, a pipe clenched between his teeth, his head wreathed in the most horrific foul-smelling cloud.

'What on earth are you smoking now, Mr Grant?'

The lack of tobacco on the island was a serious issue, but one which the men had decided to take it upon themselves to solve by smoking increasingly bizarre concoctions. Last week had featured dried coltsfoot combined with the contents of a jar of molasses someone somewhere had found in the back of a cupboard. She dreaded to think what this week's ingredients were. Strict bedrest and fresh air were the only treatments available to their TB patients. Without the roll-ups or pipes, the staff would never have been able to get them to agree. The fact they lost most of them within a year of diagnosis was something Evelyn tried not to think about.

'Only bramble leaves. I asked the wife to bring some in. An experiment to see if smoking it is any better than drinking it.'

'I think the definitive answer to that is no!' she spluttered, handing round the teacups, trying not to breathe in any more of the foul odour. 'Do remember the fire buckets in the corner. I'll be back to check on you after I've sorted out the dishes and alerted the fire brigade to stand by.'

'Hah, very funny. More to the point, what have our boys been up to?'

Evelyn, like many of the islanders, was desperate to hear news of what was happening in the war but with all the media outlets in the occupiers' hands she had to use nefarious means to get her daily updates. Crystal radio sets were relatively simple mechanisms for someone friendly with the head of chemistry at Blanchlands Ladies College, the only problem was hiding them. There was a huge bunch of nettles growing behind the shed at the back of the cottage, which was optimistically referred to as their outside toilet. An ideal place for her violin and anything else they didn't want Lili to find.

'Not good, I'm afraid. The Japs have sunk one of our American neighbour's subs.'

'Bloody Nora. Sorry, nurse,' he apologised quickly, his face glowing a ruddy red in narrow cheeks.

'I see you're trying to improve my vocabulary again, Mr Grant, although I'm not sure what Nora has done to upset you.' She wandered over to the edge of the balcony, only to turn back almost immediately at the sound of her name.

'Nurse Nightingale, can I have a word?'

The man in the last bed at the end was called Reggie Tardiff. At sixteen, he was barely a man. A gangling youth with a shy smile, a sharp brain and unfortunate teeth. Evelyn always made time for him, which had nothing to do with the fact he didn't smoke, the only one of the men who didn't. It was also the first time he'd singled her out for anything more than a brief smile of thanks or a question related to his condition. Evelyn's interest was piqued as she arrived at the side of his bed.

'Don't look now but I think there's a stranger hiding in the bushes near the cow shed,' he whispered, leaning forward, his voice low.

Evelyn bent lower, as close as she dared. 'A German?'

'If he is, he's not in uniform.' Reggie looked worried, two bright spots of colour in the centre of his cheeks, which had her feeling his forehead. Thankfully cool under her fingertips.

Evelyn could hear Roberta calling for her in one of those muted whispers they all used at night, but she decided to stay a moment, her back to the car park and farm sheds beyond. The incident with the sentry earlier had unsettled her, a reaffirmation that their lives were a fine balancing act with the Germans controlling all the levers and pulleys. If she could come up with a way to address that power imbalance without causing repercussions for either herself or others, then she'd be first in the queue. There was also Reggie to consider. While the disease might have wrecked his lungs, his mind was a sharp as ever. If he said there was a problem, then she had every faith that he was right.

'What do you think is going on, Reggie?'

'I don't know for sure, but I don't think it's Jerry unless he's in disguise and, let's be honest, there isn't anything exciting to be found in ole Mr Guille's sheds except buckets and the like.'

Oh, there was more. Far more, the last time she'd looked, including the farm horses and farm equipment, like pitchforks. She'd made friends with Emile Guille, the farm manager, early on. An irascible ole codger but, once you managed to breach his crusty exterior, someone with a heart of gold.

She swung around, ostensibly to talk about the yellow, snow-filled sky, her hand pointing upwards, her gaze heading in a completely different direction.

With curfew and blackout regulations there should have been no one about but the snow made a completely new set of rules. The gleaming white reflected off whatever surface it could find, allowing her to see across the car park and the trees and fields beyond. The one car, belonging to the doctor on duty. The pile of bicycles. The old horse-drawn cart that had come out of storage when fuel was rationed. The sheds, the doors shut. The windows blank. Nothing untoward and, with the sound of Roberta calling her name in increasingly frantic tones, it was time to go.

'I promise to check it out. The main thing is not to worry and to try and get some sleep. I'll pop out later for a chat if I get the chance.' She raised her voice slightly on the way to the door. 'Not least in case our Mr Grant tries to burn us alive in our beds.'

'Where have you been?'

'Sorry, staff. Reggie was worried about something, so I stayed to have a quick word.'

'There was obviously nothing quick about it, Nightingale, and when do we call our patients by their first names. It's rude and disrespectful,' she stormed, her hands entrenched on her hips, her eyes bulging out of her head. Roberta Draper was in a foul mood. Nothing was right from the way Evelyn had stacked the linen trolley to the back round, where cups were collected, bedpans and bottles offered, patients turned, sheets straightened, and pillows fluffed. She was too slow, too particular and far too keen on talking to the patients when she should be working.

Evelyn let her comments drift over her head. After working at the hospital for two and a half years, she'd got used to the peculiarities of the staff. The disdain Roberta had for some of the patients was her biggest gripe and the thing she could do nothing about. As an unqualified nurse Evelyn was so low on the ladder as to not even make the first rung.

By midnight Roberta was ensconced at the desk, her knitting on her lap, a beaker of acorn coffee by her elbow. Tim had made himself scarce on the pretext of tidying out the large equipment cupboard, the cloud of smoke sneaking from under the door telling its own story.

'Alright if I take my break now, staff?'

'If you must. I want the sluice given a proper clean when you're back. Sister was annoyed about the state you left it in earlier.'

Evelyn felt a spark of anger and hurt at the words.

While she wasn't the ward Sister's best friend, Evelyn's relationship with Sister Murphy had certainly improved. Evelyn had ended up spending four months working on male medical after her initial spate on nights. It had been quite a shock given that she'd worked solely with children in her previous role, and female ones at that. She realised now how much of a nightmare she must have been in those early days, a huge liability for a ward full of sick patients and with never a spare bed to offer any slack. When Sister Murphy had finally recognised that Evelyn had a brain in her head and was keen to learn, she'd taken her under her wing and trained her up in the same way she would have if she'd been a student. There were no student nurses in Guernsey, no course materials or ways to assess knowledge, but that hadn't stopped Evelyn from procuring textbooks from the library. She didn't know it all but she knew a whole lot more than she had last year or the year before.

The canteen wasn't open at night, instead the kitchen staff left them soup to heat on the ward and slices of bread from their tommy loaf rations. If they were lucky there might even be macaroni pudding on the side, made from imported French pasta, and milk from their own cows.

With food at a premium, it was rare for anyone to miss their meals, but that's exactly what Evelyn did. Instead of making for the kitchen, she grabbed her cloak, hurried downstairs and slipped past the empty reception and out into the night, the hood pulled over her hair, her thin-soled shoes sliding and skidding on the patch of black ice just outside the door.

Everything was silent, even the cows and the old dray horse, Molly: a deep, perfect stillness now the world was enveloped in snow. If Evelyn hadn't been so concerned about someone spotting her out of one of the windows, she'd have taken a moment to appreciate the beauty of the white-washed trees and gleaming drive. Roberta wouldn't be slow in making a formal complaint about her behaviour no matter the reason.

When Evelyn reached the middle of the car park, she turned to glance at the first-floor balcony and Reggie's bed in the corner, but it looked like all the men had settled to sleep. She was on her own.

Up to the war, crime had been non-existent on the island, but it was different now and that's where Reggie's worry had taken her. Apart from the occasional boat to France for food and seed shopping, they were completely isolated from the rest of the world. Most of them got on with it, but a few had decided to take the law into their own hands which was why Emile kept a pitchfork under his bed. It would be a brave thief who chose to either steal one of his cows or, far more common, milk them. But the farm manager would be asleep, and woe betide anyone who tried to wake him without good reason. They all knew about that pitchfork.

The first shed was empty, but there were signs that someone had been there and quite recently. Evelyn stepped back before crouching down to examine the ground and the clear mottled footprint pressed into the virgin snow. Visibility wasn't great and with full blackout in place she wasn't brave enough to use her torch. It was only a slim, pocket one she'd managed to hold on to by eking out the batteries. There was no way she'd be able to get replacements. She ran her finger along the edge of the print, then pulled her hand back sharply at the tacky feel of the dark splodges.

Blood.

SEVEN

EVELYN

26 March, 1943

Blood – lots of it – trailed over the snow in a ribbon before disappearing behind the shed and under cover of the bushes beyond. Someone was injured and in need of help. That she wasn't qualified or officially undergoing training didn't matter. Evelyn had learnt quite a bit from Sister and the other nurses she worked with. She could change a dressing and make up a decent poultice. Her bed baths were second nature as were her temperature taking and blood pressure recordings... but this felt different. It was a man for a start, or a woman in possession of the largest pair of feet she'd ever come across. He was also someone severely injured, now she realised what she was looking at.

Her steps quickened, her shoes and stockings sopping as she sloshed around the snow, her breath snatched away by the wind whistling through the trees overhead.

The man lying slumped against a tree stump was dressed in tattered blue and white striped rags. His narrow face was as pale as the snow by her feet, his eyes closed, his chin and cheeks unshaven. His hair was a shaggy, uncut mess hanging down his back in unwashed cords, unmoving apart from the gentle rustle of the wind whipping his overlong fringe around his forehead. Friend or foe?

Up to that point it hadn't mattered to Evelyn. She hadn't stopped to consider the risks involved. No one knew where she was or what she was up to, apart from a sixteen-year-old lad, currently dead to the world. That the stranger might be armed and dangerous hadn't entered her mind until that moment. A chill ran down her spine as the gravity of her situation settled in, her determination to find out what was going on replaced by a gnawing fear.

'*Stop it!*' She whispered the words under her breath. The trail of blood was indication enough that, even if he was dangerous, he was badly injured.

The thought was the switch she needed to flick her back into nurse mode. She'd had enough training to know that she had to act and quickly, which meant packing up her fears and shoving them far out of sight. Sister was always telling them that the patient was the most important person in the hospital. That the man wasn't technically on the ward was irrelevant. She would do what she could to help.

Whipping her cape from around her shoulders, she leant towards him, her voice artificially soft.

'Hello there. I think you might need some help.'

No response.

As she dropped her cloak over him, she tried to spot where the blood was coming from. There was no sign of it now. Not his head or his feet, or indeed any of the places in-between. His back then.

Crouching low, she felt his neck for a pulse, not sure what to think when she finally found one, albeit thin and thready. Her gaze rested on his fingers, the nails torn and blackened, the arms thin sticks covered in bruises and welts, his clothing not even fit for burning. He looked half-dead, quite possibly three-quarters, and definitely in need of urgent medical help. The problem was from whom. Roberta the Rottweiler was the least compassionate person she'd yet to meet, inside or outside of the hospital, which narrowed her choices somewhat.

'What we got here, nurse?'

'Bloody Nora!'

Evelyn didn't swear. She'd be lying if one or two choice expletives hadn't tangled with her mind on occasion but this was the first time one had escaped. A quick glance into the farm manager's kindly face was the permission she needed to start breathing again.

'I'm not going to ask what you're doing out here at midnight, Mr Guille, but I couldn't be more pleased to see you.'

'Well, I could say the same about you, nurse.' He tipped his flat cap briefly before crouching beside her, the smell of tobacco mingling with that of Old Spice, seemingly his favourite fragrance and one he must have stocked up on by the bucket load pre-war. He'd confided in her once that his son had bought him a bottle the Christmas of 1916, within days of joining the Royal Guernsey Light Infantry. It was the following Christmas that they'd received the news that he was missing in action somewhere in France. He'd worn the fragrance ever since.

'Shouldn't you be on your break or something, nurse?'

'Or something. We need to get him inside and examine him.'

'Who have you got on with you, tonight?'

Roberta's reputation had travelled beyond her small, narrow-minded life on male medical, but it was still a surprise that Emile knew to ask. 'The Rottweiler. Just my luck.'

'Not a bother, nurse. Dr Holly has been called in for a birth. I'll sort this while you tootle off back to work.'

'I can't leave you here to manage by yourself.' She glanced between him and the unconscious man, shocked at the suggestion that she should leave him to cope. Emile Guille was one of life's copers and the next best thing they had on the island to a vet since the evacuation but there was a huge difference between animals and people. What if...

'You can and you will.' He slipped off his Guernsey jumper to replace her cloak, which he handed back. 'We can't have old Roberta on the warpath. Off you go but if you could have a whisper in the good doctor's shell-like ear on the way. He's been in an hour so should be finishing about now, God willing.'

There was nothing she could do. It wasn't as if she had the experience or physical strength to manhandle the man onto one of the hospital stretchers. Instead, she placed her hand briefly on Emile's rounded shoulder before turning and heading back into the building. She bumped into the doctor inside the door, his black bag in one hand, his old, battered trilby in the other.

'Evening, nurse. Not the kind of weather for a midnight stroll.' Dr Holly dropped his gaze briefly to her feet and the puddle forming. 'If you're not careful, you'll catch a chill.'

Evelyn liked and respected the four doctors that managed the health of the islanders, day and night, often having to resort to using a bicycle to get around when they'd exhausted their scrappy petrol allowance, but Dr Holly was by far her favourite. A pragmatic man, who'd decided to grow a beard when he'd used up the last of his razor blades.

'There's an injured man behind the first cow shed. I've left him in Mr Guille's capable hands, but I said I'd fetch you.'

Dr Holly placed his hat on his head, pressing it down into place as he hurried to the door. 'How injured?'

Evelyn shrugged. 'Bleeding but it might have stopped. He's unconscious so difficult to tell.'

'The snow might have been a help. Acts as a vasoconstrictor so one of the best ways to stop blood flow.' He paused a second, catching her eye. 'A German or...?'

'No way of telling until he wakes but he doesn't look

German,' she replied, thinking of the tall, broad-shouldered blonds that marched the streets and lanes, their voices lifted in song.

She watched the door close behind him before speeding back to the ward to try and dry off in the forty-five minutes she had left.

Evelyn wondered what had happened to the man as she raced round the ward carrying out her duties, but there was no way of knowing unless she heard it on the hospital grapevine, which was usually under power during the small hours. Roberta kept her busy, getting her to run from bed to bed while she worked on her knitting. As a mild-mannered woman who attended church on Sundays whenever she was able, Evelyn felt compelled to hide her murderous thoughts under a calm exterior, refusing to show her annoyance. She was finally able to escape to the annex on the pretext of checking the hot water bottles, her hands raised as she secured her mask. The other men were asleep under their mound of blankets. Reggie was awake.

'Alright, Reggie? Can I get you anything?

'Apart from a new pair of lungs, not a thing.'

She tucked the blanket further around his neck, already starting to shiver under her thin dress and wet feet.

'Do try and get some sleep, dear. You were right about that man. Dr Holly is looking after him but keep it to yourself.' She flicked her head in the direction of the other beds. 'The walls have eyes and ears.'

'Not a word.' He sounded sleepy. She watched as he rolled on his side, his hand tucked under his pillow.

It was half three when Roberta joined Evelyn in the sluice, where she was turning out the specimen cupboard, the counter littered with glass jars. 'You're wanted in theatre. Apparently, we're getting an admission although goodness knows where we're going to put him. Be sharp about it.'

Evelyn spent a moment washing her hands and rearranging her apron and cuffs before hurrying across the corridor, her still damp shoes sliding on the polished floor.

The theatre block was in full swing, the blackout blinds secured to the windows, shielding the central light from the eager eyes of the Germans. With power now at a premium they had to use lamps on the wards to preserve electric light for when they needed it, like during an operation.

'Ah, there you are.' She was met by Carla Harris, one of the theatre nurses, a feisty redhead from London who'd decided to come to Guernsey to work for six months shortly before the Germans had arrived. Carla had been given the opportunity to leave in the last of the boats. Luckily for them she'd opted to stay.

'Am I pleased to see you, duckie. Only fit for my bed. Dr Holly is just writing up his notes.' She leant closer, her eyes bright over her mask, her head tilted in the direction of the trolley and the man on top. 'Shot in the backside would you believe. Lucky to be alive, Nightingale, and, if our esteemed doc is to be believed, all down to you and your bleedin' lamp.' Her eyes crinkled up in amusement at her little Florence Nightingale joke, which Evelyn took in good spirits. She knew she was liked in the hospital, by everyone except Roberta.

'Any idea of who or what he is?' Evelyn glanced around the room for any signs of his clothes. 'We'll have to get in touch with his relatives.'

'Hasn't woken up yet, ducks, and nothing in the bag of rags he was wearing. Only fit for burning. If I'm not very much mistaken, he has brought some passengers with him too. You'd best let your senior know as soon as you get back.'

'Great. Thanks for that.' Evelyn matched her look with one of her own. If there was one thing she hated, it was head lice. She was already starting to itch.

Carla chuckled. 'You're welcome. Anything to upset The

Rottweiler. Grab an end and I'll help you take him up. The sooner he's warded the sooner I can get on with my cleaning and sterilising.'

Roberta was in a worse mood than before, if that was possible. All short words and harsh whispers as she took the handover from Carla with barely a word of acknowledgement. Carla, for her part, threw Evelyn a wink before skipping from the ward and back to her cleaning.

'Get a move on, nurse. We'll have to push him into the isolation ward. There isn't room anywhere else. Half-hourly obs if you please and do something about his hair.'

'Like what? We don't have anything.'

'Then tie it back.' Roberta secured the brakes and spent a moment staring down at him. 'Highly irregular. Probably a wanted man too. I don't know what Sister will say in the morning.'

EIGHT

EVELYN

'Nurse Nightingale, I'd like you to stay back after report. It won't take long.'

Evelyn caught Roberta's smug expression, before turning back to where she was helping the colonel with his drink. The staff nurse had collared Sister as soon as she'd entered the ward, no doubt full of complaints about what a bad night she'd had down to Evelyn's tardiness. The fact they'd hardly seen Tim all night was neither here nor there. He wasn't a bad man but crafty in the way he could never be found when he was most needed. Of course, he made sure he looked busy in the ten minutes it took for the day staff to arrive, peculiarly in possession of a rather authentic-looking limp that he hadn't appeared to suffer from earlier.

'Hope I haven't got you into trouble, Evelyn.'

'Not a bit of it, Colonel. It would take a lot more than me helping you with your drink for that.'

'You're a good woman. Don't let anyone persuade you differently.'

Evelyn patted his hand, distressed at the continued deterioration in the man's condition. Nurses, like mothers, weren't meant to have favourites but the colonel was more like a dear friend than a patient. As the only diabetic left on the island he got special treatment, which wasn't much. A carefully controlled diet when the fresh, wholesome food he needed was almost impossible to come by. They all knew it was only a matter of time. He'd seen the vicar and made peace with his God, and his family. The only thing left was to pamper him in every way possible.

'I won't, thank you. Now, there is a little bit left. Best drink it before it gets cold.'

He pulled a face but opened his mouth, swallowing the remains before nodding at the room opposite and the closed door.

'Who's the new recruit?'

'Now, you know I can't tell you that but,' she lowered her voice, 'in this case it's true. No ID and, as he hasn't woken up yet, no name. We're hoping he's not *one of them*. Matron will go ballistic if we've let Jerry the German in, albeit accidentally.'

He struggled back up the bed, his gnarled knuckles pressing into the mattress as a shout emanated from the room. 'I think you're about to find out. He's waking up.'

Evelyn placed the feeder cup carefully down on the colonel's locker before making her way over to the room, feeling the gaze of the ward on her. All except for Tim who'd disappeared outside on to the balcony for a sneaky cigarette now the day staff were ensconced in Sister's office for handover.

'Hello there.'

'Where am I?'

'In hospital. How's the pain?' Evelyn said, taking her time in studying him. Not young and yet not old either. Somewhere between thirty and forty. A man with a thin, narrow face, his voice a rasp of sound but with a lyrical note she thought she recognised.

'Like my ar... backside is on fire.'

'Not surprising after what you've been through.' Evelyn smoothed the sheets around him, careful not to add to his discomfort. 'Staff will be out in a minute. I'll ask her to get you painkillers. What about some water in the meantime? You must be parched.'

She helped sit him up, rearranging the pillows before pouring a glass of water from the jug she'd placed on his locker earlier. 'Go easy. You might still be feeling the aftereffects of the anaesthetic.'

'Anaesthetic?' he questioned, taking small sips before pushing the glass away and easing back against the pillow, his eyes closed.

'You've been ill. Now you're getting better.'

'Right.'

Evelyn examined him as she set the glass back down on the table. A very tired, very pale bloke who'd been through the wars.

She collared staff about painkillers for him, on her way to the office. Being called in to the office was a rare event and one Evelyn didn't relish. She couldn't remember the last time – probably within weeks of starting. Her heart was pounding as she knocked, her mind churning with possible reasons for the summons.

The office was small with a window facing out front, a filing cabinet on which was perched a tray of china cups. The desk contained the report book, a flat file with details of all the patients care, which the nurse in charge updated twice daily, during the afternoon and at night. There were also two trolleys, one containing patient's medical notes and the other containing their X-rays.

'Do take a seat, nurse. I won't keep you long after your tiring shift.' Sister smiled briefly.

Evelyn did as she was told, folding the sides of her apron across the front of her dress nervously. Glancing down, she noticed the state of her shoes and hurriedly tucked her feet out of sight underneath the chair.

'Staff tells me you've had a busy night?'

'Not too bad, thanks.' Evelyn's expression was wary, unsure of where the conversation was headed.

Sister picked up her pen and started swivelling it through her fingers. 'Is there anything you'd like to tell me?'

Evelyn's mind went blank, trying to work out what she was being asked and failing on all counts. 'No, Sister.'

'I happened upon Dr Holly in the car park just now,' Sister continued. 'He also told me what a busy night you had, Nurse Nightingale. He elaborated exactly why, and how much he valued your assistance.' She placed her pen on the desk, lining it up on the edge, another small smile in evidence. 'Well done, nurse. Now, I'd like to ask a favour, if I may?'

'Yes, Sister.' There was no other possible answer she could give. A favour usually meant more work. If she'd been Violet, she'd have been able to come up with something better, but not on the back of the compliment she'd just received. They were rare enough for her to appreciate each one.

'You're due for your nights off but we're short of cover. I've just had to send Mr Le Clair off sick. He tells me he's quite unable to work the remainder of his shifts. If you could see fit to take his place and I'll tack your days off onto the end of your nights?'

Violet had told her all about Tim's medical condition at supper the previous evening. Evelyn had laughed when she'd heard about his incurable case of lazyitis but it was no laughing matter when it meant she had to forgo her nights off. She was tempted to refuse until she remembered that it would also be The Rottweiler's nights off and therefore push her out of sync with the woman's off-duty. Working a thirty-three day stretch instead of the thirty-one she was used to would be a killer, but not when the other end of the week was staffed by the sweetest woman she'd ever met.

Nurse Martel was one of the few local staff nurses in the hospital and, with general, children's and midwifery under her belt she could and would work anywhere. That she was married and still able to work was unusual in hospital circles.

Married staff were unheard of but in Abi Martel's case Matron had made an exception. It was a ridiculous rule that had lost them many a fine nurse over the years, or so she'd been told. It wasn't the first time that Evelyn had heard about what a forward-thinking nurse Matron Rabey was, not that she had any ideas with regards to finding herself a man.

Evelyn blinked, willing herself to concentrate on the conversation. 'That's fine, Sister.'

'Thank you. Now about the new patient. I hear he's awake. Do we have a name for him yet?'

Evelyn felt her cheeks redden. 'Sorry, no. Not yet.'

'What did he say to you, nurse?'

Evelyn paused a second, thinking back over their brief discussion. What he'd said. The way he'd said it. How she'd replied. His accent. There was something in the melodious tone that reminded her of one of the girls at the school. She blinked again, pulling up the memory of someone she hadn't thought of since the evacuation. Iris, that was it. With the father working away, the mother had moved back to the island to live with her parents. An intelligent girl. Glorious red hair, as had the mother although in her case faded a pale apricot in the tradition of all real redheads. Now where had they come from again? Ireland, that was it.

That he was Irish was, to her mind, astounding. They had Irish people on the island, like Sister in fact, but most of them had evacuated in 1940. There were only a handful and mostly if she didn't know them, she knew someone who did, which added to the intrigue because this man was a stranger. She could be wrong about his origins but not that she'd never set eyes on him before.

A little cough from across the desk was the reminder she needed that Sister was still waiting for an answer.

'Irish.'

'Excuse me?'

'I think he's Irish, Sister.'

Sister stood quickly. Evelyn followed her movements, thinking she was about to be dismissed. Violet would be waiting for her in the dining room and would want to get going as soon as possible. Evelyn couldn't blame her for that; after the night she'd had, she was of the same opinion.

'No, sit down, nurse. I'm not finished yet.'

Evelyn's mouth opened slightly as Sister rounded the table, stretching out a hand to close the door before retaking her seat.

'Irish? What exactly did the young man say to make you forge that opinion?'

'Nothing. We barely spoke. He asked me where he was, and I told him. Then we discussed whether he was in pain or not, and he said he felt a bit of discomfort and that was all.'

'And yet you were able to deduce that he was a fellow countryman of mine?' Sister's eyes were shrewd behind her glasses, her placid features hardening along with her jawline. Evelyn had obviously upset her, something she was quick to try and rectify.

'Sorry, I didn't make myself clear. He, well, I think that he has the same accent as someone I know, and they're Irish.' Evelyn frowned. 'Not like yours though.'

'You do realise how important this is, nurse. With the island closed, there is no way in or out unless he managed to sneak in, and with no papers on him, that's an increasing possibility.'

'Like a spy?' Evelyn said, immediately feeling foolish at her words.

'I wouldn't go so far as to call him that, remembering that

the South is neutral in all this madness. That's not to say I don't know of a fair few who decided to join up anyway.' Her gaze sharpened. 'What part of Ireland was your friend from?'

Evelyn stared down at her clenched hands, taking a moment to pull the information from the depths of her sleep deprived brain. 'Dublin.'

'Ah, that explains everything and nothing. Dublin is in Southern Ireland so not part of the war, which in no way accounts for his presence on male medical or indeed the state of him.'

'I don't follow.' Evelyn lifted her head, the depth of her tiredness making it impossible to join the conversation dots.

'No, you wouldn't but don't worry about it. That's my concern.' Sister nodded briefly. 'I'm afraid though that I'm going to ask you to do me a second favour.'

'What kept you! The maid has nearly thrown out your breakfast twice, and I've nearly eaten it once.' Violet pushed her plate of bread towards her, the thin scraping of yellow butter doing little to disguise the course texture of the loaf.

'Sister was in a snit about something.'

'I heard about your new admission, but not the details. What's all the secrecy about?'

And that was the problem. Evelyn didn't know what was going on, or what Sister suspected was going on. She had spent the time it had taken her to walk down three flights of stone steps trying to work out what it could mean, given that Sister hadn't sounded convinced on the idea of the man being a spy. Evelyn didn't think he looked like a spy either. More like a tramp, or one of those slave workers that had suddenly appeared overnight to help build Hitler's fortifications. What would a spy look like anyway? She was clever enough to guess that the most successful of spies probably looked the same as everyone else.

The cinema depiction of dark glasses and long, gabardine trench-coats would be a dead giveaway. She also didn't like lying, particularly to her friend, but she wasn't able to tell her the truth, even if she knew what the truth was.

Instead of replying directly, Evelyn broke off a small piece of her bread. 'I don't think there is a secret, really. He's far too ill to tell us how he ended up in hospital.' She popped the bread in her mouth, before picking up her cup, consoling herself that as lies went, it wasn't a complete falsehood. He hadn't told her a thing. The rest was only supposition.

'Poor man. I suppose it will come out eventually. I hear he's infectious too. Must be, to open an isolation room for him. What's the world coming to?'

Evelyn nodded, concentrating on her breakfast instead of replying. With Roberta now on nights off and Tim sick for the foreseeable there were only two other staff members to consider. Dr Holly and Carla. No, three, if she included Matron, and who could not, but that was Sister Murphy's concern. They'd arranged between them that Evelyn was to special the Irishman at night while Sister was going to take responsibility for him during the day, and not a word to anyone. His life could depend on it. The only issue left to sort was which fictitious disease to assign him.

It was something she thought about on the walk home and that kept her awake most of the day. The disease had to be potent enough to keep the Germans out while reassuring the islanders that there was no threat to them catching it. Front page headlines were something to be avoided.

Evelyn gave up on sleep at four in the afternoon. She sat up in bed, the blankets pooling to her waist, revealing the greying flannelette of her nightdress. The shock of cold made her shiver and she instinctively plucked her shawl off the chair beside her bed. With it wrapped tightly in place, she reached under the bed for her violin, Not the securest of hiding places but it was precious. Far too precious to risk being damaged by snow.

Even before she played a note, the familiar weight of the instrument caused her breath to ease and her pulse to slow. The feel of the wood beneath her fingers sent a quiet joy pulsing through her veins, igniting a flicker of optimism. *We'll get through this bloody war,* she thought. *We'll show Hitler what for.*

She played a few chords to loosen her icy fingers before slipping into Chopin and Strauss, the melodies spilling into the room. The time of day didn't worry her. Violet never slept past four, preferring to lie in bed and read until it was time to get ready for work. For Evelyn, she used this as her thinking time, only there wasn't much thinking. The music brought memories of happier times to the surface.

By the time she returned the violin to its case and snapped the lid shut, she felt lighter, energised and ready for whatever this blasted war threw at her next. She'd also remembered a rare disease that the hospital occasionally came across. It would be a perfect fit.

NINE

EVELYN

An outbreak of diphtheria was serious news, news that was impossible to contain outside of the narrow confines of the ward. That Evelyn was one of the juniors on male medical meant that she'd barely sat down to her supper before the questions started.

'How is he? Who is he? Any more casualties? I hear one of the maids has been warded too.'

'Let her eat, for goodness' sake,' Violet interrupted, happy to act referee in the knowledge that she thought she knew as much as Evelyn did about the mystery man. She didn't.

'Yes, let me eat,' she added, with a smile for Violet. She finally pushed her bowl aside and collected her cloak and bag. If she must spend her night babysitting an adult she might as well spend a few minutes with the colonel beforehand.

The ward was unusually quiet when she arrived, the men sitting beside their beds for a change and not huddled in groups of twos and threes like naughty schoolboys planning acts of mischief. The reason was immediately apparent with the sight of the red screens drawn around the colonel's bed. The screens only came out for one of two reasons. When there was a dangerously ill patient, or a death.

'You're early. Sister says to relieve her as soon as you arrive, but I reckon you're good for a few minutes,' the staff nurse said, hurrying past, her hands full of medical notes. She nodded in the direction of the screens. 'Afraid the ole colonel has taken a turn for the worse. We don't expect him to last the night. In fact, I promised his missus a cuppa. You wouldn't mind? I must sort out these before the report starts.'

'Yes, staff.'

Evelyn rattled the cup in its saucer as she approached the screened off bed. A gentle warning to the colonel's wife that she was interrupting their privacy.

'Evening, Mrs Carter. Evening, Colonel. A drop of tea for you.'

'Thank you, my dear.'

Mrs Carter looked young enough to be the colonel's daughter, even though they'd only been born a year apart, her skin smooth and her style of dress that of someone who tried to make the most of herself. There were still a few islanders who managed to retain their pre-occupation style and vigour, but none were as stylish as the colonel's wife and, by the spark still lingering in his eyes, the colonel knew it. She turned up every visiting time like clockwork, bringing a little something with her each time, even if it was only a sprig of wildflowers growing on the hedges. With the shops empty, and everyone on rations there was little enough to spare let alone give away, but she always managed.

Evelyn cast a professional eye over the colonel and noted his sickly pallor, his parchment-dry skin, which hung in folds round his neck. When he'd arrived on the ward at the start of the occupation he'd weighed fourteen stone. Now he was barely seven. They'd been lucky to keep him alive when the insulin had finally run out, but that luck was seeping away like sand through an hourglass. The most frustrating thing was the Germans had insulin. With France still open to them they had access to all the medicines needed but in the colonel's case they'd chosen not to share it.

'Pru, if I could have a brief word with nurse, please.' The colonel clutched at his wife's hand before dropping his own back to his side.

'Of course.' Evelyn watched as she walked round the screen and back into the ward, her heels making tiny clicks on the flooring.

'What is it, Colonel?' Evelyn's voice was soft as she crouched beside him, her hand instinctively reaching out to his, her throat tightening. He was her dear friend, only that.

'I don't want you to upset yourself over me, Evelyn. No tears allowed.' He managed a smile, the creases spanning out across his cheeks. 'You're a strong woman just like I've been a strong man, not that you'd notice now.' He managed a chuckle at his bad joke before adopting a serious expression, one she hadn't seen on him before. 'But the stronger you are the harder it will be. People will look to you to make difficult decisions. Make them and don't look back. Never look back at where you've come from. Only at what lies ahead.' He patted her hand, his head sunk back into the pillows. 'No regrets.'

Ten minutes later she was knocking on the door of the isolation room, the remnants of their conversation a heavy ache in her heart. It had taken five minutes to get a grip and another five to pop out to the balcony and have a brief word with the men, who would think it odd her not saying hello.

Sister stood from where she was writing up the man's notes, placing them back on the bed table before heading to the sink and washing her hands.

'He's been asleep most of the day and just dropped off again about ten minutes ago.'

'Did he say anything, Sister?'

'Not much.' Evelyn watched as she unravelled her sleeves and buttoned the cuffs. 'Other than the fact he's Irish and obviously on the run – we can probably guess who from – not a thing.'

'Is there anything you want me to do?'

She shook her head, making for the door. 'Get him to drink if you can and keep an eye on his dressing. It's been leaking quite a bit, but the saline washouts and kaolin poultice seem to be doing the trick. I've padded it as much as I can. We're short enough of kaolin for me not to want to change it anytime soon if we can get away with it. Staff will bring in his medications, but she obviously doesn't know what we're up to. Only Dr Holly. Oh, and Matron.' She smiled. 'My life wouldn't be worth living if I hadn't informed her.'

'What about Mr Guille?'

'Emile Guille hasn't asked, and he knows more than most when to keep quiet.'

Evelyn knew only too well what she was getting at. The farm manager would do anything and everything he could to thwart the Germans. Thinking that he'd helped an escapee would make his day. They still didn't know who the Irishman was or what he was doing on the island, but that didn't matter. They would do all they could for him.

She had one more question, prompted by being stopped a second night by the sentry. It was a different sentry but no less intimidating.

'And what if we get any *untoward* visitors during the night?'

'It shouldn't be a problem, nurse. The German army will be as scared of diphtheria as everyone else.'

The room was in darkness, lit by a solitary lamp, the air pungent with tallow and sweat.

Evelyn crossed over to the bed and stared down at him. He looked comfortable enough, his breathing regulated, and, when she placed her hand on his brow, his forehead cool to the touch.

With no antibiotics, infection was a huge problem and the reason all the ward Sisters were insistent on careful handwashing even though their stock of soap was in dire straits.

She took a moment to flip through his folder, reading through the notes on the operation, which didn't take long. When she next lifted her head, she found that he was watching her.

'Hello there. Not sure if you remember me from last night?' She tapped at her green mask and hat. 'Nurse Nightingale.'

'Of course you are.' His eyes scrunched briefly in amusement. 'No questions for me?'

Evelyn shook her head. 'I'm happy to listen, but it's up to you what you want to tell me. It's also fine if you don't want to tell me anything.'

He tilted his head, his gaze on the ceiling. 'A refreshing change from Sister Murphy then.'

Sister had a reputation among her staff for needing to know everything. While not necessarily a gossip, her dislike of being left out of any information loop was often seen as intrusive. During wartime, secrets abounded, and trust was scarce. Collaborators readily betrayed neighbours for a tin of tobacco and a quart of whisky. Sister, though relentless, was only curious. Her nurses accepted it as part of her nature. Strangers might be less forgiving.

'Indeed. She's only trying to be kind though and is, I believe, one of your country folk?'

He laughed at that, his attention held by the boring white of the ceiling. 'She might like to think she is, but there's a hard-won border between the two countries.'

Evelyn's geography of Ireland was sketchy, but Sister had mentioned something about Dublin being part of Southern Ireland and not the north.

'I know someone from Dublin,' she replied, filling his glass and offering it to him. 'It's important to drink.' She was as keen as Sister in discovering who they had occupying their side room but hoped to be a little more subtle about it. The man was a risk but she felt a sense of responsibility for him. If she hadn't gone to investigate goodness knows what would have happened. That didn't negate her wanting to know what he was up to and where he was from. If she was going to end up in a concentration camp, Evelyn at least wanted to know why.

'Do you, now. I hope you're not asking for information on them, it's a large place.' He raised an eyebrow, a faint smirk twitching at his lips.

Evelyn felt herself warming to the stranger. He had a strong, serious face but there was a twinkle in the back of his eyes that reminded her of the colonel. A man with a good sense of humour, someone who didn't take life too seriously.

No one was free from the scars wrought by the war. In the dark of night, Evelyn still missed her mother, and the father she'd had before bereavement had pulled him into the bottom of a whisky bottle. What saddened her most was that he'd gone willingly, choosing a path which included working for the *Feldkommandant*. She missed the life she'd known before, just as she missed her friendship with Alice. A hastily scribbled letter wasn't the same as heading out to one of the many beaches and flinging themselves in the sea. With the beaches off limits and heavily mined it was only the foolish that attempted to access them. An interesting thought. The Irishman must have come onto the island... but how?

'I think that would be difficult as they were evacuated to England, but thank you for the offer,' she finally said, hiding her feelings behind her professional demeanour. 'Any idea on what you'd like to be called during your stay?'

'You speak as if I'm on holiday instead of my backside being used as a target.'

'Yes, well the less we talk about your backside the better, unless it's to do with your dressing, or if you're in need of painkillers?' Evelyn parried, slipping her hands behind her head and removing her mask, leaving it dangling around her neck where she could get to it easily if there was a knock on the door.

'That's better. Is there a rule or something that the nurses must shroud themselves?'

'Only if we're nursing patients with highly contagious infections.'

He blanched at that. 'Something you're not telling me there, nurse?'

'It's not only you that's good at keeping secrets but, in this case, it's probably better that you know you're meant to be suffering from diphtheria.'

'Mother of God and all the saints in between. What kind of a place have I come to?' He looked bemused and well he might.

'You've come to a safe place, Patrick.' She decided to pluck a name out of thin air, the most Irish-sounding name she could come up with. 'We must send a list of our patients to the local police on a daily basis, information they share with their German counterpart if they feel the necessity. Providing you with a highly infectious disease will help you escape interrogation, at least for the time being. Unless that is, you'd like us to contact Jerry the German for you?'

'No, I'm good. But thank you for offering.'

She watched the way he shifted position, his head sinking deeper against the pillow, his eyes closing in the way of surgical patients who quickly ran out of steam for a couple of days after an anaesthetic.

'You can call me Colin. It's not my name but I'm happy to answer to it and, to my mind, better than Patrick. I've never been a fan of snakes, saintly or otherwise.'

'Thank you, Colin. I'll make a note. You'll only be seeing me and Sister for the next few days, until we decide what to do with you.' She added Colin's name to the top of his record before turning the page and adding it to where she'd been recording his temperature and pulse.

'No way off the island?'

He sounded on the cusp of sleep, so she softened her voice to a whisper. 'Only in a box.'

'Eminently preferable to where I've just come from,' he muttered back.

TEN

EVELYN

The Germans left them alone that night, but Evelyn knew the reprieve wouldn't last. She didn't know how they did it, but they always found out what was going on, from the minor to the enormous. Having their kinswomen working as hospital maids probably had a lot to do with it. Nothing was secret.

She stopped off briefly at Colonel Carter's bedside before heading home. His wife was still beside him. He was asleep, his eyes closed, his breathing stertorous. It wasn't the kind of sleep he was going to wake up from.

Evelyn had lost patients before, but this felt different, heavier somehow. She could draw comfort in knowing that his suffering was drawing to a close. That his death would only be a continuation of his sleep, his breathing slowing, his colour fading into the pillowslip. But she was still losing a friend. She didn't have that many to begin with.

She turned to leave, coming to an abrupt halt at the feel of Mrs Carter's hand on her arm.

'I can't believe it's going to end like this. After all he's done to fight Jerry and yet Jerry still gets to win.'

'He hasn't won yet, Mrs Carter, and we're certainly not

going to give up without a fight,' she replied, her voice determined. 'It's down to your husband and other men like him that we have a fighting chance of beating them.'

The grip on her arm tightened, the woman's diamond wedding band sparkling in the light. 'If you need anything, anything at all from me, I'll freely give it. In Mark's name, always.'

Evelyn had heard such fighting talk before, but never from someone so angry and upset. There was nothing she could do to comfort the woman and, as there was no formal resistance on the island, she had no contacts to share. A brief hug and tears of compassion were all she had to give.

When she arrived back that evening, she glanced briefly towards the colonel's bed, her heart shifting at the sight of the screens positioned just so to hide what was going on behind, the edges of the curtains pinned together to ensure no gapes.

'Evening, nurse.' Staff hurried over to her in a repeat of yesterday but her hands full of sheets and towels instead of notes. 'You heard we lost the colonel?'

Evelyn nodded. She'd been told almost as soon as she'd stepped into the building. Bad news always travelled quickly and there never seemed to be anything but bad news these days. She stayed quiet while she waited for her to continue.

'Got another one in straight after and it looks like he's heading in the same direction, poor man. Right, must get on. Hope you have a good night.'

'Thank you, staff.'

Evelyn scanned the ward briefly. Reggie, Pete and the rest of the TB crew had moved back onto the balcony now the weather had moderated, while the remaining beds were full of the faces she recognised.

The men were subdued. They missed the colonel. A death

among them was bound to have a negative effect but the colonel was special, not least because he'd occupied the same bed since the start of the occupation. Made them think of their own mortality and of what might lie ahead. All days were the same on the ward, the only highlight was when one of them managed to be discharged, a rare event with the paucity of much needed medicines and equipment. Good nursing had never been so important.

'How about I set the kettle on straight after report? There's plenty of milk and the sugar ration is just in, but I'll need a favour in return, Mr Bisson,' Evelyn said. If her smile was overly bright and her eyes heavy from lack of sleep, none of the men commented.

'Anything for you, doll.' Perry Bisson was another one of her favourites, not that she'd admit it to anyone. Fifty on his last birthday, looked sixty and acted six but he also had a heart of gold. A car mechanic who'd lost his job when Jerry had requisitioned most of the vehicles for their own use. He'd been admitted with a cut on his foot, which had turned septic and, without the availability of antibiotics, had nearly killed him. Gangrene had been their worst fear but, after three months of careful nursing he was nearly ready for discharge. He also had friends all over the place who seemed happy to supply anything and everything except the unobtainable tea and tobacco.

'Razor blade. Just the one and I'll let you have it back straight after.' She glanced between them, noting their glum expressions. Razor blades were another thing on the impossible to get list and yet the men still managed to appear clean shaven.

'As it's you, but I want it straight back.' Perry ambled over to his locker and after a few seconds rummaging appeared with a cut throat razor blade in the centre of his palm.

Evelyn blinked at the unwieldy tool, unsure if she was brave enough to use it. 'I'll make it up to you, Mr Bisson.'

'Promises, promises.' A reply which had her still grinning as she walked into report.

Their mystery man was asleep when she took over from Sister Murphy, the sound of his muffled breathing and occasional snore proof enough that this time he wasn't pretending.

'There's not a lot for you to do, but I would prefer if you continued keeping up the pretence until Matron and I have decided what to do with him.' Sister rolled down her sleeves and fixed her cuffs. 'We thought perhaps hiding him in the wilds of St Peter's but, wherever we put him, he'll need an ID card and ration book, and who has one of them to spare!'

Evelyn thought of her dad, a glimmer of emotion crossing her face. His job working for the *Feldkommandant* put him in the perfect position to falsify documents, but that didn't mean he'd do it. She'd ask him if she must, but if there was another way, she'd take it.

'Yes, Sister.'

'I've left my knitting if you're bored.'

Evelyn had smuggled in her own knitting, so just smiled in place of an answer. More importantly she'd also brought her hairdressing scissors, along with Perry's razor blade. The scissors were a closely guarded piece of kit, which she'd made sure to hide in the back of her drawer when she'd started working at the hospital. She rarely had a day off to waste on going to visit the hairdresser. It also made her very popular with the staff.

She tackled the issue of his hair as soon as he woke. 'Evening, Colin. How's about I try and tidy you up a bit? We still have a problem with your unwanted friends, so I was thinking a full head shave. What do you think? It will grow back soon enough,' she said, brandishing her tools.

In the small hours, the noise of motorcycles and cars entering the car park pierced the low hum of the ward. Evelyn had suspected what was coming but that didn't stop her pulse from quickening and a cold knot forming in her stomach at the sound. She'd come up with a half-formed plan in her mind but it all depended on whether the German's had Matron's up-to-date figures as to the number of patients they had currently. With patients coming and going at all hours, it was often difficult for the staff to know, let alone Matron.

She stood by the door, paralysed with fear at the clipped footsteps growing louder before coming to an abrupt stop outside. It wasn't until the loud knock and the sharp order to open the door that she jolted back to life.

'Don't forget your mask, nurse,' Colin whispered, switching quickly from deep sleep to very much awake.

'Cover yourself with the sheet, quick,' she replied, rapidly fixing her mask in place. 'Right over your head. That's the ticket! And do play along.' Then in a much louder voice. 'Just coming.'

She opened the door a crack, only to have it taken from out of her hand.

'I enter, *bitte*.'

'You can't come in here. We're contagious.'

The soldier was tall and officious, his smile non-existent. His eyes were a cold, uncompromising grey as he glanced around the room. Grey to match the colour of his uniform.

'We have an escaped prisoner. I see for myself.'

'Not without a mask, gown and gloves you don't. And I don't care who you are. No one wants diphtheria, least of all the German army, or do you have a death wish on your hands?' Evelyn felt her knees rattle along with her teeth. She had to hope that he feared diphtheria, that he knew what it was. If he didn't believe her... She tried not to think about that.

He stood over her, a good foot taller, his eyes darker than the black sky outside as he made his decision.

'I come back.'

She closed the door, pressing her hand flat against the wood for a second as she waited for her insides to settle. Then she was all action. With her pen between her fingers, she leant over the table and started to fill in the blanks left in the documentation by Sister, Colin watching her from over the top of the sheet.

'You probably won't make it out of this room alive, Colin.' Her voice was quiet, her gaze flickering to his face before returning to what she was doing. 'If you can't convince him you're dead already then you definitely won't, and neither will I.' Their eyes clashed again, his colour fading into oblivion.

There was no second knock. The soldier pushed open the door and strolled into the room, intent on the man in the bed, his green gown only reaching his knees, his helmet looking ridiculous with one of their masks dangling underneath.

'Who is this patient?'

'This was the colonel. Colonel Mark Carter. He died an hour ago. I was just about to start laying him out.'

Evelyn was terrified. She'd never been more frightened of anything. If she got this wrong it wouldn't just be her with a noose round her neck.

She deliberately placed the folder on the table before turning to the bed and gently rolling the top of the sheet back to reveal Colin's head. Her movements were slow and deliberate, her gaze fixed on Colin while she tried to ignore the man peering over her shoulder.

Sister had conveniently left out a dressing pack in case Colin's wound needed repacking. She concentrated on peeling the packet apart and removing the cotton wall, trying not to show that her hands were shaking.

Colin was putting on an Oscar-winning performance, but that's what was needed. There was one problem. Evelyn was no actress. The only thing she had to help her was her mask, which covered her face apart from her eyes.

With a small piece of cotton wool at the end of the forceps

she packed first the right nostril before packing the left, her hand shifting to Colin's chin as a ruse to inspect his mouth. There would be no point in the exercise if he was to suffocate to death.

'Still has his own teeth. Good. It's always difficult to get a good seal with dentures,' she said conversationally, turning to pack each ear. 'Relatives do get distressed at an open mouth.'

They didn't normally pack ears, but it was the only delaying tactic she could think of. She'd have to think of something else as the German was still watching, seemingly transfixed by her actions. Turning back the sheet to Colin's waist, she started wondering how far she'd have to go in the process before the soldier cottoned on to the living, breathing man under her hands.

'We have to pack all orifices before burial,' she said, turning back to the table.

'All?'

She glanced over her shoulder at where the soldier's gaze had shifted, beads of perspiration suddenly budding on his forehead, his eyes nearly popping out of his head.

'Not quite all, obviously.' She picked up the scissors and the roll of ribbon gauze, which they were using as a saline wick for the bullet hole. 'For the men, we have to tie a knot,' she said, measuring out an arm span before cutting and pulling it taut between both hands. 'I've heard reports that the diphtheria bugs can be transmitted long after death, so it really is imperative that we do things correctly.'

He wasn't convinced, it was there in the way he examined her masked face before flicking back to Colin's still body but there was just enough fear in the back of his eyes to make him head for the door. 'I come back in an hour when this is done.'

'Right. He'll be in the mortuary by then,' she said, starting to turn back the sheet.

He waved his hand dismissively, clicked his heels and was gone.

Evelyn made for the door, her ear pressed to the wood and listened, her finger to her lips. A moment, two moments. She heard his retreating footsteps, his loud boots clacking across the floor. Only when the sound faded into the distance did she hurry across to Colin. 'We must be quick. Hurry.'

'Please don't tell me how far you were planning to go with the packing,' he said, working at pulling strings of cotton wool from his nose before starting on his ears. 'You're either mad or stupid but, whichever one it is, I think I love you.'

Evelyn felt her cheeks heat, grateful that she'd finally found a use for her mask, if only to hide her blushes. 'Enough of the Irish blarney or you'll have us both arrested. And careful with that cotton wool. It's not the old days and I still might use it for something. If you were dead, I wouldn't have wasted it on you, but I didn't think you'd approve me ramming the inside of an old sofa up your nose.'

'You don't.'

She nodded sadly. 'We do. Have to if we're to preserve our dressings for the living. We use anything we can come by. The last lot came from the seats of a clapped out Mercedes that Jerry crashed into the seawall over in Perelle but not before the men had stripped everything reusable out of the engine. It's an island rule that the hospital has first dibs on any soft furnishings.'

The colonel would've liked to know that he'd been a part of this, she thought, as she worked on packing up the room, the sheets and blankets carefully folded and left on the end of the bed, spare dressings in a clean pillowcase. Then she pushed the thought aside. It wouldn't get her anywhere. 'They think you're dead, but they'll want to see the body and, luckily for you, I have one in the morgue.'

'Which is all very well, but where do you expect me to go?'

'You'll find out. Here.' She handed him her cloak, eyeing his bare feet with a frown, remembering the rags he'd been wearing. 'Whatever happened to your shoes?'

'Left them with someone who needed them far more than me, luv.'

Her look was sharp, the information filed for another time. 'Can't be helped. With a bit of luck, you'll be able to manage with the colonel's. Here, catch. Back in a second.' She threw him the pillowcase and, slipping out of the door, made for the large cupboard next to the sluice, her thin-soled shoes making no sound.

Patients' belongings were stored in a cupboard following their deaths until families felt strong enough to collect them. It was a bit of an ask, trying to disguise him as a nurse, but it was all she could come up with.

Five minutes later, and they were slipping onto the balcony and down the metal staircase into the car park, the snow now only a memory. They made an interesting pair: Evelyn shivering in her uniform, a bundle of clothes over her arm, a very tall skinny nurse decked out in thick leather boots two sizes too big beside her, a pillowcase dangling from 'her' hand.

The sight of a lone German vehicle caused them to pause, but only momentarily. They were taking a huge risk, but Evelyn had made her decision back in Colin's room. It was too late to reverse it.

They didn't have to go far, not with Emile appearing around the corner, his great coat pulled around him, his pipe clamped between his teeth, his son's army cap squashed onto his head. He'd barely taken it off since it had arrived in the packet along with the rest of his son's paltry belongings. The rumour was he slept in it.

'Mr Guille. Am I pleased to see you.' They hurried over to him, or as quickly as Colin could, his stride more of a hop. They only stopped when they'd rounded the corner and were in the farm part of the complex. He looked to be in excruciating pain, but there was nothing she could do about that now.

'At your service, nurse.' Emile lifted his hand in a half salute.

'Can we avail ourselves of your cow shed for the night?'

Emile scratched his head, tilting his cap in the process. 'Aye. Happen you can but it will have to be up the ladder. Anything to upset Jerry but not my girls. Can't afford to put them off their milking.'

ELEVEN
EVELYN

Evelyn made a brief detour to the porter's lodge before heading to the morgue. The morgue was always kept locked, but the location of the key dangling from a hook in the lodge was the worst kept secret in the hospital.

'Evening, Mr Blondel. Hope you're having a quiet one.' She'd taught the head porter's daughter previously and always stopped for a brief word.

'Not so you'd notice with the Germans turning up,' Mike Blondel replied.

'That's the reason I'm here. He wants to check on the colonel. I thought I'd better see if everything is just so beforehand.'

'Thought as much. Best be quick though. There's been another one.'

Evelyn swallowed hard at his words. 'Another one' could only mean one thing: another death, and most likely the new man on her ward, she thought, recalling the screens pinned closed.

The morgue was a windowless room, bare except for two trolleys, one of which was occupied, and a small table pushed up against one wall with a register of the patients. An important log as it detailed the name of the deceased and the date and time the undertaker had removed them. A missing body was the last thing they needed.

Evelyn filled her lungs with air as she turned back the sheet, the colonel laid out before her. Cold and pale as white marble.

'Sorry about this, Mark. I don't think you'd have objected, but I am sorry.' She spoke as if he was in the room. She couldn't not. There was little she could do to make the colonel look like Colin except trim what was left of his hair.

After, she scanned the dark room briefly. There were no windows, the only light from the lamp she carried with her.

It might work. No. It must work!

She was about to re-enter the ward and report to the staff nurse when she was stopped by the same soldier, this time minus the gown and mask.

'The colonel, *bitte?*'

'What's got into you, Evelyn?' Violet tapped the edge of her untouched breakfast with a tip of her finger. 'You're not coming down with something?'

'Just tired. It's been a hell of a night.'

Violet returned to scooping porridge into her mouth, barely pausing between mouthfuls.

'So, I heard the Germans came looking for an escapee. Good luck to them, I say. How's that new admission by the way? You haven't said.'

'Passed away.' Evelyn nodded, picking up her spoon. She wasn't hungry, but she knew she had to eat. There was nothing in their kitchen cupboards and it was a long time until supper.

'I hear they're due back this morning but this time to tear the farm apart,' Violet said, changing back to the topic everyone was discussing. 'Emile had better hide his Old Spice or we'll have the whole German army reeking of the stuff!'

Evelyn managed a smile, her spoon in the empty bowl, her hands cradling her tea.

'What about your man in isolation, Evelyn?'

'Disappeared. I nipped to the loo and when I came back, no man. It's bound to cause a stink. Who wants diphtheria walking around?'

'What did the officer say?'

Evelyn lowered her voice to a whisper. She didn't want the maid to hear. 'Not sure he was aware or even interested. It's not as if we can hide anyone with their barracks so close.'

'More tea?'

The German maid plonked the pot down on the table, her piercing gaze roaming between them. Evelyn didn't think she'd heard, but it was impossible to tell.

As it was officially the end of her nights tomorrow, and with three glorious days to look forward to until she was rostered back onto days, she decided to ride into St Peter Port. The snow had melted, and the roads were now relatively safe.

The ride was exhilarating, with the wind in her face, her cloak tucked around her, her feet primed in case she had to come to an emergency stop, a common occurrence due to the many potholes and the fact that one of the first things the invaders had done when they'd arrived on the island was to change the rules of the road. Cycling on the right instead of the left was all very well, but not when her brakes had given up in the first year, and with no spare bike parts, she was stuck with having to put her foot out.

She pulled into the car park of the Grange Lodge Hotel, slipping her bike behind the many army vehicles parked at the back. It wouldn't be the first time an officer had requisitioned a civilian bicycle he took a fancy to, although he'd have to be particularly needy to fancy Evelyn's. It was a relic from World

War I found in a mangled heap at the bottom of the shed when her first bike had gone missing.

Grange Lodge Hotel was where her father had been working since the late 1920s. He still worked there, despite the building being commandeered as the headquarters for both the *Feldkommandant* and the *Geheime Feldpolizei* within days of the island being occupied. He was a hotel manager by trade but with half of the islanders departed, they offered him employment as general odd jobs man, which he'd accepted. It was either that or working in the greenhouses on minimum pay. As he rarely left the confines of the building except to head to the pub, he didn't suffer the same kind of abuse other so called sympathisers were privy to.

Evelyn negotiated the meandering corridor through to the kitchen where her father had a small flat in the basement. As it was not yet eight, she found him sitting in his shirt sleeves over a copy of the local newspaper, a heavily censored missive since the Germans had arrived on the scene.

'Morning, Pa.'

'I thought it was you. What do you want?' He didn't bother glancing up, instead he turned the page and continued reading, his glasses perched on the end of his nose, giving him a studious look when nothing could be further from the truth. An honest man who'd left school at fourteen and slipped in and out of whichever job he fancied until he'd settled in the Grange Lodge in his forties. Now mid-sixties, he looked ten years older and acted it too.

Evelyn bit her lower lip at his abrupt tone, clamping down on words she'd only regret.

She examined the top of his head, his hair combed back from his high-domed forehead. After all these years she should have got used to his behaviour. Underneath it all she knew he didn't mean it but that didn't make his offhand manner any easier. It had been better when her mother had been alive, now it was worse. Evelyn didn't believe he thought twice about his behaviour or the effect it had on his only child. The truth was she had no expectations from him but that didn't make their exchanges any easier. It hurt and kept on hurting.

Understanding why he was the way he was only partially softened the blow. Losing his own father, her grandfather, when he was a toddler had left him to grow up in a house burdened by grief. His only sister had ended up raising him until her own tragedy had made her turn to Les Cotils Convent in despair. He'd never learnt how to express warmth or affection, and by the time he was a man, it was too late.

Evelyn knew he loved her in his own way, but she still felt battered and bruised at the loss of the loving father he could have been.

'Do I need a reason to visit my father?' she finally replied, fetching a cup from the shelf and helping herself to tea from the pot in the centre of the table. Strong tea, so strong she could stand a spoon up in it but none of the bramble nonsense she had to put up with at the hospital. If she had an excuse to visit, it was right there in the teapot.

She wrapped her hands round the cup, her fingerless gloves looking the worse for wear. 'We lost the colonel.' Her attention was on her drink but she knew he was listening to her, the paper ignored.

'I'm sorry to hear that. A good man.'

'I thought you should know.'

The colonel lived in a large townhouse in an area known as Les Gravées, which was five minutes' walking distance of the hotel. While Evelyn hadn't met him prior to working at the hospital she'd known of his friendship with her father.

'Thank you and, sorry if I was abrupt. I'll put on a fresh pot.' He shuffled to his feet, and made for the kettle, the pot in his hand as he emptied the leaves into the dish set out for that purpose. Later he'd spread them in a thin layer and leave them to dry before storing them in a glass jar in the back of the cupboard. He'd stockpiled shelves of the jars since taking up the job and, on occasion let her have one or two to take back with her. A rare luxury and one which, like the scissors, made her very popular with the nurses.

Evelyn pulled the newspaper towards her, her attention caught by the headlines. The *Evening Press* was still only a penny, but its popularity had tanked since being turned into a propaganda machine. There was no news, or none that the islanders could believe, only decrees, dictates and war updates heavily skewed in favour of the invaders.

Escaped prisoner. Dangerous.

Patrick Brady, a prisoner of Lager Sylt Camp, went missing on the 23rd March. It is thought that he might have managed to stow away on one of the boats back to Guernsey.

Do not attempt to apprehend. Report any sightings to the local constabulary or the military police.

And underneath it was the photograph. A man with a long, narrow face. Clean shaven and with short cropped hair. Evelyn squinted down at the image in alarm.

Colin.

She managed to arrange her features into a suitably indignant expression by the time her father returned with the teapot and retook his seat, massaging his right shoulder before pushing closer to the table. He didn't look well, a little bluish around the lips now she looked at him closely. She wanted to ask how he was feeling but already knew how he'd respond. '*My health is my business.*' A phrase he'd used so many times she'd begun to believe him. Instead, she turned back to the newspaper.

'That's all we need. A dangerous man at large, and from Alderney too.'

Evelyn had heard snippets of the happenings in Alderney and Lager Sylt concentration camp in particular. Mainly rumour spread by the occasional brothel worker they got in the maternity unit. The other mothers soaked up their salacious gossip, a deviation from their staple conversations of how to make do on nothing.

She was starting to warm up, all apart from her feet but her shoes were still damp from trekking through the snow. 'We had a soldier sniffing around last night, come to think of it. Good to know why.'

He finished topping up his own cup before answering, his eyes guarded. 'They'll catch him, always do. No way off the place and always someone willing to sneak.'

'What will happen to him?'

'Deported again but this time to Germany.'

'This time?' she asked, her tone curious.

He frowned, realising his slip, but continued anyway. Her father for all his staunch ways liked a gossip in the same way the men on the ward did. Having worked on both male and female wards, she now knew that men were far worse for this than their oft maligned counterparts.

'Managed to give them the slip in Alderney and for a second time too. I hear the secret police are furious.'

'The secret police. You mean the Gestapo are here?'

He pointed to the ceiling and the offices above. 'The *Geheime Feldpolizei* but as good as. Equivalent powers and just as vicious.'

She made a point of reading the rest of the article although it didn't tell her anything she didn't know. 'Patrick Brady. Sounds Irish.'

'Probably because he is. He'd better hope he has all the luck his race is renowned for. He'll be needing it.'

She hesitated briefly. 'What he needs is a new identity but there's no chance of that.'

'Absolutely none,' he said, glancing at her keenly over the top of his spectacles. 'The *Feldkommandant* keeps the blanks locked up in his safe and there's only one key. With no incomers and children only having to be registered when they reach fourteen, they're rarely needed.'

He stood abruptly, his tea hardly touched, his good humour disappearing. 'Work calls. You can finish your drink, but I must get on.'

'No, me too. Thank you.' She drained her cup and collected the teapot, mirroring his actions with the tealeaves, disappointed about the ID cards but far from surprised. They had a problem on their hands and no way of resolving it.

'Here.' He placed a couple of jars of tea on the counter. 'It's not much. I'll drop in to see the colonel's wife when I get a chance. A nice woman not that he ever allowed her into the bar.'

'Of course not!' Evelyn had only been into the bar the once at the Grange Lodge, and that with a male escort when she was in her twenties. There were many things still out of reach of the women of Guernsey and walking into a bar unescorted was one of them. 'I think I'll drop in on her myself on the way back.' She glanced at her watch, a tiny gold one inherited from her mother and her most treasured possession, which was never off her wrist unless she was on duty, when it was in her pocket.

'You're on tonight?'

'Yes, but then off for three. As long as I'm in bed by eleven I'll be fine.' She'd have to be. Evelyn owed Mrs Carter an explanation for her actions not least in case she caused a ruckus about her husband's missing great coat and boots.

'Remind her to hand in her husband's ID and ration card. I'd hate for her to receive any unwanted callers.' He slipped on his jacket, avoiding her suddenly interested gaze.

'They're really that hot on getting them back?'

'Absolutely. All must be accounted for. What easier way of hiding someone than using someone else's ID?'

That topic was at the forefront of her mind when she walked into male medical later that evening.

'Evening, Sister.'

Sister nodded her regal head on her way into the office. 'A word before report if you please, nurse.'

'Yes, Sister.' Evelyn beckoned to Perry Bisson, who was hovering at the end of his bed, looking guilty, a half made roll up sequestered between his fingers. While Sister didn't object to smoking on the ward, she preferred that it was done out of her sight and preferably out of range of her nostrils.

'Be a love and start with the tea, please, Mr Bisson and...' She winked as she passed across one of the glass jars. 'Make sure that Sister has left the ward before pouring out. Oh, and...' She slipped her hand into her pocket, withdrawing the razor with care. 'Sorry I didn't have time to return it to you earlier.'

The blade disappeared before her widening eyes, his attention on the jar. 'You doll. Just what the men need after...' He didn't need to complete the sentence, his eyes flicking towards the colonel's bed and back again before removing the lid and burying his nose in the smell. 'I think I've gone to heaven. I'd marry you if the missus would allow it.'

'Hah, two proposals in as many days. I'm honoured. Look, I have to go. Sister wants a word. Enjoy the tea.'

'I'll bet you a sixpence she's going to move you. A real shame that will be too.'

'Move me, Mr Bisson?' Evelyn hovered between feet. Perry was the eyes and ears of the ward and obviously knew something she didn't. They never got moved even in a dire emergency when the hospital was only left with a skeleton staff.

Matron would rather call someone in from outside than shift staff between wards. She viewed it as difficult enough for the nurses in wartime without the added insecurity of never knowing which area they were working in, from one shift to the next.

'Where to?'

He tapped the side of his nose. 'A couple more cases of diphtheria. Should we be worried?'

He looked worried, as did the other patients. An outbreak of diphtheria wasn't as unexpected as it might once have been, with difficulties in getting the vaccine shipped to the island and their inferior diet only a whisper away from malnutrition. There was no protection from getting the disease and nothing they could do for the patients except get them to drink and lower their temperatures with tepid sponges. Not surprisingly, an outbreak invariably meant deaths.

Evelyn wasn't a nurse and had little formal training outside of the sessions provided when they weren't busy, but she'd never let a question go unanswered. Perhaps it was her age or her background in teaching, which had left her with an uncanny ability to spot when one of her pupils was in difficulty.

'I think we're all worried. Mr Bisson, but we have a good team here and, remember you're in the right place if any of you start to feel unwell.'

'Righty-oh. Sister's on the lookout.' He backed away with a brief wink before turning and heading into the kitchen with a little whistle.

'Close the door, nurse.' Then, after a moment: 'It seems as if our Irish gentleman is a wanted man, which complicates matters somewhat.'

Evelyn hid her amusement, her hands folded neatly in front of her fresh apron. After all, what other reason could he have had for hiding out in the hospital. 'I read about it in the paper, Sister.'

'Good, no need to explain then. It does mean I can't risk leaving him with my friends in St Peter's, so it looks as if we're stuck with him.'

'How is he, Sister?'

'The wound is healing well although goodness knows how. The man needs rest and good food, neither of which he's going to get in Mr Guille's cowshed. The only problem is what to do with him now. He can stay with Mr Guille in the short term. That old rogue has more hiding places than the Germans have had hot dinners, but it can't last. Anyway, that's my problem.' Sister leant forward in her chair, her expression souring. 'As the ward is quiet this evening, I've been asked to loan you to obs and gynae. They've had a rush on with expectant mothers and a nursery full of babies.' She lowered her voice. 'They've also had to ward one of their nurses with suspected diphtheria.'

'That's worrying.'

'You're telling me!' She waved her away. 'Report to Matron before you leave in the morning for your days off. I'm not sure if the move is temporary or permanent. You can tell me tomorrow night at our musical evening.' Her gaze sharpened. 'You are still thinking of attending, I take it? I've been looking forward to hearing you play again. I particularly enjoyed your interpretation of Mendelssohn's "Spring Song".'

'Thank you.'

Evelyn left the office feeling far happier than when she'd entered it. Deserting her men would be a challenge. She'd miss them dreadfully but she tempered that with the knowledge she was in need of a change since losing the colonel.

However, it wasn't the thought of moving wards that lifted her mood. It was the promise of music. In a world where everything felt like a struggle, music was her escape. It gave her a sense of purpose beyond the weight of her responsibilities. For those brief moments when the violin was in her hands, she lost herself in the melodies.

Evelyn wasn't a natural performer, far from it. If given the choice she preferred playing for herself in the quiet of her room but she'd had to learn to conquer her anxiety and, in a funny way the music helped her. Once the notes filled the air, her nerves unravelled, and the music took over.

The thought of music carried her from the ward and up a flight of stairs to where the maternity unit was situated, but no further. A new ward meant new faces, new challenges and an unsettling reminder that the only children she had experience of up to now turned up to her classes fully formed, wearing their regulation uniforms.

TWELVE

EVELYN

The maternity unit was situated at the front of the building on the second floor. A long ward split in two with the nursery at one end and the mothers' ward at the other. As well as the prerequisite sluice, linen cupboard, treatment room, ward kitchen and storage cupboards there was a large birthing room fitted out as a small theatre, with a trolley in the middle.

Evelyn was trying to take it all in when a busy-looking woman with a furrowed brow raced up to her, her grey hair escaping from what must have been a tight bun at some point.

'You must be Nurse Nightingale. I'm Sister Jehan. Flung in at the deep end, I'm afraid. Can't be helped. We have a woman delivering now.' Her expression hardened in distress. 'It's not looking good for either of them. Too early by a month but we'll do what we can. It does mean we're short as I have a midwife with her, and one off sick.' She shifted from one foot to the other, her eyes everywhere, obviously keen to get on. 'If you can join Nurse Naftel in the nursery. It's time for the babies' eight o'clock feeds. Gloves and aprons on the trolley by the door, masks in the jar alongside. You're used to babies?'

'It's been a while,' Evelyn replied, trying to remember the last time and failing. It couldn't be that difficult surely.

'You'll soon get the hang of it and, you won't even notice the noise,' she said, a brief smile transforming her face. 'If you need anything ask Nurse Naftel. I've asked her to mentor you while you're with us.'

The noise behind the thick door wasn't so much deafening as heartbreaking. Eight newborn babies whimpering for their feeds and only one nurse in attendance.

'It's not as bad as it looks. It wouldn't look this bad if one of our regulars hadn't decided to collapse into her macaroni pudding last night. Never mind. You're here now. Only two more to bottle feed, I believe, Nurse Naftel? The rest are on breast.'

Evelyn nodded, remembering the mask just in time. She recognised Ivy Naftel from her first day and their brief meetings in the canteen. But she'd never worked with her or spoken to her much after she'd started work. They were far too tired at the end of a shift to do more than ask to pass the salt and, with salt now rationed along with everything else, she didn't even do that.

'Hello there. This must be a shock after all those men,' Ivy said, smiling with her eyes, a mask hiding the rest of her face. 'Don't worry. It's pretty straightforward once you get over the blessed noise. Spare nappies and what have you on the trolley along with fresh bibs and baby clothes. All the dirty nappies in the labelled buckets on the right, the bibs and baby clothes on the left for soaking,' Ivy continued. 'Nappies are the father's responsibility and collected daily. The rest ours. Feed, burp, nappy, back in cot. Got it?'

'I think so.'

'Here.' Ivy vacated her chair and handed her a baby. 'If you finish Sarah, I'll start taking the others in to see their mums. She's a bit of a guzzler, aren't you, my pet. Try and slow her down a fraction or you'll be seeing it again, right down the front of your pinny!'

'Right.' Evelyn watched as Ivy started pushing a couple of the cots through the door.

'Back in a moment.'

Sarah used the time to scrunch up her face to that of an overripe prune, although the colour was angry tomato, her body stiff at the disturbance to her feed.

'It's alright, sweetheart. You'll get used to me in a minute.' Evelyn tucked the tiny head on her arm, securing the rest of her in place with her hand. 'Just as I'll have to get used to you, eh.' The mindless conversation continued as she tried to remember Ivy's brief instructions. It was a nice enough job not least because she was able to rest her feet.

After thirty-two nights without a break, Evelyn had a great appreciation of anything that allowed her to take the weight off. That it was while she was at work was a bonus she intended to take full advantage of. She had plans for her days off, which didn't include staying in bed like her last one. She'd slept round the clock only to realise that she'd wasted her only day off in its entirety.

'That's it, my sweet.'

With the bottle empty and back on the table, she carefully positioned Sarah on her shoulder and started rubbing her back, the smell of clean baby making her close her eyes. Motherhood hadn't been on her mind for years but cradling Sarah brought it into clear focus along with memories of Joseph. A little house on the island, maybe a couple of children running around.

The sound of Sarah's loud burp, quickly followed by the sound of Ivy's soft steps caused the image to dissolve, dropping her back into the present with a jolt.

'Don't forget her nappy. Then, if you can do Moses next. Here's his bottle.' She placed it on the table beside her. 'I'm off to deliver these fine young ladies to their mums. Come on, girls.'

'Righto.' Evelyn adjusted Sarah's position in her arms. 'Not just yet, sweetie. Ivy says I need to do the necessary first.' She fumbled her way through the change, all fingers and thumbs before settling her in her cot, taking a second to watch her settle into sleep.

'Oh dear, no.' Ivy laughed behind her, making her jump. 'Sarah will wriggle out of that in no time. Budge up, there's a dear.' Evelyn watched as she undid the nappy before repositioning it with a speed that was astonishing. She could never be as quick or as efficient.

'Don't worry, you'll soon get the hang of it.' Ivy tapped the next cot. 'This little grizzler is Moses.'

Moses was a totally different species to petite Sarah with her dark eyes and hair as black as midnight. The bruiser of a boy had white, blond hair and the palest icy blue eyes. Her thoughts visited that initial conversation with Matron about the Jerry babies that were starting to appear in dribs and drabs. Not many, most of the women would have nothing to do with the German soldiers, but still a steady trickle who looked nothing like the dark-haired youngsters that had attended her school.

Moses blinked as bottle met mouth, his gaze unwavering, trusting, and she put the idea of his heritage away in a box labelled none of her business. It wasn't his fault who his parents were, and it certainly wasn't any of her business.

Ivy returned but a very different Ivy to the happy go lucky girl that had left shortly before. 'We've lost the Le Pelley baby and it's touch and go whether we're going to lose the mother. Dr Holly is with her now. He had to open her up but, as he couldn't stop the bleeding, he's also had to remove her uterus.' She leant against the doorframe, her eyes glimmering bright. 'Forty-two, no children or husband. He's halfway to Germany for some minor infraction or other.'

'That Le Pelley?' Evelyn had heard about the man shipped off to the continent for six months after being caught syphoning petrol from one of the Germans' cars. It wouldn't have been so bad except that he'd chosen the wrong German to thieve from. The *Kommandant*.

'They've been trying for ages. They thought their luck had changed when she fell pregnant, and now this. Some of the women pop them out like peas only to abandon them like little Moses here, while the ones who'd make fantastic parents never get a look in. It's times like these that I hate my job.'

'Moses was abandoned?' Evelyn's eyes rounded in shock, her arm instinctively tightening around his tiny body. 'How could anyone!'

'A foundling, my dear, and hence the name. Moses Raven, poor little chick,' Ivy replied, running a finger down his cheek. 'Placed in the entrance to the town church within minutes of the service starting. The vicar, Reverend Raven, found him as he was opening the doors. Poor little mite wouldn't have survived otherwise.'

Evelyn nearly dropped the bottle. She would have done if it wasn't for Moses's firm grip on the rubber teat. 'How could anyone?' she repeated, her eyes glazing.

'For numerous reasons. It was probably a choice between the workhouse for the duration of her pregnancy or hiding it as best she could. Remember, she might be married to a man who was going to take offence at her giving birth to someone who clearly didn't resemble him.' They took a moment to glance over at the remaining cots of almost identikit dark haired babies before turning back to the only blond.

'At least someone found him,' Evelyn finally managed, distress and disgust warring for pole position. Whatever the reason there must have been a better option than a doorway on what would have been one of the coldest nights of the year.

Ivy shifted her position against the wall. 'Don't mind what I say, Nightingale. I'm just so bloody annoyed at the unfairness of it all. His mum was probably at her wits' end and he was wrapped up warm. So many layers that the vicar mistakenly thought someone had left a clothes donation.' She laughed gently. 'Silly man. No one has anything to spare these days.' Ivy turned her mouth down in a grimace, her attention on her legs, which were coated in stockings with so many darns that they looked patterned.

As if Matron would allow anything so avant-garde in her hospital as patterned stockings.

'What will happen to him, nurse?'

Ivy moved from the wall, reaching for the next two cots, the babies starting to make their impatience known. 'Either fostered out if we can find someone and, if we can't, sent to the Town Hospital. She could have saved her breath by going there in the first place. That's where all the orphans and foundlings end up. We'll try and find her, of course. Sister has lodged it with the police and asked that it's put in the paper in the hope that some kindly German won't censor it out. It wouldn't be the first time.'

With the evacuation of most of the children, Evelyn hadn't given a thought to the plight of those that had remained or, indeed those born during the occupation. That unwanted babies and children were sent to the Town Hospital, the former workhouse turned asylum, emergency hospital overspill and children's home combined was unthinkable and yet what other option was there?

Evelyn positioned Moses against her shoulder like she had Sarah shortly before and started rubbing his back, continuing her conversation with the little man. She'd used to joke with her fellow teachers that the best part of the job was sending their charges back home at the end of the school day. Now, she was all out of jokes. She knew she'd never be a mother, that she'd never experience that unique bond forged between parent and child. If she hugged Moses a little more tightly and placed a kiss on the top of his fussy blond hair then there was no one to see, no one to record the event. No one to sanction her.

Thirty minutes later, with feeding time over, she was sent into the ward to help the mothers change nappies and position their babies before wheeling the cots back into the nursery, Ivy's words ringing in her ears.

'Don't say anything to the women about the Le Pelley baby. There'll be time enough when she wakes, poor dear. There's no point in upsetting them until we must.'

They stood just inside the main door, surveying the ward briefly, lingering on the extra bed in the middle and the still unconscious woman lying under a mound of blankets, their ears half tuned into the ongoing conversation between the mothers.

'I wish I could do the same with the rest of mine. Shattered I am after a night's feeding and a farm to run,' Mrs Nutall exclaimed, resting back against recently plumped pillows, a cup between her fingers, a restful smile filling her hollow cheeks.

'You'll be soon back to it, eh, Julia. Discharged tomorrow, isn't it?' her nearest neighbour said, similarly positioned and with a similar smile.

'He's picking us up at three, after the best ten days I've had in bed since my honeymoon. With a bit of luck, we'll all be snowed in for another fortnight.'

Evelyn started collecting the cups to the sounds of their muffled laugher only to stop at her name being called from the doorway.

'Leave those for now. We'll have to collect them later. Sister wants you to fetch a patient from the porter's lodge. Another one. I don't know where we'll put her but there we are. It's not as if we can refuse. What a night. I've never known one like it. I'm away to clean the birthing room and set the instruments to boil. Take the lamp from the kitchen and the side staircase, it'll be quicker.'

Evelyn eyed Ivy's retreating back, her hands still clutching on to the tray of crockery. It wasn't what Ivy had said, or even the way she'd said it. It was her blank expression and the way she couldn't quite meet her gaze. As the only hospital available to the islanders, they were open twenty-four-seven to anyone who needed them. There was nothing out of the ordinary in Ivy's request, only in the way it had been delivered.

The hospital was in darkness. The long corridor and steep stairs were full of deep shadows and strange sounds. She heard the echo of footsteps, most likely hers, but she paused a couple of seconds to make sure. The creak from the wooden windows as the wind picked up speed. And other sounds she tried not to think about. Evelyn wasn't a coward, but she'd never had to make her way down from the second floor by herself with only a hurricane lamp to light the way.

The sight of the small posse of soldiers in the reception area at the bottom of the stairs had her nearly dropping the lamp.

The Germans were a suspicious lot, who didn't seem to understand the life-and-death scenarios the staff had to work with in the hospital. They viewed it their prerogative to walk into the place day and night, their guns armed and loaded, their appreciation of patient privacy non-existent. One, two, three of them standing beside the porter, who was doing a good job of ignoring them cluttering up his reception.

'Ah, there you are, nurse,' the head porter said, his shoulders heaving in relief. 'I told them to leave the er... young l-lady in the car. She's in a bit of a bad way. I've had to send Mr Guille for Dr Jones. The poor doc will hardly have had time to take off his coat, but it can't be helped. He's bound to be needed. It's a godsend he happens to live at the end of the road. An absolute godsend.'

Evelyn stopped a beat on her way to the main door. The head porter was a hospital stalwart but without a medical bone in his body, which in no way altered the fact he knew a whole lot more about patients and what ailed them than most of the nurses put together. But that wasn't why she'd paused. He was also a family man who attended mass whenever he could. A man with high values who was very quick to act judge and jury when he was presented with something untoward. That he'd stuttered over calling the woman a lady was telling. Evelyn had a pretty good idea of what she'd find outside.

'Hurry.' The tallest of the men, and the oldest by a decade spoke in German, which she pretended not to understand. Her proficiency in languages was something she was determined to keep out of the hands of the enemy. It felt as if working as a teacher had been in another life.

'Hurry,' he repeated, this time in English, his hand shifting to the gun belted to his hip. She didn't wait to be asked a third time. There was no choice. There was never a choice.

'What's her name?' Evelyn asked, rushing across to the car.

'Marise.' The word was forced from reluctant lips, and she knew there wouldn't be any more. No surname for the unconscious woman slumped across the back seat, a black-haired woman stroking her hand.

'Come on. *Ma petite.* Hold on a little while longer.' The accent was French as was the perfume, the woman's face pale under the powder and paint, her attention exclusively on her companion.

Evelyn called over to the porter, who was hovering by the door. 'A stretcher. Stat, if you please.'

She hurried into the car, her fingers reaching for the girl's pulse. Marise was young, barely out of the schoolroom and yet dressed in a way that caused Evelyn's cheeks to redden, when she'd thought herself of an age long past blushes. It was the first time she'd seen a heavily pregnant woman in anything other than loose fitting and functional garments. There was nothing functional about skintight black satin ruched around her distended abdomen or the red silk blouse, which was so low cut as to be indecent, a gold locket plunged into the cleavage. The black hair artfully arranged. The cheeks rouged. All unimportant when compared with the faint thready pulse and shallow breaths.

'You and you.' Evelyn beckoned to the two soldiers, embarrassed-looking young men who were standing back, their heads averted. 'You need to lift her. I'll direct you.'

THIRTEEN
EVELYN

·

The soldiers weren't prepared for negotiating two flights of stairs in possession of a stretcher and a heavily pregnant woman, but with the electricity rationed there was no other way of reaching the second floor. Another reason she'd chosen the two younger and decidedly fitter looking of the three for the task. The head porter was all very well but pushing sixty. She sent him on ahead to warn the staff. She'd like to have sent the senior German packing but with his hand still resting on his gun she wasn't that brave. His uniform was different for a start. An officer's uniform. His shoes more polished. His attitude as intimidating as his expression.

Sister was waiting at the entrance and, with one swift look at the stretcher, directed them into the delivery suite. With an oxygen mask in place over Marise's face, she placed her hands on her hips and eyeballed the officer, the one obviously in charge.

'What happened?'

'Pain here, and here.' He pointed to under his ribs before shifting his finger to the centre of his forehead and tapping sharply, his face pale where seconds before it had been glowing with health. 'Then she collapsed.'

'I told him we shouldn't have attempted the boat trip, but he insisted. We could have managed. We've done it before,' the black-haired friend said, taking over the conversation. 'The pain, and I couldn't stop the bleeding.' Her expression said it all and more. A medley of distress, frustration and anger.

'Alright, dear. You're welcome to stay and offer any comfort you can while we do our very best for your friend and the babe.' Sister turned to the soldiers, her face souring along with her tone.

'No men are allowed in the delivery suite. You'll have to wait in the canteen. It's not fair on the other mothers to have you cluttering up the ward.' Her words dismissing them was a surprise. What was even more surprising was the way the two younger men trooped out in a line but then the situation must have been a scary one for them. A heavily pregnant unconscious woman was difficult enough for those who were meant to know what they were doing.

Evelyn watched as the officer clicked his heels, taking one last look at Marise before making for the door, his voice a harsh note in the otherwise quiet room.

'If you must make a choice, prioritise the baby over the mother. A child of the Reich.'

Evelyn was horrified, but Sister Jehan, an old hand, displayed no emotion at his words. It was almost as if she'd been struck down by a sudden case of acute deafness and without a remedy in sight. Then Evelyn forgot everything except the orders that Sister started barking out, staccato style. 'Set out the instruments, nurse, and if you can pop Baby Le Pelley into the nursery on the way back, if you please.' She nodded to the steaming steriliser and then the cot set off to one side. 'We've got to get Marise's baby out now.'

'I can still stay?' The friend was crouching down beside Marise, holding on to her hand.

Sister's taut expression relaxed slightly. 'Yes, m'dear. Your friend needs all the help and prayers on offer. Keep holding her hand like you're doing.'

Evelyn had never been into the delivery room, which was essentially fitted out as a small theatre but with a cot next to the wall. She glanced in the cot with idle curiosity on her way to the stove then wished she hadn't.

The image was one she'd never be able to forget. It stayed with her when she reached the stove and the bubbling steriliser on top and the thick gloves to the side, and it would still be there hours later when she finally tumbled into bed, just as it would be when she woke two hours later.

The Le Pelley baby was perfect in every way, apart from her alabaster skin and still lips, her tiny body encased in one of their little pink gowns, her fingers crossed over her chest in death, her fingernails half-moons of perfection, the softest of black down smoothed across her head.

Evelyn stood in front of the stove, mechanically removing item after item of the strangest looking instruments, seeing none of them. Only seeing the baby. It was far easier to equate death with the old and the infirm than with the young and innocent and what was more innocent than a newborn.

The colonel's fate was sealed the day he chose to stay on the island instead of evacuating on one of the steamboats. The Le Pelley baby had no such choice. Her death was a tragedy in comparison. Her life stolen before it had begun.

Evelyn knew she was just doing her job, but nursing wasn't something you could leave behind at the end of a shift. It clung to you, much like teaching had. She remembered countless evenings fretting over certain pupils – the hungry ones, the friendless, the bullied, the bereaved. Even the tormentors, oddly enough. Who would've thought nursing and teaching could be so alike?

The sharp gasp from Sister jolted Evelyn back, that and the sight of a stream of blood staining the trolley sheet, the black of the girl's skirt having disguised the truth. Then she was too busy to think about moving the cot. Dr Jones hurried into the room, his coat off and already in the process of rolling up his sleeves.

'What have we got, Maureen?'

'Pre-eclampsia at a guess,' Sister replied from the head of the table where she was trying to locate a pulse in the neck. The short shake of her head said it all, her fingers shifting to the girl's face and closing her eyelids.

'And a ruptured liver to boot I'm guessing if the sight of all that blood is anything to go by. Bled out, poor woman.' He reached for a gown and one of their precious pairs of gloves; there was no way of obtaining replacements. Evelyn rushed to help him to tie the tapes at the back 'What's her name?'

The friend answered, her voice thick, her cheeks streaked with mascara-tinged tears. 'Marise, doctor, and I'm Camille.'

The doctor nodded in Camille's direction, his full focus on his patient.

'Right. Marise, we're going to have to get your baby out.'

Evelyn hadn't had much to do with Dr Jones, one of the two general surgeons left on the island. Superhuman individuals in her opinion, and that of the rest of the nurses. Men who had to wear many different hats in their current roles from orthopaedics, gastric, eyes, delivering babies and anything and everything in-between. A tall, slight, serious man in his early forties, whose wife and young children had been evacuated at the start of the occupation. She'd heard that he'd had to take up cycling to eke out his petrol allowance, which wasn't nearly enough for his home calls. She'd even passed him wobbling down the road on his bike with his black bag chucked into the basket on the front; balancing clearly wasn't one of his many talents. Evelyn had smiled, thought it amusing. Now she felt guilty, her gaze resting on his deft hands as he helped Sister to quickly cut the skirt off to free up the distended belly. She watched as Sister handed him a scalpel, soft words on his lips as he sliced into Marise's skin before working down through the layers. 'This won't hurt, my dear. You're long past that and, in a better place I'll bet than this hellhole.' He paused, working carefully now the baby was close. 'Only one layer left, Marise. We'll get your baby out and give him, or her a proper... My word! Get a warm towel, nurse. Quick.'

'On the side of the stove, Nightingale,' Sister said, picking up a clamp, her voice as calm and unhurried as if asking for someone to pour the tea. 'Quickly now.'

The baby didn't look like any baby Evelyn had ever seen. She was easily identifiable as a girl, her skin a deep, almost navy blue, and she was still attached to her mother by a long tube. Evelyn presumed the umbilical cord, but she couldn't be sure of anything as the towel was snatched from her hands and Dr Jones started rubbing her skin. There was no cry, no sound in the room, nothing apart from the thrumming of her heart in her ears. Thump. Thump. Thump. The silence said it all and more to her untutored mind. They were too late.

Evelyn felt sick and more, her gaze sliding between the dead woman, the cot and the continued endeavours of Dr Jones and Sister Jehan as they worked on the baby, her gaze finding and holding Camille's stricken face.

'It's alright, ladies. You can cheer up. Not all babies cry, you know.'

'What was that?' Camille said.

'Not all babies cry, especially prem ones who've just had the biggest shock imaginable.' Dr Jones handed Sister the baby, pausing a second to run a finger down her cheek. 'Poor little motherless mite. At least she has a father, of sorts.'

'Over my dead body, as well as Marise's.' Camille was on

her feet, hovering over the baby. 'He's no father. An absolute beast of a man. Marise had to service him whenever he wanted.' She spat out the words before running the back of her hand across her mouth, her face flame red. 'He promised to replace her with her sister if she as much as squeaked her displeasure. Her twelve-year-old sister currently living on a farm somewhere outside of St Malo. At least Marise is out of it now. At peace.' The tears were flowing, her mascara making inroads on her rouged cheeks and reddened lips.

'Here you go. Your friend would have wanted you to hold her.' Sister placed the baby in her waiting arms. Evelyn would have done the same, but it was all so pointless. A short reprieve until this mite, this child of the Reich, was sequestered back to the fatherland. She felt the harsh burn of bile race up the back of her mouth at the thought.

'I'm sorry, Miss...?' Sister said.

'Camille will do. There is no place for surnames in my line of work.'

'Well, Camille, with the father waiting I'm not sure that there's anything we can do to prevent it.' She damped the end of the towel under the running tap, wiping away the worst of the blood from the baby's cheeks. 'She'll be well enough looked after. One has to hope that will be the case.'

'There must be an alternative,' Camille hissed. 'Surely you're not intending to hand her over like a parcel?' She clutched the girl to her breast, her arms a protective cradle, the baby's wrinkled face worldly wise. That she'd managed to sleep through her birth and all that had followed was a miracle. That she was now facing a future as a child of the Reich was a travesty.

Evelyn blinked then blinked again, her lips firming along with her thoughts, her attention on the closed door and the shadow of the officer pacing up and down outside.

She agreed with Camille, every word. There had to be another way.

FOURTEEN

EVELYN

Evelyn had never been the kind of person to push herself to the front of any given situation and this was even more the case since swapping teaching for nursing. The likes of Violet and her were there to do what they were told by their trained counterparts. If Sister had asked her to jump, she wouldn't have stopped jumping until someone told her. Doctors were on a completely different plane. She didn't speak to them unless they asked her a question and, as she usually took herself to the sluice during the daily doctor's round, she rarely got to see them. That Dr Holly had been in the right place when she'd discovered Colin was a miracle. Now she had plans for a second one.

'There is another way.' Her voice was breathless, her words hesitant when she needed them to convey her utter conviction in what she was about to do. 'You'll have to trust me.' Instead of wasting time on further explanation or argument, there wasn't time for that, she took Marise's baby from Camille and handed her to Sister. 'Take the "Le Pelley" baby into the nursery where she belongs, Sister. It's about time mum and daughter were introduced.'

'Nurse Nightingale, I don't think...'

But, with the sound of clomping boots coming to a stop outside the room, it was too late for that.

'Camille, you're with me. Just play along.' Dr Jones was hunched over Marise, taking his time in sewing up the gaping hole. That he didn't say anything was indication that he was happy enough. She had to hope that was the case.

Evelyn watched Sister race into the next room but only from the corner of her eye. She was too busy scooping up the baby from the cot in the corner before placing the Le Pelleys' long awaited child within the circle of Camille's arms. 'I'm sorry, my dear, but it's the only way.' Whispered words as she partially covered the dead baby with the edge of the blanket to the sound of the door crashing open behind her.

Dr Jones eased into standing with a pained expression, a needle in his hand, a long thread hanging from the end. 'Really! This is intolerable behaviour. We said we'd call for you in due course and we would have.'

'Where is my son?'

The room stilled a second, just one. Evelyn kept her eyes front and central, the scene unfolding in a series of vignettes. The doctor turning his back and, with the needle back on the trolley, pulling a clean sheet from the pile and proceeding to unfold it, the sharp creases in evidence. The slight movements visible through the glass panel piercing the door of the nursery, the muted cries as one of the babies decided it was time for a snack. Camille hugging the Le Pelley baby to her chest, in the same way she had Marise's moments before, the track of tears still visible.

'Here's your daughter, Yannick. Your child of the Reich, and welcome.' She pressed her lips to the baby's forehead briefly in silent tribute before strolling to him, her hands extended as she offered him the bundle.

He looked stunned, his skin a ghostly grey as his body caught up with his brain. 'What is this?'

Doctor Jones stood back from shrouding Marise from head to foot, still wearing his bloodied gloves, his gown stained. 'We did our best. If you'd brought her here sooner perhaps we could have saved both but...' He shrugged, making for the sink, his back rigid with annoyance and distress.

The officer looked grim; his expression impossible to read but a slight moisture on the rim of his lids where his eyes were squeezed shut told a story he would never share. Evelyn felt guilty then, but it was only a fleeting emotion tempered by the youth of the woman and the pain she must have gone through. The child would be brought up by a loving mother and given the kind of life Marise would have wished for her. She couldn't care about anything else.

'Would you like to be left alone with Marise and your daughter?' Evelyn approached the officer, her shredded nerves making her braver than she'd ever felt before.

'No, I would not. Neither are of any use to me now.' He handed her the baby without a second glance and stormed back to the door, pausing briefly in the entrance, his hand fisting around the frame before leaving.

Dr Jones opened his mouth to speak, only to close it again at the sharp shake of Evelyn's head, a finger to her lips. The corridor was too quiet. No sound, apart from the gentle baby snuffles next door. No click clack from steel capped army boots. She made for the still open door, grabbing a pile of bloodied sheets on the way as an excuse.

The officer was pressed up against the wall outside, looking as grey as his uniform. She didn't think that he had stopped intentionally but that was no pacifier for the rapid beat of her heart. Evelyn could have offered him sympathy then. She was tempted but she knew it wouldn't be appreciated. Instead, she did the next best thing. She offered him the time to gather his thoughts by sending them off in a new direction.

'Ah, I'm pleased I've caught you. Would you like us to arrange everything from here? A Christian burial in our local graveyard? I'll make sure Marise and her daughter get treated properly.'

'Do what you like.'

He nodded once and was gone. Evelyn watched as he headed towards the stairs and continued watching at the window in the hanging silence until she saw him make for the car, one of the soldiers hurrying to open it for him. Only then did she return to the room and face the three people waiting for her.

'He's gone.'

'And good riddance! Is that a problem?' Sister amended, turning back to Camille. 'We can probably arrange a lift into town later with the cart.'

Camille swept her hair from one shoulder to the other. 'Yannick will send someone back for me. Doesn't like any of his property going astray.' The bravado in her voice didn't quite mask the uncertainty in her eyes as she pulled out a packet of cigarettes from her bag. She took her time in placing one in a long black holder, her fingers trembling slightly. 'Do you mind if...?'

'Everyone else does.'

Sister continued tidying the room while Evelyn moved over to the sink and started the laborious task of scrubbing instruments before setting them aside for boiling in the steriliser later.

Camille sat on the only chair and smoked, her head back and her eyes closed, her hand holding on to Marise's.

When the room was back in order, Sister joined Evelyn at the sink, her grey hair losing the battle with her bun. 'Nightingale, you're either a genius or an idiot to come up with the plan.'

'No.' Camille spoke, her words cracking a little. 'You're a

hero, *ma petite*, and my friend for life.' She took a deep drag on her cigarette, the tip glowing red in the badly lit room. 'Now, who is this Madame Le Pelley, and will she be a good mama?'

The ward was quiet. It was long past blackout and with no alternative source of light, an ideal opportunity for the mothers to catch up on their much needed sleep.

Evelyn approached the bed in the centre, the cot's front wheels making a slight squeak against the polished floor. It was another one of Sister's rules that they weren't allowed to carry babies to and from the different parts of the ward in case of accidents. The way Evelyn was shaking, she was in total agreement. Delayed shock, Dr Jones had called it, when she'd nearly collapsed in front of the sink, a kidney dish clattering to the floor. He'd wasted no time in pressing her into the chair, which Camille quickly vacated, telling her to put her head between her knees while Sister went to fill a medicine glass with a tot of sal volatile. They were kind, kinder than she deserved the way she'd risked all their necks. They were also on a high at getting one over on a German officer.

Evelyn was more pragmatic. She'd acted on impulse and with no thought outside of the future of Marise's child. Now she fretted that she'd made the right decision. One look into Mrs Le Pelley's face fumbling its way back from sleep and she knew she had.

'Hello, dearie.' Evelyn's voice was soft.

'Mmm.' The reply was just as quiet. It was difficult enough to see in the dim light cast by the isolated lamp on the central table, the sight of Ivy pushing to her feet etched into the shadows, her startled gasp quickly turned into a small cough.

'I have your baby for you and, by the sounds of her, I think she's hungry.'

'What?'

Staring down at the woman was like reading a book: a tragedy only to find a surprise happy ending written into the final page. No one had told Betty about the baby, not after everything she'd been through. They'd left her to wake up naturally. It was there in her look of amazement, of wonder and in every tear that flowed freely down her cheeks.

'My little baby.'

Evelyn hurried to the door, her stomach cramping and her eyes blinded by tears, which she furiously blinked back. She had to believe that she'd done the right thing. Too many lives depended on it.

FIFTEEN
EVELYN

Evelyn didn't know what to do with herself when she finally got off duty. She needed to go to bed for a few hours if only to rest before playing at the musical evening scheduled for later, but not yet. Not until she'd allowed herself a little breathing space. Time to rationalise the last few days when there wasn't a rational explanation to be had. Life was cruel, with little joy, but if she didn't at least try and search for it she felt she'd go mad.

The morning was crisp and cold, the sky a heavy yellow, the wind and rain forgotten. She was almost, not quite, warm, her many layers insulating her from the elements such as they were. She stood in the car park a moment to wave to the men on the balcony, their beds pushed forward to the railings.

Her time spent on male medical had been one of the highlights, the men more friends than anything, especially the tuberculosis sufferers who had spent many months in the same position and would spend many more.

'Morning, nurse. A bit of an improvement on the ole weather,' Emile called from the other side of the car park, an empty milk churn in each hand as he left the door to the kitchen. She knew they were empty the way he swung them in the air, his cap pulled low, his lips clamped around his pipe.

'Morning. It is that.' She crossed over to him, her attention on his expression and the way his brows disappeared under his cap at something behind her, the sharp scrape of heels on concrete giving her a clue as to what she'd find.

'Camille! I thought you'd left.'

'Waiting for my lift, *ma cherie*, and as if by magic, here it is.'

The black car swung into the car park with no regard for the five miles an hour sign, its wheels scattering stones in a shower of dust, the driver barely pulling to a stop. There was no thought of the young soldier jumping out to open the door for her. Instead, he stayed where he was, his supercilious expression indication enough at how demeaning he felt the task of acting taxi driver was. But that didn't seem to bother Camille. With a gallic shrug and a small wave she opened the back door and slid inside, her legs crossed decorously under her tight skirt, her face a composed mask of indifference as he swerved towards the exit.

'Like the queen, that one.' Emile stood beside his churns, his cap now pushed back from his forehead, his expression bemused.

Evelyn laughed, threading her hand through his arm. 'You could say that, Mr Guille, but also a very kind young woman. Any chance of a cuppa? I might as well look at that little problem of yours while I'm at it.'

'Problems I have many, as I do milk. Alas, as to the tea...'

In that moment, Evelyn made a promise to share any she had his way.

'Bramble it is. I'll miss it when this war is over,' she said, her words pitched to mean the exact opposite.

The cottage was tiny. A low-ceilinged room in which to live and to sleep. A double bed pushed up into one corner, partly hidden by a wicker screen. A table and chairs. No inside toilet and the only running water a single tap in the kitchen sink. Having a bath was a huge chore, entailing dragging a tin bath through the door and filling it from water boiled on the small stove. But, as Emile had said on many occasions, his needs were simple now he didn't have a wife mithering after him. He'd been happy enough to give up his slighter larger cottage when he'd taken over managing the farm.

'It's alright, Colin. It's only nurse come to check on you.'

Colin eased out from behind the screen, the colonel's trousers and shirt hanging from his skeletally thin frame, his long arms and legs far too long for the shorter man's made-to-measure clothes. It only took a quick glance for Evelyn to notice all this and more but she wasn't interested in what he was wearing. It was the spot of colour in his pale cheeks and the lessening in the shadows under his eyes that caused her to relax. The change wasn't great. It would take time for the haunted look to disappear and better food than they had available to fill out the hollows in his cheeks and add muscle to his stick thin bones. But it was good to see that he was on the mend. She needed a bit of good news after the night she'd had, for all her high jinks with baby swapping. A dead woman and a dead baby wasn't something she could brush off with a bit of positivity but the sight of him looking so well was enough to bring a smile to her tired face.

'I can see you're on the mend. How's the dressing doing? Any pain?'

'Fine. Only an occasional twinge. The doc popped in last night and prodded round a bit. Said it would be as good as new in a few days.'

He flicked an anxious glance between her and the door, his hands in his pockets in an air of nonchalance, which was anything but. It was clear he was concerned about something, and it didn't take a genius to know what. The risk of capture was huge as was the threat of repercussions for anyone found to be harbouring a wanted man. There was no question in her mind that he was the man the soldiers were looking for.

Evelyn knew very little about him. The newspaper headline had been sensational as opposed to informative. A dangerous man on the run could be anyone and weren't they all dangerous, given the chance. That there was rarely a chance with the number of Germans was irrelevant. He'd seen an opportunity to escape and had taken it. All she knew was his true name, his Irish roots and the little issue of someone taking a pot shot at him but, unlike Sister Murphy, she didn't need to know more. Knowing might be dangerous, and she couldn't afford to put anyone else's life at risk. His captors obviously shot first and asked second. She had to hope that he was safe enough for a few days. For a start, the strong tide between Herm and Guernsey must have them think that he'd died en route.

'You alright staying here for now? There's nowhere else but we're working on that. Can't really move you until the risk of infection has been ruled out.'

He nodded. 'I thought the game was up when I saw Camille leave.'

Evelyn examined him a moment, trying to weigh up the meaning behind his words because he was certainly saying more than the short sentence alluded to. That he knew Camille was a shock. The thought that he would have also known Marise hovered and burned, the stab of pain in the vicinity of her heart. Probably psychosomatic but as sharp as if caused by the sharpest of blade fashioned from the toughest of steel.

'You know Camille?'

He laughed, a bitter excuse for a laugh with no trace of humour lingering in the depths. 'Everyone living on Alderney knows Camille. Not so much to speak to. Her sort would never speak to the likes of me, but I've seen her around on the arm of one or other of the officers. What was she doing here or aren't you allowed to say?'

Evelyn was as surprised by his answer as she was in a quandary as to how to reply. He wasn't a relative but that didn't seem to matter. Nothing was normal about the situation she found herself in.

'Camille was visiting a patient,' she said, which was sort of the truth.

'One of the girls?'

Evelyn nodded. 'Marise.'

'Ah. She's had the kid then. Poor thing.' He dropped his gaze to the floor.

'I take it you know her too?'

'Not more than that. Seen her around the *Kommandant*'s villa. Couldn't really miss her.'

He concentrated on the tips of his boots with a fascination that far outweighed the dull leather. 'More than our life's worth to raise our heads from our jobs. More than her life's worth too, I would imagine.'

'You've never said what you were doing over in Alderney?'

His brow lowered, his forehead a concertina of wrinkles as he fumbled in his pocket and pulled out a cigarette, his hand shaking slightly as he lit it. One of Emile's special roll-ups if she wasn't mistaken. It was a great mystery that he still managed to have a ready supply of tobacco. It was also clear from Colin's fixed expression that he had no intention of answering her question and she wasn't going to press him. Instead she veered back a little on their conversation to the other thing that was nagging her. The officer who had brought Marise in. She'd felt an instant dislike for the man. There was something about him that spelled danger, which made her uneasy. After all, she'd stolen his daughter.

'Someone called Yannick brought her in.'

His head shot up; his mouth compressed into a thin line. 'Yannick Klein?'

'I guess so.'

So that's his name. Not easy to remember but one impossible to forget, she thought, making a mental note.

'Uberlieutenant Klein,' he continued. 'Luckily not as good a marksman as he thinks, or I wouldn't be standing here. The fact I have trouble sitting...'

She laughed because it seemed to fit the conversation, but it was only a brief laugh. 'He brought her over by boat and in this weather. I take it there's no doctor in Alderney then?'

He drew heavily on the cigarette before removing it and studying the glowing end. 'That's where you're mistaken, nurse. A doctor assigned to each camp, not that we're allowed to see them. Hell would have to freeze over for that. What would be the point of battering us with anything they could lay their hands on only to then patch us up. That's not the way the SS works.'

'The SS?' Evelyn was surprised at the use of the term. Word had filtered through about the atrocities that were happening across Europe and beyond, but Alderney...? 'Surely the SS wouldn't want the women to leave?'

'Would you want one of their army doctors to be looking after you? It's alright for the likes of the soldiers but...' He shrugged. 'I wouldn't let one of their butchers within a mile of my nearest and dearest if I could help it.'

SIXTEEN
KITTY

Wednesday 26 December, 2018 – Dublin

The kitchen was quiet apart from the odd swish of water and chink of china. A haven in Aunty Min's manic house, with her three dogs and what seemed like fifteen cats, but was only two. Her aunt volunteered at the local animal shelter and invariably came home most weeks with a new foster to add to her menagerie. Last week it was a one-eyed cat with a torn ear called Ambrose, the week before a budgerigar she'd named Sam.

Washing dishes wasn't a pastime Kitty normally volunteered for but, with her dad and aunt huddled around the fire nursing glasses of sloe gin, it was an ideal opportunity to puzzle out what was going on with him. She needed to think and there was nothing better to set her brain cells alight than a mindless, repetitive task like scrubbing pots.

He hadn't strung more than two words together since yesterday and those consisted primarily of yes, please and no thanks. The violin was the obvious cause. No, the photograph hidden within the case.

Kitty stopped a second, working on a stubborn mark on the edge of the pan, her attention on the metal feeder dangling from the bird table outside the window, her mind going round in circles. What was it about a photograph that could cause him to blow all his gaskets in such a spectacular fashion?

'Thought I'd keep you company for a bit.' Her aunt joined her at the sink, plucking a tea towel from the back of the chair on the way.

'Dad resting his eyes?' They shared a conspiratorial smile at the sound of a deep rumbling snore rattling through the open door.

'It's his age catching up with him.' Aunty Min chuckled as she picked up a plate and started running the tea towel over it before adding it to the growing pile. At seventy-five she was only a year older than her brother but as different as could be in both looks and attitude. Where her dad was tall, dark-eyed and skinny, her aunt was as round as she was short but with an energy that outstripped both her brother and her sister. Kitty felt dizzy hearing about her day, which included Pilates in the morning, dog walking and volunteering in the afternoon and Irish dancing in the evening.

'So, what's going on between you two then?' Min added, starting to slide the plates into the built-in rack to the right of the sink.

Her aunt was also intuitive. It was impossible to keep secrets when she was about, not that Kitty had the kind of life that attracted secrets. The most exciting thing to happen to her in the lead up to Christmas outside of the violin was selling the epergne to that lawyer, which said more about her life than she'd admit to anyone, including herself.

'You spotted that, eh?' She tipped the water out of the bowl and started refilling it in preparation for her aunt's best tea set. Paper thin Royal Albert bone china and as fragile as it looked. As a child she'd craved drinking her milk from one of the pink floral cups. As an adult and in the business of antiques, she knew the value of the set and was rightly terrified.

'Would you prefer if I washed? You know it's only a tea set, don't you?' Her aunt pressed her soft body into Kitty's side, the scent of her eponymous Chanel No 5 bringing an ache to her throat and a tear to her eye. Kitty had always been close to her aunt but, with the death of her mother their relationship had shifted, the gap in their age closing with every breath.

'You mean the gift from your husband? The one you'd been eyeing up in Switzers department store for weeks before the wedding? I'm terrified. How about I make coffee and watch as you wash and dry?' Kitty lifted an earthenware mug from the shelf and tilted it back and forward. 'I think I'm safe with your Denby.'

Aunty Min laughed, the flicker of a young girl lingering in her sparkling eyes and wicked smile. 'I've obviously overshared at some point in my life, except it was Arnotts and not Switzers,' she said, swapping positions with her. 'It will also be an opportunity for you to tell me what's up with your dad.'

Kitty knew when she was beaten. With her hip against the counter, she gave up any pretence of making drinks, her attention on her aunt as she deftly worked her way through the cups and saucers. It was a task she'd carried out many times before.

'Did I tell you we'd agreed not to buy gifts this year?'

Starting at the beginning was probably the best place. There were still questions. Why the woman had happened on their shop for one. Kitty was no further forward in how to find out, as the address she'd been given was a fake. Villiers Road existed but not the number 307.

'I seem to remember something, although it's not what your mother would have wanted.'

'I know but...' Kitty swallowed the persistent lump in the back of her throat that popped up every time she thought of her mum locked up in a padded cell, her mind stolen away like a thief in the night. Her mum but not her mum, nothing left apart from a frail body wrapped in a hospital gown, the hair wild and uncombed. The nurses did their best but were limited by what she'd allow before lashing out. Biting, scratching, screaming, kicking and punching. Her mild-mannered mother changing into someone she hadn't recognised by the end.

'There was this woman. Just a walk-in off the street with something to sell. You know how Ma was about musical instruments,' she finally said, her voice taking on a husky undertone.

'I do indeed. You too until recently,' Aunt Min replied, pulling out a chair and waiting while Kitty joined her at the table, all to the backdrop of gentle snoring coming from the lounge. It was impossible to tell how long they had before he woke, probably only a few minutes.

'Yes, well. She brought in an old violin. Ancient and in need of a lot of work.'

'Interesting she chose White's?'

Kitty glanced at her. 'Not really. I've never given up on the instrument side of the business, only the playing part and I'm thinking I might take it up again now I have a decent fiddle.'

'I'm delighted to hear it. So I take it you bought it?'

Kitty nodded. 'It needs a lot of work, but I couldn't resist.'

'I'd think my brother would have been ecstatic in how thoughtful you'd been in buying your own present,' Aunty Min replied, her voice tinder dry.

'He was at first. That is until I showed him what came with it.' Kitty slipped her phone from her pocket and slid her finger across the screen before pushing the device across the table, the image clear to see. 'There were some photos tucked down the side of the case.'

Aunt Min removed her glasses from the top of her head, propped them on her nose and glanced down at the phone. It was only a brief look but enough for colour to flood her cheeks.

'What did you say the woman's name was again?' Her aunt's chin lifted, her expression suddenly difficult to read.

'I didn't but it was Caroline Raven.' Kitty leant forward. 'Why are you so interested all of a sudden?'

'I don't think I should...' Aunty Min pushed her glasses back up her forehead, the arms snagging in her blonde hair. 'It's up to your father. It's not my place.'

Kitty ignored her hesitancy, instead scooping back the phone and sliding to another image. 'There was a notebook too. A kid's schoolbook would you believe, full of spellings until nearly the end. Then it's a diary headed up by a list of names.'

'I can't.'

Kitty stopped her. 'You can, Aunty. You must. Please.' She stretched out the image with her fingers. 'There's a name too. Look, just visible on the cover below that of Susan Martin. Miss E Nightingale. What does it mean. What do they mean? I've searched and searched for both of them but there's nobody the right fit.'

'That's because you're looking in the wrong country – or should that be island.'

'What do you mean?' Kitty said, trying to contain her frustration.

Min's shoulders slumped, her defences cracking under the weight of Kitty's blank stare. 'You probably don't remember your uncle Mo, do you? He'd pretty much left the family by the time you arrived on the scene.'

Peering into the past for Kitty suddenly resembled searching through thick treacle. She'd always known her dad had a brother but as for more.

'He had a daughter,' Min prompted. 'Caroline. Nice little thing. Not sure what happened to her.'

Kitty knew or thought she did, remembering the pale shadow of a woman standing in her shop, a tatty carrier bag clenched between work-roughened fingers. 'My dad never mentioned him, not for thirty years or more.'

'He wouldn't. They never saw eye to eye. Sibling rivalry.' Aunty Min tapped the phone. 'That's him. Moses Raven. Not so much a black sheep as a misguided one, or should that be confused.'

'Hang on a sec,' Kitty interrupted. 'Our family name is White, so what's with the Raven?'

'He was born Raven. I know it's difficult to get your head round. Think back to when your aunt Ena retired and decided to move away?' she continued. 'You couldn't understand what had prompted her to retire to Guernsey.'

Kitty swallowed, uncertain at the conversation shift but happy to go along if it meant she'd finally learn what was going on. 'I'm still not a hundred per cent sure where it is.' She shrugged. 'When Uncle Gerry died and with no children to tether her, I just thought she was taking the opportunity to spread her wings while she could.'

'You're right and you're also wrong.' Aunty Min glanced across at the dresser and the two cards propped up side-by-side. One from her oldest son living in Brisbane, the other from the youngest, in Hong Kong. She was about to embark on a six-week tour to see them both.

'So, what does Aunty Ena moving to Guernsey have to do with an old violin and a crazy diary ending up in the shop? I don't understand.'

Aunt Min's gaze shifted from the cards, a smile lingering in the back of her eyes. 'Everything and nothing. Miss Nightingale was a nobody. Someone you wouldn't look twice at but that didn't stop her from being a hero. All nurses are heroes in my book but none of them are a patch on Evelyn Nightingale. What she did in Guernsey during the occupation was quite frankly remarkable. She's also why you're here, why we're all here. Our family owes a debt of gratitude, one that we could never repay,' she said, idly flicking through Susan Martin's Year Four homework. 'It was much later, after Evelyn had finally decided that nursing wasn't so bad that she got dragged into a situation she had no control over.' Aunt Min topped up their mugs from the brown earthenware pot. 'Your aunty Ena knows the ins and outs.'

'I never realised that part of Britain was occupied during the war.'

'Most people don't, Kitty. Not unless they have a particular interest for some reason or other. Remember, Ireland was neutral, although many of our men decided to up and join in spite of that ruling.'

Kitty was at a loss as to why she'd never heard of Evelyn or their own family links to the Channel Islands. Not a whisper even when her aunty Ena, sister to both Aunty Min and her dad, had decided to move over there a few years back. She'd invited her to stay many a time since but with the shop and her mother's illness it was something she'd never taken her up on.

What was all the secrecy? Her aunty Min hadn't told her anything that would explain the reason for the list. What was it about this Evelyn Nightingale that had made her so special to their family?

It was a question she didn't get to ask with her father wandering into the room, his eyes flipping between them before landing on her phone on the table.

'Any chance of a cuppa before we get on our way?'

Instead of the leisurely evening she'd planned in the company of her aunt, who was fun in a way that her father was incapable of, Kitty found herself packing a pile of Tupperware dishes full of leftovers in the boot. Her father had suddenly decided he didn't want a late night. She had no say in that.

'Sorry, I didn't expect him to drag me away so soon. I have so many questions, Aunty Min.' Kitty embraced her, the smell of her perfume tickling her nose.

'Don't be too hard on him. He finds it difficult what with losing your mam. He'll come around though. It always took him a while as a child to adapt to change.'

'You two seem to be as thick as thieves.'

Once in the car, she'd scarcely released the handbrake before the interrogation began. Kitty retracted the thought as being unworthy. There was nothing combative in his words only the way he said them. While her dad had never been the life and soul of any party, he was a good, solid bloke who cared for his family in the best way he could. He'd been devastated when her mum had died and had never managed to reignite the spark he'd lost after but that didn't make him unfeeling. His behaviour since yesterday was completely out of character.

'Just talking about Aunty Ena and what drove her to move to Guernsey.'

Kitty felt his stare boring into the side of her head before he replied.

'Tax exile. I told you that when she left. Hoarding her gold offshore while the rest of us have to slave for a living and pay for the privilege.'

There was no talking to him when he was in one of his moods. Instead of replying they moved on, chatting about the shop and their next buying trip, which was planned for February. Topics that were as familiar as sliding into an old pair of slippers. However, Kitty was determined to revisit the question of his sister's move to Guernsey when his temper had cooled and, if he wasn't willing to share, she'd have to start unraveling the mystery on her own.

SEVENTEEN
KITTY

Many of the shops on the quay had decided to stay closed in the lull between St Stephen's Day and New Year's but that had never been the case with White's Antiques and Curios. Come ten o'clock the next morning she was turning the closed sign to open while simultaneously unlocking the door. There wouldn't be much trade but hopefully not the kind she hated. People in possession of a receipt returning unwanted gifts as part of their thirty-day returns policy.

She dropped into the chair behind the desk, a mug of tea pushed to the side to make room for a shoebox full of family photographs, content in the knowledge that her father was lolling about in bed. If she was lucky, she'd have a good hour before he wandered downstairs. At seventy-four he'd all but passed over the running of the shop to her but he still liked to potter about even if it only consisted of moving the items on display to their best advantage.

She'd barely lifted the lid from the box when the sound of the doorbell heralded her first customer.

Kitty managed to restrain a grimace at the sight of the man busily shaking his umbrella onto the pavement before propping it up against the inside of the door to drip all over her original parquet floor, for the second time. The solicitor who'd purchased the awful epergne!

He was dressed in casuals instead of a suit, but expensive ones that came with discreet logos embroidered onto shirts and jumpers and hand-tooled leather brogues. The fact he didn't have an epergne-shaped bag with him was irrelevant. He wouldn't be the first person to visit the shop to check the refund policy before lugging the item back.

'Hello there, hope you had a good Christmas?'

'No, not really.'

It wasn't the standard response she'd expected. 'I'm sorry to hear that.'

'Not your problem.' He approached the desk, his attention on the photographs. 'Actually, you've come recommended.'

Kitty wasn't sure how to respond, not least because of the look of surprise on his face. Jeans and a T-shirt, with her hair tied back in a scarf because of the dusty job she'd planned, obviously wasn't a look that inspired confidence.

'Well, it's always good to come recommended. How can I be of help?'

'With photographs actually.' He touched the pile of images with the side of his finger. 'I have a similar pile of these, stored in a similar shoebox, would you believe, that I need to get mounted, and I don't know where to start.' He lifted his head, and met her gaze, a fleeting look of uncertainty quickly disappearing. 'Is that something you can assist with?'

'It certainly is,' Kitty replied, leaving the security of the desk and beckoning for him to follow her over to the other side of the shop to where the albums were stored.

The assorted albums took up two shelves, each one placed in its own velvet bag before being secured in an expensive-looking box. When they'd been brainstorming how to increase their income a few years back her mother had come up with the idea of offering a bespoke album-making service. This had evolved into utilising both repaired albums rescued from previous eras and expensive hand-worked leather and hessian bound ones imported from France. They quickly found out that the service they offered was a luxury few could afford but those who could kept coming back again and again and told their friends far and wide. Barely a week went past when she didn't have to visit the post office with one of their albums ready for posting. It broke her heart that her father had always pooh-poohed any suggestion of giving their own family photographs the same treatment. The shoebox had remained untouched until earlier on this morning when she'd clambered to the top of the wardrobe to retrieve it.

'It's all very well keeping them in a shoebox. To be honest it's better than having them exposed to the light so well done for that, but fading isn't the only problem.' Kitty pulled out a black album, the one she used for explanation purposes, and started leafing through the pages. 'Air and humidity can do as much damage, as can be seen from the yellow and brown marks here and here,' she said, tapping the edge of a photograph. 'There's also cracking and creasing to consider and even the odd tear to address.' She turned to the next page where the same photographs were displayed but this time computer enhanced copies. 'You still get to keep your original images, but you also have ones as good as the day they were taken.'

She stood back and watched as he skimmed between the before and after pages before closing the book and handing it back. 'That's amazing. Just what I'm looking for, however there's a problem.' He studied his hands briefly. 'I need it done ASAP?'

'ASAP as in...?'

'Tonight, tomorrow. The next day at the very latest.'

Kitty scrutinised him from her inferior height. She'd like to know what the rush was but there was a desperation about his reply that told her any intrusive questions wouldn't be welcome. An ill relative at a guess. Either way it wasn't her business.

'I would need to see the images before I can answer. I take it you've brought...?'

'Of course.' He unzipped his bag and withdrew a brown A4 envelope. Not the largest envelope she'd ever seen but that didn't mean anything. Vintage photographs tended to be a great deal smaller than they were today.

The envelope contained about twenty images, although the pictures couldn't be said to be in the best of condition with fading and colour spotting appearing on nearly all. They'd take hours to sort.

She inspected each one before collecting them into a neat pile and placing them back in the envelope. 'We can certainly do something with them but as for the timescale—'

'I'll pay double,' he interrupted.

'I haven't even told you our fees,' she said, shocked.

'It doesn't matter. Please. It's important.'

Kitty relented. Helping people was in her nature, a trait her father called being a soft touch. Her aunts, on the other hand, said she took after her mother. Either way, it meant the same thing, but she was learning. Refusing to be bartered down on the price of the epergne proved it.

'What firm did you say you worked for again?'

'I didn't, Miss er...?'

'I'm Kitty. Kitty White.' She paused, her eyes widening in expectation.

'I'm Thomas Bradbury from Bradbury, Peters and Bradbury.'

'Which one?'

'Does it really matter?' He looked exasperated.

'It will if I'm ever in need of a solicitor.' She smiled. 'I'll see what I can do. Leave me your card.'

She waited while he scribbled down his personal email and

phone number under the information presented about the firm before walking him to the door, the rain hurtling from the sky in thick rods.

'Don't forget your umbrella. I'll be in touch.'

She locked the door after him and switched the sign to closed, thinking of the oddest of looks he'd given her when she'd presented the umbrella, then forgetting all about it. There was no point in staying open. Instead, she went back to the desk and her laptop, the photographs spread out in front of her but before she started scanning them into the system, she decided to dial up her aunty Ena on WhatsApp. A catch-up was long overdue. She could pop her on speaker and work on the images at the same time. Her own family photographs would have to wait.

'Hello.'

'Aunty Ena?' It didn't sound like her aunt unless she'd taken to smoking twenty a day along with dropping her voice an octave or two. 'I'm looking for my aunt,' she added belatedly, feeling a fool as she ran over the number she'd dialled and the number at the top of the screen. It was the same.

'I'm Police Constable Thompson. There's been a bit of an accident. In fact, I was in the process of dropping off Mrs Beatty's phone to her when it rang in my hand. She left it, and her bag, at the scene.

'She's alright, is she?' Kitty's voice was sharper than she intended but she couldn't bother about that.

'I take it you know Mrs Beatty, Miss...?

'White, and, yes, she's my aunt.'

'You'd be her next of kin then, so to speak?'

'As good as. Technically it's probably my father, her brother, being as he's the eldest but he's seventy-four and will be happy enough to be passing on that mantle.'

'Right. She's been taken to the emergency department for a check-up.'

'She's alright then?' she repeated. The relief came with a flood of emotion, her voice cracking.

'As well as can be expected for someone who wandered into the path of a bull. Mistook it for one of Mr Ingrouille's prize-winning Guernsey heifers, would you believe.'

Kitty rolled her eyes. That would be her aunt Ena. As daft as a whole box of brushes. 'If you can tell her I'll be over as soon as I can. Might take a day or two to arrange flights.'

EIGHTEEN
KITTY

The flight from Dublin to Guernsey was short. In less than two hours she was craning her head to look out the window as the plane circled over the small island. The steep cliffs on the south to the stretches of white-sanded beaches to the west. The spans of greenhouses that crisscrossed the countryside, a remnant from the days when tomato growing was the order of the day until imports undercut their prices, and the islanders had to scrub around for an alternative way to make a living.

It suddenly felt as if she was on holiday, even if her first stop was the hospital. A few days away from working or studying for her master's, suddenly felt long overdue. She didn't even have to worry about preparing Thomas's album as she'd managed to complete it before leaving for the airport.

Her gaze dropped to her lap and the book she'd picked up in departures. *A Comprehensive Guide to the Bailiwick of Guernsey*. An impressive title for a slim volume, which detailed the story of Guernsey, Herm, Sark, Jethou, Brecqhou and Alderney, from William the Conqueror's conquest years before the more famed 1066 battle to the occupation during World War Two, right up to their role as an international finance centre. It told her everything and yet nothing of what she wanted to know about. The people and what made them tick. How the past had influenced their present Guernsey way of life and, far more importantly, what had prompted Aunty Ena to up sticks for a new life on an island where she knew no one.

She switched on her phone as soon as the plane had screeched to a halt in case of messages, the small travel book tucked in her pocket. The plan was to drop her bag at her aunt's house – the neighbour had a spare key – before trekking up to the hospital to meet with her aunt's doctor. In the absence of anyone closer she'd been nominated to the scary role of next-of-kin. It was one thing to race across the Irish sea, the English Channel and all the land in between, but the thought of perhaps having to make some serious decisions on behalf of someone else was something entirely different.

There were two emails: the first confirming the time of the meeting with the doctor looking after her aunt, the second surprisingly from Thomas Bradbury.

Thank you for completing the album so quickly and taking the trouble to drop it off at my office.

I was wondering if you'd like to grab a coffee or lunch sometime this week. It would be nice to chat more. Let me know what you think. Thomas.

The message gave her a little thrill and got her through the baggage hall and the queue for taxis outside the entrance. It was only when she climbed into the taxi that she finally shrugged off the spark Thomas's note had ignited.

'Rue de la Croix, Bailiff's Crossroads please,' she said to the driver, settling back into the seat and closing her eyes. She wasn't the best of travellers, particularly in the backseat of a strange vehicle, which stank of aftershave. Lynx or something housed on the same shelf in the supermarket. A far cry from Thomas's subtle scent.

Stop it!

'Visiting relatives, are you, love?'

She sat up slightly, wondering how he'd guessed. 'That's right. My aunt is in hospital.'

'Ah. Sorry to hear that. At least you won't have far to walk and there's a nice little shop up the lane a bit for all your groceries. House only a few down from the Hangman's. Course, not the Hangman's Inn now. One of the best pubs in the island and they had to turn it into a funeral directors. Apt enough.'

'I take it they called it the Hangman's because...? Actually, don't answer that. If it's not far then best you drop me at the hospital.'

'Right you are.' He indicated right at the traffic lights. 'Just around the next corner. Which ward?'

'Hold on a sec. I'll just check my phone.' Then, after a moment. 'Lincoln Ward.'

'The new entrance so. Have you there in a jif.'

Within twenty minutes she was being escorted into the doctor's office. Her aunt had been asleep when she'd been shown into the light, airy four bedded bay. The other occupants were in their chairs and surrounded by what seemed like an army of visitors but in reality were two per patient, the hospital rule. She had stood at the end of her aunt's bed, trying to equate the small, hunched figure with blankets up to her chin. Her tinted hair was showing its white roots for the first time since she could remember, her face clean from the powder and paint she liked to coat herself in. Her shield and one she was never without.

'Ah, Miss White. I'm Dr Sara Yonkmans. Do take a seat. I hope you had a good trip over. Dublin, I believe?'

'Yes, not too bad, thank you.'

'A lovely place. Right, to your aunt. This is her first time at the hospital, but I believe she's relatively new to the island?' She lifted her head briefly from a thin set of medical notes, housed in a buff-coloured folder.

'About four years but she hails from here, or so I've recently found out. She's also always been as fit as a flea. Nothing serious apart from the occasional cold.'

'That's good to hear. Well, your aunt has taken a nasty tumble and, while there are no injuries as such apart from the odd bruise and scratch, her heart is giving us some problems.'

'What does that mean exactly?' Kitty said, feeling a flutter of anxiety spreading in her chest.

'It means that your aunt is getting on a bit and her heart is feeling the strain. In this case her blood pressure is abnormally high, and she'll have to go on medication to bring it back under control. I've made an appointment for her to see one of the cardiologists.' She paused briefly. 'Until the appointment comes through it would be best if you or another member of her family tries to curtail some of her more adventurous pastimes.'

Kitty stared across at her. The doctor didn't know her aunt at all if she thought that was even a possibility.

'Give up sea swimming? Ridiculous. It's one of the best activities going, KitKat, and the reason I've lived so long.' Aunt Ena bristled, her thin shoulders lifting in defiance as she straightened in her chair. The way she compressed her vermillion lips reminded Kitty of just how stubborn her father's sister could be. And there was her thinking of the few days in Guernsey as a well-needed break, as well as an opportunity to check up on her elderly relative.

The conversation had taken a serious turn almost as soon as they'd arrived at Aunty Ena's cottage following her discharge later the same day.

'Not give up,' Kitty countered, struggling to keep the

laughter from her voice. Her aunt, both aunts, were legends in Dublin for taking life by the tail and trying to string as much out of it as they could. Her father was completely different. 'Take a break for now, at least until you've seen the cardiologist. I know you say the Bathing Pools are safe enough and there's changing rooms and a café, and what have you, but you must admit there are warmer places this time of year than the water in the English Channel. What about the local swimming pool?'

'Are you mad? I am not swimming in a public pool. That's for kids and old people. It's the sea or nothing.'

Kitty was tempted to ask at what age her aunt considered middle age stopped but she wasn't that brave. 'Then I'm afraid it's nothing until the doc gives the all clear, Aunty. I'm not having you on my conscience. Walking's good, in fact very good. The doctor said so. We can go on one tomorrow and you can show me some of the island you keep going on about.'

'Call me Ena, aunty makes me sound ancient.' She swapped her cup for Kitty's hand. 'I miss your ma, you know. It was always going to take a strong woman to manage an eejit like my brother, and your mother was more than a match. You look just like her.'

Kitty stared down at their linked fingers. Her aunt's were peppered with age spots, the joints thickened, the nails painted a vermilion red to match her lipstick. People told her she looked like her mother, but she could never see it and she'd looked often enough over the years. There was no one in her mother's family to discuss it with. No siblings or family at all. Her mother's background had been a mystery. She'd only really got to know her father's two sisters during the last ten years. They were the type to be off galavanting in far flung places until age and common sense had finally restrained their activities.

It seemed as if her life was heading for another change shortly and there was nothing she could do to stop it. No one halted old age.

'Thank you.'

'Why the serious face all of a sudden, Kit?' She felt her hands being squeezed tight. 'I'm sorry if I...'

'It's not that, Ena. Never think there's anything you could say to upset me except perhaps if it's going for a swim against doctor's orders.' They both laughed, the atmosphere softening with her words and giving her the impetus from somewhere to change the subject. 'I came across some photos, which I think might be from Da's and your side of the family. Dad won't talk about them. He's never wanted to talk about the past and whenever I asked Ma, she always used to say something about it being a sore subject.'

Ena's eyes softened. 'Ah, well, your father's stubbornness rubbed off on all of us, I suppose. He made it clear a long time ago that the past wasn't to be dragged up and, out of respect, I kept my mouth shut. But now that you've found them... Maybe it's time to stop skirting around. We've all got secrets, my dear. Secrets we don't want anyone to discover. The power only comes from sharing them and facing the truth.' She smiled a little. 'I take it you've brought them with you? There's never any time better than the present. It's important you know what stock you hail from. A strong one.'

'They're in my case but the morning will do. It's getting late,' Kitty said, not wanting to break this special moment.

'Away with you. It's only a little after nine and I've never been one for my bed. Off you hop to get them and I'll top up your glass while you're about it.'

Kitty knew there was no arguing with her aunt once her mind was set but she'd promised herself she would be a responsible adult and not drink too much while she was here. 'I don't need...'

'I know you don't, but you will anyway.' Ena frowned down at her glass with regret. 'I on the other hand had best get used to being good. Not much fun in growing old, eh, although I don't much fancy the alternative. I'll take a look at what you've brought then straight to bed. Promise.'

With the photos between them, along with a mug of cocoa for Ena and a dash more whisky in Kitty's glass, she picked up an image at random, quickly checking the back before pushing it across the table.

A tall, rangy man with thick dark hair swept back from a high forehead, dressed in baggy trousers and jacket, a cigarette clamped between his teeth.

Ena dropped her glasses in place, taking her time in scanning the black and white image, her expression unreadable as she traced over his features before speaking. 'That's your grandfather, Kitty. A true hero if ever there was one...'.

Kitty reluctantly feigned a yawn, noting the way her aunt's voice tailed off, her pallor at war with her bright eyes.

Some things were more important than others. *Other* things would have to wait.

'Let's leave it for now, Ena. All this travelling has suddenly caught up with me. You can tell me tomorrow. Something to look forward to.'

NINETEEN
EVELYN

2 March, 1943

Attending one of the hospital's evening soirees was the last thing Evelyn wanted to do when she woke up after the four hours' sleep she'd allowed herself as she was now off for three days. There was a vast difference between playing for herself and performing for others.

With Violet still asleep she had the cottage to herself, but she couldn't be inspired to complete any of the little jobs she'd been staving off until precisely that moment. Instead, she took herself out for a walk along the lanes, a crust of bread from her allowance wrapped carefully in a square of waxed paper for her supper.

The lanes were empty, but Evelyn didn't mind. She relished the solitude, using the time wisely to get her head together after the most traumatic of nights imaginable. She couldn't help grieving for Marise, a young girl torn from her family to take up work in a foreign land. Most of it was supposition, the few facts shared by Camille and supported by the French labels sewn into the woman's plain underclothing, which were out of keeping with her trashy outfit, and the small gold locket she'd been wearing.

Evelyn had been asked to start laying the girl out. She'd ended up completing the task while Sister and Ivy had been busy with the back round and all the feeds. By the time she'd gone off duty she'd forgotten that she'd popped the necklace into her pocket. It was only later back at the cottage when she was stepping out of her dress that she spotted something glistening at her feet. Then she'd sat on the edge of her bed, trembling with fatigue, the locket open in the palm of her hand, the inscription on the left hand side faint but readable.

Marise Dupont, Toujours Aimée, Mama et Papa. 3/4/1926

She stared at the inscription a long time, growing cold in the chill of the unheated room. It made a strange sort of sense, she thought, her eyes shifting to the photo and the image of a couple holding onto a small baby. Marise hadn't been a woman at all in spite of her sexy clothes. Not yet seventeen and lying cold and still on that hard trolley. Alone.

The locket was now safely around her neck as she strolled out the cottage to clear her muddled thoughts. The safest place she could think of until she got a chance to hand it over to Sister Jehan.

The hedgerows were alive with ferns, ivy and pretty red campion, or soldiers' fleas as they were known locally. Soon she had an armful of what most people would term weeds, but they made her happy. When she got back to the cottage it was already dusk but with no sign of the snow and, thankfully no sign of the rain that had threatened to take its place.

The first thing she did when she arrived back was to wake Violet with soft words and a cup of bramble tea before returning to the kitchen and dividing the flowers into bunches, placing the largest in a jar on the kitchen window. By then they were both ready to leave for the hospital, her forgotten bread in one hand, her violin case clutched in the other. Violet grumbled beside her as she banged the door shut behind them. She didn't bother to lock it. It would only be Jerry sniffing around and if he found a locked door he'd most likely kick it in, causing a host of problems for them both. The only time they locked it was when they were home alone and who could blame them with the sound of drunk troops roaming the lanes of an evening, their strangely melodious singing at war with their stamping feet and the occasional sound of enthusiastic gunfire released into the night air.

'It's not fair that I'm having to miss it, it's always me.' Violet moaned all the way down the hill, forgetting that she'd attended the last soiree and the one before when it had been Evelyn who'd had to work. If Evelyn could have swapped shifts, she would have but their schedules were set by Matron. She was a nice enough woman until she was crossed, or so the rumour went. They'd decided early on against testing it.

They parted company at the entrance. 'I promised Mrs Le Pelley that I'd pop up and see how she was getting on. Have a good shift.' Evelyn slipped off her cloak and bundled it under her arm on her way up the two flights of stairs. It was another one of those strange hospital rules she couldn't get her head around that cloaks weren't allowed to be worn on the ward. That she also wasn't meant to be on the ward when she wasn't working was another one, but she ignored that. Instead, she lifted her knee to balance her violin case before withdrawing one of the small bunches of flowers and heading for Sister's office.

'Shut the door, nurse,' were Sister's first words, closely followed by, 'and do take a seat.'

The flowers were an excuse, but she laid them on the desk all the same, smiling slightly. 'I know it's against the rules, but I thought Mrs Le Pelley might like them.'

'I'm sure she will.'

Evelyn wasn't scared of Sister Jehan, but she was worried about the mess she'd got them into. 'Everything alright with the baby and...?'

'She's named her Wilhelmina, after her mother. We've sent a letter to the chief of police with the news to see if it can be forwarded onto Mr Le Pelley in prison but who knows. Wilhelmina is a beautiful little girl who will be well loved and taken care of, thanks to you.'

Evelyn felt her cheeks heat. 'And Marise and the baby?'

'Will be buried together in the Câtel Church graveyard. The vicar won't need any persuading. Uberlieutenant Klein has sent word through, reiterating that he is happy to leave all the arrangements to us.'

Evelyn placed her cloak by her feet and, reaching up, unfastened the necklace, placing it on the desk between them. 'I found this when I was washing her. I'm sorry. It was a genuine oversight not to mention it to you this morning. It should go to her parents but...'

Sister touched the locket with her fingertip briefly. 'Camille may know, if she ever comes our way again.'

They exchanged a look. Rumour had it that there were over a hundred prostitutes working across Guernsey and Alderney in the five German-run brothels. Finding, or even asking for the whereabouts of one of them would only engender suspicion, the last thing any of them wanted.

'Best if you keep it *pro tem*. It will be safer that way. Now, onto cheerier topics. I believe you went to see Matron earlier?'

Evelyn refastened the necklace with reservation, but she wasn't prepared to argue the point. She'd keep it safe but only until she could pass it on to Marise's family, if that was even possible. 'Yes, Sister. She'd like to make my move permanent, if you'll have me?'

Sister smiled briefly. 'Well, so far, you've been an asset,

although I'd appreciate a little more warning if you do decide any funny business. I'm not sure my heart can take many more of your ad hoc decisions.' She checked her watch, pushing back from the desk with a small laugh. 'I hear you're to play for us this evening.'

The soiree was in full swing by the time Evelyn slipped into the room unannounced, taking up a chair at the back.

There was Matron Rabey in the front row surrounded by the ward sisters and two of the doctors. The other two, Dr Holly and Dr Jones, were on the impromptu stage dressed in white coats and hurling their stethoscopes around while giving a passable rendition of the Andrews Sisters 'Boogie Woogie Bugle Boy' to the accompaniment of Jack, one of the male orderlies, on his tin whistle. That the audience were singing along to the words was proof that the ban on radios wasn't as successful as Jerry thought. Most people either had crystal radio sets of their own or access to one, even her although she rarely troubled to listen to it now.

When the claps had died down someone spotted Evelyn from her hiding place. She was persuaded to make her way up front to where Dr Jones had placed a chair at a right angle to the audience, a smile of what looked like relief on his face.

Evelyn wasn't a performer. As a music teacher she was far happier encouraging her students from the wings but once her talent had been spotted, she'd had little chance to evade the spotlight.

She opened the case, pausing to admire the way the dull red of the lining complemented the burnished tone of the wood. Evelyn had owned many instruments over the years, but none were a patch on the clarity of tone she got from this violin. It was nothing to look at. The case battered, the leather covering coming away from the frame. The violin in need of a polish, the varnish flaking in places. The label with the words *Made in Germany* scrawled across it, just visible through the F hole, was proof enough that she was dealing with a fake, a good fake but still a fake. Her father wouldn't have passed it on to her if he'd thought he could turn a profit. That was her dad. It didn't matter. None of it mattered, only the sound. The music was everything.

Evelyn tightened the strings before positioning the chin rest in place and lifting the bow. A few tester notes to get the feel of the instrument.

Her eyes slipped closed, the room fading and all the people with it, not that there was a sound, unless bated breath made a noise.

It took a lot to forget a war, to forget the suffering and starvation they faced from one day to the next, to forget the threat of the enemy just outside the gates, and oftentimes inside their homes as accommodation became scarce.

Evelyn had the power to do all that, but her music had the ability to do much more. It helped her make sense of a world that she'd failed to understand for a very long time. The images slid behind her closed lids. Marise, still beautiful in death. Betty Le Pelley's baby girl. A girl without a name. And finally little Wilhelmina and the future she'd manipulated. No one had given her the right and yet... she viewed she had every right to change this slight course in history.

The music flowed. Chopin, Vivaldi, Debussy. Music she'd played to her Joseph, so long ago now she could barely bring up an image other than the small pasteboard photograph of a soldier standing proud in his uniform. They had been so young when they'd met. Their plans delayed until after the war. She would have cried at the thought, but she'd promised herself a very long time ago that she'd shed the last tear for memories as faded as his photograph.

She stopped then, she had to. On the edge of what she knew

too well. One more note and she'd tumble and embarrass herself. No one knew about the death of her fiancé during the last war except Violet and that's the way she intended to keep it.

'I'm sure someone else must want a turn in the hot seat.' Her voice was a dry rasp, a husk of emotion, her smile laboured as she went to return the violin to its case, her heart bled dry.

'No. More. More.' They started shouting out songs, happy tunes to mitigate the sad, to shift the melancholy and she let them, picking up the tempo and ditching the chair for the floor, her hips and shoulders swinging to the beat. 'Pack Up Your Troubles in Your Old Kitbag', 'It's a Long Way to Tipperary' and finally, 'Wish Me Luck as You Wave Me Goodbye' before she determinedly placed the violin back in the case and snapped it closed.

The evening was finished for her but not for everyone else. She endured praise over a long hoarded half-bottle of sherry, the dark amber liquid barely coating the base of the glass, her taste-buds reneging at the unaccustomed taste after months and months of the blandest diets where salt didn't feature, and sugar was a rarity. Without their Guernsey cows to milk they'd have starved long ago.

'That was wonderful, nurse.'

'Thank you, Dr Holly. I enjoyed your and Dr Jones's performance immensely,' she replied, finishing her drink and placing the glass on one of the trays circulating. The clock was ticking on their curfew time. Spending one of her hard-earned days off in the clink was the last thing she needed.

Dr Holly jerked his head slightly, manoeuvring her into a corner out of earshot of the others. 'I'd like to escort you home if I may? I have something I'd like to discuss.'

Evelyn had been worrying about the walk for most of the evening. Guernsey was one of the safest of places to live but that had been before the war. Attacks on women were rare and dealt with harshly by the German police but that didn't mean they didn't happen. Dr Holly, in his role of doctor, was in possession of a pass, which meant that he could escort her before making his own way home without the threat of a night in the cells for breaking curfew.

She nodded her reply, her cloak in her hand. 'We'd best hurry.'

The night air was cold, the ground icy underfoot as they rushed up the hill past the sentry box outside the battery in the pitch black of the evening. No streetlights or chinks from windows, blackout blinds drawn. Nothing to light their way and a few stumbles until their night vision sorted itself out.

'What we need is carrots. You know, to see in the dark.'

'Good luck with that, nurse. Can't remember the last time. You need to love the turnip to enjoy any kind of a diet in this place. At least Marjory and the boys should be faring better.'

The last sentence was said with a heavy sigh. Evelyn knew about the doctor's wife and family. Their evacuation to London, then Coventry because of the Blitz, was something they talked about on the odd occasions they'd met outside of work. Perhaps because of their similar ages and he had to talk to someone.

'I do hope you hear from them soon. The powers that be are either censoring or stopping everything and anything outside of the usual *how are you doing* platitudes, and I know you've told me how opinionated your wife can be.' Her voice was soft, but matter-of-fact instead of the sympathy she reserved for her patients. She'd learnt long ago that different people and different circumstances demanded a different approach.

'Thank you, m'dear. I appreciate it.' They continued an ambling conversation, which shifted from the weather to work and back again until they arrived at her cottage. It wasn't only the Germans they had to worry about. The occupation had set friends and neighbours against one another, tales of collaboration rife. They were all starving but some less starving than others.

'Do you want to come in?' She was outside the front door, her hand on the latch.

'No time. I just thought you'd like to know that I've solved Colin's little problem,' he replied, leaning against the wall, his eyes fixed on the lane ahead, his voice a breath of sound.

Evelyn was astonished. She'd thought it might have been something about Wilhelmina or Marise. That he'd found a work around to Colin's problem... Impossible.

'How on earth...?'

'Trust has to be earned in this war and you've earnt mine, Nurse Nightingale.' He flicked her a smile before continuing with his scrutiny. 'However, I don't think I should risk involving you further. This is a very serious business. If any of our friends in grey get to hear...'

'Now, hold on a minute. You can't start to tell me something only to stop. You must know I won't talk.' She pulled her cloak around her, tucking her hands underneath for added warmth, her violin now by her feet.

'I'm not sure you know what you're getting into but so be it. It is probably too late to change things anyway. Just remember you can always trust me to come to your aid, if it's within my power to do so.'

She nodded, impatient for the update and not really understanding what he was getting at.

He pushed away from the wall and moved to the gate. 'It might be better if I tell you. Not so much of a shock as you'll be seeing him around the grounds. Mr Guille has finally admitted that he needs help on the farm. An ideal job for Mr Edgar Falla, now he's in possession of the right...' He paused, picking his words. 'The right implements. Although a bit of a change from his greenhouses out in the wilds of Torteval.'

'One of your patients? The poor man.'

'Not so poor. As rich as Croesus but, as he sadly learnt, you can't eat money and too proud to ask for help. I found him earlier on today after the postman realised his mail was adding up on the doormat. Must have been bedridden days before finally succumbing.' He stepped back, his hands in his pockets as he prepared to depart. 'Now all I need to do is find a way of burying him.'

With a wave of his hand he was gone, making fast work of the lane.

She continued watching until he faded from sight, then picked up her violin and made her way inside, remembering to bolt the door behind her.

TWENTY
EVELYN

Tuesday 6 April, 1943

Evelyn pulled her cloak more firmly over her knees, the bitter cold of the church leaching through the patches in her stockings. She felt cold all over but it was a cold that came from within. A cold that couldn't be stemmed by a hot drink or a blazing fire. Numb with cold. The cold of death.

She was here because Sister had asked her but also because she wanted to come out of respect for the bravest of young women, and a little baby.

The funeral of Marise Dupont and her supposed child wasn't on anyone's social calendar. An event to be brushed under the carpet along with the dirt on the end of the broom. There was no missive or announcement shared with the parishioners.

As a group, the brothel workers were viewed on a tier below those poor unfortunate local girls who deemed it fitting to drop their drawers for any passing German that asked. That didn't stop Evelyn from feeling a huge sympathy for the women. Many were prisoners of war with no choice in their role. Society always needed someone to oppress just as they celebrated underdogs and heroes alike, and the brothel workers, as a group, were easy to hate. Parading around St Peter Port in their finery when everyone else was forced to wear rags only fit for the bin was one thing. The fact they were assigned special rations designed for manual labourers was a thorn in the side of everyone in possession of a ration book. An insult. Evelyn wondered how these women coped with the harsh reality of their lives under German rule and in a society that acted both judge and jury. She couldn't but help admire their resilience while also deploring their provocative ways.

The pews were empty but not totally. Not the second row. The nurses on the unit had come out in force, led by Sister Jehan in a battered felt hat with a feather sticking out the side.

Evelyn was on a split shift, which wasn't a bad thing as she had a ready excuse to go in her uniform. It meant she didn't have to worry about what to wear. She sat hemmed in by a pillar one side and Dr Jones the other. Sister Jehan on the end. On the opposite side sat Camille, flanked by three similarly clad young women. Their make-up flawless, their outfits sexy but seemingly toned down for the occasion. No flaming reds or iridescent whites and pinks. Black with little lace trifles to cover their immaculate hair, and hands, with no concessions made for the polar icecap temperatures, which always reigned supreme whatever the weather or time of year in the stone built church.

'Dearly beloved, we are gathered here today to celebrate the life of Marise Dupont and her small daughter, Cozette.'

The door to the church didn't so much burst open as creak, the wood warped over the years, the hinges rusting up and with no spare oil in which to grease them.

Evelyn kept her gaze front, her attention on the plain wood of the coffin, at the sound of heavy-soled boots clipping against the tiled floor. The sound paused briefly before stopping. The officer flipped up the back of his jacket and settled in the pew in front, his cap now resting on his knees along with his black leather gloves, his hand smoothing his greying hair back from the broad dome of his forehead.

The vicar looked alarmed above the white of his dog collar but, after a brief cough into the cone of his curled palm, started repeating his words.

Evelyn was also alarmed but for completely different reasons. Her view of the coffin was obliterated by the steel of his hair, her heart making a fair attempt at trying to climb through her chest wall. She glanced sideways out of the corner of her eye at the doctor and Sister Jehan, who both appeared to be going through the same metamorphosis. Hands gripped into fists. Skin the colour of porridge, eyes determinedly glued to the coffin, the vicar's speech going over their heads. His words were superfluous when taken alongside the crime they'd committed, the crime they were still committing.

They had to keep up the pretence that they were just attending the funeral of a patient, in the same way they'd attended many other funerals. Not so easy in the presence of the enemy. She hadn't thought he'd suspected a thing, now she wasn't so sure. Why leave all the arrangements to someone else only to turn up at the eleventh hour? A crisis of conscience or a growth in the suspicion that all wasn't as it seemed. Whatever the reason, Evelyn bent her head for the last prayer, not hearing a word. She was thinking of her pending arrest and what that would mean for her father and Sister Thérèse. When she finally opened her eyes, she'd decided to take full responsibility for the baby swap whatever the penalty.

The vicar was on his round up, careful to avoid the gentleman in the front row. 'Thank you for coming here today. As you know, I never got to meet Marise or her child but from the stories and memories you've shared, I know that she would have appreciated your attendance. Go with God.'

Evelyn closed her eyes, concentrating on her breathing and

her hands, which she loosened against her lap in a semblance of normality, Sister Jehan following her example. The funeral was the easy part. If they were going to be discovered, it would be now.

Dr Jones was on his feet and heading for the coffin, along with three pallbearers from the funeral directors. They exchanged measured whispers before they braced their knees and lifted the coffin onto their shoulders.

'Halt.'

Yannick made his way over, his bare head bowed, his cap and gloves left in the pew. Evelyn wanted to run out of the church, Doctor Jones's steadying hand on her arm the thing that prevented her. A brief gesture hidden behind the hat on his lap. A gesture that said *be brave*; they had to see the tableau played out to the end.

'Marise.'

The name was soft, barely a name at all and pierced with an acre of emotion dragged from the depths. More of a cry than an intelligible sound, the m barely distinguishable from the r and the s.

Camille joined him, her tight outfit concealed by a silky shawl. 'Come now, Yannick, *mon chéri*. Marise wouldn't have wanted this for you. You know as well as I do how much she loved life and it goes on, you know. Yes, it's sad that you've also lost your child. *C'est tragique* but you still have me.' She threaded her arm through his and gently led him back to the pew to collect his cap and gloves, nodding her head for the procession to continue.

Instead of joining them at the graveside, Camille led Yannick to his car, the door opened by the waiting chauffeur but not before the requisite exchanges of 'Heil Hitler'. She threw a fleeting glance over her shoulder through the window before they drove away at speed, so fleeting that no one spotted it apart from the one person looking. Evelyn.

'That woman has saved our bacon, Nurse Nightingale. I was convinced we were about to spend the night in prison while awaiting deportation.' Sister Jehan bent forward, her hands on her hips as she heaved air into her lungs. 'I've never been so terrified in all my life. If he'd asked to open the coffin, he'd have found a third...'

'Shush,' Evelyn whispered and then in a much louder voice: 'I think we should spend a moment on that bench over there, Sister. Just until the blood gets back where it belongs. All this working on short rations is catching up with us both.'

They moved across to the graveside when the pallbearers started lowering the coffin into its final resting place, Marise's friends huddled in a tight-knit group, their rapid, colloquial French causing Evelyn to frown in concentration. She tried to keep fluent by speaking the local patois when she could but there was a wealth of difference between the two languages and indeed the accents in which they were delivered. The only parallel was in the rapid delivery.

'It looks as if Camille has made her decision. Rather her than me.'

'She'll have her reasons. Better her than one of the young ones. At least she knows not to involve her heart. Poor Marise never had a chance. He likes it rough. An absolute beast in bed, that one.'

Evelyn scrunched her eyes shut at the word beast, not truly understanding and yet still able to form a picture in her mind. After all, she'd met Yannick twice now. It didn't take much to appreciate what he would be capable of if he didn't get his own way.

Her attention was diverted to the men releasing the ropes, the chief pallbearer going round shaking hands. 'Thank you for helping, doc. Fred hurt his back on her earlier. Not sure what Jerry's been feeding his whore.' He spat out the word along with a globule of spittle, dragging the back of his hand across his mouth. 'Rock cakes probably.'

They laughed. Men jesting after a job well done. There was no humour in Dr Jones's face or sombre gaze despite the pretence of camaraderie. He was only playing a part like they all were.

The graveyard cleared. The brothel workers tottered off on the arms of waiting Germans and the vicar ambled back to the church. There was a grave, a floral basket to one side and Evelyn, Sister Jehan and Dr Jones paying a silent tribute before the gravedigger arrived.

One coffin. Three bodies. One thought.

The greatest sacrifice of all must be the giving of a life to save one.

That thought lingered while the trio made their way back to the church and settled on the back pew, waiting for the second act to commence, their eyes skimming over the gentle procession of plainly clad men, women and children, in an assortment of Sunday wear although it was still only Tuesday.

A baptism so quickly after a funeral might have been seen in bad taste but not to the vicar, who was used to performing a variety of services on the same day. Apparently, he hadn't even blinked when Mrs Le Pelley had asked about an early ceremony during one of his regular visits to the hospital. Evelyn had been the one to plant the idea in her head. An opportunity to celebrate little Wilhelmina's discharge by a gathering of family and friends. Who knew what the invaders might have to say about religious ceremonies next week or the week after.

Introducing the topic was easy. There was no guilt in her actions, only a realisation that the more official documentation Betty had proving her daughter's identity, the better. Birth certificate. Baptism record. It all served as validation of the truth, even if that truth was riddled with lies.

As Betty carried Wilhelmina to the font, a hush fell over the small congregation. She looked radiant, a vision of motherhood that transcended her hastily arranged appearance. It wasn't the voluminous dress or the hurriedly pinned hair that made her beautiful; it was the fierce love and protection radiating from her very being.

The cold touch of water against Wilhelmina's forehead elicited a startled yell, followed by a full-throated scream that echoed through the church. In that cry, there was life – raw, undeniable, and full of promise. It cut through the somber atmosphere, reminding everyone that even in the darkest times, new beginnings emerged.

Hope.

It was a small word for such a powerful force. But as Evelyn watched Betty and Wilhelmina, surrounded by love and support, she knew it was enough. It had to be.

TWENTY-ONE
EVELYN

Evelyn was back in the unit at ten to five. Just time to pick up her post from the porter's lodge before nipping into the kitchen. Only one letter waited for her. A thin envelope addressed in her aunt's sloping handwriting, which she read while leaning against the sink drinking a filthy brew of stewed bramble tea left over from the afternoon drink's round.

Dear Evelyn,

I hope this letter finds you well. I was overjoyed to receive your kind note thanking me for the eggs. It warms my heart to know that you enjoyed them so much.

We've had to adapt our arrangements somewhat since the forces confiscated the wooden henhouse for firewood but we're managing with the chickens using a flap in the kitchen door to roost under the stairs at night. It's provided the added security from those who fancy them for their pots.

The days are slow now the children and patients have gone but we are getting by. It could be so much worse.

May God bless you abundantly, dear niece, and keep you in His loving care. I look forward to hearing from you again soon.

With all my love and prayers,
Sister Thérèse

She was tucking the envelope back in her pocket when the door pushed open.

'Ah, there you are.' Staff nurse was in the doorway, her hand on her watch as the little hand shifted to five. 'You can wash your cup later, nurse. Hurry up now. There's the bread still to butter for the mothers' tea and the soup to warm. Then I'd like you to stay in the nursery and start the teatime feeds and what have you. I'll try and help you after the med round.' Her voice was kindly but her manner strict. There was never any skiving when staff was in charge, not that any of them had time to skive, but chatting to the patients, especially the ones that never got any visitors, was something Evelyn viewed as an important part of the job. Staff nurse less so.

With the bread buttered and the dishes tidied away, Evelyn washed her hands a second time before walking swiftly to the nursery, tying an apron around her narrow waist and pulling a clean mask from the jar by the door before entering.

'How was it?' Ivy asked, in the act of plucking Moses from his cot, his cheeks an angry bright red to match the hungry mewing wail from his lips.

'Awful and horrible.' Evelyn didn't dawdle in picking up a bottle of warmed milk from the counter and testing it on the inside of her wrist, her eyes scanning the room and settling on Jill, who had her fingers stuffed in her mouth. 'Come on, poppet. I've lots to tell you and none of it of any importance, my sweet.' She picked her up, her dark head pressed into her neck a moment as she placed a kiss on the top. 'The vicar was excellent though.'

Jill stared back at her with trusting blue eyes, taking in every word.

'Why so awful then?' Ivy settled back in her chair, baby and bottle positioned with the expertise of someone with three younger siblings and two years spent in the unit caring for other people's babies.

'Yannick turned up. I thought Sister Jehan and Dr Jones were going to have a coronary when he stalked in and settled on the pew in front of us.' Evelyn followed Ivy's actions almost completely, still feeling awkward as Jill nestled further into the crook of her arm.

'Blimey! What was he doing there?'

'Presumably mourning Marise, poor woman and poor little Cozette. Camille managed him superbly.' Her voice was crooning soft, at war with her words.

'Well, as she's in the game so to speak.' Ivy settled Moses on her shoulder now the bottle was empty, a loud burp causing them both to grin.

'I felt sorry for her. He's a brute. Who'd want to...?' She

shook her head, unprepared to send the conversation in that direction. 'Why not leave him in the cot, Ivy, and run along? I'll sort him out after I've sorted Jill.'

'I won't say no. My feet are killing me. Staff has had me marching from one end of the unit to the other for this and that. In a huff at Sister deserting her, no doubt.' She studied Moses, her eyes creasing with concern. 'Poor little dot. He's off to the Town Hospital tomorrow for his sins. Why is it always the kids that must pay for their parents' indiscretions? News only came in today not that there's space. Heaving they are. No room to swing a cat let alone room for this little charmer, and you are a charmer, my sweet. Don't let anyone tell you otherwise.'

Evelyn concentrated on the way Jill was guzzling down her milk, her blue eyes latched onto her brown ones, a glow of anger filling her chest. 'How can we let that happen after everything that's already happened to him in the first few days of his life?'

'I'm not sure there's anything we can do about it, dearie,' Ivy replied from over her shoulder, as she soaped her hands in the sink. 'At least he'll be hidden away. I can't see our German friends being tempted to visit a pile of motherless chicks.'

'And not provided any love, which is the right of every child.' Evelyn smoothed her hand over Jill's hair, thinking through their options. By the sound of it the Town Hospital wouldn't care. What Moses needed was a woman to love him, a family. Neither of which he'd get at the former workhouse. There had to be a way even if she didn't feel she was the right person to suggest it. That hadn't stopped her when she'd interfered with Marise and Colin, she remembered. But this was a different situation. A situation that required careful handling.

'What time is Matron's office open to again? I think she'll have something to say about this.'

'But no power to do anything. It's not as if we can keep him. Our beds are full as soon as they empty.'

'I still think I should try.'

'Why? What are you up to, Evelyn Nightingale?' Ivy said, drying her hands.

'I have no idea. The nurse who voluntarily goes to see Matron needs her head examined.'

'You're right there. She takes her supper at seven so you should be able to catch her on your way to your break.' Ivy picked up her bag and cape and made for the door. 'I'd love to know what you're planning.'

'It's really best that you don't,' Evelyn replied, her voice dry. 'Before you go, you don't have a couple of stamps on you by any chance? I'll pay you back tomorrow.'

When she finished her shift, Evelyn made her way downstairs. She stopped at the porter's lodge to drop off a couple of letters. One a reply to her aunt over at Les Cotils Convent, the other to the Town Hospital requesting a delay in the date of Moses's arrival. That she still had to get permission from Matron was only part of the problem she was facing.

TWENTY-TWO
EVELYN

The following day, Evelyn was on a late shift and, with the bad weather holding off, she decided to visit her aunt.

It was guilt that had driven her to write to her last night, guilt laden with necessity. Determined to follow up on her letter, she had decided to spend her morning cycling into St Peter Port and to the convent, which stood on the hill at the edge of town in a panoramic position overlooking the other islands. The beauty of the landscape felt at odds with her racing heart as she neared her destination, the vibrant sky in stark contrast to the shadows lurking beneath her cloak.

It was a journey she'd made many times before but as she turned the corner into the road leading up to the convent, it felt different.

What she'd forgotten was that the enemy occupied the string of houses bordering the tree-lined avenue. An ideal location with room to tunnel under the road to the green field of Cambridge Park opposite for their stables, and with the added advantage of the upper rooms overlooking the harbour beyond.

What was scenic to the locals was viewed as strategic positioning to monitor the comings and goings on the stretch of water between Guernsey and England.

There was a congregation of officers mingling on the pavement outside a large double-fronted Georgian residence, their hands raised in greeting at the arrival of a black car. She watched out of the side of her eye as the back door opened, a tricky exercise given the state of the road, which was mostly dirt track laced with potholes.

'Stop that woman.'

She'd just cycled past, the convent up ahead, when a tall, thin soldier stepped out in front of her, his rifle tilted in her direction.

Evelyn put out her foot to act as a brake and wobbled to a halt, her hands relaxed on the handlebars as she waited, neither looking left nor right. Her heart was galloping and anxiety coiled in her stomach but she did her best to conceal her nerves.

The soldier was young, scarcely out of his teens and with a square, spotty face under his helmet. He also looked as nervous as she felt at the sound of boots approaching from behind. Evelyn stayed resolutely facing forward.

'Your name please, *Fräulein?*'

Evelyn didn't react in any way that was noticeable to her group of onlookers when her gaze lifted to meet his. Her face was flushed from the cycle and if her fingers tightened around the handlebars, it was an infinitesimal tightening.

'Evelyn Nightingale, Uberlieutenant Klein'

'You know my name?'

'From the hospital, yes.'

'And what are you doing so far from the hospital, *Fräulein?*' He flicked a gloved finger over the wicker basket strapped to the front, intent on the well packed contents.

'Items for the poor.' She risked nodding her head at the entrance up ahead. 'Sister has been having a clear out of clothes and nappies and thought the nuns would know of some families in need.' As an excuse for riding halfway round the island on her precious morning off, it was a stupid one. All families were in need.

She picked up an item at random, a small white cardigan, and followed it with a white bonnet.

He stared at her from the top of her greying hair, partly concealed by the hood of her cloak, to her darned stockings and plain lace-up shoes. Silent seconds, which went on and on until Camille came to stand beside him, her hand on his arm. 'Come and rest before we catch the boat back, Yannick.' Her voice was an intimate caress, her meaning reinforced by the curl of her fingers around the sleeve of his jacket.

He didn't move. Evelyn had to drop her gaze before he finally allowed himself to be led into the house. The soldier was still barring the road until, with a shout from one of his friends, he finally stepped to one side, waving her past.

Evelyn glanced back over her shoulder before making her way up the steep drive to the convent. Yannick was paused in the doorway staring after her.

'Evelyn, my dear. It's so good to see you. I got such a surprise knowing you'd be able to visit.' Her aunt was waiting for her by the gates, her long, black habit dusty from a morning spent working the land.

'Just sorry it's been so long but you can understand the urgency,' Evelyn replied, trying to get her breath in order along with her pulse. As close calls went that was by far the closest. 'You're looking well, Aunty.'

'Which is more than I can say about you.'

Evelyn shrugged, dismissing her comment. 'Hard work never did anyone any harm.'

'And what was that little scene I just witnessed with that

officer?' She stood back while Evelyn leant the bicycle against the wall and unclipped the basket. 'Let me take that off you.'

'Nothing. He recognised me from the hospital.'

'Hmm.'

Evelyn followed her aunt into the kitchen and closed the door behind her. Instead of joining her at the table, she leant back against the wall and closed her eyes, waiting for her pulse to settle, her hands cradling the bundle strapped to her chest.

'I don't know, Cissie. A group of old women.' Her aunt tutted, her gnarled hand reaching for the small wooden cross dangling round her neck, the use of her nickname drawing a smile from Evelyn.

'The nicest, kindest, group of women, who need some happiness in their life and what brings more happiness than a baby. Chickens are all very well but nowhere near as loving,' Evelyn replied, undoing the tie of her cape and swinging it from her shoulders, revealing Moses cocooned in a silk scarf borrowed from Matron. 'We made sure to give him a good feed as well as waking him up early from his morning nap. The poor mite is rightly shattered.' Evelyn blinked, remembering the fear of moments before. She had every right to try and find a loving family for Moses, but she didn't think that Yannick would see it in quite the same light. The boy's blond hair and blue eyes would have seen to that. She grimaced, remembering his words.

A child of the Reich.

One last hug and a sweet lingering kiss on top of his downy hair before she unravelled the scarf and placed the sleeping baby into her aunt's waiting arms. Aunt Thérèse's beatific smile said it all as did the herald of feet racing across the courtyard only to burst into the kitchen, the small group of nuns twittering excitedly. All things considered it felt like the right thing to do even if Evelyn felt she was leaving a piece of her heart at the Convent.

She left shortly after, her basket empty of baby supplies

except for an egg, carefully wrapped in Matron's best silk scarf. She'd decided to curtail her visit, after she'd given instructions about the powdered feed and the bottles hidden under the baby clothes. Yannick had unsettled her, which was hardly surprising after what she'd stolen from him.

The avenue was empty of soldiers apart from one solitary guard outside what must be where Yannick stayed when he was visiting the island. She sailed past, pedalling fast now she didn't have to worry about her cargo.

If she'd glanced up, she'd have seen Yannick standing in the front window, his hand on the curtain watching her until she disappeared out of sight.

TWENTY-THREE
EVELYN

31 August, 1943

The only thing that seemed to change were the seasons and the names and faces of the patients, Evelyn thought as she made her way into the ward, her cape draped over her arm, her eyes readjusting to the brightness after the darkness in the corridor. She was back on nights and dreading every minute. It was completely different trying to sleep with the air heavy with the scents and sounds of summer instead of the half-light of winter.

There was nothing she could do about the weather just as there was nothing she could do about her father taking up a bed on male medical. Evelyn had been up to see him not that he recognised her, his narrow grey face huddled under a pile of blankets with no thought for the streaming sunshine on the balcony. Fresh air and good food were all they had to treat tuberculosis with, the new-fangled antibiotics still far out of their reach.

She sat beside him as the afternoon dwindled into evening, regretting the many missed opportunities she'd let slip through her fingers to tell him how she felt. She knew that time was running out, and yet she still couldn't find the right words. It would soon be too late.

'Evening, Sister.'

'Evening, nurse. I hope you managed to get some sleep?'

'About two hours' – which was five short of the plan but Sister Jehan hadn't asked because she'd wanted to know. They'd become firm friends over Marise's death but that didn't change who was in charge and it wasn't Evelyn.

'That's good.' Sister followed her into the kitchen and watched from the doorway as she hung up her cape. An unusual occurrence made more unusual by her closing the door behind her as Evelyn started settling the heavy pan on the stove in preparation for the evening drinks.

She stopped what she was doing, her hands behind her back, a look of enquiry on her face: the go-to stance of any nurse when accosted by one of their seniors.

'I thought I should warn you that we have one of our old friends on the ward, in case it comes as a shock. An emergency admission as female surgical is full.'

'Yes, Sister?'

Evelyn didn't have any friends outside of the hospital now. She couldn't remember the last time she'd written to Alice or whether she'd even bothered to reply. She was working through a list of possible names in her mind when Sister spoke.

'Camille Le Blanc. Don't upset yourself too much. She's in a bit of a mess, poor woman. I'd like you to special her tonight. She's in need of a friend.'

'Yes, Sister.'

Evelyn turned back to the stove, her hands shaking as she started to pour milk from the large jug resting on the side. Five months without a word or a ripple in her perfectly ordered life. There was work, the occasional social evening and treasured times spent at the convent with Moses to break the monotony. Now this, and right on top of her father too. She hadn't been able to forget the trick she'd played on the Uberlieutenant but with nothing to remind her, she'd pushed it into a dark corner.

Her breath caught in her throat the moment she laid eyes on Camille. To say that the French woman was in a bit of a mess was an understatement. A fractured eye socket to match severe concussion and an arm broken in two places – it was worse than she could have imagined. Her mind crammed with a thousand questions, topped with how and why could anyone do such a thing. She didn't need to ask who. She knew who.

Yannick.

Dr Jones stood at the end of Camille's bed, his fingers curled around the metal rail, his knuckles whitening under the thin layer of skin. 'She hasn't regained consciousness yet and there's a possibility she never will if her brain continues to swell. Keep her on hourly observations and ask staff to call me if there's a widening in the gap between her systolic and diastolic blood pressure, along with a slowing of her pulse.'

'I'm surprised they didn't take her to the German Hospital?'

'I'm not,' he retorted, ramming his stethoscope into his pocket. 'Remember, nurse, while Germans might be the enemy they're also husbands and fathers. This is bad for everyone. He'll be lucky to get away with it and the reason he came running in our direction.'

'It was Yannick Klein? The father of...?'

'Yes to both. Now *Kommandant* of Lager Sylt camp so a very dangerous man, nurse, as Mademoiselle Le Blanc has found to her cost.'

'But people will surely know? She'd have had to come over on the boat for a start.'

'Happened in Guernsey from what little I can gather, nurse, so, no. He brought her in himself. If I'd been there, I wouldn't have been able to restrain myself. To call him an animal is doing a disservice to those noble creatures.' He stood and stretched, his lean face grey in the dim light leaching through the corners of the blackout blinds.

She readjusted the screens surrounding the bed on three sides, trying to offer a small reassuring smile to the anxious faces of the other women. Being in hospital was part of being a family, albeit an extended one. There'd be prayers said tonight, no matter the religion, and Camille needed all the prayers she could get.

Evelyn began gently cleaning the make-up from her face before applying cold compresses to her bruises and bathing her cuts. She took particular care with the swollen skin around her eye, her jaw hardening at the state of the tender flesh. In between, she sat and held Camille's good hand and spoke of everything and nothing in her perfectly accented French, her voice calm when she was anything but. She'd imagined Camille worldly wise when she'd first met her. A woman who'd chosen to follow a certain path, in the same way Evelyn had decided on teaching and nursing. But now, stripped of her powder and paint she looked young and fragile. That someone could do this and to someone who wasn't in a position to defend herself was monstrous.

During her break, Evelyn decided to escape the suffocating confines of the ward. The air was warm and muggy, the temperature still in the high teens almost as if someone had forgotten to reset the clock to early morning. With a slice of bread in her pocket, she ambled downstairs and out into the car park and the fields beyond, her spirits flagging under the pressure of having to remain in the same position for hours on end. She didn't stay long, just long enough to fill her lungs with clean air after the stuffiness of the ward before making her way back upstairs to the congealed milk pudding waiting for her in the kitchen. As unappetising as it was, she wolfed it down. There was never any excuse for leaving food. Nothing got wasted whether you liked it or not. It was starvation or eat what you were given.

An hour passed. Then another. Evelyn replaced the cold compresses with fresh ones, noting that the swelling had started to ease, the bruising more apparent. A slight clenching of Camille's fingers underneath her enclosed palm was the first indication that things were shifting, along with the time. A flicker of an eyelid, just the one. It would be a few days before her left eye responded to any commands other than pain.

'Hello, my dear. Remember me? Nurse Nightingale.' And for the second time in her career, she broke the first name rule. 'Evelyn. You have been in the wars but you're better now.'

'I...I...'

Evelyn smoothed her fingers over the back of Camille's hand in a feather light touch. 'Just rest, my dear. That's what you need more than anything.'

The weather broke on her way back to work that evening. The heavens opened in a downpour which had her thankful of her cloak, her head bowed against the worst of the drops as she pushed open the main hospital gate and ran for shelter through the formal front garden. Not the usual way she took but it was the quickest. There was a letter waiting for her in her pigeon hole, which she tucked under the bib of her apron to read later. She always enjoyed news from her aunt, even more so now that they were caring for Moses. A reminder that she was overdue a visit but with her father now poorly all her spare time seemed to be spent at the hospital, whether rostered to work or not.

The first thing she noticed when she entered the ward was Ivy carrying bunches and bunches of red roses, so many bunches. Flowers were one of the things she missed the most. Oh, there were still wild flowers to be found on the hedgerows and some of the bushes, but most people were too busy growing vegetables to waste time and money on something so non-essential. The reality was if it couldn't be eaten it wasn't grown. She couldn't recall someone receiving any kind of a floral tribute that wasn't cobbled together from this and that found growing wild.

Evelyn's thoughts shifted onto a different track, a band of cold almost a physical presence squeezing her tight. There was only one person on the ward currently who might have received them but surely he wouldn't dare. Not after what he'd done.

'Off to the sluice?' Her question was casual. The normal type of question in a situation that was anything but. 'You're going to be busy arranging that lot.'

'I'm not arranging a thing,' Ivy replied with a disdainful sniff. 'Off to the bin and good riddance was what she said. I just hope she knows what she's doing. He went to a lot of trouble to get them. Straight from Brittany too. A waste but not a waste if you get me?'

Evelyn's eyes rounded in surprise. 'From Brittany. How?'

'Sent a plane over specially first thing this morning, would you believe, and if you think I'm jesting...' She pulled out a ripped card from between the blooms and passed it over. 'No idea what it says but it's stamped with the name of the grower on the back.

Evelyn noted the name but was far more interested in what was written on the other side.

You need to be more careful in future. Goodness knows how much damage you might cause yourself next time. With warmest affection

With warmest affection. Evelyn was hard pressed not to growl at the sign off coming after such a blatant threat. Instead, she managed a passable impression of someone annoyed at their inability to read even a word of German as she handed back the card.

'Shame it's not in French. I might have been able to understand the odd word here and there. I have met him, sadly. A horrible man.'

Ivy nodded in agreement. 'Poor Mademoiselle Le Blanc. Can you believe that he said she walked into a door. No pretty petals can excuse his actions.'

Evelyn wasn't specialising Camille that night. Now she was conscious, she was off the danger list. The bruising had come out in all its technicolour, causing the other women to twitter around her like a pack of clucking hens. There were no thoughts about who or what she was. A woman in need was only that, and one so far from home too.

Instead, Evelyn was back in the nursery, her favourite place in the hospital now she was used to the noise. They were full again. There was always an influx of pregnancies in August and September. The effect of the Christmas period on marital relations was one of the first midwifery lessons she'd learnt, along with how to clean around the baby's cord and prevent nappy rash in the absence of any of the usual barrier creams to hand.

It was midnight before she remembered the letter inside her bib. She was alone in the nursery finishing off the last feed before tucking the little boy into his cot. With the bottle on the counter, she balanced his head against her shoulder and started rubbing his back, Aunt Thérèse's letter on the table in front of her.

Dear Evelyn,

I hope all is well at the hospital.

Thank you for the clothes and nappies. They will certainly be put to good use by those in need. We had some visitors to the convent earlier who took a particular interest in how we came by these items. Their curiosity was quite thorough, though I assured them everything was in order.

Please continue to pray for us as we navigate these times.

*With all my love and prayers,
Sister Thérèse*

Evelyn hugged the tiny body, reading between the lines of the letter with ease. Yannick had somehow learnt about Moses and visited the convent, trying to ferret out the truth. She knew all too well what Yannick wanted with Moses or, at least, what the man suspected. Her stomach twisted, her macaroni supper a heavy weight. The thought of the German taking the baby made her heart ache. It was a cold comfort that his suspicions were unfounded. With Moses's distinctive colouring, his pedigree was indisputable. Both the Emergency Hospital and the Town Hospital were aware of the convent's role in fostering the baby. With places at a premium no one was bothered as to the little lad's future, it seemed, except the nuns and now Yannick. He was closing in fast.

A tiny mew reminded her of what she was meant to be doing.

'Sorry, my pet. Yes, bedtime, sweetie, but first your nappy.'

Evelyn moved him to the table, her normally capable hands fumbling as her mind raced. What if they came tonight? What if Yannick acted before they could hide Moses?

She was folding the letter and tucking it in her pocket to read again later when the door opened behind her.

'Finished?' Ivy whispered.

'Only just. The last one is settling now,' she said, gently tapping on the end of the baby boy's cot and where he was trying to find his thumb.

'Great. Hop off for a quick cuppa. There's fresh in the pot. All the mums are asleep, so I'll take over here for a bit.'

Evelyn only managed the door of the kitchen when a low muttered '*Nurse*' had her change direction back into the ward where Camille anxiously awaited her.

'I was hoping for a word, Evelyn.' Her English was perfect apart from the accent, which was pure French.

'You should be asleep, my dear.'

'Can't. Too worried.'

Evelyn took a chance and sat on the edge of the bed, the corners of her apron flipped up over her lap, forming a V.

'Yannick?'

'Among other things. I think I've got your aunt into a lot of trouble.'

Evelyn was surprised she knew of her relationship with the nun but let it pass. Her aunt must have told her, which meant Camille must have gained her confidence.

'You know Sister Thérèse?'

'A little.' She smiled gently. 'I walk that way when I'm here. The view from their gardens out across the other islands is astounding. I never realised that Yannick must have had me followed.'

Evelyn suspected that there was more to her visits than just the view, like seeing Moses, a baby with colouring so similar to Marise's daughter, but she let it lie. Camille had a right to her secrets. 'Sister Thérèse will be fine and there's nothing Yannick can do. Moses was a foundling, and born a good two weeks before...' She stopped short of completing the sentence. A hard learnt lesson that the only person she could depend upon was herself. 'Is that why?' She waved her hand briefly in the direction of the fingerprint bruising on the young woman's wrists.

'The story about the door still stands, *ma cheri*.' Camille hesitated slightly over the word door, her gaze not quite reaching hers. 'All my stupid fault.'

It took a lot to shock Evelyn but the changes since she'd last seen Camille were heartbreaking. Gone was the confident young Frenchwoman. In her place was a woman stripped of her spirit. A woman defeated. Her passive acceptance of the situation had Evelyn thinking she was speaking to a stranger, not the fearless woman who had helped orchestrate the baby switch, and distracted Yannick with calculated charm.

She found herself at a complete loss for words. It was in her nature to help but nothing in her experience could prepare her for such a situation. Camille was both beaten and broken in ways Evelyn didn't know how to mend. She only knew how to heal the body. This required much more. More than she knew how to give.

'No one deserves to be beaten, Camille. There is nothing I can think of, no reason – or am I wrong? Tell me if I am and I'll be quiet.'

Evelyn wished the words unsaid as soon as she'd uttered them. The only relationship she'd ever had ended in a bunker in France, along with her hopes for any kind of a normal future. There were plenty of spinsters left over from the Great War, she was only one of them. That she'd tried to make the best of things in no way excused her meddling in someone else's life. Relationships were complex, unwieldy things. She only had to listen to the mums on the ward to realise how complex.

'You don't understand. How could you. He's kind mostly, as long as I do as he says.' Camille pressed her fingers gently to the puffy skin below her eyes, the area a mottled palette of navy and black. 'I should have read the situation better, agreed to his terms. This... the accident,' she amended. 'It was my fault, completely.'

His terms? It sounded like a legal transaction instead of a relationship.

When Evelyn finally returned to the sluice to sort through

the dirty linen into piles for the laundry, the overpowering smell of crushed roses made a mockery of Camille's words.

TWENTY-FOUR

EVELYN

Evelyn sat on the balcony beside her father, her hand resting on top of his, her fingers tracing the outline of his wedding ring. Her eyes were bleary after her night shift but it was the whirlwind of thoughts in her head that truly exhausted her.

He was a pale shadow of the tall, proud man she remembered growing up. The burden of malnutrition and cold, damp conditions had left their mark, making him susceptible to the worst of illnesses. It was an illness he had nothing left to fight with. Worst of all was that he'd stopped eating and drinking. Evelyn knew what this new development meant. Time was running out and she had so much left to say. These last moments were precious. Bed would have to wait although she knew she didn't have much time until her shift began. Seven nights left until her next set of days off.

'Are you alright, Dad? Anything I can get you?' she asked in as bright a tone as she could muster.

He moved his head slightly, grimacing at the effort, his voice a hoarse croak. But it was his words that shocked her into silence, words she'd never expected. 'Sorry. I should have tried to be a better father to you.'

She squeezed his fingers lightly, a lump filling her throat. Those few words meant everything. It was the permission she needed to focus on the good parts of their relationship, and to bury the bad. The unsaid words that had lain between them for so long dispersed. They were unimportant.

'Hush now. No need for that. You did just fine. I love you. That's all that matters.'

He managed a brief smile.

Evelyn leant over him, whispering in his ear as his eyes closed and his breath eased. 'I'll stay a little longer, Dad. Rest easy.'

Half an hour passed. Time to think about leaving if she was to make work later. She was stretching out her stiff legs in preparation when a noise from below snagged her attention.

The balcony was never silent. Five men, forced together, shared stories along with cigarettes. Now silence reigned apart from the odd rasp of breath and occasional deep rattling cough, the tools of tuberculous sufferers. Camaraderie, respect or something else. Whatever the reason, Evelyn was thankful for their consideration.

The flurry of sound came from a small cavalcade, a large car flanked by two motorcycle riders. It wasn't only Evelyn who looked over the balcony as Yannick strode across the forecourt, one hand adjusting the peak of his cap, the other holding on to his gloves, his eyes suddenly clashing with hers.

'Er, what's he looking at?'

'Admiring your masculine beauty, Peter.'

Reggie laughed at his words while Peter grinned. Evelyn was too shocked to comment. The threat in his gaze was lingering. A second. Two. Ten, before he moved away, his black leather coat flapping around him despite the weather, the soldiers standing to attention until the door banged behind him.

She met him on the stairs on the way down, which was odd. She hadn't rushed off the ward, in fact she'd deliberately taken her time in saying her farewells to prevent such a meeting. Either he'd been waiting or... He'd been waiting.

'*Fräulein* Nightingale.'

'*Kommandant*.' She stopped where she was, one hand resting on the bannister, her fingers as relaxed as her expression. She wasn't going to give him the satisfaction of knowing that her heart was beating against her ribcage like a trapped bird.

'Our meeting seems to be a frequent occurrence.'

She inclined her head. If he wanted to talk, she couldn't stop him, but she had no intention of helping him out.

'I heard about your father's ill health. How is he?'

Evelyn should have known he'd have made a point of checking up on her. He had her name so it wouldn't have been difficult. It wasn't as if the island was flush with Nightingales, feathered or otherwise.

'He's ill, very ill indeed. If you'll excuse me. I'm working again tonight.'

Yannick continued staring at her as if trying to come to a decision. With a little click of his heels, he finally stepped aside but continued watching until she rounded the corner. She didn't need to be blessed with second sight to feel the beam of his gaze in the centre of her back, nor the long pause before hearing the clip of his boots resuming on the stone staircase.

Colin was waiting for her on the corner past the hospital, the colonel's great coat hanging from his skinny frame. Everyone in the hospital knew him as Edgar, or Mr Falla. For her he'd always be Colin.

'You shouldn't be here. What if he catches you?'

'He won't, and anyway, I'm legal, or had you forgotten about my documents?'

'I haven't forgotten, but you don't know what he's like.'

Colin matched his stride to her shorter one out of the gate and up the hill until they came to a derelict farmhouse set back from the road. With his hand on her elbow, he drew her into the front garden where the thick bushes had been allowed grow wild.

'I know very well what he's like. I still have the scar on my backside to prove it.'

Evelyn was too tired to be polite. 'Colin, I'm not in the mood for chitchat after the night I've had. Leave me be. We can catch up another time.' She went to move away, his hand on her arm stopped her.

'What's Camille doing here?' His question was a surprise and one she couldn't answer.

'You know I can't tell you that.'

'Come on. The porter told me she'd been beaten to a pulp. Is that right?'

'If you know, then why bother asking?'

He reached into his pocket and pulled out a squashed packet, taking his time to select a cigarette before replying.

'And you're allowing him to visit? That's clever, Evelyn. He's murdered one woman and you're going to let him murder a second.'

Evelyn watched as he struck a match, his palm curled around the flickering flame, a muscle working in his cheek, knowing he was right and yet unable to think up a reply. While Yannick hadn't murdered Marise, he might as well have. She was dead, wasn't she?

'You know that's unfair. It's not up to me.'

'That hasn't stopped you before. Saint Evelyn to the rescue or is it only to be metered out to those you think worthy of saving?' With a sudden movement, he spun away and was gone before she could come up with a reply.

Her father died in the middle of the afternoon. She'd managed three hours' sleep before she was called back to the hospital. They'd moved him into a side room shortly before and left her to it, closing the door gently behind them. She'd done the same many times before. A mark of respect to let loved ones in on those precious last moments without the intrusive presence of a nurse.

Evelyn wished they'd stayed, her eyes dry as his hand grew cold in hers, the colour leaching to a pale yellow. The colour of death. She felt numb. She was numb, from the top of her head to her shoes, which had never recovered from their time in the snow, the leather dull and scratched, the soles thin enough to let in water.

There were his belongings to pack, which meant approaching the *Feldkommandant* stationed at the Grange Lodge Hotel, and the funeral to sort. She'd have to write to her aunt too and inform his friends. Her father had a lot of friends, he seemed to adopt them like stray dogs. No doubt every one of them would want to come and pay their respects. She'd think on it later. Make a list. Her dad had always liked a good list. She'd got out of the habit when she'd shifted to nursing.

Her feverish thoughts jumped from topic to topic. Insignificant details shielding her from the truth lying a breath away. Relief came in the form of a nurse offering tea while they attended to her father. She left in a daze, blinking at the change in light, her face a sickly pale.

'You can't work tonight. It's unheard of. It's also not right.' Sister Jehan was beside herself in her attempt to follow hospital protocol, just as Evelyn was adamant to stop her.

They were in her office, the door closed and Dr Jones languishing against the wall, running the rubber of his stethoscope between his fingers after confirming what they all knew: Her father's death.

'I'm sorry, Sister, but it's not up to you.' She turned to Dr Jones. 'You can understand, can't you, doctor? I need to be busy and at least I'll be doing something worthwhile. It's not as if it was a shock. We all knew he wouldn't make it, including him.'

'I think you're going to have to accept that Nurse Nightingale is working tonight, Maureen, and be done with it. However, I will speak to Matron to see if we can't change your off duty and...' He lifted his hand when she went to speak. 'No, my dear. You can't stay on nights when there's a funeral to arrange. Work tonight then drop in to see Matron in the morning. It should only be a case of asking one of the nurses to swap their duty with you.'

'Back on the same ward?' It shouldn't be a priority with her dad recently moved to the mortuary, but she'd fallen asleep on Colin's accusation. Her father was at peace and with her mother. She had to believe that or go mad. Her responsibilities now lay with the living, which meant Camille.

'Most likely. You know how Matron dislikes shifting staff once they're settled.' He shoved his stethoscope into his pocket. 'I see you had the presence of mind to wear your uniform but there's a couple of hours yet before night duty.' He tilted his head in Sister's direction. 'I'm giving nurse permission to use the doctor's room. See she's not disturbed.'

TWENTY-FIVE
EVELYN

9 September, 1943

It was a week later and she was back at work. The funeral was over. The standing room only in St Stephen's Church and the many lovely things his friends had to say about him almost broke her. It was too much on top of fear for Moses in the wake of Yannick's visit. Her aunt was pragmatic but then she'd never known Sister Thérèse be anything else. They'd huddled in a corner of The Royal Hotel, a glass of precious sherry in their hands, as they mourned what they'd lost, and prayed for a better future.

Evelyn had hoped that the funeral would be, if not the end to her grief then a milestone to put aside in her memory box and pull out whenever she thought of her father, which seemed to be all the time. But the reality of her grief made that impossible. She wasn't sleeping. Long nights spent staring at the ceiling, following the cracks in the plaster meant her days were like working through thick, heavy treacle. Every item she possessed held a memory between its lines and grooves, from her humble hairbrush and comb set to her violin, the last present he'd given her.

Around her, life carried on but for Evelyn it was muted. Almost black and white instead of full blistering colour. There were still her father's belongings to sort but it was one step too far. The *Feldkommandant* had written to her instead of attending the funeral, a little act of kindness she appreciated. There was no hurry in collecting her father's things, which would be stored for as long as necessary. These small gestures were often followed by paroxysms of tears, leaving her limp.

As she moved through the ward, her father was only a blink away. She longed for one last conversation, even though there was nothing left to say. His last words had been enough.

The sudden influx of patients was the impetus Evelyn needed to concentrate from day to day. It was enough to divert her from the thought that she was all alone now, apart from her aunt. No, that wasn't true. She had Violet. She had friends and she still had her music.

Sister Jehan burst into the kitchen briefly, startling her from her reverie as she prepared the patient's afternoon tea.

'Thank goodness it's not a day for visitors. We have an emergency admission, if you can get a bed ready. After, join me in the clinical room. I'm going to sort the steriliser and get the trolley ready.' She passed her hand across her forehead. 'I have a funny feeling about this one.'

Sister was gone before Evelyn had time to respond. That they had no beds wasn't important. They'd make space. It was Sister's 'funny feeling' that was the worry. She was well known for her funny feelings and, up to now, Evelyn had never known her to be wrong.

It looked like they had an emergency on their hands, which filled Evelyn with a sense of dread. Most of the emergencies she'd been on duty for had turned out okay in the end but there were always the ones like Marise to remember. In her case they'd been able to save her baby, but sometimes they couldn't even do that. Expectant mothers required a good diet when even the most basic of foods were in short supply. Now it was the norm for babies to be born sickly and underweight. It wasn't in anyone's power to change that.

'Here, I take over the teas. *Vamos*. Go.' Camille had slipped into the kitchen for a chat, a frequent occurrence. Her face was now a kaleidoscope of colours, her broken wrist secured in a makeshift sling made from a colourful scarf. They'd run out of proper slings during the second year of the war.

'You're sure? You darling. Leave the washing up to me.'

Evelyn whisked out of the ward to the large storage room at the end of the corridor. A depository for old equipment, which they hoped never to use. The bed was sturdy but with enough rust to have Evelyn's namesake rolling in her grave. But it was the floor or the bed, and no nurse would dare place a patient on the floor, no matter the cleanliness.

With the frame and mattress wiped clean, she swiftly set up a post-operative pack in the centre of the tightly drawn bottom sheet before hurrying to join Sister.

The woman had arrived in a wheelchair. A pale wretch with dark brown hair hanging down her back in a thick plait, her eyes widened in fear.

'Where's her relatives?' Sister Jehan barked at the porter; her gaze drawn to the woman's hands concealed in thin grey gloves. Husbands along with marital status were taboo subjects on a maternity ward but they had to have the name of a next-of-kin in case the worst happened.

'Says she was dropped off at the gate by a friend. Wouldn't say anything more other than she's bleeding.'

'Right you are. Thank you. Send the doctor up as soon as he arrives.' And to the woman. 'What's your name, dear?'

After a slight pause. 'Mary Le Page. Mrs Mary Le Page.'

Sister didn't say anything about the name, as common on

the island as John Smith and as likely to be of as much use. 'And how far gone are you Mrs Le Page?'

The woman's face crumpled like a crushed tissue along with her voice. 'I don't know. I didn't even know I was... you know, until this morning.'

'Don't distress yourself, dear. We need to get you on the bed so that the doctor can examine you. He's on his way.' Sister rolled up her sleeves as she spoke, helping the woman remove her coat and her cardigan before working on the zip at the back of her floral dress, the pattern faded from washing. The slip was stained bright red at the hem as was the bottom rim of her girdle. Sister's eyes shot up at the sight. There was little call for girdles on a maternity unit unless worn by the nurses and it was a long time since Evelyn could bear something so restrictive under her uniform.

'Let's get you up on the bed and I'll take a look. Don't worry, nurse here will cover you with a blanket.'

Evelyn arranged one of their red blankets over the woman's chest, the colour specially chosen in case there was blood, and there was a lot. A gush as soon as she helped remove her knickers, an old hand towel rolled up inside to try and prevent the flow.

'I'll manage here for a minute.' Sister's voice came out in a rush, her hands octopus quick as she juggled what appeared to be three tasks at once, stemming the flow with one hand while pushing Mrs LePage into a flat position with the other. 'Run down to the lab and get two units of packed cells, nurse, while I pop the end of the bed on bricks and start a drip. Type O neg. There's no time to group and cross match, and if you see the doctor tell him where we are, if you please.'

Evelyn didn't wait. She lifted her skirt and ran, the power coming from somewhere to reach the pathology department on the floor below in record time. She barely had breath left to speak to the man behind the desk, certainly not enough for the niceties.

'Two units of packed cells for maternity stat. Type O neg.'

'I'll bring them up for you now, nurse. Glass bottles. Wouldn't like to see them dropped.'

'Thank you.' She smiled over her shoulder briefly, already half out the door, only to meet Dr Jones in the corridor outside.

'An emergency, nurse?'

'Haemorrhaging patient.'

'And I see you've already got the necessary replacement blood from the lab. Off to put my four-minute mile to the test. Wish me luck. Might even break the Mighty Atom's record. Here's hoping!'

Evelyn managed to match him stride for stride, pausing a second to let him through the door first, thankful now of the lack of cars and buses, which meant cycling up and down the many hills on the island was a daily occurrence.

'At last,' were Sister's first words. 'I think it's placenta previa. Mrs Le Page isn't sure of her dates.'

'Morning, Mrs Le Page.' He spoke on a huff of breath, working on removing his jacket as he headed to the sink to wash his hands. 'I'm Dr Jones. Baby is coming but it looks like she's in need of a little help.'

Dr Holly burst through the door, his hair flying back from his forehead, his cheeks red. 'Need any help?'

'An anaesthetic, if you please. Sister has already got a line in place. We need to get baby out now.'

There was no sense of urgency or panic in Dr Jones's tone, his hands clasped in front of him while Evelyn tied the tabs at the back into neat bows. He even took the time to thank her before putting on his gloves, while Dr Holly injected something into the back of Mrs Le Page's hand.

They watched her eyelids flutter closed. A tableau of masked and gowned statues, one standing at the head of the bed with an endotracheal tube between his hands, the other hovering over the draped instrument trolley, staring at the scalpel with a gimlet eye.

'That's her. I'm going in.' And after a few seconds: 'Another correct diagnosis, Sister. The placenta is totally occluding the cervical opening. When this blasted invasion is over I suggest you have a try for medicine. The pay's better for a start.'

'But not the hours. You work even longer ones than we do.' She passed him a retractor before peering into the wound over his bent shoulder. 'Babe doesn't look to be a bad size.'

'Mmm, five, six pounds at a guess, Sister,' he said, testing the weight briefly as he lifted the crying baby into Evelyn's waiting arms before starting work on the placenta. 'A little girl, noisy too. How's the mum holding up, John?'

'Not too bad.' Dr Holly stretched out a hand to increase the rate of the blood falling through the glass drip chamber. 'How long more?'

'Five minutes tops before I start sewing.'

'When this blood's through I reckon she'll need another two.'

Evelyn looked up from the baby, her hands pausing mid-wipe as a soft mew broke the silence. Her eyes crinkled with an unexpected smile, the mask concealing it from view but not from the warmth in her voice. 'Do you want me to go to the lab, Sister?'

'How's she doing?'

'Seems hardy enough.'

'Okay, you go but shift the cot a little nearer. I can keep an eye on her until Dr Jones is finished.'

Evelyn leant against the cool windowpane on the way back from the lab, grateful for a moment's respite now that the frantic rush had ebbed. The bottle of blood still needed to warm so another minute wouldn't harm. Her gaze wandered across the hospital grounds, unfocused – until it snagged on two familiar figures near the wrought-iron gates. Camille and Colin stood close, their heads bent in conversation. Colin's hand rested on Camille's arm, his fingers curling with a tenderness that felt almost too intimate.

A sharp chill sliced through her, as precise and sudden as a doctor's scalpel. She blinked, her breath catching in her throat, and the moment shattered. Camille and Colin were already turning away.

Evelyn pushed herself away from the window, unsure of what she'd seen, the blood bottle cool against her skin. She blinked then blinked again but it was no good. The image remained.

There was work to be done. Patients waiting. Whatever she had seen – or imagined – would have to wait. Yet as she hurried back to the ward, the image of Camille and Colin lingered, a shadow at the edge of her mind, refusing to disappear.

Later, much later, she would remember this moment with painful clarity. But by then, it would be far too late to do anything about it.

TWENTY-SIX
EVELYN

The following day, she was in the kitchen getting the drinks ready after supper when Camille wandered in with her cup.

'Where's Mrs Le Page?'

'On her bed last time I looked. Perhaps she's popped to the loo?'

Camille shook her head, her pinned curls refusing to move. 'Not in bed or the loo, and neither is her bag.'

Evelyn added the last of the cups and saucers to the trolley before replying. Missing women were one thing: Camille had been missing for a good hour before supper yesterday. But a missing handbag was something else. The women on the ward guarded their bags with, if not their life, then with a healthy respect in the knowledge that there was no way of replacing whatever items they contained. Hairbrushes, combs, compacts, photographs, lipsticks. All irreplaceable and therefore priceless. The money didn't matter. There was nothing to spend it on.

'I'll have a look. You stay here.'

'Nowhere to go, nursey.' A lie if ever there was one but Evelyn couldn't be bothered about that as long as Camille didn't send Yannick after her. The man was a scourge the way he tracked her movements on the ward. Every time she lifted her head from whatever she was doing he was watching her, his fingers beating a tattoo on his leg, waiting. He thought he knew something but he couldn't prove a thing. That made it worse.

People knew her secrets, too many for her to feel safe.

Instead of checking all the possible places on the ward, Evelyn headed in the other direction, where Ivy oversaw the nursery. It only took a swift glance to see that the Le Page baby was exactly where she should be, asleep in the second cot closest to the door. She stared down at the five pounds three ounces of beautiful blonde baby, her heart skipping a beat. Surely Mary Le Page wouldn't have deserted her daughter?

It took ten minutes and the help of Sister, who delayed night staff handover to assist in the search to confirm just that. Mary Le Page had upped and gone, managing somehow to take all her belongings with her apart from the most important. Her child.

'I don't know how she did it.' Sister was bemused as well as affronted at the idea of someone leaving the ward without her say so. That she was still in need of medical care went without saying. There were sutures to remove and the wound to redress not to mention her general fatigue at the loss of all that blood, despite the replacement units. How would she cope?

'I can guess, Sister,' Evelyn replied, thinking back to the morning and how Mary had manipulated the situation. She'd thought her kind then. Kind and considerate to the other women. She'd also thought what a good mother she was. Keen to learn the basics under an experienced eye. What an utter fool she'd been not to suspect a thing.

'Well, nurse?'

'She requested to use the bathroom last this morning, in fact made a point of it.' Evelyn stood in front of her desk, her hands tucked behind her back, her eyes fixed on the floor. 'The other women thought she was being considerate. Now I think she was being crafty, leaving her clothes on the hook behind the door.' Evelyn lifted her head, her voice tightening. 'It wouldn't have taken much to get dressed at the end of evening visiting and join the throng of relatives heading home for their supper. If it hadn't been for Mademoiselle Camille noticing, we wouldn't have found out until night-time drug round. I'm sorry.'

Evelyn felt her cheeks flood with colour under Sister's watchful gaze, but forced herself to carry on. 'She took me in completely, even down to sharing what she was going to call the baby. Serena.' She swallowed, the name catching in her throat. 'Her name is Serena.'

Sister sighed, running her finger down the report book before closing it with a snap. 'Try not to be too upset. I'd like to say it's never happened before but that would be a lie. However, it was a very long time ago.' She looked at Evelyn, her expression softening. 'And no family details to help us. Oh well. We need to search the grounds to be sure. Ask Mr Guille and Mr Falla to help. The police will expect it. I'd do it myself but I must tell Matron.'

Evelyn nodded but didn't move immediately. She couldn't shake the image of Mary – pale, withdrawn, yet fiercely protective when she'd first arrived. She wasn't heartless, Evelyn knew that much. Desperate, maybe. Trapped by circumstances Evelyn could only imagine. No family, no support... who knew what had driven her to abandon Serena? Mary didn't seem the type to try and catch Jerry's gaze. While young, she wasn't pretty, the opposite could be said to be true with her straggly unkempt hair and fusty clothes. So very different to Marise and Camille. But there was the baby to consider. The cutest bundle with, it must be said, the whitest of blonde hair and the palest of colouring. She'd bet on the fact that Mary loved her daughter. It wasn't something she was able to hide, sitting in the nursery with her cuddled up on her lap, which made the reason for her desertion something insurmountable. A husband overseas or perhaps no husband. Both would have caused difficulties in the tight-knit community where stepping outside any of the ten commandments was viewed the greatest of sin.

'Serena's a beautiful name.' Sister's voice brought Evelyn back, and she glanced up. "We'll make sure she's well taken care of.'

'Yes, Sister.' Evelyn left the office and headed outside to find Emile and Colin, her thoughts in disarray. She'd been trying, ever since the news broke, to put herself in Mary's position. What would she have done if their roles had been reversed? Could she have made the same impossible choice? She was yet to come up with an answer.

Evelyn found the two men in the cottage sitting round the table smoking, the remains of what looked like some kind of vegetable soup supper still in front of them.

'Missing? And left her babe. What's the world coming to.' Emile pushed his cap back from his forehead, his brow a map of wrinkles. Colin was silent but his dour expression said it all. 'I'm not sure where Sister thinks she might be hiding but we'll look, eh, lad? You do the fields while I check the outbuildings. Nurse, you stay right there and rest up.' Emile shifted back from the table and plonked a cup down. 'There's tea in the pot. A bit stewed but you'll be used to that.'

The grounds were extensive, with the formal garden at the front and the farm behind, which tracked right up to the German gun emplacement boundary at the top of the Rue Des Cauvains. Evelyn was on her second cup, her shoes on the floor beside her, her feet propped up on the rung of the chair opposite by the time they returned, bringing the night air with them.

'No luck?'

''Fraid not.' Emile placed his pitchfork against the wall before removing his boots. 'Ran into a German up to no good at the back of the second cowshed.' He tapped the wooden handle of the fork. 'I don't think he'll try and milk someone else's cow any time soon, eh, Colin?'

'You were lucky you weren't shot for poking that in his backside. I can tell you what that feels like, any time you like.' Colin slapped his bottom to emphasise the point, but it was a gentle slap.

Evelyn bent, working on putting on her shoes. 'I'm still trying to work out why she'd do such a thing and only a day out of surgery too. She could have at least waited until her wound had healed. I can't begin to tell you the risk she's put herself in without medical care.'

'If she was consorting with the enemy...' Colin glanced at Emile briefly. 'There's been quite a lot of rumours coming out of France as to how the local folk are treating collaborators.'

'Jerrybags.' Emile spat out the word, along with the end of his pipe, which he managed to catch before it landed on the floor.

'Excuse me?' Evelyn and Colin stared across at him.

'Heard the term only last week in town. That's what they're calling them women.'

'That's awful,' Evelyn spluttered. 'What about the likes of Camille and Marise? Not all women have a choice, Mr Guille.' It took a lot to enrage Evelyn but once the fuse was lit her temper went off with a bang. 'For some of them it's the distance between consorting with the enemy or starving. The Germans have food and we don't. I've even considered it myself. A quick fumble for the price of a decent supper. What woman hasn't with a houseful of starving kids and a husband run ragged with the worry of it all, and I don't even have that extra baggage to use as an excuse. Women are damned if they do and damned if they don't.'

Emile tapped his pipe against the ashtray in the middle of the table and started to refill it. 'Don't shoot the messenger, luv. I can see where you're coming from being a nurse and all, but feelings among the locals are running high. If the little lady in the nursery happens to have a German dad, you can imagine what the mother must have been going through. Torn in two. It's all very well having a quick fumble but not with the price set so high.'

With her shoelaces tied and her cloak around her shoulders, Evelyn made for the door, feeling sick at the thought of what must have driven Mary to abandon Serena. 'Thank you for the help. I'm only sorry we haven't been able to find her. I'll tell the night sister before heading home.'

'Not on your own this time of night, you won't.' Colin grabbed his coat from the peg, waving her through the open door.

'Are you sure it's safe?'

'Why wouldn't it be?' he said, his accent switching from Dublin to broad Guernsey. 'I have me papers, like.'

Evelyn remembered the last time he'd accompanied her. It would take a long time for her to forget his comment about Saint Nightingale. Like everyone else she was trying to do the best she could with what little there was on offer, and for no other reason than it was the right thing to do. Her steps quickened when they came to the deserted farmhouse, and they didn't slow until they'd passed the sentry stationed outside the entrance to the gun battery. There was only fifteen minutes left until curfew.

'Thank you.' The first words she'd spoken since she'd questioned the wisdom of a wanted man putting himself in a position of risk.

'I take it you're going to do something about the little girl?'

That was exactly what she had planned. The nuns had proved to be worthy and, more importantly, kind nursemaids as well as substitute parents to Moses. Far better than the Town Hospital or some adamant officer trying to claim Serena as his own. She would like to get to the bottom of why Mary had chosen to give up her baby, but with a false name and address she had no idea where to start looking.

'Why would you think that?' She went to insert the key in the lock.

'I'll do that.' He took the key off her. 'About time you saw sense about locking the door,' he said, going to follow her into the hall.

'You can't. What about curfew?'

'To blazes with it, it might be better if they do catch me.' He slammed the door shut behind him but instead of entering further, leant against the wood, the keys still in his hand. He twisted the bunch through his fingers, over and over. 'You do know what will happen if Yannick or another Jerry finds out what you're doing, what you've done?'

'And you're worried, are you?' She laughed as she removed her cloak, setting it on the end of the bannister. 'There's no need to be. He can't do anything about Moses, or Serena.'

'But he might have something to say about his own child.'

Evelyn paused in the act of slipping off her shoes. She'd wondered if Camille had told him. Now she had her answer. They were obviously closer than she thought.

'Which again he can't prove unless...'

'He decides to go digging in some graveyard or other.' Colin smoothed his hand over his head, the hair starting to grow back in clumps. She'd have to remind him he needed to attend to it soon. 'I know it doesn't look like it but I'm only trying to keep you safe. If it wasn't for you, I'd be...'

'Hush now. There's no need for that. To answer your question, I would like to contact Serena's mum. I think she'll be in need of a friend as well as medical care but, in the meantime, her daughter has a lovely home waiting with a relative of mine.'

'If only you could do the same for me and Camille.'

'What...?' But he pulled the door open and slipped outside before she could question him further.

Evelyn stood in the doorway watching until he disappeared out of sight before heading back inside and locking the door behind her, a hollow feeling settling deep in her chest. It wasn't news, or, at least not to her. She'd expected something like this ever since she'd seen them together the other night.

She wandered into the kitchen and closed the door, the silence echoing her own sense of loss. With Violet on nights, she was alone with her thoughts, the last place she wanted to be. The war, her dad, Camille and now Mary. It was too much to bear.

The banked up stove was a luxury, but the room was small and didn't take much to heat. A hot drink. Tea. Evelyn decided to treat herself to the last of her father's. There was only enough left for one pot after she'd shared it with the patients and given Violet some to share with her parents, enough for two or three cups, no more.

With the kettle on, she settled on the chair, a woollen shawl wrapped around her as she relived the last few minutes on the doorstep. Colin had unwittingly told her more than he probably intended. His love for Camille. There was a softness in his face and his eyes had lit up when he'd spoken her name. Camille would head back to Alderney, and soon. Yannick was already muttering about the camp doctor being able to attend to her needs once the bruises had faded a little more. There could be no happy ending for the pair, that was their tragedy.

With her cup cradled in the palm of her left hand she settled at the table with an old notebook, one she still had from her days as a teacher, the front marked with writing

Susan Martin, Year 4
Miss Nightingale.
Spelling List

She remembered Susan fondly. A sweet girl but dreadful at spelling.

Instead of opening the cover, she flipped the notebook to the back pages and withdrew a photo, the image of a young man in uniform, which stopped her in her tracks. She'd forgotten she'd slipped it between the pages. Joseph. Dead and buried some twenty-four years. Over half her lifetime and yet it felt like yesterday. No, it felt like forever. An eternity.

She blinked and, with the photograph on the table beside her, started to write their names. Moses. Wilhelmina. Serena.

A record. Nothing official but nonetheless important. Her way of setting the facts straight in case something was to happen to her. In case something happened to the children. If she was to die who would set the record straight?

She gripped the pen, already planning on where to hide the notebook once she'd finished. They'd had proof enough of what the Germans could and would do. Colin was right. She wasn't safe. No one was safe in this hellhole. She'd been a fool to think she ever could be, not after what she'd done. Not with Yannick on her trail. A man like him wouldn't have been content with her aunt's explanation about Moses. One glance at the baby's aryan looks would have been enough to seal his fate as a child of the Reich. That he seemed to accept the death of his daughter was surprising but he'd been beset by grief at the time. His suspicion was growing. The truth wasn't far behind.

Evelyn knew she had to be careful but she also needed to make a record of events.

The babies had a right to know their parents, their history; their roots.

Her list of lost children.

TWENTY-SEVEN
EVELYN

The police weren't interested in an abandoned child or indeed the welfare of Mrs Le Page. Evelyn was shocked by their response but the bitter reality was that they simply didn't care. She'd been told by Sister that Matron had decided to get in touch with one of the board members of the hospital to inform the *Feldgendarmerie*. A list of admissions and discharges were collected every couple of days anyway so it would be stupid to try and conceal the matter from them. It was the truth or risk some soldier or other turning up to try and claim their child. What he'd do with Serena was another matter.

Evelyn had used up all her contacts in trying to trace Serena's mother. She'd even asked Dave Le Page, her friend from the ambulance station, but the only Marys he knew of were either too young, too old or had left the island as part of the evacuation. A dead end, until two days after her disappearance.

She was in a rush home after her eight-hour shift. It was another music night, and she'd decided to go home and change first. There was also supper to make. A treat of an egg and a bunch of carrots from a thankful father, which she'd been drooling about all day. The plan was to share it with Violet before cycling back to work with her violin balanced in the basket. It was only by luck that the porter managed to stop her as she skipped out the door, waving an envelope in her direction. 'A letter for you, nurse, and one for your friend too.' He scratched his head. 'Yours was hand delivered. Probably didn't have a stamp. You know how we've pretty much run out of the things. Would you believe I found it on the counter after my rounds'

'I'll believe anything these days, Mr Blondel.' She barely looked at the letters as he handed them over. There'd be time enough after work. Something to look forward to. 'Everything all alright with you and the family?'

'Fine, thanks. Looking forward to your playing later. Wasted on nursing with that talent if you don't mind me saying.'

She smiled in response, tucking the letters safely in her pocket and soon forgetting about them in her excitement over the thought of making home-made carrot soup.

Later, as she stood over the stove, carefully slicing the egg in two and placing the halves on top of the steaming bowls, she heard Violet's voice from the doorway.

'You haven't seen a letter for me by any chance, have you? I can't think what Mum is up to. She promised that recipe for braised seaweed.'

'I have it! Sorry, I forgot. Fetch it from my uniform pocket while I dish up,' she said, drizzling the soup with cream. The only thing it was missing was salt, but she couldn't help that. With the beaches mined, Jerry had cut off their last means of harvesting it from sea water.

'There's one for you too,' Violet said, slipping into her seat, her nose nearly in the bowl. 'That smells like heaven. Dear Ma can wait!'

'As long as it tastes it.'

The next few minutes were taken up with pure enjoyment,

their bellies full for once by the time their bowls were scraped clean. They'd each used up a slice of their tommy loaf as an accompaniment, keeping a corner to mop up the remains instead of letting any go to waste.

'Now for mother.' Evelyn watched as her friend unfolded the letter, the writing tiny in order to accommodate as much news as possible in a short space. Her own letter was also a single sheet and in the same handwriting as the envelope; one she didn't recognise.

'Got a secret beau, Ev?' Violet had finished her letter and was in the process of clearing the dishes.

'Hardly. Can't think of anything worse. Leave the dishes a sec and have a look at this.' Evelyn pushed the letter across, her elbows on the table, feeling slightly sick at the fullness in her stomach after what felt like a period of sustained fasting.

The letter was single-sided and written in a sloping hand, the words running into each other.

Maison des Fleurs

Rue des Friquet

Dear Miss Nightingale,

I hope this letter finds you well. Please forgive my forwardness in writing, but I find myself in a situation where I do not know to whom else to turn.

The absence of my child weighs heavily upon my heart, but I hope you can believe me when I say that I had no other option. If I had, I would have taken it, and I knew that you would ensure little Serena is well looked after.

There is also the issue of my wound. It has started to leak. I fear it may be infected or otherwise not healing properly.

I am in desperate need of your assistance and guidance as well as news about Serena. I hope you might find it in your heart to help me during this difficult time.

I am most grateful for any help or advice you can provide.

*Yours faithfully,
Mary Le Page*

'You must go,' Violet urged. 'Rue des Friquet is only a few minutes away. That narrow lane on the way to Cobo Bay. If you leave now there'll be time before the concert.'

Moments later Evelyn was freewheeling down the Rue des Cauvains hill, her cloak billowing out behind her, her hands stinging from where she'd hurried in collecting her violin from under the clump of nettles, still unsure of the wisdom in what she was doing. It wasn't her place.

Rue des Friquet was a long winding dirt track of mainly fields and greenhouses interspersed by the occasional house. Evelyn missed the entrance to Mary's home the first time, but she wasn't surprised when she finally did find it.

The gate was rusted, the bushes on either side overgrown and straggly. The path rutted and uneven. She abandoned her bicycle just out of sight of the road, not wanting to risk her tyres any further on the uneven ground.

The house wasn't much to look at. A one-bedroomed cottage by the look of things. The paintwork peeling on the windows and the frames rotting. Evelyn's mood darkened at the depressing sight. Was this really where Mary was living?

There was no answer when she knocked and, peering through the window, no sign of anyone in the kitchen.

She tried the door handle, shouting as she went. 'Hello, anyone home? It's nurse come to check on you.'

Mary was slumped in the lounge, her chin on her chest, a slight snore filling the air with a gentle rumble.

Evelyn paused on the threshold, her gaze darting around the small, stuffy room, taking in the heavy furniture and general air of genteel squalor. She'd been to many such homes but this one, for some reason upset her the most.

'Hello, dear, it's Nurse Nightingale, come to check on you,' she repeated, her voice gentle, not wanting to scare her.

The woman stirred, the flickering grimace of pain as fleeting as it was heart-rendering.

'Didn't expect you so soon.' She struggled to sit, only to stop at Evelyn's next words.

'No, you stay where you are.'

Evelyn watched as Mary leant back, her face blending into the cushion, her cheeks devoid of colour, her eyes feverishly bright. Evelyn hadn't been sure why she'd visited instead of telling Sister. But now she understood. She cared deeply for this woman – someone who wouldn't have abandoned her baby without a heavy heart.

'How is she? How's Serena?' Mary broke the growing silence, her eyes closed, her voice resigned.

'She's well. Taking all her feeds. She'll grow stout at this rate. But how are you?' Evelyn felt herself relax as she crouched beside her. This was something she could cope with.

'Just sorry for the trouble I caused.'

'It was no trouble, only people worrying about you. Up and leaving hospital so soon after surgery is never a good idea.'

'You're so kind.' She grabbed onto Evelyn's hand; her grip was remarkably strong. 'I knew that the first time I saw you. I shouldn't have run away, but I didn't have...'

'Dennis, you there? Who you talking to?' The shout came

from the room next door, probably the bedroom, the voice a croaky rasp.

'That's Mother. I'd best go.' Mary's grip tightened briefly. 'She doesn't know about... anything, and she mustn't.'

'Would you like me to?'

'No!' Her reply was short. Emphatic. The one word filling the space between them. Evelyn's eyes widened but there was nothing she could say to that. She was in Mary's home and by invitation too.

She clambered to her feet and offered Mary her arm to pull against, worried beyond measure at the way she pressed her hand into her abdomen, her gait a shuffle. Infection was bad news after any surgery but impossible to contain in conditions like the room she appeared to be living in.

Evelyn glanced from the pile of blankets on the end of the sofa and the single pillow, to the window coated in dust. Everyone was finding it difficult to manage but some far more difficult than others.

Instead of waiting in the lounge, she made for the kitchen and the kettle. While no one liked bramble tea, at least it was something everyone had access to. With the kettle on the stove, and the cups set out, she pulled back a chair and waited. It didn't take long for Mary to join her.

'You live here with your parents?' Evelyn pushed the cup of tea into her hands as soon as she'd settled, her face drawn.

'You might think that but it's only mum and me. We lost my dad a few years back.'

'But she was asking for him, or am I mistaken?'

Mary sighed, her attention on her cup of milkless tea. 'No, you're not mistaken. Some days she's not as lucid as others.'

Evelyn absorbed the information with a nod. She'd cared for several patients with dementia during her time at the hospital and found it one of the most difficult types of nursing. Demanding and relentless in all the ways possible. Round-the-clock care and this poor woman appeared to have no one to help her.

She finished her tea in silence before getting to her feet. 'How about I take a look at your wound? No, stay there. No reason to move.' And a minute later. 'Any more bleeding?'

'It seems to have eased.'

'Good, it's doing surprisingly well. The stitches need to stay in for another ten days. I can come back then if you like?' She dug into her pocket and pulled out a small brown bottle, a few tablets rattling around in the bottom. 'I brought a few painkillers with me. They should ease things a little.'

'Thank you.' Mary stared up at her through tear-filled eyes. 'I'm not sure I deserve all this after what I did.'

Evelyn swallowed, suddenly knowing what was needed and it wasn't nursing care. It was the validation that the woman had no choice in what she'd done. There were plenty of islanders who viewed being judgemental as a national sport. Evelyn was proud that she wasn't one of them. Who was to say she wouldn't have done what Mary had in the same set of circumstances?

With her hand on the table, she straightened from where she'd been crouching, her back twinging in protest. Her brain twinged too. This wasn't the kind of conversation she'd signed up for when she'd been forced to change career. There were too many pitfalls looming for her to have any confidence in her ability to give the sort of answer needed.

'I suspect you only did what you thought necessary, Mary. You certainly seem to have your hands full with your mother. It can't have been easy with the pregnancy?'

'No one suspected, and they can't.' Mary's gaze sharpened; her pupils dilated. Two black holes of despair.

'I'm not going to tell anyone, my dear, but I do think you're in need of some help.' Evelyn replied, noting the dark circles under Mary's eyes, the slight tremor in her hands.

'The neighbours were good enough to offer when I told

them I had to go in to have a tooth removed. I'm fine now, really.'

'I'm worried about you. How are you managing for money if you haven't been able to work?' Evelyn remembered the bare cupboards she'd glimpsed earlier. The milk-less tea staining the bottom of the cups between them. The memory of her own full stomach was a sharp stab of guilt. 'And food? I... I noticed your cupboards were rather empty.'

A sudden shout from the other room made them both flinch. Evelyn's brow furrowed as she watched Mary's shoulders tense. 'Are you getting any sleep at all with...?' She left the question hanging, not wanting to pry but unable to hide her worry. 'You don't have to face this alone. What about Serena's father? Surely he's...'

It wasn't a question she should ask. It was none of her business, but Evelyn couldn't help feeling confused by the situation. The nurses had made assumptions that Serena must have had a German dad with that colouring but maybe they were wrong.

'I don't know where he is.'

'I'm so sorry. Why don't you let me help?'

'Dennis? Dennis, where are you?' The shout from next door turned into a piercing scream.

'I must go. Thank you for your visit.' Mary pushed away from the table, and made for the door, her words an end to the conversation and not the beginning Evelyn was hoping for.

'Please, Mary. Let me help.'

Mary paused in the doorway, her shoulders stooped, her belly protruding from under her thin, faded dress.

'You can't help me. No one can. All I ask is that you help my daughter.'

TWENTY-EIGHT
EVELYN

September 1943

A week passed, then ten days.

Evelyn cycled to Mary's house in the afternoon, the three-hour break before she was due to go back on duty enough time to remove her stitches and have a chat, if that's what Mary wanted. She knew that removing sutures would be the easy part, the internal scars caused by separating mother from baby were more difficult to treat but far more important.

The house looked and felt the same, apart from the dearth of noise coming from the room next door.

After the stitches were removed, they settled down to chat, and Evelyn noticed the deep shadows under Mary's eyes, the lines bracketing her mouth, the shake of her hands as she tried to control her cup.

'You are getting enough rest, dear?'

'Mother had a bad night.' Mary shrugged, the teapot between them along with a jug of milk Evelyn had brought with her. 'I'll wake her up when you go, or she might not sleep tonight.'

'I hope she does for your sake.' Evelyn picked up her cup and took a small sip before placing it back in the saucer, the china rattling. She wanted to say more but there was little point. Mary had declared conversations about her mother out of bounds and there was nothing she could think of to change that.

'Any idea what will happen to Serena?' Mary blurted out suddenly, her fingers gripping onto the edge of the table, her knuckles showing white. It was the only thing they hadn't discussed. The entire conversation had revolved around the baby, after Evelyn had checked Mary's wound and removed the stitches.

'I don't know if I'm honest.' Evelyn flicked her a glance before losing courage and returning to her tea. 'I do know that Sister is determined to ensure the very best for the babies under her care and that includes babies like your daughter.' She fiddled with the handle of her cup. 'You said there's no chance of the dad...?'

'Gone.'

Evelyn glanced up to see Mary's grief-stricken expression, her face streaming with sudden tears. 'Oh, my dear.'

'Don't bother yourself.' She scrambled to remove a handkerchief from up her sleeve and dabbed her eyes. 'Hormones. Can't seem to stop them.'

'Sometimes having a good cry makes me feel better.'

'Only thing to make me feel better would be having my Wilbur back, along with Serena.'

'Serena's dad?' Evelyn pressed gently.

'I have a photograph, if you'd like to see it? He also gave me his signet ring, in lieu of an engagement one.' She blushed, the wash of colour causing her eyes to sparkle.

The image was of a blond-haired man barely out of his teens, with a receding hairline and shy smile decked out in his uniform, the swastika insignia on display. Mary hadn't heard anything from him since he'd left for the Eastern Front and she didn't know who or how to ask. What she did have was now hidden away in the nursery along with his promise to return, and his signet ring.

The next day, the hospital was again open to visitors and, as Yannick hadn't missed one yet, Evelyn was expecting him. The sea between Guernsey and Alderney was visible from the top of the hill outside her cottage. Since Camille's arrival on the ward, it was something she'd taken to checking on her way to work. She'd mostly been hoping for rough weather, the one person she could do without seeing today was Yannick.

Evelyn was making Camille's bed, straightening the sheets and plumping up the pillows, the opening of the pillowslips turned away from the door, just as Matron had shown her.

Camille was sitting in the chair by the window staring into the distance, a little smile playing on her lips. Her bruises had faded to a faint discolouration. It was her broken arm that was causing concern. The continuous pain had necessitated two adjustments to her plaster of Paris. A puzzle to Dr Jones as the X-ray plate showed the bone knitting well. Evelyn was amused but remained silent. The peachy glow of Camille's skin told its own story as did the faint sound of a whistle from Colin outside when the wind was blowing from the south. Evelyn didn't recognise the tune, but she'd taken to humming it on and off during her journey to and from work, the chords tunnelling through her mind and lifting her soul.

'I'd like to ask a favour if I may?' She tucked the end of the red counterpane under the mattress and readjusted the envelope corner, already thinking of the next task.

Camille turned as if forced out of a trance and in a way that's what it was. Allowing reality to intrude on her fairy tale wasn't what Evelyn wanted but there were others to think of. While Mary's life was very different to Camille's it was no less tragic. If she was going to be accused of being an interfering old busybody, then so be it. She viewed it as helping a friend.

'Anything.'

'I know someone who's trying to find out about her boyfriend, and I was wondering if Yannick might be able to help?'

Camille's expression froze.

Evelyn felt the guilt slap at her like a physical blow. Reminding Camille of anything even indirectly linked to Yannick was to cause the woman pain. The longer the Frenchwoman remained on the ward, the more she started to resemble her former self, and not a pale imitation. The thought that Evelyn would soon have to discharge her back into Yannick's care was an abomination. Reminding the woman of it felt tantamount to a betrayal.

'Of course, *ma petite*. The name?'

'Wilbur Schwarz, middle name Klaus. He was sent to the Eastern Front last January.'

'I will see what I can do but it depends.'

Evelyn smoothed her palm over the top of the bed to remove an imaginary wrinkle. It was too late to take the request back but she could soften it. 'I'm sorry to have to ask. If it's going to cause a problem for you...'

'It won't! Now, a little walk I think before lunch.' Camille smiled a second time, but it was a very sad arrangement of her lips. 'I have to make the most of my time here.'

Evelyn watched her leave the ward as she started on the next bed, her pink dressing gown belted in a bow around her narrow waist, her hair a bouncing set of waves.

'Fancy a hand, nurse? I have a few minutes before Dr Jones arrives for his round.' Sister was at her elbow. 'Poor woman. Can only end in tears.'

Evelyn shouldn't have been surprised by Sister Jehan's response. The woman appeared to have eyes in the back of her nursing cap. Nothing happened on the ward that she wasn't aware of even if she wasn't on duty at the time. Evelyn didn't know if she knew about Colin – she still couldn't get used to calling him Edgar – but the inference was clear about his relationship with Camille.

'I fear you're right, Sister, but she might as well grab whatever happiness while she can.'

'Sometimes the price of happiness is too much to pay, Nurse Nightingale. Now, what about these beds.'

Evelyn pondered her words as she raced around the ward tidying lockers and arranging bed tables in preparation for lunch.

What would she do if their positions were reversed? Colin was a good man and a kind one too, but goodness and kindness didn't come into it. Not with a brute like Yannick as the opposition. They wouldn't be able to keep Camille for much longer.

Evelyn crossed the ward to wash her hands at the sink before starting the long journey back and forth to the kitchen in the basement with trays of food, her gaze on Camille's empty chair. It remained empty until ten minutes before visiting time. Then she returned with her secret smile, her hair as neat as ever, the bow of her dressing gown now tied on the other side.

It didn't take long for her smile to fade. It disappeared completely within seconds of Yannick entering the ward. There were no flowers. There was nothing apart from the stern man clipping across the floor before flipping up the back of his jacket and settling on the edge of the bed, his gloves, a permanent feature, crushed between his fingers.

Evelyn was busy pushing the last of the cots from the nursery in time for the influx of visitors to coo over, her ears trying to tune into the conversation being carried out on the other side of the room.

'I have good news, *liebling*. The plaster comes off tomorrow in preparation for your discharge.'

He didn't stay long now he'd got his way. Half an hour at most but long enough for the bottom to fall out of Camille's world.

Evelyn only managed a brief word when she was turning back the bed covers and replenishing the water jugs. The nursery had welcomed another new baby that afternoon and she was still trying to catch up with her chores.

'I'm sorry.' It didn't seem enough, but it was all she could think of.

'I know, *chérie*.'

Camille looked diminished, the glow of her skin fading to a dull mask, her rouge-reddened cheeks taking on the look of a painted china doll. 'You've been very kind, but I have no choice but to go back. If I disappear, he'll find me, and if he doesn't, he'll choose someone else to take my place. Someone younger, and not as well equipped to manage him.'

'Camille, he broke your arm. How does that sound like you're managing him?'

'It was an accident. The door. Remember?' Her sad smile said more than her words. 'And, anyway, it won't happen again.'

Evelyn took a chance and settled on the locker seat a moment, one eye on Sister's closed door. 'How do you know that? He can't be trusted.'

'Because I've agreed to his demands,' she said simply, smoothing a thick layer of cream over her arm where the skin above the plaster had dried and was starting to flake. 'It won't be so bad, and he won't touch me when I'm...'

'When you're what?' Evelyn gasped as she realised what Camille had promised him. 'You've agreed to have his baby, haven't you? Oh, my dear.'

TWENTY-NINE
EVELYN

Evelyn was on another split shift the following day.

In the morning, two of the mums had been discharged but they were replaced almost straight away by two women well in the throes of labour. Evelyn ran around trying to fit a morning's work into an hour or two. Packing up babies and bags was squeezed in with flitting between lockers for an array of essential items from combs to mirrors and scissors, cleaning the sluice and sterilising the gloves. A tricky job which they used an egg timer for. More than a minute and they turned into lumps of jelly. It was a mistake she'd made in her first week and had never made again.

When she looked back at those first few days at the hospital, she barely recognised herself. The way her heart had thumped every time a bell rang, terrified of the patients and staff alike. She had worried constantly both on and off duty that she'd never achieve the confidence and speed of the other nurses. She couldn't remember now when that fear had changed, replaced by a gentle awareness that she was good at what she did. More than that. It had become even more fulfilling than teaching. She'd found her calling.

The hospital had become a second home, and the staff, a kind of family. There was camaraderie in the shared struggle, a sense of belonging she hadn't expected to find. She took joy in the small victories – making a patient comfortable, seeing them smile after a tough procedure, or simply knowing she had made someone's day a little better. It wasn't just about the tasks anymore; it was about the human connections, the trust patients placed in her hands. The quiet moments of care that often went unseen by others but meant everything to her.

If she thought of the future, a future after the war, it was along the lines of career progression. Adding a formal nursing qualification to the job she was mostly carrying out already.

Evelyn cast a curious glance in Camille's direction, watching as she dropped her untouched breakfast back on the trolley and made for the door, dressed in a black dress with a red bow at the collar. It wasn't the first time she'd strolled off the ward with her head held high but this time there was a sadness clinging to her. None of the joy in her face like the other times. The hospital wasn't a prison, nor the wards its cells. The patients were free to come and go as they pleased but most chose to stay, the gardens holding little attraction.

Her hat remained on the bed, ignored. It was a new outfit. She couldn't very well wear the torn gown she'd arrived in when she'd been admitted. The dress suited her, but it also transformed her back into the woman Evelyn had first met at Marise's side. No, not quite. She was softer but also more resigned. Evelyn struggled to put it into words. It was as if the fight had been beaten out of her.

The boat back to Alderney wasn't leaving until midday because of the tides. A short reprieve, which she appeared to be taking full advantage of, and good luck to her.

Yannick was already on the ward by the time she returned. Evelyn had made up an excuse about Camille being in the bathroom. Whether he believed her was irrelevant. It was whether he believed Camille.

'Oh, *mon chérie. Je suis désolée.*' She didn't elaborate as to why, instead perching her little trifle of a hat at an angle while she waited for him to pick up her case. 'It will be so lovely to get back home and see all my friends.' She hooked her good arm through his, tilting her pretty face, her heels tripping along to keep up.

There was no thank you, only a wave and a smile from Camille for the other ladies watching them leave. A glamorous bird of paradise, with all her plumage on display, her wings soon to be clipped.

Evelyn continued tidying the ward in preparation for lunch and afterwards fetched her cloak from the hook in the kitchen and headed into the nursery as planned. Sister Jehan was already waiting for her, Serena wrapped in a white cardigan and matching bonnet. 'Are you sure the nuns won't mind? It's a huge responsibility.'

'They're loving having little Moses. Adding a girl to the mix will be perfect. Something to make their life meaningful now they've lost their remaining patients.'

'I still don't like it, but anything must be better than the overcrowding at the Town Hospital.' Sister gave Serena one last hug. 'Come on, cherub, time to meet your new family.'

'I'll try not to be late.' Evelyn adjusted the scarf to even out the weight before flinging over her cloak and looking up. 'Will I do?'

'No one would know any better.' Sister picked up a bundle wrapped in hessian sacking and tied with a scrap of string. 'A few bits and bobs to help tide them over.'

Evelyn didn't get very far but that had never been her intention. Maison des Fleurs was on the way. She propped her bicycle in the usual spot and unclipped the basket from the front, her free hand pressed against a sleeping Serena cocooned to her chest.

'Mary, it's Evelyn.'

She pushed the front door open and placed the basket on the kitchen table. Mary hurried to greet her, tears tracking down her cheeks at the sight of Serena partially hidden by Evelyn's cloak.

'You came. I didn't want to believe it in case something happened to stop you.'

'Of course I came.'

Evelyn dropped her cloak on the table and started fiddling with the knot in the scarf.

'Here, help hold her while I undo this. There.'

Mary cradled Serena in her arms, a look of pure love causing her skin to glow with contentment and her eyes to shine.

Evelyn watched a second, a tender smile appearing at the sight of their reunion after a two-week separation. She'd been present at many meetings between mothers and babes but none as heartfelt, none that felt like a physical pain under her ribs. There was little that was perfect in her life, little that she wanted to remember from her days at the hospital and sparse off-duty. This reunion of mother and baby was something she'd take to her grave.

'I'll make us a tea.' She turned to the stove, her fingers gripping onto the edge of the counter, the pressure the only thing anchoring her feet. If she could will one thing it was for mum and baby to be reunited permanently instead of this half measure. What she was able to do for them wasn't nearly enough.

Evelyn busied herself with unpacking the basket, while she waited for the kettle to whistle. She'd managed to hide a few slices of bread and a small macaroni pudding in a container under the baby clothes and baby milk. It wasn't much but when you didn't have anything it didn't need to be. There was also Serena's birth certificate in an envelope, with the name Mary Le Page as mother, the father left blank. Evelyn had learnt that Mary's surname was Laine and not Le Page. It was a subterfuge she'd reluctantly agreed to sign up to. A protection for both Mary and Serena if the Germans, or indeed the islanders, learnt the truth about the little girl's parentage.

They sat in the kitchen over their cups, Serena cradled against Mary's shoulder. The clock stretched relentlessly to four, the time Evelyn had to leave if she wanted to be back at work on time.

Just a few more minutes, she told herself, blinking rapidly to chase away the sting in her eyes.

The clock on the wall ticked, each second dragging her closer to four, closer to the moment when she'd have to take Serena away. She glanced to where Mary was resting her cheek next to Serena's, the bond between mother and child clear on both of their faces.

How can I take her away? How can I not?

Evelyn poured more tea, the warmth of the cup offering little comfort as she sat across from them. Her hands trembled slightly, and she wrapped them around the mug, trying to steady herself. She didn't know what to say. Time was running out, and there was nothing she could do to stop it.

She looked at the clock again – three forty-five. *Fifteen minutes.* She wanted to stretch time, to give them both more than this fleeting hour, but she couldn't. The convent was waiting, and so was the reality of their world. A world filled with choices no one should have to make.

It was time. With the cups collected and in the sink, Evelyn turned back to them, her hands fiddling with the scarf.

'I've asked about Wilbur for you, Mary.'

'You promise you'll tell me the truth, whatever it is?' Mary rushed, the words hurried, her body a coil of tension, her expression hardening.

She hesitated then nodded briefly, for the first time feeling the sharp stab of stupidity. Ruining the perfect moment for this. What if it was bad news? What then?

'I'll let my aunt know to expect you. There's no need to write first. She'll be happy to see you.'

Evelyn left shortly after to cycle to the convent. Again, she decided to only spend a couple of minutes with her aunt. Just time enough to pass over the basket and the baby before popping back on her bicycle down the short hill past the German house. The road was empty, with no sign of the *Kommandant*'s car or, indeed any of his soldiers. There was also no sign of Yannick or Camille. They were probably back in Alderney by now.

Like many locals, Evelyn had never been to the island but, before the outbreak of war, she'd heard reports of its wild beauty. Guernsey but in a bygone era. Colin had told her of the changes. The boundaries of barbed wire. The brutality. For Marise to have had to live through that. For Camille to agree to return. She'd said there'd been no choice and, reluctantly, Evelyn had finally agreed with her. If there had been a way, she'd have found it.

She was tired when she finally arrived home after work, tired and dispirited. The cottage was quiet and cold, the stone walls doing little to warm its only occupant.

Instead of losing herself in her playing, she got ready for bed, a hot drink beside her and Susan Martin's spelling book balanced on her knees. She picked up her pen and began to write…

Serena Le Page, born 9th September, 1943.
Mother. Mary Laine. Father Wilbur Klaus Schwarz.
Current address. Les Cotils Convent.

THIRTY
EVELYN

November, 1943

Weeks passed, the days shortening and the nights lengthening on the countdown to Christmas, not that there'd be any turkey to look forward to. Meat was a luxury that even the wealthy were finding difficult to obtain. The nurses at the Emergency Hospital fell well outside of that bracket.

Evelyn worked and slept, apart from the necessary chores required to sustain life. Washing. Cooking. It wasn't much. There wasn't the energy for meaningless walks now. She didn't need the exercise, couldn't afford to use up the hard earned calories. Everything had to be preserved, including her energy. Letters remained unanswered. Clothes were repairs on top of repairs, faded and falling apart at the seams. No one had anything but, what they did have, they mostly shared. There were the occasional vipers. Usually women who seemed to have more than everyone else. The rumours abounded about what they'd had to do for the price of a meal, a packet of cigarettes, a silk scarf. Evelyn didn't participate in these conversations. That didn't stop the bitching and moaning but people quickly learnt not to do it when she was around.

On her days off, she made the extra effort to visit Mary, finding her own quiet joy in their budding friendship. What began as polite, slightly awkward conversations soon broadened and deepened over cups of bramble leaf tea. They talked about Serena but also of the difficulties they both faced. Women who'd both loved deeply and, in Evelyn's case, who'd lost everything on Joseph's death. Of Wilbur there was still no news.

Some days, Evelyn volunteered to spend the afternoon sitting with Mrs Laine, while Mary borrowed her bicycle to go and visit Serena. It wasn't much but it was all she had to give and she gave it gladly. Like Violet, she viewed her in the same light as the sister she never had.

The list remained just as it was but, instead of being concealed in the wall, it was wrapped in a scrap of oiled cloth and hidden in her violin case because they now had a hospital maid billeted in their cottage, a change which had meant Violet sharing her bedroom, as it was slightly bigger. She didn't mind about that. She would trust her with her life and knew the reverse was true. The one person they'd learnt very quickly to distrust was their lodger. Within a week of whey-faced Gerta arriving they'd both been aware of items being moved in their room. Nothing had been taken. Neither of them left anything of any value at home apart from the crystal set and the violin, which remained untouched in the garden surrounded by an ever increasing patch of waist high nettles.

The day the letter arrived began like any other. Evelyn was on a late so had woken at eight and bumped into Gerta coming out of the kitchen. There were no words. They weren't on speaking terms since Violet had caught her stuffing the last of their tommy loaf into her mouth. Now they always kept their small stash of food with them, a chore but a necessary one if they weren't to starve. When they slept it was under their beds in an old hessian sack, a chair propped up against the door handle with an old broken pot on top for good measure. When at work they took it with them, a cumbersome exercise but not without its reward when they spotted Gerta's increasingly dour expression.

At least working at the hospital they were guaranteed meals and with only one day off a fortnight it was a rare day when they weren't assured of something to eat, no matter how small.

'Afternoon, nurse. On a late shift?'

'For my sins.'

The head porter stepped out of his tiny office. 'There's a letter for you.'

'Thank you. Must dash if I'm to make dinner.'

'You don't want to be missing your macaroni pudding.'

The dining room was quiet, everyone trying to work through their breakfast before Home Sister stood up and led the procession to the wards. Evelyn was late and had missed grace, a fact that Sister noted with a frown. Instead of bothering about it, she peeled the envelope open before propping the letter against her glass of water and started mechanically scooping in her pudding.

After, she wished she hadn't. She wished she'd waited until she was alone to absorb the contents of the letter. She had made a solemn promise, but with all her heart, she now wanted to break it.

'Hey, you're not eating. Sister will be on her feet in a minute.'

Ivy's voice intruded enough for Evelyn to lift her head and watch her friend folding her own letter and placing it back in the envelope, her bowl empty.

'Not hungry. You have it.' She shoved the letter in the envelope any old how before pushing her bowl over and watched as Ivy started on it without a second's pause, her own stomach shrinking against her spine at the thought of food.

With Sister on her feet, they left the dining room for their respective wards.

'Hope you're feeling better. You can have my supper bread later. I'll keep it for you.'

It was a rare day when food wasn't at the front of their thoughts. Where their next meal was coming from. How long the stocks would last. What about when they ran out but today that wasn't important, not with the envelope and its contents burning a hole in her head and her heart.

'You're a good friend, Ivy,' she said automatically, the letter back behind her bib as she forced herself to follow the throng of staff on duty.

Ma chère amie,

I hope this letter finds you all well.

Yannick is here with me so I will be brief. He has had news today about Wilbur Klaus Schwarz. I am afraid it is not good. Herr Schwarz was reported to have died during the battle to keep Rostov-on-Don from falling into the wrong hands. I don't have any further news on this except to say that his family in Germany have been informed.

THIRTY-ONE

EVELYN

The medical and surgical wards were increasingly full of patients with a combination of conditions, with malnutrition at the heart. People too frail and weak to coordinate their footsteps meant an increase in a variety of fractures from arm, leg and pelvis while poor diets lowered resistance to illnesses like they'd never seen in the hospital before. Healthy men and women dying from what would have been viewed a minor injury in the old days. The days when the island had belonged to the locals.

Evelyn arrived on duty, her mind preoccupied by the letter. She wanted to head to the sluice to read it properly but the thought fled as soon as she heard that Betty Le Pelley had been admitted with trench mouth, a disease Dr Jones hadn't seen since working as a medic in the Great War. Betty couldn't eat or drink, her infected gums bleeding and swollen while little Wilhelmina, by contrast, was thriving on the children's ward.

'I think Mrs Le Pelley has done what any mother would and deprived herself in favour of the girl and this is the outcome. With no news of her husband, she's thrown everything into being a mother.' Sister and Evelyn didn't need reminding that it was Marise's daughter they were talking about. Some things were best left unsaid. It was safer that way.

'Poor woman. No news about him?'

'Nothing.' Sister raised her eyebrows. 'At Naumburg Camp but that was over a year ago. She has no one now apart from Wilhelmina. I've popped her in a side room. I'd like you to special her.'

The afternoon was busy and, with sister off, staff nurse was in charge, not that Evelyn was aware of much, sitting beside Betty hour after hour to the sound of her struggling breaths. There was little they could do for her apart from try to lower her raging temperature with cooling bed baths and a frequent change of a cold flannel applied to her forehead. With still no access to penicillin the disease had to follow its own course. Evelyn was left with trying to chivvy her along with news of Wilhelmina's exploits, some true, many from her imagination.

Betty's breathing worried her more than anything. Evelyn had never heard of trench mouth let alone nursed anyone with it but how a mouth infection could cause the deep, heaving breaths was a mystery and, with staff in one of her moods, there wasn't anyone she could ask.

'I've come to relieve you.' Staff pushed open the door an inch, the sound of her disgruntled tone filling the room, her meaning clear. That Sister insisted on all her staff having their breaks was a huge inconvenience and, for once, Evelyn agreed with her.

'I'm not hungry, staff, so I'll stay.'

'As you like but no tittle tackling to Sister tomorrow.'

The words floated across the room, finding no purchase. Evelyn was as immune to her dictates as she was to her nasty comments.

She was feeling faint by the time she was finally relieved by the night staff. Twenty minutes late and with no apology forthcoming.

'Sleep well, Betty. I'll be back tomorrow with more news about Wilhelmina and how she's getting on with that front tooth.'

She paused in the corridor and collared Abi Martel, the staff in charge over night.

'I'm a bit worried about Mrs Le Pelley, nurse. It's her breathing. It's not right.'

Abi gave her a searching look before nodding her head. 'Off you pop. Leave her to me.'

Evelyn made her way to the changing room to divest herself of her apron before reclaiming her cloak. A glass of water helped fill the void from a day of unintentional fasting, as did the slice of bread she found tucked into her pocket, wrapped in a scrap of paper with I scrawled on the back.

'God bless you, Ivy. I'll do the same for you some day.' As the last nurse off, she spoke the words to the empty room, the bread folded in two and already heading for her mouth.

Colin was in the yard, helping Emile unload barrels from the back of the trap, when she left for the evening. It was a full moon, a rare enough event for them to take full advantage of the free light. Molly, the old Shire horse, was taking no notice, her head buried in a bucket.

Evelyn started to walk past only to stop abruptly, her hand to her mouth. Seeing Colin was the prompt she needed to drag her back into the dining room with Camille's letter propped up against her water glass.

There'd been something niggling her about the letter since she'd read it but the business of Betty Le Pelley along with the shock of its contents had pushed the thought to the back of her mind, Colin was the key needed to bring it into sharp focus.

It didn't take a moment to whip the envelope from her bib and pull out the thin sheet of cream paper, her heart in her mouth as she slowly turned it over and read what was scrawled on the back.

There is good news, however. I hope you will share in our joy when I tell you that I am two months pregnant. Yannick and I can't wait to welcome our child into the world.

Take care and be safe.

Avec toute mon affection,
Ton amie

She blinked, then blinked again, feeling the colour drain from her face as the letter crumpled between her fingers. The words burned, scorching her skin, her chest tightening with each passing breath. The news of Wilbur was hard enough. Devastating but not as devastating as the two decisions she now had to make. To tell Mary and Colin, or to stay quiet.

With the letter smoothed out, she reread both sides, her mind churning along with her stomach. What kind of a friend would she be to even think of withholding news about Wilbur? Yet, what kind of friend would she be to deliver it, to break the fragile peace Mary had managed to find? But Colin was different. He'd hear about Camille. He was bound to with the hospital grapevine the way it was. Evelyn knew that Camille would want to have her baby on Guernsey, it stood to reason after what had happened to Marise. Surely it was better to warn him even if every cell and nerve told her to run, to not get involved. And, finally, what would she want if she was in his place?

She heaved a breath, one of the decisions made. The other one didn't need to be made yet.

'Evening, Mr Guille. Lovely evening. Hello, Colin, a word if I may.'

'Sure. Back in a minute, Emile,' he replied, following her to the corner of the building, where the moon was shaded by the angle of the roof.

There was no prevarication. There was no need. His expression and the way he instinctively reached behind his ear for a cigarette with a trembling hand said it all and more.

'Here, I've had a letter from Camille.'

She pushed the envelope across and turned on her heel, unwilling to watch his world collapse. It was all a bit too close to a repeat of the telegram she'd received from the War Office all those years ago. It might be a different war but that was irrelevant. The devastation remained unchanged.

THIRTY-TWO

EVELYN

Evelyn was bone-tired when she left the hospital after lunch. The morning had been busy but also emotional with Betty moved from the seriously ill list and onto the dangerously ill one. While they weren't sure what the diagnosis was, TB had been mentioned, in combination with the trench mouth they already knew about. Evelyn wasn't surprised. She tried not to worry unduly about something she couldn't change. Life was hard enough worrying about the things she could.

Wilhelmina was now her biggest concern. The few weeks it would have taken Betty to recover would be prolonged by months, if she did recover.

Betty might have passed the infection on to her. Wilhelmina was being kept quiet in a side room away from the other children until such a time as they could rule out transmission. After that...

She'd write to her aunt. One more mouth to feed shouldn't stretch them too far.

Decision made, Evelyn climbed on her bicycle, a small jar of milk tucked away in the bottom of her basket. It was all she had to spare, the remains of the urn from the night before, which was already starting to curdle, but when you had nothing you weren't fussy as to what you ate. It wasn't theft if it was only going to waste. A thought that she measured her life against. Mary and her mother were in a desperate situation. It was only with the help from their neighbours, Evelyn and now the nuns that they were in any way managing.

If Evelyn ever thought her life hard, she only had to think of Mary, Betty, Camille and Colin to feel ashamed of the thought. Mary was a carer night and day, with no respite and with her child living with strangers while Betty was solo parenting with her husband locked up somewhere in Germany. As for Camille and Colin...

She couldn't bear to think about what was happening to them, as she pedalled furiously along L'Aumone and round the corner onto the Friquet. There was a hidden message in Camille's letter, she was sure of it. A slight slant to the words, *our news*. Only time would tell if her suspicions were correct. People lied. Dates didn't, although she'd have to wait until Camille went into labour for full confirmation. There was no way she could share her suspicions. What if she was wrong? What then?

Evelyn had been keeping up with Matron's weekly lectures, in the hope that she'd be able to train as a midwife at some point. She didn't like to dwell on the future more than that. There were too many variables. She lived from day to day, however the dream lingered, where all her other dreams floundered. Matron was meticulous in her record keeping of the lectures delivered, determined to assist at some nebulous point in the future if any of them decided to follow up on their training.

Evelyn, Violet and the rest of them were in that difficult no man's land where they had to perform duties carried out by senior student nurses, due to the lack of qualified staff, but without any of the exams to prove their application or level of expertise. However, she didn't need a pass mark, or a certificate to know that the typical gestation period for a baby was between thirty-eight and forty weeks, nine months was cutting all the corners. If... No, hopefully *when* Camille came in to give birth she'd know. Camille would want to give birth at the hospital among friends instead of the male-dominated and, quite frankly, spartan Alderney landscape. There was nothing wrong with spartan, but it also meant no access to any of the specialist equipment they could cobble together at a moment's notice to aid a difficult birth. Camille wouldn't need to be told that and neither would Yannick, not after what had happened to Marise.

Mary's cottage was gloomy in the dull, overcast day, but that wasn't a surprise. With fuel stocks at an all-time low there was nothing spare for heat or light. When normal, hardworking Guernsey folk ran out of oil there was nothing to replace it with and Mary didn't have a drop left. If it wasn't for the woodburning stove they'd starve or freeze, whichever came first.

'Hello, anyone home?' Her knock was soft, her words softer. Mary had told her not to stand on ceremony with her visits, but she was still reluctant to walk into the house unannounced.

Manners weren't the only reason for Evelyn's hesitation. She'd spent most of last night trying to work out what to say to her friend about the letter. The truth was she knew she shouldn't have interfered. Being soft hearted was no excuse for being soft headed. There had always been the chance the news would be bad. If only she'd thought it through properly before involving Camille.

'In the lounge.'

Evelyn placed the basket on the table and hurried to join her.

Mary was lying on the sofa, her eyes closed, the thin curtains pulled against the weak afternoon light, the house quiet for once.

'Another bad night?'

'Aren't they all!' She struggled to sit.

'No, don't get up.' Evelyn perched on the hardwood dining chair. There was only one chair left but probably not for much longer. When she'd first visited, the lounge had been full of outdated, heavy mahogany furniture; now all that was left was the table, one chair and the sofa. The stove had been fed the rest.

'You can't keep going on like this, my dear. There are places she can go.'

'I promised I'd look after her.' Mary's voice was resolute, her expression belligerent.

'But no one would expect you to go without sleep, not even her,' Evelyn pressed, unwilling to give up just yet. Surely she must see reason. What was going to happen when the furniture ran out? Without her mother to look after, Mary would at least be able to work and bring some money in.

'Hah.' Mary propped herself up on one elbow, her hair falling in a greasy wave around her shoulders, her face strained, the skin stretched over bone. 'You don't know my mother. She'd expect it and more besides.'

'Then you shouldn't have any loyalty to someone who thinks that you're only there to meet her needs,' Evelyn said, trying to keep the frustration from her voice. It was a difficult situation but Mary making herself ill wasn't going to help.

'You don't understand.' Mary swung her legs down and pushed to her feet, her big toe poking through a hole in the right slipper, her cardigan a matted grey in need of a wash. She wasn't coping but, as she wouldn't let Evelyn help her apart from accept the odd bit of leftover food, there was nothing she could do. Pride and poverty were the deadliest of combinations. Her greatest fear was that she'd do something stupid and the main reason she'd finally decided not to tell her about Wilbur.

'Heard anything from your friend?'

Evelyn followed her into the kitchen where the stove was pumping out a low heat, pleased that Mary had her back to her so she couldn't see her startled expression. Proof enough of the time they'd been spending together if their minds were running along parallel lines. She'd hoped for a little longer to plan an answer but perhaps it was better this way. Act on instinct instead of a preprepared little speech. Gloss over Camille's news instead of leaving the letter to fester.

'Fancy you asking today of all days.' She fussed over her basket, rearranging the contents to reveal the container of milk, her face averted, her voice taking on a breathy quality, which she tried to disguise with a little cough. 'Received a letter yesterday.' She raised her head, the milk in her hand, to find Mary staring at her, an unhealthy brightness in her cheeks and her eyes. 'There's no news other than she's pregnant. I'm sorry.'

'Not as sorry as I am.' Mary changed the subject with a speed that made Evelyn blink, her face still warm from the lie. 'Milk. You are kind. I'll boil some for Mother. She enjoys hot milk.'

'There's more than enough for both of you.'

'I'll have mine later but thank you for thinking of us.' Her words had a finality etched between the letters, the hidden message clear. *I don't want the milk. Just go. Leave me alone.*

Evelyn lingered for as long as she could even though she knew she was outstaying her welcome. Moments passed, the stand-off clear until she finally relented. With a gentle goodbye, she picked up the basket and slipped out of the cottage.

She'd reached the bottom of the hill up to her home when she suddenly came to a stop, her legs shooting out for balance, the truth taking away her breath. Mary always asked for news of Serena in case Evelyn had received something in the post from her aunt. She managed to visit when she could but was always keen to hear any additional scraps.

In all Evelyn's months of visiting, today was the first time she hadn't asked after her.

THIRTY-THREE

EVELYN

Evelyn had barely stepped back into the ward when Sister collared her.

'I'd like you to special Mrs Le Pelley, nurse. She's in need of a friendly face.'

Evelyn didn't need to read between any lines to recognise what she was telling her. In that second she pushed all thought of Mary to the back of her mind, her nurse's hat clamped firmly to her head.

Betty was attached to one of their precious oxygen cylinders. Evelyn propped her up against a bank of pillows but, apart from holding her hand while she spoke quietly there was very little she could do. The pharmacist in Boots worked magic in producing a range of tablets and creams from seemingly nothing but, as yet, the penicillin they'd heard much of, was as far out of their reach as it had ever been. Dr Jones had put in a special request with his opposite number over at the German Hospital only that morning. The doctor hadn't even bothered to reply.

Evelyn sat with her heaving thoughts at the injustice of it all when the poor woman's chest rose and fell for the last time. A quick feel of her pulse told her what she already knew.

She remained frozen, Betty's hand cooling under hers, not quite believing that a seemingly healthy woman of thirty-six could die and without anyone being able to do a thing to stop it. The sounds of the ward formed a dim background behind the thick wooden door as the work carried on outside. There were tasks to be done now she'd gone, but Evelyn didn't have either the energy or impetus to move. It took a sharp knock on the door to pull her out of her trance and hurry to her feet.

'Time to get off duty, nurse.'

It was Sister at the door, and it was Sister that stayed to help her lay out Betty's body. Having a death at any time was an extra burden on the staff, but that wasn't why Evelyn stayed. She stayed for Wilhelmina, and she stayed for Marise. But she also stayed for Betty's daughter, buried in an unmarked grave on the border of the cemetery.

Sister was inclined to be chatty as they rolled Betty between them, performing the last essential tasks before manoeuvring her onto the mortuary trolley. 'A nice woman. Such a shame. I wonder what will happen to her daughter. This bloody war.'

Evelyn didn't respond even though the thought gnawed at her. Her mind drifted to the letter she'd write to her aunt and how she'd ask the porter to send it out with the horse and cart first thing in the morning. Eight old ladies looking after three babies was too much to ask but she couldn't bear the alternative of sending Wilhelmina to the Town Hospital.

The ward was subdued the following day. The women were aware that they'd lost one of their own. The babies were also restless, after their morning spent with their mothers, and difficult to settle after their midday feed.

'I'm afraid you're going to have your work cut out,' Sister said, standing in the doorway, the noise from the wailing babies filling the air, her smile as serene as ever. 'They know something's up, just not what. As soon as their mums settle, they will. At least it's visiting later. Our mums will be spending the evening moaning about their husbands instead of thinking about poor Mrs Le Pelley.'

Evelyn's answering smile was troubled. Humour was a panacea but today she found it difficult to laugh at one of Sister's well-meaning observations. She'd been nursing long enough to know that life had to go on when tragedy struck. For her, the clock had stopped with Betty's death; she was struggling to restart it.

Everything seemed to take longer that morning. The water was cold. The stove light went out with the damp wood they were forced to use. The laundry ran out of sheets. When she was finally sent to lunch it was an hour late, the kitchen staff aware that they were to hold back her meal.

She was slowly negotiating the corridor down to the dining room when the porter stopped her.

'Hold on, nurse. Mr Guille dropped this off from Sister Thérèse over at the convent in reply to your letter.'

Evelyn thanked him briefly, her fingers already starting on the envelope. It was unlike her aunt not to take council with Mother Superior on any of the issues facing the convent. She was already expecting a refusal when she pulled out the reply.

Dear Evelyn,

While I don't want to refuse, I am very aware of the extra burden this baby will bring even if it is only for short time until her mother improves. Therefore, with a heavy heart I must tell you that this must be the last child we take.

It is a difficult decision, but I trust that with God's guidance, we will find the strength to carry this additional responsibility.

With all my love and prayers,
Sister Thérèse

Good for you, Aunty.

Evelyn almost ran down the last few steps, slowing her pace to a glide at the sight of Home Sister standing to her feet to lead the procession out of the dining room.

'What kept you?' Ivy whispered out of the corner of her mouth as she pushed away from the table.

'Letter from Aunty. Nothing to worry about.' Evelyn nodded at the maid, who'd plonked a bowl of what smelt like turnip soup in front of her.

She concentrated on her meal, ignoring the clatter of chairs and the sound of feet until a pair stopped beside her. She dropped her spoon into her bowl and started to stand at the sight of Matron Rabey looming over her.

'Matron.'

'Stay where you are, nurse, and finish your meal.'

'I'm finished, Matron. Only my tea and I'm quite happy to give it a miss.'

Matron nodded, pulling out the chair recently vacated by Ivy and sitting down, taking a moment to check the buttons on her sleeves, her attention on her cuffs. 'If you're not as sick of turnip soup as me then there's no justice in the world.'

Evelyn had no idea what Matron was doing in the dining room let alone sitting beside her, but she replied in kind. 'I know I should be thankful but if I never see another turnip again I'll be a happy woman.'

Matron smiled; it didn't reach her eyes. 'Dr Jones asked specially for me to have a word away from the ward, nurse. I thought it best to have it here instead of asking you to visit my office. For some reason nurses seem to dislike my office. I have no idea why.'

'I understand, Matron.' She didn't but it was better than

saying either yes or no. Her brain was in such a muddle that she couldn't work out which response fitted best. There was no attempt to add a smile at Matron's joke. Her lips suddenly weren't obeying commands.

'I believe you know a Mary Laine?'

Evelyn stared at her, unable to read her expression but that didn't matter. Her mind took on a turn of speed to hurry across the finishing line. She'd known yesterday that something was up. Now here was the proof. She took a breath, a steadying breath to ensure there was enough air in her lungs for the next bit.

'Yes, Matron. We're friends.' She didn't mention the baby or Mary's stay in the hospital under an assumed name. She didn't know why, only that the information in the wrong hands could be incendiary. Matron was implacable in her stance on nursing and the preservation of patients' rights, but she was also a woman who'd come out of retirement to head up the hospital when the Germans had landed. A woman like that wouldn't last two seconds if the likes of Yannick ever decided to question her.

Matron nodded, her attention back on the button of her cuff and a thin strand of white thread that had worked loose. 'Miss Laine told her neighbours as much when they asked about your visits. They immediately thought of the hospital when they were disturbed by shouting and yelling in the small hours.'

Evelyn relaxed. 'That would be Miss Laine's mother, Matron. She gets confused, particularly at night. I have tried to persuade Mary to speak to someone about getting some help. Hopefully now we'll be able...'

'I'm afraid it's a little too late for that.' Matron pulled the thread free, finally meeting her gaze. 'When the neighbours went in to see if they could help, they found Miss Laine hanging from the ceiling. Sadly, they were unable to revive her.'

Evelyn closed her eyes as the room started to spin, her hands tremouring in her lap. As shocking as it seemed to her now, Mary must have known. She must have sensed the news, news that would have shattered her. Wilbur had been the love of Mary's life just as Joseph had been the love of hers. But unlike Evelyn, Mary had no career to anchor her, no supportive mother to lean on. Without them, she might have...

The unfinished thought slammed hard, bile rising in her throat. She was as much to blame as the person who'd pulled the trigger on Wilbur's life. The acrid taste of turnip soup filled her mouth, and she gagged, the shame burning hotter than the soup itself. Poor Serena, left with neither mother nor father. It was all her fault.

'Oh, my dear. Head over your knees.' She felt a gentle hand pushing her forward, the ground racing up to meet her. 'That's it. Deep breaths. In through your nose, out through your mouth. You'll feel better in a minute.'

Evelyn didn't believe her even as the room started to straighten, the sudden darkness brightening round the edges. She'd known yesterday that there had been something up. She could have stayed. Staff like Tim Le Clair missed work all the time and no one ever did anything about him.

'You can sit up now.' Matron lifted her hand and pressed her cup into it. 'That's right, have a drink. It's a long time since I've done any proper nursing, too long. Not that I'm giving you an excuse to collapse again.'

'Thank you, Matron, and I'm sorry for being such a nuisance.'

'No need for that.'

Evelyn managed to finish the tea. Slow sip after sip. 'What happens now?'

Matron reclined in the chair, her back ramrod straight, her cap immaculate as was her uniform when Evelyn felt as limp as a lettuce leaf. 'We've taken her mother in for assessment but it's likely she'll be moved over to the Town Hospital for continuing care. As to the rest. Dr Jones has asked if you know of any relatives? The neighbours couldn't help on that point.'

'No, I don't think there are any. I asked her often enough about getting someone in to sit with her mother to give her a brief respite.' Evelyn's heart squeezed tight at the words. *Keeping Serena safe has to come first. Focus on the baby.*

'Thank you for that.' Matron patted her hand, rising to her feet. 'I know this can't be easy. We will need someone to go into the house to help sort out some belongings for her mother. I don't like to ask but.'

'No, that's fine. I'll be happy to.'

'You're a good person, nurse. A credit to us.'

Evelyn cringed, her heart rebelling at the unworthy praise. 'Yes, Matron. Thank you, Matron.'

Mary might still be alive if it wasn't for her, and Serena would still be in possession of her mother.

THIRTY-FOUR
EVELYN

Evelyn was rostered to work until 5 pm the next day but that changed with Matron's request for her to retrieve some of Mrs Laine's personal possessions.

Instead of going back to work after lunch she hopped on her bicycle with Wilhelmina strapped to her chest. After passing over the baby, she reached round her neck and unfastened the gold locket, which she'd worn ever since Marise had been brought in. It felt a part of her, but the necklace had never been hers, not really. It had only ever been on loan until it reached its rightful owner. Now it was time to hand it back.

She cycled back to the hospital via Mary's house, with a reluctance which far outweighed the task of bagging up a few frocks. Evelyn had been in the presence of death too many times to be scared but Mary had been her friend. To see where she'd died and within hours of her visit lay heavy, the blame a burden she could barely function under. If Camille hadn't written, or if she'd been a better actress... Pointless observations, which refused to be dimmed. She was responsible. That thought outstripped the rest.

With her bicycle parked, she decided to approach the neighbours first. People were increasingly touchy about strangers, which had probably prompted them to ask Mary about her own visits.

The door was answered by a stout woman with a formidable bosom and iron-grey hair set in rag rollers.

'Hello, sorry for troubling you. The hospital has sent me to see about some things for Mrs Laine.'

'You're the nurse. Her daughter's friend.' She sniffed, eyeing her up and down, from the top of her grey head to her pathetic shoes.

'That's right. Nurse Nightingale.'

'An awful business.'

'Tragic.' Evelyn changed her position slightly not sure what to say next, even less sure what was expected of her.

'You might as well go along so. I can't stomach it again. Having palpitations at the thought. Her hanging there, the chair kicked out...'

Evelyn dug her nails into her palms until she couldn't stand the pain a second longer. 'I'll take what I can now and leave a case to be picked up by a Mr Falla either later today or tomorrow.'

'Leave the case with me. Wouldn't want anyone ransacking the place now there's no one to look after it. I'm Mrs Sarchet by the way. Her things will be safe enough with me.'

Evelyn walked down the narrow drive, turning right at the gate then right again to where she'd placed her bicycle in its usual hiding place, collecting her basket on the way. She'd heard enough stories about ransacking to appreciate how neighbourly the woman was being.

The house had the same air of neglect and smell of mould but without any of the signs of the tragedy that had unfolded within its walls. The chair was back in its place. The sofa with the blankets neatly folded, the single pillow on top. The kitchen had been tidied. The cups hanging from hooks over the sink, the draining board shining. The larder bare. The glass jar she'd brought placed in the centre of the table. Empty. Accusing.

She turned away and made for the bathroom only to find a similar air of genteel poverty. A tiny sliver left from a tablet of soap. A pile of face cloths and towels. The surfaces wiped clean. The toilet lid closed.

It was in Mary's mother's room that things were less orderly. The bed unmade, pillows scattered, a broken lamp pushed into one corner, but inside the wardrobe the clothes were hung up, bags of lavender draped with scraps of ribbon. In the chest of drawers, Evelyn found underclothes and nightwear, which she piled onto the bed before starting a second pile of dresses and jumpers. A single coat and one good hat. A warm black felt Mrs Laine had probably kept for church. There was a jewellery box tucked away in the back, which she added as an afterthought, reluctant to leave anything of value if looters found the property unoccupied.

She found a suitcase on top of the wardrobe, which she dusted down before packing it firmly, keeping back a cardigan, a couple of nightdresses and the jewellery box, which she placed in her basket.

That was the job done, everything that Matron had asked of her, but she didn't leave. She couldn't. There was more and she was determined to find it instead of leaving it to the looters, who seemed to have possessed her mind, along with that of Mrs Sarchet's. Serena might not ever be able to remember Mary, but Evelyn could ensure she knew a little of her mother and father, and the background surrounding her birth. She'd seen Wilbur's photograph, and it was with this determination that she set about working through the cardboard box of papers set in the corner of the lounge, where up to recently there'd stood a solid mahogany bureau.

There was Mary's ID card on top. Her face serious. Fuller. Prettier. She'd have liked to have kept it but, remembering her father's words, she added it to the top of the basket. There was also an ID card for her mother, which quickly joined it. Underneath these two items she found what she was looking for. A creased brown envelope with her name written across the front.

Evelyn sat back on her heels, her eyes slipping closed briefly before peeling it open. First came the letter. She wasn't expecting that but, remembering how organised Mary had been, she shouldn't have been surprised.

Dearest Evelyn

I am sorry to have let you down, but you must not blame yourself. There is nothing you could have done and there is no one to blame.

Can I ask that you help me one last time, dear friend. I know that you will ensure my mother receives the care she requires but there is one thing more.

I can't bear to think that Serena will never know about her parents and that they both loved her above all else. If it is at all in your power, please can I ask that you keep these for her until she is old enough to understand.

With my love and eternal gratitude,
Mary

The envelope contained a photo of Mary in a floral dress and summer bonnet, Wilbur standing beside her, his hand on her shoulder. Tall and proud, decked out in his grey uniform.

She was about to place the letter and photograph back in the envelope when she realised there was something else at the bottom. Turning the envelope up, a large signet ring dropped into the palm of her hand.

'Hello, my dear. I wasn't expecting to see you again today.' Sister Thérèse was unpegging sheets from the line before carefully folding them into neat squares, her habit billowing around her thin ankles.

Evelyn had decided to cycle back to the convent before handing the few items of clothing into female medical. She needed company. Company from someone who might be able to help her make sense out of what had happened. Sister Thérèse was now her only living relative as well as being the most reasoned person she knew. She lifted her gaze from where she was working on the button at the neck of her cloak and straight into her aunt's concerned face.

'What is it, child? What's happened?'

Evelyn never cried or, not recently. After Joseph's death it had felt as if there were no tears left. Her mother had helped her then and her father, in his own way. She hadn't been able to cry after she'd lost him too, instead she'd come around to accept that it had been a merciful blessing. A relief that he hadn't lingered like many of her patients. The world was becoming an increasingly terrifying place. Her father had found the changes impossible to accept.

It almost felt as if the war was coming to a head. They were standing on a precipice, all it would take was one little shove to topple over the edge.

Her tears dried as suddenly as they'd started. She was in her aunt's arms and, being the taller by a good five inches, she was able to see down the drive to the cavalcade of cars screeching to a halt outside the *Kommandant*'s residence below.

'So sorry.'

'Never apologise for your tears, child. Like all emotions,

tears are hard earned. It will be an opportunity for you to have cuddles with Mo, Mina and Ena. They'll be delighted to see you.'

Evelyn smiled at their shortened names. 'And I them.'

'We'll have tea, and you can tell me about it, but only if you want to.'

THIRTY-FIVE
EVELYN

5 June, 1944

Evelyn climbed out of bed, rubbing her painful shoulder before reaching for her threadbare dressing gown and shuffling to the kitchen. Every footstep was an effort. She'd lost more weight but so had everyone else. A week didn't go by without her having to safety pin her uniform skirt a little further closed. She didn't bother to shift the button. One of the nappy pins from work took much less effort.

There was no sign of Gerta, their live-in German maid. She spent increasing amounts of time down the road at the barracks where she and Lili were reputed to have found boyfriends among the officers. As long as they weren't at the cottage stealing their food, not that there was much with the rations cut again. Any more cuts and they'd have to start giving back food instead of collecting it. No one had laughed when Dr Jones had made the joke. It was a little too near the truth to be amusing.

With the kettle boiling, Evelyn used some for the teapot and the rest for a strip wash, using a tiny sliver of soap from the tablet they'd been given. There was a slice of bread, but she left it. The less she ate the less she wanted to eat. The thought of food took her breath away. Over recent weeks she found the walk up the hill after work increasingly difficult. The unsettled weather of recent days was a bonus, a break from the oppressive heat but it also brought heavy black clouds and rain. She'd be cool but soaked by the time she arrived at work.

She felt a little better after the walk, the rain deciding to stop for the twenty minute journey down the hill to the hospital. With her cloak on the hook, she made her way to Sister's office for handover. After almost four years there, she was viewed as a stalwart of the ward with Sister Jehan increasingly relying on her to carry out a range of duties only usually performed by trained staff. The blurring of boundaries between staff nurses and auxiliaries was necessary as serious sickness was now as common among the staff as it was the patients.

So far Evelyn had been lucky, but she knew that her luck was about to run out. It probably had already. The pain in her shoulder was an ever present reminder as was the stabbing pain in her chest. She dreaded the thought of winter and where they'd all be the other side of it.

She was in the middle of bed bathing Mrs Malandain when Sister asked to speak to her. At seventy-five, Mrs Malandain was their oldest patient by ten years and a favourite among the staff, in the same way the colonel had been. If they spent a little more time on brushing her hair and massaging her arthritic limbs then it was only because she was unable to do these little tasks for herself. If they lingered when they helped her with the tiniest portions of food, all she could manage, then it was because they were completing the task and not laughing at her increasingly outrageous jokes.

The rumour was that the Germans were losing the war. Not such a rumour. Evelyn had elicited as much from Colin the last time she'd seen him. With Lili and Gerta becoming suspicious, paranoid even, Evelyn had decided to give her crystal radio set and her violin to him for safekeeping. There were far more hiding places at the farm than at their tiny billet. Too many secrets in the violin case for her ever to feel safe. She missed her music more than anything. Some evenings she took to dropping in on her way home and playing a few chords but even that was becoming increasingly difficult. Her health was failing along with her determination and she didn't have the strength to fight it.

'I'll be back shortly, Daphne.' She covered Mrs Malandain with a blanket before placing her bed table within reach not even realising that she'd used her first name. Sister, on the odd occasion, even called her Evelyn. Not often but enough to lessen the guilt when she did the same with their long-stay patients. The ones too ill to ever go home.

'In your own time, dear. I'm not going anywhere, unlike our friend, Jerry the German.'

'I hope!'

Evelyn picked up the washbowl and slipped out from behind the screen, almost dropping it at the sight of Sister wringing her hands. Dr Jones was standing beside her, his battered brown medical bag by his feet.

What now? It couldn't be Violet. She'd had a quick word with her earlier as she passed her on her way to bed, and there wasn't anyone else she'd allowed herself to care for, apart from Aunt Thérèse and little Mo, Ena and Mina.

Evelyn closed her eyes briefly, struggling to catch her breath. *Please, no.*

'I'm sorry to ask you, nurse, but I need you to accompany the doctor on a home delivery. The woman is too ill to journey to the hospital, and I don't have anyone else I can spare. There's a car waiting downstairs.'

'Yes, Sister. I'll just grab my cloak.'

She turned, and that's when she saw him. Yannick in the doorway, his face a supercilious mask, his uniform impeccable. It could only mean one thing.

Camille.

THIRTY-SIX
EVELYN

Evelyn was used to seeing women in the throes of giving birth. Skin drenched in sweat, eyes wild with pain, teeth bared and muscles rigid. Assisting women during labour was an honour, something Evelyn viewed as the most important part of her role. The only experience that equalled it was being present at the moment of death. It was a dichotomy she couldn't fully comprehend, only that the giving of life and the taking away were strangely intertwined. She wasn't eloquent enough with her words to explain it better.

There was nothing eloquent about the way Camille looked, no trace of the exquisite French beauty stretched out against pure white linen, her black hair matted to her forehead. The reverse could be said to be true.

Evelyn threw Yannick a filthy look as she rushed to the woman's side, only pausing a moment to dump her cloak on the nearest chair along the way. If he decided to throw her into jail for being insolent, then so be it. It would be worth it. The man disgusted her, every muscle, nerve and pore of him.

It was impossible to know where the bruising stopped, and Camille began. Her face was alive with colour, her left eye again half shut, the lower lid a bloody rim. Both cheeks and the nose this time, which looked as if it had been smashed back into her face.

'What happened?'

There was a pause, just a beat. 'A stupid accident. Silly me.'

The door slammed behind them, the sound of footsteps trailing off into the silence. Evelyn chanced a quick look over her shoulder. The room was empty apart from where Dr Jones was washing his hands by the sink, his bag open on a chair beside him.

'Okay. He's gone. You'll be safe with us.'

Camille grabbed her hand as if to speak, only for the words to dissolve as wave after wave of spasm caused her to scream out in terror, the cords in her neck rigid, her head lifted from the pillow.

'It's alright, Camille. You'll be fine. This is nothing like before. You must trust me. Now, take a big panting breath. That's right. Short, sharp breaths. Puff out through your mouth as if blowing out a candle. Good girl. You're doing just fine.'

Evelyn's words were automatic. She'd said the same words to other soon-to-be mothers, many mothers over the years but never like this. She'd told Camille she'd be fine. She had to believe it but what about the baby. The baby was something she couldn't bear to think about.

The spasm faded and Camille flopped back, her eyes closed, her hand still clutching hers.

'Right, my dear. I'm sorry, but I need to change your position a little. That's right. On your back again but this time with your knees bent. That's perfect.' Then a few moments later. 'She's ready for you, doctor. Looks to be about four inches.' Evelyn hurried over to the sink, her eyes anxious above her mask, her ears pricked for any sound from behind the stout wooden door. The lack of noise was almost as off-putting as his footsteps. What was Yannick doing? What was he planning?

Where had he gone? It was certain he'd recognised her. She knew he didn't trust her. What would that mean?

'Thank you, nurse.' Dr Jones approached Camille, stooping slightly. 'We've met before, my dear, but this will be in much happier circumstances. Now, I just need you to do as I say. When I ask you to push, you push, and when I ask you to pant, you pant.'

'I'm not in a position to argue, doctor.' She managed a laugh, which he acknowledged with a slight tilt, his hands now pressing gently on her stomach.

'Baby seems to be the right way and behaving herself and, as nurse so correctly surmised, she's also ready to come out. We wait for the next set of contractions.'

Evelyn brought a cold wrung out flannel for Camille's forehead, and reached for her hand, noting a contraction starting to build. 'Let's do this.'

The next few minutes were beautiful and fraught. Every birth was different just as every baby was different. The rudiments were the same but there was still an element of fear to overcome. The unexpected had a habit of coming out of the woodwork to pounce. They'd learnt that hard lesson too many times over the last four years to be complacent. That they'd only lost one mother, Marise, during that time was testament to the way they worked as a team and to the fact they'd barred home deliveries from almost the start. With no access to vehicles, it was the only decision to make. Women turned up with their bags packed well before their delivery date. The only two women to have missed that missive had been Marise and now Camille.

The cry from the baby was more of a mewl but a strong one.

'*Thank God.*' Camille raised her eyes heavenwards before dropping them back to the baby.

'A little boy. Congratulations, Camille.' Dr Jones passed the baby into Evelyn's waiting arms for cleaning and checking over.

'We're not quite done, Camille, but it looks like you have a healthy little lad there. While nurse is doing her bit, I need you to keep following my instructions. It won't take long.'

The door burst open, bouncing back against its hinges. Yannick charged in, an excited colour in otherwise grey cheeks.

'The baby, *bitte*.'

Evelyn ignored him, instead continuing to Camille, and settling the towel-wrapped bundle in her arms. 'Your son, Camille. Well done, you. He's beautiful.'

'I'd like to take Camille back to the hospital. Some of those... injuries from her *accident* are worrying. She needs to be X-rayed.'

'No, she is fine.'

Dr Jones pressed his lips together, his fingers working on the clasp of his bag before standing to his full height, sadly a foot shorter than Yannick's.

They were in the hall. There was no offer of refreshment or thanks. Now the job had been done they were being summarily dismissed.

'On your head be it, *Kommandant*. You might think you are in charge here but remember that your son isn't as hardy as Camille. Any more trips down the stairs, for either of them, will most likely be fatal.'

'Be very careful, doctor. It was a door, remember?' he said, carefully. 'And anyway, she'll be travelling back to Alderney later on today so that won't be your concern.'

Yannick's stare was enough to trouble the bravest of men. Dr Jones wasn't that man.

'Good God. Have some compassion.' He softened his voice slightly to more of a plea. 'At least leave it until tomorrow, with the sea state. Any fool... anyone can see it's building to a swell just by looking out the window. She's lost a lot of blood, and a day spent in bed with her son will do her a power of good instead of being bounced around on a boat. She'll be back here in any case if her milk doesn't come through,' he said, playing his ace. 'I doubt you'll be able to find a wet nurse or any baby milk over there.'

Yannick considered them, his eyes glacial chips before relenting slightly. 'One day won't make much difference.'

'Thank you.' Dr Jones clamped his hat on his head, making for the door. 'Good day to you.' Closely followed by. 'After you, nurse.'

There was a tense suffocating silence in the car as they were driven back to the hospital, the blustery weather battering at the windows. The weather suited Evelyn's mood exactly. Turbulent and unsettled. Dr Jones's usual chatter was absent, replaced by an uneasy quiet. She appreciated the silence. It allowed her the time to marshal her thoughts into some sensible order at what had just transpired. That a man, a father, could do that to the mother of his child was appalling.

Evelyn felt helpless. She was helpless, her breath coming out in short sharp gasps, which she struggled to hide from the astute doctor next to her. The thought that there was nothing she could do to change Camille's situation was blade thin and as deadly as the sharpest of knives. This feeling of futility more than any feeling that came before turned her normally placid demeanour into a blistering, red-hot anger, which quickened her pulse and flushed her cheeks to a burning glow.

Evelyn leant back against the seat as the car rolled on through the wind-swept lanes, trying to calm her mind, her thoughts in freefall.

No matter which way she looked at it there was no way out for Camille, and the baby.

Yannick had finally won.

THIRTY-SEVEN
EVELYN

6 June, 1944

Evelyn lay in bed, unable to sleep. It didn't help that Violet had dropped off as soon as her head hit the pillow, the sound of her gentle breaths and occasional snore heightening her frustration.

She missed everything about her former life: her father, her pupils and her friendship with Alice. She even missed her cherry-red gloves, which she'd lost in the second year of the war, or was it the third? But what she missed most was playing her violin. The ability to lose herself in the music. If she'd had the energy she'd have crawled her way to the farm and her violin after work but she had none left after her run-in with Yannick. She needed sleep to recharge. Sweet elusive sleep.

There was a noise overhead, growing louder. The drone of planes, closely followed by the distinctive pop pop pop noise the guns made from the battery down the road, as they released shells into the sky. It felt as if the world was ablaze with the sound of planes and shells. She stayed in bed staring at the ceiling and listened, too tired to move, her brain a fog of fatigue while she tried to process what was happening. They occasionally heard the odd plane overhead but rarely at night. This constant roar was nothing like that.

There'd been rumours for weeks that an invasion was being planned, but no one knew when or where.

'What's happening?' Violet lifted her head in a cloud of hair, dragging her hands down her face to brush away the sleep.

'No idea but I'm going to check.' Evelyn swung her legs out of bed, consoling herself with the thought that no one would be getting any sleep with the racket overhead. Now it seemed important to find out exactly what was happening in the skies. Their futures might depend on it.

She belted her dressing gown and slipped her feet into her shoes before striking a match and lighting one of their precious candles. It was an extravagance they could ill afford but far better than risking a broken ankle in the dark. 'Coming?'

'If I must, but it better be good, Ev,' Violet grumbled.

The sky was thick with cloud. It was impossible to see anything despite the full moon, but the misty grey night couldn't affect their hearing, and the roar of engines continued, one after the other and, if Evelyn wasn't mistaken, all heading towards France.

'What's happening?' Violet repeated, standing beside her in her nightgown, the cool night air at war with the calendar month of June.

'Let's get you back to bed before you freeze.' A sudden stab of pain and Evelyn bent forward, coughing into her hand. Cough after cough, her chest rattling under the strain, a sharp pulse pounding in her temples, a wave of sickness inching up the back of her throat.

'It sounds like you're more in need of bed than me, ole girl. Those long days catching up with you.'

Evelyn looked up from where she'd placed her hands on her knees, managing a smile. 'You might be twenty years younger but I'm not dead yet.'

'Seriously, Evelyn. Perhaps take the day off tomorrow. No one would object.' Violet stared at her in the dim light cast by the candle. 'You don't look that good.'

'Just tired, my dear, and heart sore.' Evelyn blew out the flame, navigating by instinct now they were inside, and the door bolted behind them. The change in the texture of the flooring. The dim narrowness of the doorway up ahead.

She told her friend about Camille and Yannick as they slipped into bed and pulled the covers up to their necks, their toes wriggling to warm up. It was a distraction technique to divert attention from her health and it worked perfectly, as she knew it would. Violet was asleep in moments.

It took Evelyn a lot longer to drop off.

Violet was still asleep when Evelyn sneaked out of the house, a slice of bread lying heavy on her stomach, a cup of bramble tea sloshing around to keep it company. She hadn't wanted to eat, She'd stood by the sink forcing down mouthful after mouthful, heaving in breaths between. The only thought that kept her sipping and chewing was the image of her collapsing on duty, something she couldn't allow.

The first thing she noticed as she walked down the hill past the battery was a second soldier on duty instead of the one they were used to. She was stopped for the first time in months, her ID card examined, the photo held up against her face to check the likeliness. Evelyn hadn't resembled the stranger in the photograph for years but there must have been some point of similarity for him to wave her away with a flick of his hand and a click of his heels.

The hospital was quiet. No cars outside. No sign of anyone. No noise apart from the soft thud of hay bales landing as Colin unloaded them from the back of the cart. They hadn't exchanged more than a nod and a brief hello in months. Since the letter, he'd retreated into himself. Evelyn couldn't blame him. After all, hadn't she done the same?

She remembered the camaraderie they shared when they'd first met. She'd come to think of him as a brother. Certainly someone she could trust, someone she could turn to for advice. But that was before the letter. Before his relationship with Camille had fractured. Before her pregnancy.

It came as a surprise when he lifted the last of the bales before joining her by the entrance.

'Have you heard? The invasion, it's started,' Colin said, plucking a cigarette from behind his ear and placing it in his mouth. 'All the police officers were called to report to the *Feldgendarmerie* in the middle of the night. They think we're going to be invaded by the British.'

'At last!' Evelyn replied, a sudden weariness dulling her voice. Most days she managed to struggle through but only after a good night's sleep. 'Violet and I were woken by the aeroplanes. Thought World War Three had started.'

He chuckled, the sound muffled as he cupped his hand around the match. 'Here, give us a chance to finish this one first.' His eyes flickered to her face through the haze of smoke, only to pause a second before hurriedly shifting away, a sudden frown settling.

Evelyn felt her cheeks redden at his look of concern. She knew she was a scrawny mess. It only took a glance in the mirror to confirm that. There'd soon come a time when she'd be unable to work but she wasn't prepared to face that yet.

She shifted awkwardly, a stab of pain making its presence felt. 'What will it mean for us?'

'Nothing, I imagine, apart from stricter rules and regulations,' he said, blowing out a puff of smoke. 'The British are going to be far more interested in France than the poor ole Channel Islands.'

'I suppose.' Evelyn knew he was right. There had been no discussion about his own capture and enforced stay in Alderney, but it was impossible not to recognise someone of the colonel's ilk. Daredevil men were a breed apart but with an attitude impossible to disguise. He spoke from experience and, hearing his words, she believed every one.

She swapped feet, half thinking whether to tell him about Camille but his next words stopped her.

'I've heard she's had the baby. A boy.' His face was expressionless apart from a sharp tick flickering in his cheek.

'That's right.' She didn't ask how he knew. It didn't matter.

'How is she?'

That was the one question she'd hoped he wouldn't ask but of course he did. He loved Camille just as that love was returned. It was impossible not to see that and if Evelyn saw it everyone else would too. Love was powerful stuff. She knew that from her little taster, but some things were insurmountable. Their situation was one of them.

She paused too long, long enough for him to start to move away. 'I can see you're not going to tell me.'

'It's not that. I don't know how to or even if it will make any difference.' She glanced at her watch. 'Maybe we can talk later?' she offered gently.

'I'll walk with you. Emile won't mind. Those blasted planes had us up half the night but he's older than me.' He stamped out his cigarette butt, screwing it into the ground before bending to pick it up and place it in the sand bucket at the entrance.

'What about the cows?' Evelyn asked, her foot poised on the first step.

'Fed, watered and milked, my girl. Now, what about...?'

'It's not good, Colin.' She coughed suddenly.

It was a sharp rasp that went on and on. This was a train she couldn't stop. There wasn't a set of brakes strong enough.

He waited, his expression fixed but the twitch was back.

'He's taking her to Alderney later,' she finally managed, dabbing her lips with her handkerchief. 'God only knows how she'll cope because I certainly don't. Camille is a brave woman, very brave but Yannick is a...'

Colin muttered a curse under his breath. A word she'd never heard and didn't want to hear again. She glanced at the trail of staff making their way up the stairs but no one was interested in them and their small troubles. Lack of sleep always made things worse, the planes had guaranteed that.

God bless the planes!

She stepped a little nearer, placing her hand on his arm. 'I'm so sorry.'

'Not as sorry as I am. He'll kill her one of these days and most likely the babe too.' His voice was gruff and she could hear the mix of anger and sheer sadness within it. But there was something else – a steely determination. This wasn't Colin the farmhand anymore. This was Colin the soldier, a man who was fighting his own war now. Yannick was a bully and a beater of women. Colin was the only man who could stop him.

THIRTY-EIGHT
EVELYN

After her early shift Evelyn made Colin head for the convent instead of the *Kommandant*'s Guernsey residence. With a milk churn in the back of the trap she had the perfect excuse to hitch a ride to see her aunt.

The troops were out in force, but no one was interested in them and what they were doing, a couple going about their business. The streets were alive with soldiers stopping everyone but with their papers in order and a ready reason for their travel, they were left alone. No one looked anything like their identity photographs after four years in captivity with a rudimentary health service, no creams, potions and lotions, very few hairdressers and a starvation diet. It was a joke even checking them, but orders still had to be followed with no thought to the stupidity of them. While there might be some fight left in the odd local, most of it had been driven out by the need for survival. Old men and women might bitch and moan over the garden gate or in the privacy of their own four walls but that was about as far as it went. Too many had been deported to the camps for the most minor indiscretions for them not to have learnt that particular lesson very early into the four years.

'You can leave the cart here,' Evelyn said. 'I'll just pop in to let my aunt know what we're up to.'

Colin hopped down from the trap, holding out his hand to assist her before walking around to the front and rubbing Molly's ears, her back coated in sweat, her ribs visible. 'Tell the good sisters to put the kettle on, my girl, because you're not going anywhere.'

'You can't stop me and, before you say anything, have you ever been in the house? Know which room she's in, what about how to access the building in the first place? By the front door?' Evelyn held his gaze, feeling brave but she knew she was right. They were in a dangerous situation, where every move needed to be calculated with precision, like pieces on a chessboard.

'Women will be the death of me,' he grumbled, his hands digging into his pockets but with an edge of a smile flickering at the corner of his mouth. 'Hurry up, we don't have all day.'

She didn't bother to answer, instead flinging herself into her aunt's waiting arms. She was careful to avert her face just in time. The threat of a cough was driving her movements, the prevention of infection as ingrained as the beating of her heart.

'It's good to see you, child.' Sister Thérèse pushed her away gently, the wide arms of her habit dangling around her arms. There were no questions, intrusive or otherwise. Evelyn wouldn't have answered them anyway. She knew how she looked. It was enough to see the love and concern flowing towards her from someone who'd never demanded anything in return.

'We need to ask a favour, Aunty. Colin is going to try and see Camille. She's had the baby and, well...'

'You don't need to tell me more. Go. I'll look after Molly.' Sister Thérèse wandered over to the elderly dray, plucking a straggly bit of grass from the edge of the path. 'Mol and I are old friends, aren't we, girl?'

Evelyn watched her a second, Colin hopping from one foot

to the other but not saying a thing. 'Actually, you don't happen to have some baby clothes going spare by any chance?'

'As a reason for the visit?' Her aunt turned without further comment and was back shortly with an old bag full of pressed clothes. 'We've been saving these. Not so many babies in need of them now.'

Evelyn handed him the bag as they walked down the hill. 'I'll do the talking. Your role is purely to carry that.'

'Yes, sir.'

She'd have smiled if she wasn't scared out of her wits at what they were about to do. The excuse was genuine enough but sending Colin, a convicted prisoner, into the enemy camp on such a flimsy pretext was foolhardy. She didn't want to consider what might happen to him, to both of them, if Yannick was to open the door.

The maid was the same one as before. A German *Fräulein* with a face like a squashed strawberry and a body to match.

'Yes?'

'Afternoon. I was here yesterday. Your mistress asked me if there was a possibility of getting some baby clothes to her before she left today.' Colin lifted the bag slowly, as if it was far heavier than the size warranted.

'You'd best go up. Top of the stairs like before.' Her voice was a guttural rasp, her head tilting dismissively.

The hall was different to yesterday. Then it had an air of busyness. Officers in and out. Now it was silent. Empty. Deserted. Evelyn restrained from glancing across at Colin, her hand curled around the bannisters, her feet like lead, a fine sweat beading her brow and pooling under her arms. Violet had been right. She shouldn't be at work just as she shouldn't be here, in the home of a newborn. Pausing on the landing, she slipped her hand in her pocket and pulled out a mask, her breath coming out in a sharp gasp from the strain of the short walk.

Colin's tall frame cast a shadow over her as he leant in, his brow furrowed with worry. 'You're not well, are you?' he asked softly, his voice unexpectedly laced with more concern than she'd expected.

Evelyn shook her head, grateful for his attention but unprepared to answer him with the truth. She'd need to accept it herself first. 'I'm fine. Just a cold but you go on ahead while I catch my breath.'

She felt dizzy, the landing starting to spin, black weaving its way in from the edges before darkness pulled her under. When she came to, she was lying on a chaise longue in Camille's bedroom, her feet on a pillow, her cloak nowhere in sight. She knew it was the chaise longue by the velvety feel of the fabric, luxurious to someone accustomed to rough and worn, torn and tattered furnishings. There were muted sounds coming from across the room. She couldn't make out the words, only the tone, Colin's Irish accent imploring, Camille's soft replies.

'Ah, you're back with us, *ma petite*.' Camille drifted over, her hair loose around her shoulders, a thin kaftan belted across what was left of her waist, the black accentuating the vivid browns, blues and greens of her skin.

'So sorry. I don't know what came over me.' Evelyn struggled to sit; it was easier when she was upright instead of lying flat.

'Worn out probably. Rest there a while. I've asked for tea to be brought up.'

The maid was the same, the scowl deep, suspicious, her gaze sweeping between Evelyn, still on the chaise longue and Colin standing looking out of the window, his hands buried deep in his pockets.

The tea was a lifeline. A proper pot, which brought up memories of her father, a tear brushing her cheek, until the whispered conversation pulled her out of the past and straight into a nightmare.

'We'll leave tonight while he's tied up with the invasion. I know of a man with a boat.' Colin tapped the side of his nose, a knowing smile planted on his mouth.

'I won't leave my babies.' Camille spluttered, her eyes darting to the cot.

'I wouldn't expect you to. Joseph comes too.'

'I don't think you understand, Colin. I refuse to leave Serena, Wilhelmina and Moses,' she said, her expression set. 'Yannick knows I go up there. He'll do something, I know he will. For him, revenge will be a bitter comfort, a pleasure he'll take the greatest satisfaction in extracting.'

'What have I missed?' Evelyn placed her cup down, the china rattling against the saucer. She'd guessed what he was planning but to hear the words was a shock.

'Nothing apart from my future wife proving yet again why I love her so much.'

Camille blushed to Evelyn's frown.

'Please don't tell me you're thinking of taking Camille and four children on a boat...?'

'It's been done before. That time there were eight.'

'Eight grown men and women are very different to—'

'There is no choice, Evelyn,' Colin said, his voice thick. 'Camille is right. Yannick will have his revenge but, being a God-fearing man, it's likely the nuns will be spared and you too, being a nurse.' He stood tall. Proud. Resolute, the slight gurgle from the basket in the corner causing the three heads to swivel as one. 'We leave tonight. There is no other choice with Yannick out of the way until tomorrow. Camille says that he's returning at first light to accompany her back to Alderney.' He tapped on the window, the air still misty thick with low cloud. 'There'll be enough light and with the full moon to guide us, we should reach land sometime tomorrow.'

'Camille. Surely you can't mean to...? This is madness.'

Her thin shoulders sank, her eyes filling with tears but her voice was filled with a quiet determination. 'Yannick is going to kill me one of these days. We all know that. If it wasn't for little Joseph, I'd stay, but we have this one chance, and we must take it. I don't care about myself but my son deserves a future without a monster in it.'

Evelyn knew, then, that she'd lost. Her heart stretched to breaking point at the thought of what Colin and Camille were about to do, but there was no way to stop them. Instead, she'd help in any way she could.

'Colin, bring the violin with you when you've sorted out the boat.'

THIRTY-NINE
EVELYN

Evelyn retraced her steps back to the convent and waited, the baby items disguised in a bundle of old clothes intended for the poor. Colin and Camille had agreed to take nothing with them, except for the babies. That still meant smuggling out the few essentials Evelyn told them they'd need. She didn't ask about the boat, what kind or where it had been hidden all these years. Colin told her she didn't need to know, that the less she knew the better, and she believed him; she had to.

Those last hours both dragged and raced by at top speed as she sat at her aunt's kitchen table, the babies on a rug by their feet as they talked. Evelyn didn't discuss what they were up to, it was better that way. Better not to get her aunt into trouble. They also didn't mention her health, the hacking cough that seemed to have no end. When the time came, Evelyn held her tight, the scent of lavender indelibly stamped in her mind, a scent that lingered, along with the small sachet she pressed into her hand.

'I'll see you tomorrow, Aunty,' she said, swallowing down the tears forming in her throat.

Colin sneaked Camille and Joseph out through the garden

gate and helped them up into the cart, where Evelyn was waiting with three children, a blanket and a small pile of supplies in a hessian sack. They had two hours in which to travel from town to St Sampson Harbour before the eleven o'clock curfew kicked in. A small group going on an evening ride to see friends. It wasn't much of a story. There hadn't been time to invent one. They hoped the presence of the children would add the layer of truth needed if they came up against a road block.

She sat in the back, her heart unravelling every time they spotted the enemy on the side of the road.

They thought they'd made it when they reached Bulwer Avenue, the sea on the right, a few random houses on the left. The road block up ahead to the approach to St Sampson Harbour was a shock.

'Camille, take my cloak, quickly now. And my cap.' Evelyn pulled out her crumpled nurses' cap from where she'd tucked it in her pocket, taking advantage of the soldier's view being obstructed by Colin sitting behind Molly. 'That's right. Pin it to your head. You're me and I'm you. Play along.' The last words were uttered under her breath as two soldiers approached, rifles in their hands.

'Halt. Where are you going this time of night?' The German was young, barely a man but his words were still a threat, his gaze steady and assured.

'Evening. Just a ride before curfew. Heading back to the Town Hospital shortly,' Colin replied, tipping his cap, his accent a fair imitation of Emile's broad Guernsey one.

'ID!' There was no please.

'Certainly.' He rummaged in his pockets, taking out his tin of tobacco, an old hankie and a pile of coins before pulling it out with a flourish. It was lucky it was dark, the only light from the swaying lantern held aloft by the other soldier, but if they checked Camille's ID their luck would run out.

Evelyn forced a cough, it wasn't hard. A cough that went on and on, zapping her energy, her hands clenched around the edge of the trap, the knuckles nearly breaking through their thin covering of skin.

'What's the matter with her?' It was the other soldier. Older and more experienced.

'She's very sick.' Colin threw her a brief glance over his shoulder, his voice lowered to a mere whisper. 'Her and her children too. A very sad story. She'll end her days, what's left of them, in hospital. Nurse and I are taking her children to her sister first. She lives up the road a bit.'

'Infectious?'

Colin shrugged. 'I'm only the driver. Nurse may know.'

Evelyn tried heaving air into her lungs, one eye on the soldiers, and the look they were exchanging, praying as she'd never prayed before.

'On your way.' The words were hurried and accompanied by the sound of thick soled boots backing away. Evelyn didn't think she'd ever heard a sweeter sound than the army in rapid retreat.

'Gee whizz, that was close,' Colin said with a sharp intake of breath. 'Come on, Molly, giddy up.'

'Not too quickly, Colin. Remember how ill I am. We don't want to make them suspicious,' Evelyn managed, her voice a shallow, gasp of sound.

'Right you are. Not long now anyway. Five, ten minutes max.'

Evelyn was dreading it. She was comfortable propped against Camille, the smell of newborn baby an inch away. The journey back would have to be the long way if she didn't want to run into the same road block. It would take her hours.

She didn't know if she had hours in her.

The trap finally pulled to a stop.

'Thank you, Evelyn.' Camille started to remove the cloak, Evelyn's hand on her arm stopped her.

'No, take it. You'll need it more than me.'

'I can't...'

'You must. I'll say I lost it,' Evelyn said, her hand pressed up to her mouth, her mask somewhere back on the road.

'I wish you'd come too,' Camille said, pulling her into a gentle hug, Joseph still strapped to her chest, Moses clinging to her side. His face was pale, his eyes huge as they darted right and left. Old enough to sense the tension between the adults even if he couldn't fully understand it.

'I can't leave but you take my very best wishes with you.'

Evelyn stared across at the children with regret, suspecting she'd never get to see them again. Life was fragile, never more so than that night, the sea a dark loaming presence in the distance under the hint of the pale, bitter moon. The haze that had never deserted the day. A requiem.

She blinked back the tears, her hand grazing Molly's head as Colin grabbed their meagre belongings and flung them over his shoulder. Then he hurried them away, Wilhelmina clutching onto his hand, Serena in his arms.

'Wait.' She rushed after them, her breath catching at the effort. 'My violin. Take it. It might be worth something and you'll need as much money as you can get.'

It was only later in the cold darkness that she remembered the secrets hidden in the depths of the case. The photographs and letters. Susan Martin's spelling book. The ring. She'd saved them all. A blessing but also a curse, depending on whether they were discovered and by whom.

FORTY

KITTY

Saturday 29 December, 2018 – St Andrews, Guernsey

Kitty sat in the bright kitchen, concentrating on the picture of her grandfather, the soft tick of the clock above the door the only sound. Her aunt sat quietly across from her, hands wrapped around her mug of tea. After a lazy morning, which had included a gentle stroll to the shop for bread and milk, they'd settled back to continue their dip into the past.

Kitty's gaze was riveted on his face, her finger tracing the worn edge of the image, as if by holding on, she could bring the past into the room with her. 'Tell me about my grandmother. Tell me about Camille?'

Her aunt picked out a studio portrait of a young woman with perfectly waved dark hair and a youthful smile, and placed it on the table.

'She's beautiful.' Kitty stared at the photo of the glamorous woman reclining on a chaise longue, a cigarette holder dangling from her fingers.

'She was that.' Ena smiled. 'We felt so lucky having her

walk us to school every morning. All the other mothers were dowdy in comparison but not Mama. She could turn out a frilly blouse and one of those A-line skirts she favoured from a leftover scrap of fabric only fit for the bin. I never saw her looking anything but immaculate until just before she died.' Her voice faded to a thin thread before rebuilding momentum. 'You remember her, don't you?'

'Yes, but not like this. She looks like a movie star.' Like with her grandfather, Kitty's memories of Mamie, as she'd liked to be called, were different to the photograph. Her French grandmother had died when she was ten or eleven, and too tied up with her move to secondary school to spend much time or thought on the woman she only saw a couple of times a year, her dark hair streaked with grey and pulled back into a chic chignon. 'We didn't see much of them.' Kitty looked up, catching her aunt's eye. 'Why not? They lived in Dublin, didn't they?'

'North of the Liffey. Your dad couldn't wait to cross that bridge to the south and leave them behind.' Ena stared down at the photograph of her mother with an expression Kitty couldn't begin to read.

'But why, Ena?'

'Because your father was ashamed, my dear. And, sadly, he's still ashamed. Ashamed of his parentage and what happened long before he was born. Ashamed of something that wasn't his fault, and he couldn't change so instead he decided to alienate himself from the people who cared for him the most.'

The pinging of Kitty's phone interrupted the conversation, like a bucket of ice-cold water being flung across the table and equally as effective.

'Your young man?' Her aunt relaxed against her chair, cradling her mug in her hands.

'He can wait.' Then she blushed, a stupid schoolgirl trait she couldn't seem to get out of.

'Hah, I knew it. I knew there was someone. Do tell. Is there a photo?'

No! And, for your information we're not dating. We're not even friends.' Her phone pinged again.

'Well, for someone who's not a friend he certainly seems to like texting you.' Ena's eyes sparkled with mischief, pulling her own mobile towards her. 'What's his name?'

'Ena, I'm warning you.'

'Warning me of what, dear? I just want to see if he's going to be good enough for my favourite niece.'

'I'm your only niece. Aunty Min had boys, or have you forgotten?' Kitty replied playfully as she checked her phone.

> I'm sorry to hear about your relative. I hope everything turns out okay. Of course, we can definitely take a rain check. Just let me know when you're back and settled, and we can arrange something then.

It sounded genuine enough. Perfect even. Possibly too perfect. No, she was overthinking things. There was also no need to reply. He'd know she'd read it, assume she was busy and leave her alone.

'Right then,' she said, turning to her aunt as she chucked her phone into her bag. 'What about my dad and this mess he got himself into with Grandpa and Mamie?'

'What about we head out for an early lunch, and I'll tell you then. I fancy a bit of fresh air after being cooped up the last few days. The bus passes right by my gate.' Ena glanced at the kitchen clock. 'In fact, if we leave in the next five minutes we should catch it. I hope you've remembered your bathers. There's no reason for you not to have a dip even if I can't.'

'In December? You need your head examining.' Kitty could feel the goose bumps on her arms at the thought of getting into ice-cold water.

'No, only my heart and that's being seen to. Now, scoot. I have my bag and my phone. Oh, and my glasses,' Ena added, tapping the top of her head. 'So, I'm ready apart from my coat. I'll wait by the door.'

The bus trip down to St Peter Port was uneventful, a short journey of ten minutes but all downhill and with the opportunity for Kitty to catch sight of the harbour full of fancy yachts, and the castle in the distance. The walk through the Victorian Gardens took them to the Bathing Pools with the café perched above.

'What are those islands in the distance?'

'Herm and Sark, the tiny one in between is Jethou and private.' Ena lifted a hand to the horizon. 'There's Jersey and France on the right and Alderney on the left, not that you can see them today.'

'Alderney? Isn't that where Grandpa was sent?' Kitty squinted at the skyline but all she could make out was a bank of cloud.

Her aunt nodded. 'I've never been. Now, you go for a quick dip. No excuse not to. Far warmer than the Irish Sea and plenty of people in already to keep you company. I'll order us lunch. Soup do?'

It wasn't only her aunt that needed her head examining; Kitty had been toying with the idea of all-year-round sea swimming in Dublin for ages. It did look inviting, with the winter sun bouncing off the sea to the backdrop of the islands.

It wasn't. It was freezing. She came out shaking from every muscle group, her teeth chattering and her skin a peculiar shade of boiled lobster for some strange reason.

'First time, luv? You'll soon get used to it,' the woman changing beside her said, balancing on one leg while she threaded her knickers onto the other.

'First, and possibly last. How do you do it?'

Why would probably be more relevant but Kitty was having

trouble stringing one thought after the other as she searched around on the bench for her underwear. She remembered at the last minute that she'd stuck them in her pocket.

'If I knew that I'd bottle it and sell it on Amazon. I just do and I feel wonderful after. You'll see, give it five minutes and you'll feel king of the hill.'

'I believe you!'

Ten minutes later and she was feeling remarkably different, sitting in front of the wood burner with a mug of home-made vegetable soup in front of her, but she was also on a mission. Kitty didn't know why her aunt was dragging out the big reveal unless she was about to tell her something she wouldn't want to hear. That didn't matter. As family she needed to know.

'Right, now that you've made me freeze my what-nots off in subzero temperatures you can tell me the rest of your story.'

'It's not my story, remember? It's yours too. You're Camille's granddaughter.' Ena lifted her bag onto her lap, withdrew a small photo album and passed it over. 'Turn to the first page and tell me what you see?'

It was a small album with only room for one photo per plastic slot and the first photo was one she recognised. Her and her mam standing on a beach together, their arms wrapped around each other and with the biggest of smiles. 'I love this photo. I have a copy beside my bed.'

'And what do you see in it, child?'

'Me and Mammy.'

'What else?'

Kitty squinted down at the photograph, not really understanding the question. 'I don't get you?'

'You and your mammy. Two peas in a pod. Isn't that what we used to say about you? The colour of your hair and your eyes, even the shape of your lips.'

'I don't see how that's relevant?'

'Now, turn to the next page and I'll tell you a story.'

The photograph overleaf was a wedding one. Her grandfather to her grandmother. There were no wedding clothes. She wouldn't even have known it was a wedding photograph if she hadn't seen it before. Her grandfather, tall and proud in an ill-fitting suit. Her grandmother, still gorgeous but instead of wedding finery, she was dressed in a simple pale-coloured knee-length frock with a fussy collar.

The café was full of people warming up after their lunchtime swim, all gravitating around the small stove, the smell of steaming clothes rivalling that of the spicy soup.

Ena lowered her voice as Kitty dragged her chair a little closer.

'All romances should start with Once Upon a Time but I'm afraid that what I must tell you has its fair share of wickedness. When your grandmother married your grandfather, he suspected that she might be carrying another man's child – a man who was a member of the SS. He wasn't certain though, and it didn't mean he didn't love her. They adored each other but things happen in wartime that would never happen outside. That child, their only child, is your father.'

'You mean my dad's father, my real grandfather is…?' Kitty was horrified, her healthy lobster pink glow drained to a sickly yellow. She'd heard about the SS through books and documentaries. Her father had never been one for war movies, now she could understand why.

'Before you make assumptions, let's compare the two photographs again because, as with everything, the truth lies somewhere in the middle.'

Kitty placed the images side-by-side. Her grandparents, their serious expressions. The way they were standing, before turning to the previous photo, the one of her and her mum, which she knew by heart. Their windswept dark brown hair and wide mouths. Grins so large as to take over the picture. Kitty had always moaned about having a too wide mouth but it was her mother's mouth, or so she thought... She switched between images again, this time cutting out her grandmother from her thoughts and concentrating on the man she'd always thought her grandfather. The height. The shape of her face. The tilt of her nose. 'Me and Grandpa. We could be twins. And I think I have Mamie's mouth. How?' She finally lifted her head at the sound of her aunt's chuckle. 'What? What's so funny.'

'You and your father, my nincompoop of a brother. What man wants to be told that his daughter is a cross between his parents, parents he'd grown to despise? Both your grandparents were dark-haired and dark-eyed and you're just the same. You're Colin and Camille's granddaughter, Kitty, whatever strange nonsense your father spouts, and they loved you very much indeed. They'd have loved you anyway but when it was clear who you'd descended from it was like an extra stamp of happiness for them. It must have broken their hearts when Moses walked away from the family when he was old enough. It took guts in the first place for my father to change his family name from Brady to White. Something new for his blended family.

Kitty remembered Aunty Min telling her about Moses. Her uncle. It was starting to make sense. Kitty wasn't good at French but she was pretty sure Le Blanc, her grandmother's name, translated into White, or similar. She opened her mouth to ask, only to close it again, noticing the dark shadows under her aunt's eyes. Instead, she smiled softly. 'How about a cup of tea and a piece of cake before we head back?' she suggested, already standing to make her way to the counter.

FORTY-ONE

KITTY

'Why did you decide to come to Guernsey, Ena?' Kitty asked as she switched on the table lamp in the lounge, the soft glow casting a cosy warmth against the closed curtains.

They'd spent the rest of the afternoon at home. Kitty had gently suggested her aunt rest while she busied herself in the kitchen, preparing their evening meal. Now they were in the lounge with a tray of tea, waiting for the news to start. It was the question that had been burning a path across her brain ever since she'd learnt of Ena's plans to leave Dublin. A question that her family had swept under the carpet until Kitty's mother's illness had made it irrelevant. A question she'd forgotten about until now.

She watched her aunt as she toyed with the handle of her mug, her fingers knotted, the skin on the back of her hand threaded with veins, a thin band of gold the only ring, a discordant note among the chunky bangles. She'd learnt from Aunty Min how Uncle Leonard had been the love of Ena's life. She'd still been a relatively young woman when he'd died but there'd never been any thought of finding a replacement. Instead, she'd filled her days with work, amassing a tidy fortune before up and moving to Guernsey. Kitty was determined to know why.

'To find my roots, love. Only that. Your dad and your uncle Mo always felt hard done by being brought up in a house full of such wondrous love. Our parents, and that's what they were even if we didn't have any genetic links, gave us the best of starts and none of us thanked them for it.' Her face was stony grey, her wrinkles showing through the make-up, her eyes red-rimmed behind the Kohl.

'I'm sure they knew, just as I know how much Dad loves me even if he has trouble expressing it. My parents were lucky, and you were lucky in finding Uncle Len. Romances like that don't grow on trees.'

'What hurt me the most,' Ena pulled out a crumpled tissue from her pocket and dabbed her eyes before continuing, 'was that if your father had bothered to use that brain of his he'd have known who his parents were. There was nothing to be done for poor Mo and it ruined him in the end.'

'How? Nobody ever speaks of him.'

'A lovely lad,' Ena continued, almost as if she hadn't been interrupted. 'My best friend until he learnt that someone had abandoned him in the doorway of the Town Church as if he was a bag of spuds. Went completely off the rails. Broads and booze until the latter finally caught up with him.'

Kitty felt her throat close. 'How did he find out? Surely, Granny and Grandpa wouldn't have...?'

'He went looking where he shouldn't.' Ena shook her head. 'You know kids. Impossible to hide things from. He was searching for Christmas presents. As the eldest and the smartest he'd put two and two together years before. Came across his birth certificate. Moses Raven of all things. Something to do with the name of the vicar who found him in his church doorway. I know, right! Bad enough for any of us but Mo was only twelve. To discover blanks instead of his parents' names must have stung hard. I was younger but not by much. I still remember the row now. We lost him that day. Oh, he was still a presence in the house until he was sixteen, our parents made sure of that, but he left as soon as he could. Went to sea and barely spent any time on dry land again until he became too ill to work. We met occasionally. Got to know his daughter, Caroline. Tried to reclaim some of the time we'd lost.'

'I am so sorry. I had no idea,' Kitty said, the pieces of the jigsaw finally fitting together. She knew she had to track Caroline down when she returned home. Family was family and the woman was clearly going through difficult times.

'It's alright, luv. No need to trouble. It was a long time ago.'

'What about Aunt Min then? Was it not the same for her?'

'Your Aunty Min is a breed apart, dear. She knew who her mother was right from the beginning, her French roots shining through with that wondrous black hair of hers. Her real mother died giving birth to her, but Mama knew enough to satisfy her questions. You know your aunt, Kitty. She's always been a contented soul, unlike the rest of us.'

'I still can't get my head around the boat trip and everything that led to it,' Kitty said, her tea forgotten as was the news, the programme running along without them, the sound muted. 'You're making it out to be romantic when the reality was twelve hours on a tiny rowing boat with two very scared toddlers and two babies, one only a day old.'

'Your grandfather got us through, KitKat. He got us through with his will and determination, powering through the waves like a machine. Right up until the day Mama died, she talked about that journey and what they'd had to endure. Waves lashing into the sides while she held fast to four little bodies. If it wasn't for the weather they'd have been spotted. But who'd be fool enough to head out in a tin can of a boat with no engine and no navigation and on the same day as the D-Day landings? They had nothing apart from your grandfather, a set of oars and an old compass that had once belonged to Emile's son. They were heading for the south coast of the UK instead of France. He guesstimated that, with the invasion, the sea around Normandy and Brittany would be chocka and he wasn't wrong. They were picked up by a Higgins boat somewhere off Cherbourg.' She placed her mug down, staring at the liquid rippling the surface, a smile glimmering. 'We teased him right up to the end about his lack of navigation skills.'

'I'll bet.'

Kitty glanced at her phone as a message pinged. Her lips twitched at the sight of Thomas's name. A man she wasn't dating, she reminded herself, though their growing camaraderie made her heart stir in a way she hadn't expected.

'What's lover boy got to say now?' Her aunt's voice cut through her thoughts.

'He's at a drinks reception at Dublin Castle and bored to tears. Asking me what I'm up to.'

'What did you tell him?'

Kitty looked up from where she was typing. 'That I'm having a wonderful time with my joint favourite aunt in Guernsey. I'm asking him what the food is like. That meet with your approval?'

Ena nodded. 'Absolutely. You'll be married by the spring. Babies the following.'

Kitty rolled her eyes, eager to change the subject. Somewhere in her childhood, she vaguely remembered being told that her father's siblings had been adopted but adoption now felt like too simple a word for the complicated truth. She knew about Uncle Moses but what was Ena's story? Instead of blurting it out she decided on a circuitous route. 'Back in a minute. I have something I brought with me that I forgot to show you in all the excitement.'

It had felt stupid and impractical to bring the violin all the way to Guernsey and as hand luggage too. They'd scanned and swabbed it in departures, their noses turned up at the state of the instrument. Kitty now thought it in rather good nick considering a twelve-hour boat trip across enemy waters but there was no pleasing some people.

Slowly, carefully, she opened the clasps. The creak of the hinges seemed to echo in the space between them.

As she lifted the lid, her aunt let out a soft, choked sound – somewhere between a gasp and a sob.

'My God,' she whispered, her voice heavy with emotion. 'I remember this.'

Kitty's hand froze mid-air, hovering over the open case. 'You do?' she asked softly, her heart starting to gallop.

The older woman's face had transformed, as though the past was rushing back in vivid detail. Her hands, usually so steady, trembled slightly as she reached out to touch the case with her fingertips, her bangles catching the light.

'Tell me where you found it?' she asked.

'It found me, Aunty.' She told her the story of how she came to buy it, how the woman had walked into her shop during the lead-up to Christmas. She even included a little of Thomas's visit for colour. 'I now know that it must have been Uncle Mo's daughter,' she finally said, sitting back in her chair with a sigh.

Her aunt nodded, her fingers tenderly moving across the strings of the violin.

'There's this too.' Kitty leant forward as she slipped the signet ring off her thumb, where she'd placed it before making her way downstairs. 'It was hidden along with the photographs.'

Her aunt took the ring, weighing it in her palm before picking it up between finger and thumb and concentrating on the design etched into the metal. 'This I haven't seen before.' She frowned. 'I wonder why it was hidden? The photographs, yes, but a ring. Strange. It's obviously got some value. Any idea what the crest is?'

'Not yet. I've done a search but nothing's coming up. It was made in Germany though so I'm guessing that it's part of the story somehow.'

'Mina has a locket, which belonged to her mother. Mama gave it to her on her eighteenth birthday.' Ena's usually expressive face was suddenly a mask of composure. Kitty could guess as to why. Mina knew her roots. Ena was still trying to navigate hers.

'Did she ever try to trace her family?'

'Mama and Papa took us to St Malo in the late 1940s or thereabouts. Our first holiday. Min will know more, she's older. I remember the sadness of the place.' Ena passed the ring back. 'It was heavily bombed during the war. So many lives lost and so many people failing to find their loved ones.' She shook her head, as if trying to dislodge an image, a memory that would never fade.

'I wonder how the violin ended up in the shop? We can guess it was Moses's daughter but how did he come in possession of it?' Kitty said, placing the signet ring back on her thumb.

'Moses's final stand I'd imagine. That boy was a trial, but Mama loved him as much if not more than the rest of us put together. Felt sorry for him, I expect, being found that way. As their oldest child she made him her executor so first dibs of her stuff, not that there was much. When he died it must have got passed on to his daughter.' Ena glanced up from where she was twisting her wedding band round her finger. 'You come from humble stock, my love. Nothing to be ashamed of in that but not much in the way of goodies to pass on except stories and there were few enough of those. No one liked to talk about the war, certainly not your grandfather, and it would have been even worse for your grandmother, I suspect. There was always a huge question mark over Mama's life on Alderney before they escaped, one we agreed not to delve into, in case we found what we were looking for.'

Kitty's phone pinged through another message, the noise slicing through the atmosphere like a sharpened blade.

'What does he say?'

'Mini quiches and those tiny chocolate eclairs that aren't enough for even one mouthful. The plan is to pop into the chipper on the way home for a fish supper along with a side order of Alka-Seltzer, to soak up the cheap wine they're serving.'

Ena laughed, reaching for her tea. 'I do like the sound of your young man. No sides to him.'

Kitty was thinking the same as she typed out a quick reply, then pushed to her feet.

'I think it's time for wine. The doc said you can have one, and I hate drinking alone.'

Ena laughed, waving her towards the kitchen with a flick of her hand, her other hand fiddling with the volume on the TV remote.

In the kitchen, Kitty plucked the wine bottle from the fridge and arranged it on a tray with two glasses. But instead of heading straight back to the lounge, she paused, propping her hip against the table. Her arm rested on the back of the chair as she gazed through the window into the blackness of the night sky, her thoughts drifting.

For all their talk about the past, she couldn't shake the feeling that Ena was still grappling with what had happened all those years ago. Searching for her roots on Guernsey was one thing. Finding them was something else entirely. She'd learnt more about her family history in the past day than in all the years she'd lived with her dad, but there was more. She could feel it. If she could just probe a little deeper, maybe she could unlock the mystery of Ena's birth. And maybe, just maybe, that would help her aunt heal.

FORTY-TWO
EVELYN

June, 1944

By the time Evelyn reached the corner of Les Friquet, she was barely holding it together. Her chest felt tight, each breath shallow and sharp, her vision blurring at the edges. Molly, steady as ever, guided them along, the gentle rhythm of her hooves lulling her into a false sense of calm. If it wasn't for the old horse's unerring sense of direction, and the promise of a hay supper, Evelyn doubted she'd have made it this far.

Seeing the babies for the last time had hit her harder than she'd ever imagined. Sister Jehan had called her a born children's nurse. It had taken until just now for her to appreciate the implications. She loved children, she always had and, at the back of her mind she'd hoped to be a mother at some point. At nearly forty-four it was unlikely even if still a medical possibility, but saying goodbye to the babies was different, heartbreaking. To know she'd never see them go through any more of their milestones. Flashes of little Moses with his two front teeth and quiff of blond hair, and Wilhelmina's widest brown eyes, so like her mama it hurt, kept looping in her mind. Serena and Joseph were too small to have started developing their little personalities, but she loved them with an ache, an ever present throb somewhere in the vicinity of her chest, which had nothing to do with her rattling cough and heavy limbs.

The pumping adrenaline had waned to a trickle by the time they reached the bottom of the hill, leaving a sloppy mess of tissue and bone. There was no strength left. No power. No determination. She sat hunched over the reins, her chin resting on her chest, her eyes closed. For the first time in her life, she didn't care.

Evelyn was past caring about anything not even the sharp order to stop.

When she finally came to, she knew she wasn't sitting in the trap, the wheels snagging against the ruts in the road. Instead, there was silence. A dense, thick silence so heavy she couldn't seem to hear anything apart from the rattle as she tried to drag air into her lungs, damp musty air coating her mouth and making it difficult to breathe.

She was lying on something hard, bones digging into flesh. But she didn't have the energy in which to rearrange her position. Her eyes were glued closed, a combination of fear and lethargy keeping them that way. She'd know soon enough where she was and why. She was apathetic to the rest.

She could tell it was dark, an inky blackness the way the space pressed against her eyelids with none of the layered browns filtering through the thin layer of skin.

She was alone. That was enough.

With a suddenness that had her heart pounding in her chest there was noise and light, her privacy invaded. If she'd been thinking, she'd have realised the solitude couldn't last but her mind had gone rogue, drifting back to the past. To the time she'd been happiest. Her time with Joseph.

She still couldn't move but she managed to creak open her eyes to see two figures in the doorway, one with a white coat hanging off his skeletal frame, the other Yannick, which confused her as he wasn't meant to be back until the morning. Either it was much later than she imagined, or he'd arrived back early. She baulked at the thought, her ears picking up their muted conversation.

'I must be allowed to interview her.'

'Prisoners have rights, *Kommandant*. Even you must know that. I will examine her first to see if she is well enough. Leave us if you please.'

'I will stay.' Yannick's words were coated with steel.

'Then you won't be interviewing her because I am not examining her with you here.'

The doctor turned, only to stop at the sight of Yannick pushing past him.

'Five minutes then you're done. Remember your rank, doctor, and who is in charge here.'

They spoke in rapid German but that wasn't a problem as Evelyn had been honing her prowess in the language for four years. She couldn't do much with the skill, but she always made a point of standing close enough to hear what was being said in case it was something to her advantage.

'Hello, Miss Nightingale. I'm Dr Kaufmann. Here, let me help you up a little.' He was kindness itself, his manner switching as if speaking to a child or someone ill, very ill indeed. A salutary thought.

He spent a moment assisting her before joining her on the bench, his eyes bright in a weathered face, lines fanning out in a crisscross of creases. 'I'm afraid the facilities at the prison aren't what they should be.'

Evelyn blinked, the pieces finally sliding into place. 'I'm under arrest? For what?'

'You'll have to wait to ask the *Kommandant* that.' He spread his hands, his elbows resting on his knees. 'I'm only a cog. As the prison is still, on paper at least, the responsibility of the local authorities I've been called in to examine you. Did you know they couldn't wake you? Have you suffered blackouts before?'

She shook her head, wanting to shift the conversation forward. Her health was the least of her worries. 'What time is it?' She wanted to ask the day, but she was too scared of the answer.

'Two o'clock, in the afternoon,' he elaborated. 'You were found collapsed after curfew and that's why they brought you in.'

Evelyn didn't have an answer, only that it was a lie. She'd been well under the time but had no way of refuting it. So, Yannick must have returned early only to find that Camille and baby Joseph had flown. Good! She only hoped they hadn't been picked up. She placed one hand over the other feeling for her watch. No watch!

'They've removed your valuables,' he said, guessing what she was up to. 'Although how they expect someone to kill themselves with their watch is beyond me.'

'My aunt should be given it.'

'Of course! Now, how are you feeling?'

'The same as anyone with end stage tuberculosis I suspect, doctor.'

He didn't move a muscle at her diagnosis, despite the highly infectious nature of the disease. She liked him for that until she remembered they had access to the drugs needed to cure it. Not so heroic after all.

'Coughing up blood? Night sweats? Pain on inspiration? Fatigue?' She nodded at each one.

'We have treatment I can get you. The new…'

She rested her hand on his arm briefly, the bones shining through, her skin slick with sweat. 'I fear it's too late for that but thank you for offering.'

'I won't allow him to interview you.'

'I can't see how you can stop him.'

'I'll stay.'

She managed a smile before the door was pushed open, Yannick filling the space with his presence.

'Miss Nightingale is seriously ill. I'm going to arrange for transport back to the hospital and, under the circumstances I—'

Yannick slapped his leg with his gloves. 'No one is going to stop me, and certainly not a jumped-up medic like you.'

'I'll speak to him, doctor, but if you could stay and...' Her voice dried, her tongue thick and furred. 'If I could have some water, please.'

'Of course.' The doctor poured it himself from the jug brought into the cell, and held the glass as she took sip after sip.

'Where is she? Where are my wife and son?'

The truth or another lie? While he could have forced Camille to marry him, Evelyn didn't think it likely.

'I don't know where they are.'

'You're lying.' He bent over her, spittle landing in the middle of her forehead, ignoring the doctor who had retaken his position beside her, a quiet comforting presence. 'You were seen heading out with her and yet you came back alone.'

Evelyn tried to pull the strands of the conversation together, but it was like working in fog so thick she couldn't see where she was going. Her vision shrunk to tunnel tight, black bleeding into the grey.

'Miss Nightingale.' Then slightly louder but oh-so gentle. 'Miss Nightingale. Good God, man. Why didn't you listen?' These were the last words she heard before her grey world merged with the black.

She didn't hear the doctor calling for a stretcher. She didn't feel the tilt of the canvas as she was lifted out of the prison and into the back of the horse-drawn ambulance. She didn't know her old friend Dave Le Page was behind the reins, his face set into unaccustomed grim lines, the sorrow acute.

The room was light behind her eyelids, the air cool on her fevered skin, the slight breeze playing with her hair, the bed soft.

'You're back with us, my dear.' The sound of Sister Jehan's voice was all she needed to knit the pieces together.

Evelyn had been drifting in and out of consciousness for the last week but it didn't matter. As long as she was away from that man.

It still hurt to breathe. It hurt to move too so she didn't, her eyes closed to everything and everyone.

'Sister Thérèse is here to see you again.' There was the sound of a shuffle of chairs and then her aunt's voice, carefully modulated to bland but Evelyn knew enough to know how upset she was.

'How can I help, child?'

'Nothing for you to do, Aunty.'

She was tired again. When wasn't she? Sleep dragged at the folds and grooves of her mind to take her to blissful oblivion, but before it could claim her, her aunt's next words cut through the mist.

'Mother Superior has a message for you.' She patted her hand. 'Goodness only knows what will happen to us if the Germans ever find her radio set. She said to tell you that Moses has his third tooth. Fancy that nice Mr Snagge from the BBC being interested in something like that.'

With the last of her strength, Evelyn's lips curved into a faint smile. Faces began to swirl and dance in front of her. Those she had loved the most and who had loved her in return. Her beloved parents. Colin and Camille, strong despite everything. Her aunt, steadfast and enduring. Alice and Violet. Moses, Wilhelmina, Serena and little Joseph.

Her smile wavered, her gaze glued to a figure in the distance. Tall and handsome as if fixed in amber. Time paused, breath stilled. Heart stuttered to a halt. *Her* Joseph, his hand outstretched, beckoning for her to follow.

There was only room for one more thought before darkness was replaced by a blistering light. Despite everything – the war, the occupation, Yannick's cruelty – they had protected what mattered most. Love had found a way.

FORTY-THREE

KITTY

Saturday 29 December, 2018 – St Andrews, Guernsey

Kitty reached for the wine bottle and topped up her drink, not surprised when Ena placed her hand over the glass. Though the story was new and shocking to her, for her aunt it was ancient history. There was also the little issue of her health, Kitty remembered, feeling suddenly guilty at the wine.

'No, best not. I'll grab a cocoa in a minute.'

'I'll get it,' Kitty replied, just as her phone bleeped with another message.

'You stay there and see what he's up to.'

'Ha, I think you're more invested in Thomas than I am,' she said, swiping her phone.

'You might be right.'

Five minutes passed as messages pinged back and forth to sounds of crockery chinking and the fridge being opened and closed. Kitty felt another stab of guilt at allowing her aunt to boss her into staying in the lounge but that's the way it had always been whenever the family had got together. Ena and Min had taken charge. Kitty had learnt to follow.

She watched her aunt pad back to her chair. She arranged her mug and plate of ginger biscuits just so before choosing one with care and studying it as if it was the best biscuit in the world. Her voice when she spoke was matter of fact, the retelling of an old, oft repeated story.

'After the war, Mama chanced writing to the convent. Sister Thérèse was still there and was happy to tell her what had happened.' She nibbled on the edge of the biscuit. 'Mama also said the nun was delighted to have news about her babies, as she called us. Evelyn is buried in Le Foulon Cemetery along with her parents. It had to be hush hush with the *Kommandant* out for blood.' Her voice dropped an octave, her eyes scrunched up in disgust. 'He wanted to fling her into an unmarked grave so there are no records, only those kept at Le Foulon Cemetery. I just wish Sister Thérèse had been able to tell Mama a little more about me.'

Her aunt lifted her mug to her mouth, her hand trembling slightly but less than Kitty feared after their day. Getting Ena to wind down was as impossible as asking her to follow doctor's orders. Kitty promised that tomorrow would be quieter. Perhaps she could hire a car. Ask her to show her the island from the vantage point of the passenger seat.

'I'm so sorry, Ena.' She leant over, reaching for her hand.

'Just ignore me. The foolish meanderings of an old woman.' Ena waved her hand dismissively, but the pulse throbbing in her voice told a different story. 'It's just the older I get and the closer to meeting my maker the more I want to know about where I hailed from. There's an empty part of me, a space that keeps on growing. The not knowing ruined Moses but he was worse off than me.' She stopped for breath, her finger tracing the pattern on the arm of the sofa, her half-eaten biscuit neglected on her lap. 'Mama and Sister Thérèse were able to tell me I was loved very much by my mother, but they never learnt her name, or not her real one. Mary Le Page.' Ena shook her head, a grim smile brewing. 'You haven't been here long enough to realise that it's probably the most common name on the island. I've searched. More than anyone knows, and nothing. Not a trace.'

Kitty felt a shiver of injustice run down her spine. It was an injustice she couldn't shake. The sheer unfairness of it all. Ena had done nothing wrong. In fact, she was the type to give a beggar her last coin, to open her door to strangers, always with a soft heart for those who had less than her. And yet, here she was, left with nothing but half-truths and mysteries about her own life. A woman who had given so much but received so little in return.

'What about one of those ancestry sites?' she finally said with a sudden shot of inspiration.

Ena nodded. 'It's a last resort I was hoping not to have to take.' She laughed, a sound so bitter Kitty knew that the step she was about to take was the right one.

Kitty had been in two minds whether to share the notebook lingering in the side pocket of her handbag. The problem was she didn't know how her aunt would react. With Ena's dicky heart, how big a shock was too big? She had been turning the problem over in her head ever since arriving on the island, but in the end, one thought swung the balance: it wasn't her news to keep or withhold. Ena deserved the chance to know.

'There's something I need to show you.' She delved in her bag and pulled out the old, faded green notebook and slid it across the coffee table, watching a beat as Ena picked it up and started flicking through the pages.

'What is this?' Her aunt glanced up from the list of spellings, confusion warring with tiredness.

'I know. Right! It doesn't look anything but check the name on the cover. Miss E Nightingale. It was hidden in the violin case. Evelyn's violin case.' Kitty drew in a deep breath, hoping and praying that she was doing the right thing. 'I don't know if it will help to know your parents' names, but I think it might. Turn to the back page. There's a list... A list of lost children but, before you get your hopes up, I have spent hours searching the internet for more and this is all there is. I'm so sorry.'

Moses Raven, date of birth unknown. Parents unknown. Place of discovery. St Peter Port Town Church.

Cozette Le Pelley. Date of birth 28th March, 1943. Laid to rest. Câtel graveyard 6th April, 1943.

Wilhelmine Le Pelley, born 29th March, 1943 to Marise DuPont and Yannick Klein.

Serena Le Page, born 9th September, 1943 to Mary Laine and Wilbur Klaus Schwarz.
Current address. Les Cotils Convent.

Ena stared at the list, her eyes wide with disbelief. Slowly, she traced her fingertip over the names, coming to a stop at her own. When she finally spoke, her voice was barely above a whisper. 'Mary Laine and Wilbur Klaus Schwarz. My... parents?'

'I think that's all it can mean,' Kitty said, her earlier excitement fading as she watched the emotions play across her aunt's face.

She gently took Ena's hand in hers. The flame of hope that had burned so brightly moments ago flickered and dimmed as she prepared herself for what she had to say next.

'I know it's likely too late.' Kitty's throat tightened. 'I think I might have found some information about your mother, Mary, but I'm afraid it's not good news.'

The words lay heavy in the air between them.

'Well, it's not going to be after all this time.' Kitty watched as her aunt took a deep breath as if preparing herself. 'Out with it then.'

'I came across a notice in the local paper about the sudden death of a Mary Laine but there wasn't much other than that she was only twenty when she died. No mention of you but there was a mother. Mabel Laine. Might have been your grandmother.'

'And nothing about my father?' Her voice was composed, her expression anything but.

'Not a trace but that doesn't mean he's not...'

'But highly unlikely.' Her laugh was bitter. 'With a name like Wilbur Schwarz, he's bound to be German. Good to know where I get my height from if nothing else. Stood out like a sore thumb in an Irish playground, I can tell you.'

'You don't mind that...?'

'The war was seventy-five years ago.' Ena sounded resigned as she picked up the last biscuit and broke it in two with a little snap, a shower of crumbs littering her trousers. 'It's off to bed for me and I suggest you do the same, my dear.' She rose slowly from her chair, placing the broken biscuit back on the plate, untouched. 'Perhaps we're best leaving the past in the past.'

FORTY-FOUR
KITTY

31 December, 2018 – Dublin

Kitty stayed for three days in total, long enough to check that her aunt was prepared to take notice of the doctor's advice. She would have liked to stay longer but she also had to consider her father and what he'd do when the cupboards ran out of food. He seemed to think they restocked themselves, which her mother used to find hilarious. It was far from funny now it seemed to be her responsibility.

That it was New Year's Eve was a shock, the streets of Dublin thronging with early revellers. The end of the year had almost passed her by but it hadn't been a great twelve months. In fact, it had been an awful year, surpassed only in the depth and breadth by the year before. The year her mother had deteriorated and died.

Her dad hadn't been in touch and he hadn't been answering his phone. There was nothing new in that but her heart still tripped in her chest as the taxi pulled up in front of the shop, the lights off in their flat above.

What if?

There was a thin layer of dust on the table in the window and a smattering of post on the mat inside the door. She spent a second flicking through the small pile of junk mail, bills and one late Christmas card before hurrying to the back of the shop and the stairs beyond, her carry-on discarded. The sound of the television at the top of the stairs was the first sign that she'd find things exactly as she left them.

She paused a second, her hand on the door handle. No. She'd make sure that they were better. It was time.

'Hi, Da. Miss me?' Her voice broke the silence, nervousness battling bravery.

There was a grunt from the chair in front of the television, a sound so familiar that warmth filled her chest. 'I brought you back some Guernsey Gâche. It's some kind of fancy cake I thought you might like. Full of raisins. Fancy a cuppa to go with? I'm parched.'

'If you like.'

Kitty flicked on a lamp on the way to the kitchen, pulling the curtains closed against the dull afternoon. She'd seen him like this a thousand times. Fallen asleep after a liquid lunch, a habit that had become his escape. But it felt as if there was something different in the air today. Something softer.

They sat around the table, her mother's old brown earthenware teapot between them, steam rising from their mugs, the thick slabs of fruitcake slathered with Guernsey butter, as yellow as the sun on a summer's day.

'So, how's Ena, then?'

'She'll do as long as she takes it easy.' Kitty took a sip of tea, savouring the warmth. 'Fancy mistaking a bull for a cow.'

Her father chuckled, a low rumble that Kitty hadn't heard in so long. 'A blessing in disguise though, Da. If it hadn't been for her fall they never would have spotted the problem with her ticker.'

'There is that.' He leant back in his seat, his hands resting on his round belly, his gaze wandering to where the violin lay propped against the dresser. 'Let's hear you play then.'

Kitty, warmed by the thaw in his manner, teased, 'On your own head be it. You know I'll never be as good as Ma.'

His smile was soft, wistful even. 'As long as you're better than me you have nothing to worry about.'

'Hah, very funny,' she snorted, the old banter slipping back into place, familiar as throwing on an old, comfy jumper. 'Wouldn't be hard seeing as you're tone deaf!'

She opened the case, positioning the instrument in her hands, feeling its familiar weight. Her eyes closed against the intensity of her father's stare. Kitty wasn't being modest about her mother's skill. She'd been extraordinarily talented but she also knew she had no intention of trying to replace her. Her mother was there in the spaces between each heart beat and breath. A constant reassuring presence.

'I've been practising while I've been away. Just the same piece of music. The one hidden in the case. I think it must have belonged to your da,' she said softly as she drew the bow across the strings, the opening chords of Londonderry Air filling the room. 'I recognise the melody. "Oh Danny Boy", isn't it?'

He nodded but stayed silent until she finished. The violin was back in the case. The music lingered between them far longer than the final note soared before swiftly dying. Fresh mugs of tea were poured, untouched before he finally spoke.

'Not my father, KitKat.' His voice was low, pained. 'I'm sure you know that by now.'

Kitty froze, the words catching her off-guard. 'No I don't!'

His face was pale as he picked up his mug. 'I'm not going to argue with you over the truth. It's irrefutable. My father was a monster. There, I've said it.' His voice cracked, the next words tumbling out. 'The worst kind of man imaginable.'

Kitty reached across the table, gently taking the mug from

his hands and cradling his fingers in hers. 'You must be tone blind as well as tone deaf, Da. You're the image of your da, the spitting image of your father. Your real father. Wing Commander Patrick Brady, aka Colin White, whatever whispers you heard. War hero and rescuer of women and children alike. Ena showed me the photographs. There's no mistaking it. You're Colin's son.'

Her father pulled his hands free, running them down his face as if trying to scrub away the past. 'I can't do this, not now. Not after all this time.'

'Yes, you can, Da.' Her voice was firm but kind, her heart aching for him. 'They were your parents and parents are hardwired to love their children. They may have made mistakes, they may have struggled, but their love for each other and for their blended family is clear to see. If you truly felt that badly about them you wouldn't have made the effort at Christmas. I don't remember much from those days but what I do remember was that they were always filled with love.'

He let out a long, raggedy breath, his eyes filling with tears. 'I've been battling it all these years. Blaming Mo when it could have been any of us who decided to go sniffing about. Poor Mo. And my poor parents, trying to pick up the pieces. I'll never forget the day he ran away. The row they had. The accusations he flung at her. The way I behaved after. It must have broken their hearts.'

'I doubt you'd have been able to do that, Da. Maybe a little bruised but the pair of them were made from very stern stuff. They loved you and with love comes forgiveness. Now it's time to forgive yourself.'

He plucked a tissue from up his sleeve and wiped his eyes. When he removed the tissue, he looked at her. Really looked in a way he hadn't since her mother had become ill, his words raw and tender. Heartfelt.

'I love you, KitKat. You do know that, right?'

Kitty's heart swelled even as her eyes filled. She hadn't heard those words in so long, but she'd never needed them more.

'I know, Da. I know. Love you back.'

FORTY-FIVE

KITTY

2019

Finding a place that was open on New Year's Day was difficult enough. A neutral place in which to meet Thomas for the first time was almost impossible.

They ended up in the Westbury, an elegant five-star hotel in the centre of the city with a suited and booted doorman and wall-to-wall waiters.

'This is nice.'

'Indeed. Good suggestion, Kitty. What would you like? Tea, coffee or something stronger?'

'It's a little early in the day for me. A white coffee would be grand, thanks.'

'Too early for me too if I'm honest. Two coffees please.'

She eyed him as he settled into the plush sofa opposite. They'd both made an effort in their dress but in different ways. Instead of a suit, Thomas had opted to dress down in an open-necked shirt and chinos. Kitty had dragged her only dress from the back of the wardrobe and given it a quick iron. A turquoise hippy affair with an uneven hem, which she'd teemed with boots.

'I can't...'

'How was...?'

They spoke in unison and stopped in unison. 'You first,' Kitty said, her dark hair tied back in a neat ponytail, a few loose strands framing her face.

'No, you,' he replied, a small smile playing on his lips. 'I insist.'

She acknowledged his words with a slight incline of her head. 'All I was going to say was that I can't believe that yesterday I was still in Guernsey.'

'How is your aunt?' he asked, his grey eyes wide, attentive.

'Better, thanks. Just needs to behave herself while the doctors run some tests.'

'I take it she's not one for following orders?' he said, shifting the small bouquet of flowers on the table, making room for the tray of coffee. His dark hair caught the light as he leant slightly forward.

'You could say that. A free spirit, just like me,' she said, a glimmer of mischief lighting her warm gaze.

'Nothing wrong with being a free spirit, Kitty, unless someone tries to cage you.'

Kitty smiled at that. A very slick reply from a very slick solicitor, which was what she should have expected. She picked up her spoon and stirred her coffee before sitting back and crossing her legs, careful to arrange the drape of her skirt over her knees. 'I've never asked what kind of law you practise?'

'Hah. Not really the topic of conversation to have while visiting an antique shop unless there's been a theft or some other nefarious dealings.' He sugared his coffee, taking his time to stir it. 'I'm a family solicitor, so even if you did have a theft or nefarious dealings, I'm not your man.'

'What kind of things does a family solicitor do? Wills and so on?' She relaxed back into the chair, allowing her gaze to sweep over him and liking everything. His strong, handsome face and broad shoulders – but it was his intelligent eyes and kind smile that caused her heart to ratchet up a notch. For her, it had never been solely about looks, although she freely admitted that they certainly helped. It was the depth behind his gaze, the hint of compassion and understanding that drew her in and made her feel seen.

'Among other stuff. I tend to concentrate on divorce, child law and of course domestic violence.' He picked up his drink and took a sip, probably unaware of the way she'd been studying him. Hopefully.

'That must be harrowing.'

'It has its moments.' He set the cup down, his hand raking through his hair. 'Enough about me. What about you? What drew you into stepping into the family business. I take it that White's is a family business?'

Kitty didn't reply immediately, absorbing the difficulty he had in talking about his job. No, not a job, she thought. Being an antique dealer was a job. Doing what he did, helping families torn apart by pain, stepping into the worst moments of people's lives – that wasn't just work. She didn't have a word that encompassed what he did.

And that he'd asked her out. It would be interesting to know why. She glanced down at her dress in alarm, for the first time feeling self-conscious at the differences between them.

'Lack of imagination and an interest in history,' she finally said, aware that he was still waiting for an answer. 'I have a degree in it, not that I get to use it much.'

'You could probably say the same about mine. All I seem to be doing recently is mediating between unhappy couples.' He pulled a wry grin.

'That must make you cautious in the dating scene.' Kitty's

tone was light, but she couldn't help wonder what a man like him saw in her.

'You could say that.' He toyed with his cup then stopped himself, his hand back on his lap as if he realised what he was doing. 'I have to say I was surprised when you accepted my invite. I thought someone like you would be partnered off long ago.'

She laughed. 'Is that your way of calling me old?'

'No! of course not!' He sounded shocked. 'I think you're... You're beautiful.'

Kitty felt her face redden but all she said was, 'Thank you.'

She always wondered why women like her had difficulty in accepting compliments. She was proud of having inherited both her mother and her grandparents' amazing genes. From now on she was determined to appreciate that. 'I'm thirty-nine by the way, with no dependants of any description, although I am thinking of getting a cat.'

'Same. Same age and dependant status,' he qualified. 'I also like cats.'

She rested her chin in her hand. He'd called her beautiful. Those words more than anything emboldened her to ask him something she'd wanted to know ever since he'd stepped in the shop. 'So, who was the epergne for if you don't mind me asking?'

'My boss's wife.'

Kitty grinned. 'Thank God for that! Bloody horrible.'

He chuckled. 'I'm pleased you think so.'

'And what about the photographs?' she probed.

'Ah.' He glanced up before dropping his gaze to his drink. 'I have a confession to make.'

Kitty sat back, uncrossing her legs, one brow arched. *Oh, here we go. Skeletons out of the cupboard time.*

'They're mine. I asked my mother to cobble together something after I met you, not that I told her that was the reason,' he added quickly. 'I went online and read about the image touching-up service you provide.'

She smiled. 'I'll bet she was intrigued?'

'I've yet to hear the end of it!'

Kitty glanced in her cup only to find it empty and, with a glance at her watch, couldn't believe where the time had gone. 'I could really do with a drink. Do you think the bar is open?'

'Can I ask you a question to do with work?'

It was half an hour later and they were settled on a sofa in the bar, this time side-by-side. She wasn't quite sure who'd engineered it or even if it had been engineered. She felt comfortable enough to discuss her family after his little confession about the photographs.

'Don't tell me. You've been arrested and want to employ me to get you out of the clink? I'm not that sort of lawyer, Kitty.'

She grinned, liking him more and more. 'As if I'd do anything even remotely illegal! Shame on you for thinking it. I'm trying to find out what happened to one of my aunt's relatives. Any ideas how I can go about it?'

'Tell me a little more and I'll see what I can come up with.'

'Well, I'm guessing he was in his late teens during the war. A German soldier going by his name. Guernsey was occupied by the Germans so that's most likely where my adoptive grandmother met him. I've found her, or I think I have.' She paused a second, trying to convert her muddled thoughts into words he'd be able to work with. 'I guess what I'm trying to say is that given the times and his age, we're looking for a grave, or a war memorial but there might be nieces, nephews. Cousins maybe. Sorry, I'm rambling.'

'No, just acting a concerned relative. What's his name?' He picked up his phone from where he'd placed in on the table beside hers. Up to now they hadn't even looked at them. A good sign.

'It's Wilbur Klaus Schwarz. Sounds German doesn't it. Sorry, that's all I have.'

'How about you catch the eye of the waiter and see if they have space in their dining room while I see what I can find? My mother is expecting me for supper but I don't think I'm brave enough to undergo more of the Spanish Inquisition.'

'I'll pop to the ladies' while I'm at it.'

She was gone for longer than she thought but she'd decided to phone her dad to let him know what she was up to and, for once, he'd picked up the phone and had wanted a chat.

'All done We can have a table at seven,' she said, settling back and picking up her glass.

'Great.' His phone was back on the table. 'I think I've found him, but it's not good news I'm afraid.'

Kitty wasn't surprised. Wilbur would have been a good age although that didn't stop the disappointing swell and burn. The difference between hope and truth.

'Gosh. So quickly.'

' Only took seconds to track him down to Heidelberg.'

'That's... I don't know how to thank you. At least my aunt may be able to contact his family.'

'I'm confused, Kitty. What about contacting him or is there something I'm missing?'

She nearly dropped her glass, the wine lapping against the edges before settling. 'But I thought you said it was bad news? I took that to mean, given his age that...' She dry-swallowed the sudden lump. 'Let's back up a bit. How did you find him?'

'Easy enough if you know how.' He gave a shy smile, nothing like the arrogant man she'd thought him to be. 'And he's ninety-five. The same age as my grandfather, who spends most of his life checking up on me.' He grimaced. 'The other Bradbury in Bradbury, Peters and Bradbury.'

Kitty was suddenly desperate to ask about the Peters in the trio but it would have to wait. 'Getting back to how you found Wilbur?'

'Germany has a similar land registry system in place, something called the Grundbuchamt. I entered his name, and it came up with an apartment in Heidelberg.'

'And the bad news?'

'The apartment block is scheduled for demolition. In fact, it's been delayed twice already. I won't be able to help if he goes into a care home. GDPR will prevent that. It looks like you're heading to Germany.'

FORTY-SIX
KITTY

4 January, 2019 – Heidelberg

Kitty had never been to Heidelberg. She'd never even been to Germany and neither had her aunt, but it showed her what they could achieve if they put their minds to it. She met her at Gatwick so that they could travel together. A girls only trip. Her father had chosen to stay at home and she hadn't pressed. Their relationship was at that tender stage where they were still finding their way after the emotional upheaval of the last year. It wasn't a boat she wanted to rock. They'd survived the storm but the waters were still choppy.

The flights were business class, Aunty Ena's treat and the trip taken, if not with Dr Yonkmans' blessing, then her understanding when Kitty had phoned to explain the circumstances for the rescheduling of her appointments. With airport assistance and a taxi waiting to meet their plane into Frankfurt, they were walking into their hotel room three hours after arrival, where Kitty had arranged room service and an early night for them both.

Ena was quiet at breakfast, the dark circles ringing her eyes telling of an indifferent night. Kitty took her time over her toast, although most ended crumbled on the plate. It was all very well deciding on a last-minute, harebrained trip but she hadn't thought it through, any of it, and neither had Aunty Ena. Wilbur could be married. He could have a partner and a collection of children and grandchildren who'd know nothing about what had happened in Guernsey all those years ago. She wished that she'd listened to Thomas instead of discounting his words of caution. Wilbur was old, at ninety-five very old indeed, the one thing they'd forgotten in their eagerness to close the loop on Ena's history. It suddenly felt like an intrusion, but it was too late to back out, not with the sight of Ena gathering her bag and phone, her stare pointedly directed at Kitty's full plate.

Apartment 54 was situated in a three-storey complex set in its own grounds with no sign of the redevelopment planned apart from a billboard displayed in front of the entrance. There were a few people milling about. A stooped, grey-haired man with a dog. A couple sitting on one of the benches. A small queue on the other side of the road at the bus stop.

Kitty dithered in the back of the taxi as to whether to ask the driver to wait. In the fuss of helping her aunt out and grabbing her coat, she forgot, only remembering when he was pulling away from the curb.

'Come on. Let's get this over and done with. Then we can head home.' Ena, back straight, head erect, plunged towards the entrance. Resolute. Determined.

Kitty followed, but at a much slower pace, the enormity of her worries in each step, her gaze on the ground instead of the building ahead and the gardens off to the side.

'*Guten morgen.*'

She glanced up. The stooped man had shifted to the bench to the left of the door, a brown stick in one hand, a dog lead in the other, his skin concertinaed into a myriad of wrinkles but it was the eyes that held her attention. A colour she recognised.

She'd been looking into them a lot recently over cups of tea and illicit, against doctor's orders, glasses of wine and whisky.

'Hello there. What a beautiful dog.' She dropped her hand to pet the friendly black and white terrier, aware that her aunt had stopped by the entrance, probably confounded by the number of buttons in front of her. 'What's her name?'

'Sark.'

'What a beautiful name for a beautiful girl.' She looked up from where she was stroking the dog's ears. 'Named after the island next to Guernsey?' Her voice was deliberately tailored to soft and impersonal. It surely couldn't be that easy but, maybe after all these years they deserved easy.

His eyes widened under bushy eyebrows. 'You know of the islands?'

'My aunt lives there.' Kitty gestured for Ena to join her as she spoke. Her gaze shifted between the elderly man and her aunt, debating the wisdom of taking this leap of faith. If he was who she thought. If this was her adoptive grandfather, for want of a better label, then what came next would be a huge shock.

'We're looking for someone,' Kitty continued cautiously. 'You don't happen to know a Wilbur Schwarz, middle name Klaus, do you?'

He shot to his feet, his eyes wide with surprise. His dog, a small bundle of energy, quickly mirrored his stance, a low growl rumbling in her chest as she faced the newcomers.

'It's alright, Sark. Lie down. These are friends.' He paused a second, waiting for the dog to settle. 'I take it I'm not wrong in saying that you are friends? Sark has killer tendencies wrapped in her one-foot frame.'

'Do sit down, please. Aunt, you sit too and, yes, we're friends. I take it you're Herr Schwarz?' She joined him in a smile as he dropped back onto the bench, Ena sitting a foot away from him, her expression one of cautious incredulity.

'My aunt and I have been looking for you. I know this is

going to come as a huge surprise but I think we might be related.'

'Might be related?' He looked across at Ena briefly before turning back, puzzlement mingling with curiosity. 'I don't quite see how.'

She hesitated briefly before reaching into her jacket pocket and pulling out the signet ring. The ring that had been crucial to unlocking the mystery of her family's story.

'And if I'm right, then this must belong to you.'

FORTY-SEVEN

KITTY

March, 2019 – Guernsey

They parked the car on the narrow lane at the bottom of the hill and slowly made their way to the Little Chapel.

A procession of the most senior members of the White family along with Wilbur, and Caroline, Moses's daughter. There was also Thomas, the newness of their relationship belying the feelings Kitty had for him.

It was a pilgrimage of sorts. Kitty couldn't remember now who'd suggested it but once the idea had been broached, the trip had taken on a life of its own. After two months to arrange flights, accommodation and health insurance for three octogenarians and one feisty nonagenarian, with more energy than the rest of them put together, they were ready.

The rain had stopped earlier, leaving the grass in the adjacent field a lush green, a crowd of brown Guernsey cows happily chomping away.

Joseph stopped in the middle of the dirt track, a smirk on his face. An opportunity to needle his sister that he couldn't miss. 'Ena, these are cows. COWS.' He spelt out the words with a laugh, tucking his hand through her arm, which she immediately shook off.

'Hah hah, very funny not. You and your jokes, Joseph Patrick Colin White. Never try stand-up!'

'Shut up, you two, and let me enjoy the peace and quiet,' Mina joined in, not wanting to be left out.

Kitty grinned across at Caroline, enjoying the antics between the three siblings, which had progressed to frank insults in the three days they'd been on the island.

A warm feeling spread in her chest. It was a long time since she'd felt such happiness.

The Little Chapel was a slice of paradise with its patchwork exterior surrounded by a tree-laden glade. The small church barely accommodated their small party. Wilbur and Thomas had to stoop low but Wilbur was determined to revisit one of the places he'd been happiest.

They'd already visited the cemetery to lay flowers on Mary and Evelyn's graves, and spent an afternoon at Les Cotils to pay their respects to the memory of Sister Thérèse. Neither Mina nor Ena could remember their stay there but they spent a happy time trying to find the exact location of the photograph taken with Mo and Evelyn.

Moses's ghost sat heavily on their shoulders but it wasn't a time to be sad. They couldn't change the past. Accepting that was the first step in learning to live with the present. That Caroline had finally agreed to accompany them on the trip was the next step in trying to rewrite their family story.

Kitty's determination to find Caroline had led her to knock on every door along Villiers Road, the fictitious address she'd given turning out to be not so fictitious after all. The fragile first step towards healing old wounds.

Wilbur came out of the chapel, his handkerchief pressed up to his eyes, Thomas holding on to his arm, directing him to one of the benches. Kitty joined them, a little unsure as to whether to intrude or not.

'Okay?'

'I will be in a minute.' He took a deep breath, stuffing the handkerchief into his pocket. 'Mary loved this place. Said she felt close to God. We used to come here a lot. It was where I proposed.' He twirled his signet ring round and round, lost in thought.

Kitty placed her hand over his, feeling the shape of the ring pressing into her skin. This lovely man had never married, had never had children, had never known a family until now.

It was the last day of their holiday, the five days shrinking into mere moments, but leaving a kaleidoscope of memories and a phone full of photographs.

With their bags packed and waiting collection at the Fleur du Jardin Hotel, they decided to squeeze in one last excursion.

St Sampson Harbour, with its fancy new marina, wasn't quite what they were expecting. They drove past and, rounding the corner, found themselves in a little lay-by with views over Bordeaux Harbour. There was a convenient café and a couple of park benches facing out to sea, all to the backdrop of Herm.

'Right. What's everyone having?' Thomas stood by the car while the little group rattled off an array of drinks with the precision of seasoned café regulars.

'Got it. Anything else? Snacks? Pastries? Some of that Guernsey Gâche?'

'I'll help,' Kitty said, joining him at the back of the small queue, her hand tucked in the crook of his arm. 'I could get used to all this spoiling, you know.'

'I'm counting on it.' He dropped a small kiss on the tip of her nose before turning to the woman behind the counter and placing their order.

Ena, Mina and Caroline were sitting on a bench with Wilbur, their quiet conversation punctuated by the occasional laugh. Her father had wandered off a little, staring at the way the tide was lapping against the rocky shore, his hands clasped behind him. It was becoming a familiar sight.

Over the course of the last five days, she'd noticed, with a little tightening of her chest, the way he'd distanced himself from the group. It wasn't in a way anyone else would have noticed but she knew him far better than his sisters.

'I'll take my dad's over to him.'

A moment later, she reached her father. 'Here's your coffee, Da. Okay if I join you?' She didn't wait for an answer. 'It's beautiful here.'

Kitty took a moment to soak up the view, the breeze a gentle waft of air instead of the Irish blustery wind she was used to. The difference in the weather this far south was going to make the return to Dublin extra hard, if leaving her aunt wasn't going to be difficult enough. Thomas was already talking of returning in the summer, a thought which made her heart swell.

'I can't imagine what it must have been like for your parents, and you. Stepping into a boat that was scarcely seaworthy. Camille having only just given birth; you strapped to her chest.' She stared out at the heaving sea, hardly able to believe that it was the same waters that her grandfather had rowed across to reach safety.

'It was a risk worth taking, KitKat,' he said after a long moment, his gaze never wavering from the view. 'The alternative was my mother being whisked back to Alderney. I owe her everything and I never bothered to tell her.' His words faltered, his hand reaching out for hers.

'You never owed her a thing, Da.' Her voice was calm but firm. 'Love doesn't work like that. It's the giving and not the receiving that would have given her the most pleasure. One of the most important gifts a parent can give their child is their independence.' She squeezed his hand gently, willing for him to understand. 'And she gave that to you. The freedom to make your own choices, to live your own life.'

'Maybe you're right but I wish I'd told her how much she meant to me. Before it was too late.'

Kitty leant into him, her head resting lightly against his shoulder. 'She knew, Da. In the same way I've always felt yours and Mam's love for me like a comforting cloak round my shoulders. There are some words that never need to be said, some emotions that speak louder than any words.'

The tide was coming in, the waves crashing against the rocky shore with a steady rhythm. Across the water, Herm Island emerged from the hazy mist, just as it had on that fateful night when her grandparents had risked everything for love and family. Behind them, she could hear the gentle murmur of voices – Wilbur sharing another memory with Ena, Thomas's warm laugh mingling with Caroline's. The sound of a family knitting itself back together after so many years apart.

Her father patted her hand gently. 'You know what, KitKat? I think they'd be proud of us. All of us.'

She smiled, knowing he was right. The past couldn't be changed, but its legacy lived on in the bonds between them – bonds that had survived war, separation and silence to emerge stronger than ever. As the sun broke through the clouds, casting golden light across the harbour, Kitty felt a deep sense of peace settle over her. They were exactly where they were meant to be.

A LETTER FROM THE AUTHOR

I hope you enjoyed Evelyn and Kitty's story.

If you'd like to join other readers in being the first to know about all future books I write, just click the link below for my email newsletter. I'd be delighted if you choose to sign up.

www.stormpublishing.co/jenny-obrien

If you enjoyed *The Book of Lost Children* and could spare a few moments to leave a review that would be hugely appreciated. Even a short review can make all the difference in encouraging a reader to discover my books for the first time. Thank you so much!

This is a book I never thought I'd write, and yet I've been falling towards it for the last forty-three years. That's how long I've been nursing. Or alternatively you could say thirty-seven years, the time I've been living and working on the island of Guernsey. In short, it's taken eighty years of experience. Fitting as the eightieth anniversary of the D-Day Landings occurred as I was writing this. It will be no surprise that it gets a mention.

As a writer I've always tried to avoid writing the same book over and over but coming up with interesting plots that haven't been already written is difficult, particularly when dipping your toe into World War Two. The occupation is a unique part of that history and therefore very popular with writers from all over the world and the reason up to now I've avoided it as a topic. I have set two books in Guernsey already (*The Stepsister*, and *Granny's Gone AWOL in Guernsey*), but they're contemporary. This is my first historical novel.

So, why now? The easy answer is why not, but the true answer is more complex. I've mentioned why I think I might be experienced in making a decent stab at this book but that's only part of it. My husband is local, as are his family. It's a generation that is fading with time and, for me it was now or never.

I came to the decision in January 2024, and discussed it with my agent, Nicola Barr. There was no plot and, as someone who plots as they write, Nicola had the great pleasure in dragging something out of me that she could present to publishers. It wasn't pretty. In fact, it was pretty ugly. Pages and pages of ideas that I binned. It took three months immersing myself in books from the Guille Alles Library and the Priaulx Library to cement the idea into a book set in the Emergency Hospital.

I veered towards true-life accounts and diaries from the time as opposed to historians' thoughts on the subject. There are pros and cons to each approach. People's memories fade and alter over time unless they are writing in the present but, for me it was the only way I wanted to approach this. I have friends and family who were here during the occupation. This was my starting point along with wanting my book to be inspired by fact. My research only underpinned what I knew already. Most of the island resisted, in any way they could.

This is a work of fiction, but it has its roots in fact, and the fact was at the height of the German occupation in Guernsey, the proportion of soldiers to islanders was close to one to one. The locals couldn't move for bumping into one of them. They were even billeted in their houses, and it wasn't just the soldiers. The Germans brought in German women to work on the island in a variety of jobs, some at the hospital as maids.

I have a name for this resistance. Petite Resistance, or small resistance. It wasn't about blowing up bridges, there weren't any bridges in Guernsey. There still aren't, except the Bridge which isn't a bridge these days.

It was about the little inconveniences like the bicycle repairman who every time he got a German bicycle in for repair, he changed the inner tubing for one that was about to wear out. The locals who ended up working for the Germans in a variety of roles and how they managed to manipulate the system so that they could misappropriate food and fuel from Jerry's table to feed their family. The small boy who decimated a German crop of cabbage by climbing through the broken window of one of the many greenhouses on the island in the middle of the night and pulling up every plant. I have a thousand similar stories I could tell you that underpin how they resisted. The one about the pig is a favourite but it's not my story to tell in print. You'll have to ask me about it in person. In short, many locals did what they could and faced harsh punishments when they were caught, from imprisonment to transportation to one of the camps. Even breaking curfew meant an overnight stay in the local prison, not that this was thought too harsh a punishment by the islanders. At least they were assured a good breakfast.

What's true and what's fiction?

Writing historical fiction is always going to be about a blend, trying to have a factual base but coming out with something that's enjoyable to read at the end.

It is fact that nurses hid patients during the occupation. They couldn't hide them for long, bearing in mind that soldiers had free access to the hospital, including the maternity suite and operation suite. They were a frequent presence. There are stories of them interrupting operations and births. Suspicious of everyone.

My story of a brothel worker having an extended stay at the

hospital is true. There was a brothel in Alderney. On April 10th, 2020, in an article in the *Guernsey Press*, they unearthed a tunnel from the *Kommandant*'s house to inside Lager Sylt, concentration camp, run by the SS from 1943. In Brian Bonnard's book, *The Island of Dread in the Channel*, the story of Georgi Ivanovitch Kondakov, he mentions two of these brothel workers and how one of them used to throw food at the forced labour camp workers. They are named in his book. However, Camille and Marise are fictional.

In *A Doctor's Occupation*, by Dr John Lewis, one of the doctors in Jersey during the occupation, he recalls all these young women being repatriated to France after liberation.

Dr Rose was one of the doctors working in the Emergency Hospital. I chose the name of Holly instead as a nod. Matron Rabey is the only true figure working at the hospital at the time, someone who I felt unable to replace. Evelyn Nightingale is fictitious as is *The Book of Lost Children*, however Les Cotils Convent isn't. The convent was running throughout the war, and they even kept chickens. They also looked after a child during the occupation, which is why I decided to mirror fact by choosing this place in which to house the children. St Peter Port Hospital, formally the workhouse, existed too and the Royal Hotel. Grange Lodge Hotel is still open for business. They make a mean coffee. The Victorian Bathing Pools, where Kitty and Aunty Ena went, is going from strength to strength as is Les Fleur du Jardin Hotel.

I work at the hospital so obviously wasn't going to use a real ward in the book for Aunty Ena's stay. Elizabeth Lincoln, MBE, was an inspiring addition to the island in the 1950s. Her research into breast cancer is still being used as a base for studies today. Also, naming a local ward after a female, local (ish) hero was a pleasure!

Escapes. There are well-documented escapes off the island

by boat during the occupation. One of the last was in 1944 and left from St Sampson. After D-Day, 6th June there were repercussions, as there were bound to be. On 7th June curfew was changed from 11 pm to 9 pm, which is the reason I chose the 6th for the day of Camille and Colin's escape. It is difficult to know what the island was like on the 6th, but my friend's father spoke about his daughter, (my friend, a small child at the time) keeping them awake in the small hours with the sound of planes on their way to Normandy overhead. The book, entitled *Guernsey Greene*, is out of print but available at the Guille Alles Library. I am lucky to have a copy. Thank you, Maggie.

Captain Colin White was inspired by true Irish war hero Wing Commander Paddy Finucane. In 1942 he was the RAF's youngest wing commander in its history. Sadly, he was forced to ditch his Spitfire into the English Channel in 1943. He was never seen again. A hero from Rathmines, Dublin. I used to live in Rathmines.

Yannick, the *Kommandant* of Lager Sylt at the time my story was set, is fictitious. There was an SS *Kommandant* running the camp in the later years of the war. I won't name him here.

Evelyn's story naturally came to an end after D-Day but that wasn't the end of the Occupation, far from it. There was worse to come for the islanders with France closed. By the time of Liberation, May 9th the following year, they were literally starving. If it hadn't been for an escapee getting word to the British, and arranging food drops via the SS Vega their plight would have been much worse, but that's another story.

Before I close, a quick note about local names and pronunciation.

For those of you listening to the audio version of this book I have tried to be true to the way Guernsey people pronounce their names. It might look like a French spelling but, as with any language, variations sneak through. I have also raided my own family tree for this book. My grandmother was called Violet. My father Reggie. My sister Caroline. My father's aunt was called Evelyn. Cissie was a recognised, relatively common, shortening of this name during the period the book is set.

Jenny O'B

ACKNOWLEDGEMENTS

I never know what to write in the acknowledgements page but, true to form, I will start with the dedication.

To this day, there are still many Dave Le Page's living on the island but for me there will only ever be one. Dave was a constant presence, taking part in many local activities from the Sailing Trust to Scouts. It's not accidental that he appears at the start, the middle and the end of the book. He was well known for always popping up when most needed. We miss you, Dave!

Brenda Hervé was an auxiliary nurse at the Emergency Hospital in the 1940s. Her son and daughter-in law, Pierre and Bev, have been a constant source of material. Thank you both!

Thank you to my agent, Nicola Barr, from the Bent Agency, to help turn an idea about a nurse into this! I'm lucky to have an amazing editor in Claire Bord, who gets what I'm trying to put down on paper. Also, thanks go to Oliver Rhodes, Alexandra Begley, Naomi Knox, Anna McKerrow, Elke Desanghere, Chris Lucraft and all at Storm along with Dushi Horti and Shirley Khan. A strong team of talented professionals. I couldn't ask for better editors if I tried. Thank you, Shelley Atkinson for the wonderful narration and for making sense of my voice mail. Thank you also to the cover designer Chris from Ghost.

Valerie Keogh is my writing buddy. We talk every day. Thank you, Val, for your faith in me. This book, more than any other nearly broke me. You were the glue I needed.

Thanks too to fellow 'keyboard writing friends' Luisa Jones, Pam Lecky, Jane Mosse, Theresa Le Flem, S E Lynes and Sam

Tonge. Also thanks to Kelvin Whelan. Island expert, writer extraordinaire and owner of the Writer's Block book shop on the Island.

A huge thank you to Maureen Jehan. A swimming friend who always wanted to be a midwife. Better late than never, Maureen!

Thank you to Liz Walton for coming up with the name Laine (pronounced locally as if there is an accent on the final e).

Thank you to Sara Yonkmans for agreeing to be included as a character. Sara's father-in-law was one of the TODT workers enslaved on the island during the war: a very special inclusion.

Also thanks to Jason Orton, who was instrumental in this story ever being written. Keep up the good work.

Thank you, CHOG. If you know, you know. No space for you this time, Kari!

Also thank you to my Dream Team: small but it's not about the number. In no particular order, thanks to Beverley, Michele, Diane, Elaine, Susan, Lesley, Tracy, Amanda, Sarah, Sharon, Pauline, Jo, Daniela, Carol, Madeleine, Tracey, Terri, Maggie, Lynda, Hayley, Donna and finally Maureen. (Last because it's summer in Auz and I'm jealous, as Storm Bert rages overhead and, as I'm editing, it's Storm Darragh. Role on spring, although we did see our first daffodil today.)

A final mention as always to my family. I couldn't do what I do without the four of you cheering me on from the sidelines. Buns for tea!

.

Printed in Great Britain
by Amazon